AF267743

Publisher's Note:

Thank you for purchasing this book. It began as an idea, was shaped by the creativity of its talented author, and was subsequently molded into the book you have before you by a team of editors and designers.

Like all EDGE books, this book is the result of the creative talents of a dedicated team of individuals who all believe that books (whether in print or pixels) have the magical ability to take you on an adventure to new and wondrous places powered by the author's imagination.

As EDGE's publisher, I hope that you enjoy this book. It is a part of our ongoing quest to discover talented authors and to make their creative writing available to you.

We also hope that you will share your discovery and enjoyment of this anthology on social media through Facebook, Twitter, Goodreads, Pinterest, etc., and by posting your opinions and/or reviews on Amazon and other review sites and blogs. By doing so, others will be able to share your discovery and passion for this book.

Brian Hades, publisher

GASLIGHT GOTHIC
STRANGE TALES OF SHERLOCK HOLMES

EDITED BY J. R. CAMPBELL AND CHARLES PREPOLEC

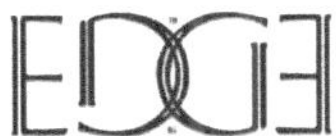

EDGE SCIENCE FICTION AND FANTASY PUBLISHING
An Imprint of HADES PUBLICATIONS, INC.
CALGARY

Gaslight Gothic
Strange Tales of Sherlock Holmes

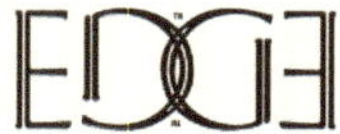

EDGE SCIENCE FICTION AND FANTASY PUBLISHING
An Imprint of HADES PUBLICATIONS, INC.
P.O. Box 1714, Calgary, Alberta, T2P 2L7, Canada

The EDGE Team:
Producer: Brian Hades
Acquisitions Editor: Michelle Heumann
Edited by: J. R. Campbell and Charles Prepolec
Cover Design: Charles Prepolec
Frontispiece: Charles Prepolec
Cover Art: Dave Elsey
Book Design: Mark Steele
Publicist: Janice Shoults

ISBN: 978-1-77053-159-8

EDGE Science Fiction and Fantasy Publishing and Hades Publications,
Inc. acknowledges the ongoing support of the Alberta Foundation for the
Arts and the Canada Council for the Arts for our publishing programme.

Library and Archives Canada Cataloguing in Publication
CIP Data on file with the National Library of Canada
ISBN: 978-1-77053-159-8
(e-Book ISBN: 978-1-77053-158-1)

FIRST EDITION
(20180630)
Printed in USA
www.edgewebsite.com

Books in the Gaslight Series

Gaslight Arcanum: Uncanny Tales of Sherlock Holmes

Gaslight Gothic: Strange Tales of Sherlock Holmes

Gaslight Grimoire: Fantastic Tales of Sherlock Holmes

Gaslight Grotesque: Nightmare Tales of Sherlock Holmes

Contents

It Is Not the Cold Which Makes Me Shiver

Charles Prepolec

Time flies. It's hard to believe ten years have elapsed since we launched the 'Gaslight Sherlock Holmes' series of anthologies with *Gaslight Grimoire: Fantastic Tales of Sherlock Holmes* at the 2008 World Fantasy Convention and seven years since the third volume, *Gaslight Arcanum: Uncanny Tales of Sherlock Holmes* debuted in 2011. In the interim, we took a little side trip to present new stories featuring another of Arthur Conan Doyle's iconic characters in *Professor Challenger: New Worlds, Lost Places* (2015). While Professor George Edward Challenger is a wonderful and fantastic character, allowing for the exploration of all kinds of stories, the siren-song lure of playing in the Sherlock Holmes sandbox has, as always, proven irresistible. It's time, once again, to make eliminating the impossible a much harder proposition for the Great Detective. So, welcome, dear reader, to *Gaslight Gothic: Strange Tales of Sherlock Holmes*, the fourth in our series of anthologies pitting the supreme rationalist, Sherlock Holmes, against the weird, the supernatural and the uncanny in ten all-new stories by a selection of the finest writers working today.

Having explored the outright fantastic, the nightmarish and the uncanny in previous volumes, this time out we take our thematic cues from the legacy of late Victorian gothic fiction (the revival, rather than the first wave that ended around 1820 with the publication of Maturin's *Melmoth the Wanderer*), the breeding ground for what we now consider 'modern horror'. It's a perfect fit for Sherlock Holmes, as he was, of course, created in the same literary crucible that produced Dr. Jekyll and Mr. Hyde, Dorian Gray, and the most Byronic of all gothic villains, Dracula. While Shelley's Frankenstein sits somewhat awkwardly between the two waves of gothic fiction, the influence on the material that followed is undeniable. Authors like Le Fanu, Poe, Dickens, the Brontës, Henry James, Richard Marsh, Gaston Leroux, etc... also heavily mined the gothic vein in their literary excursions. Arthur Conan Doyle, being a voracious reader from early on in his life, was very familiar with the work of his contemporaries and the gothic writers who preceded him; in some instances, as with Edgar Allan Poe, he was quite obviously influenced by their work. So much so, in fact, that from his earliest published stories it is plain to see that Doyle was himself a gothic writer. And, really, why shouldn't he be?

At the thematic heart of the 'gothic' lies an attempt to express something of the dual nature of man and his place in an uncertain and changing world. The Victorian gothic was all about exploration and reconciliation of the dichotomy between science and nature, head and heart, the urban and the rural, new and old, the rational and the occult, tradition and change, the secular and the spiritual. The hallmarks of the Victorian gothic are stories of men and women who rage against and defy the natural order, of monsters and madmen, of the macabre and morbid, of fear and obsession, of psychological dread, allegories of psychosexual repression, or as Coleridge put it, tales of 'desire with loathing strangely mix'd.' Transgressive tales that challenge general morality and societal norms. For a young writer of Anglo-Irish background, raised in Edinburgh (a city that juxtaposes a distinct Old Town against a New Town), indoctrinated as a Catholic by Jesuits, studying medicine, and with an embarrassing alcoholic, lunatic, artist father practically locked away as a secret in the attic, and a mother with a questionable relationship with a lodger, it's no wonder that Arthur chose to write in the gothic tradition — he was living it! The duality that lies at the heart of the gothic can be observed throughout Doyle's entire life. When his first wife, Louise "Touie" Hawkins, was diagnosed with consumption (tuberculosis) in 1893, Doyle looked into every scientific possibility to cure or comfort her. However, in 1897 Doyle met and fell in love with Jean Leckie, but was committed (at least publicly) to Louise until her death in 1906. He married Jean in 1907, as soon as was decently possible. If that's not conflicted duality of nature, I don't know what is. Then there is Doyle's long-term conflict between the rational sciences and his belief in spiritualism, faeries and telepathy. On one hand, he's working to clear the likes of George Edalji of wrongful conviction through the method of scientific deduction, on the other he thought Houdini's escapes demonstrated other-worldly skills and that two little girls really did photograph fairies in Cottingley. Definitely a complex man capable of holding divided beliefs, but to be fair, he largely saw Spiritualism more as an element of a science we had yet to understand than simply a matter of religious belief. For Doyle, his longstanding support of Spiritualism was driven by a need to eliminate the impossible, but his definition of 'impossible' may have been a tad less stringent than modern readers may understand, which brings us neatly to Sherlock Holmes...

While it is a given that Doyle's stories featuring Sherlock Holmes and Watson created a template and defined the model for detective fiction that followed, more than a few of the stories fall firmly into the camp of gothic fiction. Holmes and Watson themselves are clearly a very obvious expression of Doyle's dual nature. Holmes is the head, the darkness, the scientist who questions all, while Watson is the heart, the light, in awe of the wonders in the world around him. That these two are, in the most basic terms, updated, English, and more fleshed-out knock-offs of great gothic horror writer Edgar Allan Poe's earlier detective, C. Auguste Dupin and his nameless narrator, acknowledges the influence of earlier gothic works and places Holmes' genesis firmly in the field of gothic fiction. But there is more to the gothic than simply a question of duality, there are elements, or tropes, that define the genre, such as atmosphere, a sense of isolation of location, danger, madness, sexual repression, fear, a tone of impending doom, family curses, women in jeopardy, etc... that Doyle also utilizes fully in more than just a handful of Holmes stories. In *The Adventures* and *Memoirs* alone we have 'A Case of Identity', 'The Speckled Band', 'The Engineer's Thumb', 'The Copper Beeches', 'The Cardboard Box', 'The Yellow Face', 'The Musgrave Ritual', 'The Crooked Man' and 'The Greek Interpreter' all utilizing a variety of gothic tropes for effect, with still more to be found in later collections, including the likes of 'The Solitary Cyclist', 'The Abbey Grange', 'Wisteria Lodge', 'Lady Frances Carfax', 'The Devil's Foot', 'The Illustrious Client', 'The Sussex Vampire', 'Thor Bridge', 'The Creeping Man', and 'The Veiled Lodger'. They all hold their own as gothic works, as well as being tales of detection. Of those, for my money, the most heavily and successfully 'gothic' are 'The Speckled Band', 'The Copper Beeches' and 'The Devil's Foot'. The first is an absolute triumph of the gothic on every level, and not surprisingly, identified by Arthur Conan Doyle as what he considered to be his best Sherlock Holmes story when asked to list them for *The Strand Magazine* in 1927. The gothic tone is set from the moment the potential client, a shaking and veiled young Helen Stoner, speaks:

> *"I shall order you a cup of hot coffee, for I observe that you are shivering."*
> *"It is not cold which makes me shiver," said the woman in a low voice, changing her seat as requested.*
> *"What, then?"*
> *"It is fear, Mr. Holmes. It is terror."*

It's a masterful exchange to kick off a story that goes full-blown gothic with a lonely country house, no servants, exotic animals roaming the grounds, a cruel and difficult stepfather controlling purse strings, an inheritance, a ghostly whistling in the night that presages a ghastly death, gypsies in the woods, a lonely night-time vigil, and even a snake, with all the attendant symbolism, to firmly drive the concept home. It really is a tour de force of a gothic work, and stands as a testament to Doyle's skill and ability that such a short piece is absolutely dripping with atmosphere and menace. Although more melodramatic in tone, 'The Copper Beeches' too, with it's governess in jeopardy theme, the obsession with her hair color and length, the requirement to wear a particular dress and sit in a specific place, the grotesque bug hunting child, the dour servant couple, the mastiff kept perpetually hungry, family inheritance, and of course, the locked room and occupant in a mystery wing, all demonstrate the familiar gothic tropes. The 'governess in jeopardy' theme is usually a good sign of impending Gothicism, and crops up again in 'The Solitary Cyclist' and has variations in both 'Thor Bridge' and 'The Sussex Vampire'. Drawing on slightly different tropes, 'The Devil's Foot', brings in the suggestion of a family curse when two siblings are found to be utterly mad, and a third dead, while seated around a table in a remote Cornish farmhouse. Other stories feature other gothic elements, with thumbs and ears amputated, the latter from sexual jealousy, a premature/fake burial, a mysterious prisoner covered in sticking plasters while held in a lonely house, the suggestion of vampirism, a hint of voodoo, numerous grotesque characters, a scarred and veiled woman, spurned lovers bent on revenge, etc…but, the most gothic of all Holmes tales must, of course, remain *The Hound of the Baskervilles*.

With *The Hound of the Baskervilles* being novel length, Doyle was finally able to bring the full weight of the gothic into play, and he did it with great gusto. For a start, it begins with an ancient family legend/curse and the notion that a ghostly hound, with glowing eyes and jaws, is responsible for the death of the current incumbent in a lonely, remote, ancestral home on the Devon moors. The possibility of a supernatural explanation of the crime, as much as Holmes protests against the notion, remains throughout the entire novel, with perhaps even a faint whiff of it continuing on even after a human hand is revealed to be the culprit. Adding to the gothic trappings are some of the usual suspects: minimal number of dour servants, the sound of sobbing in the nighttime, lights and mysterious figures seen on the moor, threads of sexual impropriety, inheritance, an escaped convict, the use of doubles (Selden/Sir Henry, Stapleton/Sir Hugo), the use of Watson's notes to Holmes and his journal entries echo the letter and diary format of *Dracula*, and the endlessly atmospheric fog all conspire to hammer home the gothic effect. Sir Christopher Frayling, in his 1996 television program and accompanying book, *Nightmare: The Birth of Horror*, goes so far as to consider *The Hound* one of four cornerstone works — alongside *Frankenstein*, *The Strange Case of Dr. Jekyll and Mr. Hyde*, and *Dracula* — that together formed the basis of the modern horror novel. I tend to agree with him, and see Arthur Conan Doyle's Sherlock Holmes as much a part of the gothic horror tradition as he is an icon in the field of detective literature, which, dear reader, is why you're holding this book!

In the pages ahead you'll find ten terrific stories, from ten talented authors, who were invited to play in our gothic Sherlock Holmes sandbox. Some hew very closely to the gothic tradition, while others simply make use of a point or two to tell their unsettling tales of dread and horror. Mark Latham opens the collection with about as traditionally gothic a piece as you can get when Holmes and Watson are called upon by a young woman to solve a puzzle, and a murder or two, at the lonely familial manor house of a deceased inventor relation to gain her inheritance in 'The Cuckoo's Hour'. While David Stuart Davies wrote the foreword to *Gaslight Grimoire: Fantastic Tales of Sherlock Holmes* for us a decade ago, I'm delighted to finally have a story from him! Possibly inspired by the likes of M. R. James's 'Casting the Runes' or Doyle's own short novel *The Parasite*, David, in 'The Spirit of Death' takes a rather 'scientific horror' approach in a tale of obsession and revenge. Also returning to these pages is Stephen Volk, with another new powerhouse Poe and Holmes pairing, in 'Father of the Man'. When a Pinkerton turns up in Paris looking for the fellow Poe replaced in Baltimore years before, young Holmes takes a page from Poe's own writing to avoid disaster. James Lovegrove goes straight to Doyle's friend and fellow Edinburgh writer, Robert Louis

Stevenson, for his gothic inspiration and delivers a story of duality that could only be called 'The Strange Case of Dr. Sacker and Mr. Hope'. Meanwhile, Josh Reynolds, who provided an outstanding story for our *Professor Challenger: New Worlds, Lost Places* anthology, gets in on our Sherlock Holmes fun with 'The Ignoble Sportsmen', and shows us just how effective and far a cursed talisman can go to carry out an act of revenge. Nancy Holder, takes her cue from the Sherlockian Canon, specifically 'The Adventure of the Beryl Coronet' and provides a sequel featuring the fate of her near namesake Mary Holder, gypsies, witchcraft and betrayal. We return to the lonely country house setting when Holmes and Watson are called to the scene of a double beheading, that of a lady and her dog, in 'The Lizard Lady of Pemberton Grange' by the always excellent Mark Morris. Watson gets to the heart of an impossible crime in Canadian writer Kevin Thornton's short, sharp and shocking Sherlockian debut, 'The Magic of Africa'. Holmes gets a run for his money in the detection game when Watson brings in Kit Caswell to help out with a baffling case, rife with sexual jealousy, in Australian author Angela Slatter's incredibly engaging story 'A Matter of Light'. Rounding out the volume is Lyndsay Faye's touching, charming, and subtly horrifying, piece on perverse obsession, 'The Song of a Want'.

Ten years ago, I wrote the following to finish up the intro to *Gaslight Grimoire*, and all these years later it still seems apt to me:

> "No, not your traditional selection of Sherlock Holmes stories by any means, but what is the fun of that? After all, as Watson noted in 'The Speckled Band' *"...he refused to associate himself with any investigation which did not tend towards the unusual and even the fantastic..."* so why should we?"

As it is our 10th anniversary, I can't think of a better time to thank all the amazing talented writers and artists who've given of their time and skills to make this series a success! So, on behalf of J. R. Campbell and myself, thank you David Stuart Davies, Barbara Hambly, Christopher Sequeira,

Barbara Roden, M. J. Elliott, Martin Powell, Chico Kidd, Rick Kennett, Peter Calamai, Chris Roberson, Bob Madison, Kim Newman, Les Klinger, Stephen Volk, Lawrence C. Connolly, William Meikle, James A. Moore, William Patrick Maynard, Hayden Trenholm, Neil Jackson, Leigh Blackmore, Mark Morris, Simon K. Unsworth, Christopher Fowler, Tom English, Simon Clark, Paul Kane, Tony Richards, Mark Latham, James Lovegrove, Josh Reynolds, Nancy Holder, Kevin Thornton, Angela Slatter, Lyndsay Faye, Phil Cornell, Timothy Lantz, Dave Elsey, Mike Mignola, Neil D. Vokes, Luke Eidenschink and our publisher, Brian Hades. Getting to work with each and every one of you is a distinct pleasure.

Most of all, thank you, dear reader! Every one of the folks mentioned above do what they do, because of you.

Enjoy!
Charles Prepolec
Calgary, 2018

The Cuckoo's Hour

Mark A. Latham

It was a wretchedly hot day in August — the hottest of the year so far. All of London was dry and sweltering, as though a mischievous boy had turned his magnifier upon us and we were but insects beneath the focused rays of the sun. I hastened my step as I approached 221B Baker Street, eager to get off the street and out of my jacket and hat, wanting nothing more than to drink iced water and fan myself by the window. And yet my heart sank when I arrived, for I was at once greeted by Mrs. Hudson, informing me that a client had arrived just moments before me — a young lady.

I pulled off my jacket and frowned. "Did the lady give a name?"

"Miss Estella Harding," Mrs. Hudson replied. "Here is her card."

The name sounded at once familiar, and I quickly thumbed through my newspaper. There, on page four, was a comment about one Sir Theobald Harding who died recently in suspicious circumstances. 'Sir Theobald had no heirs,' the column read, 'but leaves three nephews and a niece to inherit.'

I thanked Mrs. Hudson and made my way upstairs at once, wondering if our visitor could be the niece.

When I opened the door of 221B I was met with a wave of heat even worse than on the street. Holmes always did like a repressive atmosphere, but he clearly had little thought for our guest, a slight young woman, who sat politely with a fan in her hand.

I strode across the room and opened the windows.

"Ah, there you are, Watson," Holmes said, noticing neither my discomfort, nor that of the lady. "This is Miss Harding. Miss Harding, this is my associate, Dr. Watson, right on time as always. Now we can begin."

To her great credit, Miss Harding passed no comment upon the sweltering heat. Rather, she removed the gloves from her dainty hands and fanned herself throughout our interview.

"You are here regarding the death of your uncle?" Holmes asked.

"Why... no," Miss Harding said. "And, well, I suppose yes. Oh, Mr. Holmes, I am at sixes and sevens."

"That's quite all right," Holmes said. "I read of Sir Theobald Harding's untimely demise in the newspapers. The Police News was most illuminating, although the details of the matter are perplexing."

"My uncle's death, although suspicious and shocking in its own right, was hardly untimely, for he was an old man, and a reclusive one. His death is being investigated still by the Ipswich constabulary, although if the talk in the village is to be believed, no killer shall be found."

"Oh?"

"The villagers say he was taken by a local curse, Mr. Holmes — claimed by Jack o' the Green."

"The Green Man?" Holmes asked, an eyebrow raised.

"Yes. They say, at the height of summer, Jack walks abroad searching for guilty men to drag away to his realm. Since Atreus Manor was built, the locals say Jack o' the Green has limited his wanderings to the estate — they say the house is cursed."

"I am familiar with such legends, although I've never heard of this spirit being a murderous one."

"You believe in the Green Man?"

"Not in the slightest," Holmes smiled. "But superstitious beliefs are worthy of study, if only to understand the prejudices of my fellow man. Now, to business, Miss Harding."

"Of course. Two days after my uncle's death, his solicitor, Mr. Paxman, summoned the four heirs named in Uncle Theobald's will."

"The reading of a will during a murder investigation is most irregular."

"Everything about this matter is irregular, Mr. Holmes. Uncle Theobald made specific provision for this eventuality, and insisted that the will be read come-what-may. In fact, not one of us even knew that we would be named in the will, for my uncle had always intimated that the entirety of his estate would be left to charity."

"And so, who inherits your uncle's fortune?"

"No one. Not yet. As I said, there were four of us named in the will — myself, and my cousins, Peter and Ralph Harding, and Algernon Simmerson. We were told that the entirety of Uncle Theobald's fortune was to be left to just one of us, but only upon the successful completion of a puzzle."

"What kind of puzzle?" Holmes' thin lips curled into the ghost of a smile, his sharp eyes twinkling at the prospect of a challenge.

"My uncle, along with my father, had a lifelong passion for riddles and puzzles. Together, they designed and built my uncle's home, Atreus Manor — a most singular building, full of symbolism and hidden chambers, so I've always been told."

"Told by your father?"

"No, sir. My father disappeared when I was a little girl, shortly after completing work on Atreus Manor. My mother later learned that he had run away to Java." Miss Harding looked somewhat embarrassed.

Holmes looked thoughtful. "Your father... he was the principal architect? Or was that your uncle?"

"I... No, my father was the artistic one. Uncle Theobald financed the house, and organized the labor, but my father designed it, and even created the many bronze sculptures that adorn the house and grounds."

"Wait a moment... then your father is Erasmus Harding, the sculptor noted for his macabre bronzes?"

"Yes. Uncle Theobald built a foundry for him on site, so he could create his masterworks. You were right that my father's works were a touch macabre, for the locals soon dubbed the site the 'Devil's Forge', and... Forgive me, Mr.

Holmes, unless you think it pertinent, I would rather not speak of my absent father. His abandonment of our family is still painful."

"My apologies, Miss Harding. Do go on."

The brave young lady gathered herself visibly. "The house is a kind of gigantic puzzle-box, I suppose. Hidden within is supposedly a great treasure, presumably brought back from foreign climes by my uncle, an explorer in his youth. Each of us was given an identical note by the solicitor, which we were told was the first clue. We were invited to enter the house at noon on the day of our choosing, whereupon the gates would be locked and we would be left alone to search the house and grounds in order to solve the puzzle. We have only twenty-four hours to do this — if the treasure is not found by the time the gates are opened the following day, we have failed. And we are allowed but one attempt, after which we forfeit our claim."

"Intriguing." Holmes pressed his fingertips together. "Who locks the house?"

"The servants — the last two, for whom my uncle has made a generous provision. Mr. and Mrs. Lafferty are gardener and housekeeper, a taciturn couple, dutiful to a fault. Their task is to set the house exactly as it was left the day my uncle died. Anything unearthed by the searching claimant was to be replaced, and the servants would not speak of it to a living soul. They treat this task like a solemn duty. Mr. Lafferty patrols the grounds at night to ensure no one leaves and no help is sought."

"So, you are forbidden any assistance in the search?"

"No outside assistance. We are permitted to ally ourselves to the task, but then the fortune must be divided equally among all those present. My cousins were most reticent to do this, as they each wanted the fortune for themselves, so we drew lots to see who would go first."

"I see. And who did go first?"

"My cousin, Peter. However, his older brother Ralph persuaded him that they should enter the estate together. Ralph has always been a manipulative sort, certainly when it comes to his brother; he couldn't let Peter solve the mystery alone and take the treasure. And so, on Wednesday at noon, they took up the challenge together. When the servants returned yesterday at noon, something terrible had transpired. Peter was a gibbering wreck. He has said nothing of what occurred in Atreus Manor and only babbles incoherently. Ralph, on the other hand, was not found at all."

"He is missing?"

"Yes, and Peter will say nothing that makes any sense, except..."

"Go on," Holmes said, gently.

"He keeps repeating, 'I saw him. The Green Man,' and then he cries out in terror."

"Surely the servants broke their oath?" I interjected. "They cannot use loyalty to their former master to cover up a crime."

"There is no evidence of any crime, Dr. Watson — we do not know where Ralph is. He could have found some treasure and fled to Java, like my father, for all we know. And besides, the Laffertys are insistent that nothing was amiss. They told the police that hardly anything was disturbed, so not much progress could have been made in the search for the treasure."

"No one saw or heard anything?"

"No one trustworthy, Mr. Holmes. That is to say, a couple of local poachers were nearby that night. They told some fanciful tale of a great, high-pitched shrieking noise, and firelight on the hill within the grounds of the Manor. Similar reports have been made several times over the years since it was built. I don't have the faintest idea what they mean."

"And these reports always come at the height of summer, I presume, as per the legend?"

"Yes."

"Hmm. And what of the other cousin?" Holmes asked. "Simmerson?"

"He has lost all stomach for the hunt and will have nothing to do with the matter."

"And so, it falls to you. But you said earlier that outside help was forbidden — surely you do not mean for me to work on your behalf?"

"That is precisely what I intend, Mr. Holmes. I have here a signed waiver, giving up my entitlement to the treasure. I want you to investigate the disappearance of my cousin, Mr. Holmes, and put to rest this foolishness."

"But you do not wish me to investigate the death of your uncle?"

"Perhaps the resolution of one mystery will solve the other," Miss Harding said, her eyes reddening slightly as she hardened herself. "But my uncle has ever brought ill to our family, even in death. Perhaps there is some small comfort in him receiving comeuppance at the hands of the Green Man."

"You speak as a woman betrayed," Holmes said. I saw in his eyes the tell-tale gleam of some recondite deduction. "You were close to your uncle?"

"You are most astute, Mr. Holmes. Yes, I tried many times to reach out to my uncle over the years and show him some kindness. I stayed in the house once, just for one night, to nurse him when he was ill. He made it quite clear he would rather be alone. I took him for a foolish old eccentric, but there was a malevolence to his nature. I would not have spent another night in that house at any cost, even if my cantankerous uncle had not nigh chased me away."

"Why so?"

"There was something… eerie… about it, Mr. Holmes. All the time I was there I had the strangest feeling of being watched. And then at night I heard… discomfiting… noises."

"What kind of noises?" Holmes asked.

"Groaning, I suppose. Or perhaps weeping. A man, I thought."

"Just the wind," I suggested. "Old houses are prone to such noises. Why I remember that time we—"

Holmes cut me short with a raised hand. "Atreus Manor is less than twenty-five years old, Watson. Miss Harding, were any other men in the house when this happened? Your cousins? Mr. Lafferty?"

"No, Mr. Holmes. Just myself and my uncle. The Laffertys live in the village, and call each day."

"Unusual in itself," Holmes mused. "At what o'clock was your sleep disturbed?"

"As it happens I checked my mantel clock. I remember it well — it was shortly after one in the morning. It is a time that has taken on a greater significance since."

"Why so?"

"It was around the same time that those poachers I mentioned reported the strange disturbances at the house. The same time that... that I suppose poor Ralph..." The poor girl took a deep breath to compose herself.

Holmes nodded. "I suppose it was when you broached the subject of these noises that your uncle became less hospitable?"

"How did you guess?"

"Guessing is a terrible habit, Miss Harding."

"Well... yes. I mentioned it over breakfast, and was all but ordered to leave the house. He did not have to tell me twice."

"About your cousins — did they also attempt to extend the hand of familial fondness to your uncle?"

"Not in the slightest! I don't believe Algernon spoke to Uncle Theobald more than once these past twenty years. Indeed, Peter once tried to have him committed in order to take his fortune from him. Ironic, really, that it is Peter himself who is now in the sanatorium. He was ambitious, certainly — some might say conniving — but a man so young does not deserve so ignoble a fate."

"I am sure you are right," Holmes bowed his head. "What did you make of your uncle's mental state? You said before he was eccentric... did you think him mad enough for the asylum?"

"I... I don't know. I thought not, although something about his terrible murder has made me reconsider. A strange note, scrawled in his hand, found at the scene. It made no sense at all, and the police wonder to his state of mind."

"What did it say?"

"I cannot remember precisely. It was all about Greek mythology. Something about Crete, and Hephaestus... he called himself Zeus. He's the king of the gods, isn't he? I suppose the alienists would say that made my uncle truly mad."

"Or in fear of his life," Holmes said, frowning.

"I suppose so, Mr. Holmes. Oh… do you think there is something to this curse? Poor Peter…"

"I do not believe in curses, Miss Harding. You were right to come to me, but forgive me for saying: I cannot help but think you need this inheritance more than your cousins. Are you sure you can afford to throw away the opportunity?"

The woman's eyes moistened, and my heart melted for her. "Why would you say that, Mr. Holmes?"

"I noted you did not remove your gloves until the rather close atmosphere of this room forced you to. Your hands are soft, unused to manual work, and yet they bear the tell-tale marks of repeated scrapes at the washboard. You have lost your own servants, and fairly recently, I would say. Your clothes, too, are not best suited for this weather, as though your selection of attire has been forcibly narrowed."

"My change in fortunes cannot be remedied by blood money," she said. "Whatever fortune my uncle has hidden is cursed, and I will not touch it, even if it means the workhouse for me. But do not worry, Mr. Holmes, I have set aside enough to pay your fee, and if it is insufficient I am sure I can persuade Algernon to help. Will you take the case, Mr. Holmes?"

Holmes pursed his lips thoughtfully. "Madam, if it will give you peace of mind, I shall help you."

Miss Harding's face brightened. "Oh, Mr. Holmes, Dr. Watson, I cannot thank you enough. Here — this is the first 'clue' that we were given. I cannot make sense of it. And here is the waiver — you will need to show this to Mr. Paxman in Badingham. Thank you again, Mr. Holmes, and goodbye!"

No sooner had the young woman gone than Holmes stooped over the paper she had given him. This so-called "clue" took the form of four lines of verse, running thus:

> *The progeny cursed by Myrtilus points*
> *With shadows cold cast by the sun at its height*
> *And beneath the bower of the one who hunts,*
> *The cuckoo's hour shall herald the night.*

"What does it mean, Holmes?" I asked.

"I shall know for certain once we have inspected this mysterious property, I'm sure."

"You really intend to go?"

Holmes frowned. "Why ever wouldn't I?"

"This infernal puzzle has already claimed one victim."

"My dear Watson, your concern for my well-being is touching. But the thickest case in the past month was that affair at Norwood, and that barely tested my faculties. I would rather face mortal danger than stagnate! Tomorrow, we go to Suffolk, and find out what this strange affair is all about."

— «» —

For all of his glib assertions, Sherlock Holmes was no fool. Holmes packed his revolver and ensured I took mine. Before leaving for Suffolk, he exchanged messages with Inspector Stanley Hopkins, acquiring the official report into Sir Theobald's murder, and securing the Inspector's services. While we were investigating the strange house, the Inspector would be at work in Badingham, on hand if needed. Given the danger, I suggested that the police should accompany us into the house itself, but Holmes wouldn't hear of it.

"A horde of clumsy policeman fumbling about the house? I think not, Watson," he said.

We first called at the office of Mr. Paxman, the Harding family solicitor. A stern man in his twilight years, of a disagreeable disposition due to gout, Mr. Paxman was not at all pleased to see us. Indeed, the solicitor only acquiesced after the most obtuse legal arguments that Holmes could muster. There was but one outstanding complication: Holmes and I were to sign a waiver of our own absolving Paxman's firm, and the servants of the Harding estate, of any liability for harm that might befall us during our time on the property. I confess, the thought that we might meet with some dark fate, and that no one should be held accountable for it, was a grim one. Were it not for Holmes' unwavering determination to go on with the assignment as planned, I should have turned about and boarded the next train back to London. As it was, we barely had time to rendezvous with Inspector Hopkins before we went on to the house itself for our fateful midday appointment.

"Here is the information you requested." Hopkins handed a piece of paper to Holmes. "It was wired to me this morning."

I squinted over Holmes' shoulder. It was a transcript of the mysterious note found on the night of Sir Theobald's death. It read:

> *Is this then my punishment? Am I not Lord of all I survey? Am I not a bountiful lord? I thought myself Zeus upon Olympus, granting Europa a mighty gift — a tower from which she might survey the land of Crete, and all that she loved. For she never returned the love of her Zeus, her God, it seems. And like Zeus, I bade Hephaestus to create for her a Talos, who protects fair Europa as is his duty, long after she is gone, and long after I have joined her.*
> *He has called, and tonight, I shall answer.*

"Do you know what it means?" Hopkins asked.

"No," said Holmes. "But before the day is through, I'm sure I will."

Atreus Manor was indeed the house of a recluse. Our carriage followed a winding, three-mile trail through a thick forest that encircled the boundary of the property. At last we approached a massive pair of iron gates set into a high wall. There, a glowering servant-woman and her stooped husband awaited us.

"Mr. and Mrs. Lafferty?" Holmes called. The woman nodded. Holmes hopped from the carriage. "Excellent. I believe we have five minutes to spare."

"Two," replied the woman. "My instructions are most precise.... Mr. Sherlock Holmes."

A thin smile crossed Holmes' features. "My good woman, you know that terrible things have befallen the occupants of Atreus Manor ever since the death of your master, Sir Theobald. I must ask, have you checked and secured this house today?"

"I have."

"And you did the same on the night the two young Harding men began their treasure-hunt?"

"The very same."

"And you were satisfied then, as you are now, that there is no one else in that house?"

"None who's livin', sir."

"What?" I interrupted. "Are you implying that there are ghosts in the house?"

The woman's expression grew sterner; there was a glimmer of annoyance in her eyes. "I never said that."

"One more question, Mrs. Lafferty—" Holmes began.

Mrs Lafferty swung open the gate, its hinges squealing loudly. "Time's up. You go in now, or I lock it up an' your chance is gone."

Holmes smiled somewhat knowingly, doffed his hat to the woman, and strode through the gate.

"What was that about, Holmes?" I asked as we trudged along the path.

"Watson, that woman had every opportunity to give a straight answer to a simple question. When a straight answer is not forthcoming, and the interviewee is not a politician, I always presume they know more than they wish to tell."

Atreus Manor rose before us almost organically, every inch the enigma it had been reported. It was built along the lines of geometric shapes — a square central wing, a pentagonal east wing, and an octagonal tower. Flying buttresses, crenellations, gargoyles and tall steeples gave the house a jagged, forbidding appearance. Most of its dark windows were tall arches, though some were round, or hexagonal, or little more than arrow-slits. There was no symmetry to its outline, no logic to its form. The only uniformity at all came from the materials from which it was built: a dark gray stone that lent a forbidding, ancient air to a house that should by rights have been modern and warm.

"To the house, Holmes?" I asked, though with some reluctance.

"No time for that, Watson. We must search the grounds for a bronze statue of Atreus, and we must be quick about it."

"Atreus? Why?" I was somewhat irked that my friend had come to some conclusion without informing me, though that was his way, infuriating as it was.

"The verse, Watson. The progeny cursed by Myrtilus were Atreus and Thyestes. Given the name of this house, I would think Atreus was the obvious answer. The shadow cast by the statue points to a clue. The verse read 'cold cast', however — an obvious reference to the bronze casting process. The statue should not be too hard to find — Erasmus Harding is noted for his sculptures of devils and monsters. Noble Atreus should rather stand out."

And yet, it did not. Holmes and I spent over an hour pacing the grounds in blistering heat, across overgrown lawns, past the old ice-house, over the bridge and up the hill to the "Devil's Forge", which we found locked and chained up. We searched the kitchen garden and the orchard, the orangery and the family cemetery. The only statues we found were grotesque gargoyles — a pantheon of beasts and grinning demons. As the sun began to descend in the afternoon sky, so too did Holmes' shoulders sink, his energy evaporating. Could this be one of those rare occasions when my friend was simply wrong?

Dejected, Holmes eventually relented to my plea to go inside for shelter. We returned to the front of the house, crossing the threshold into a hall, in which tangles of roots and ivy had been allowed to grow, creating the illusion of a house in ruin. A loud cry almost scared me out of my wits, and a great black crow hopped down from the boughs of one of the indoor trees, and fluttered past us through the front door. How long it had been trapped in the house, who could say?

Once through the entryway we entered a second hall, more traditional in style. Sunlight streamed in through a stained-glass dome high above, casting ominous hues of purple and blood-red across every surface. Numerous rooms lay to our left and right. Ahead, a sweeping staircase curled up to a balcony. Beside it, a passageway stretched off to the back of the house, although one door lay open, leading off the passage.

Holmes looked about and at once his eyes sparkled with life again.

"Look here on the floor, Watson," he said.

"Cracked tiles, scuffs and grime," I said. "Is that unusual?"

"In such a new house, upon which a fortune has been spent, perhaps. The dirt, when all else in this hall has been scrupulously cleaned by our good Mrs. Lafferty, certainly. Light a lamp, Watson, I must have bright light unsullied by this stained-glass."

I did so, and held it over the scuffs as Holmes took out his magnifier and a pair of tweezers.

"Here," he said, holding up some fibrous material. "It is some kind of algae, perhaps, embedded in the cracked tiles. And it is flecked with... metallic particles, I think."

"Is that bronze?" I asked.

Holmes nodded. "And look — the broken tiles form a pattern. Indeed, they mark a trail to that room over there." My friend led the way at once to the door that was open. Within was a large study, cluttered with books and exotic curios, taxidermy and statuary. What strip of carpet was visible through the clutter was stained blackish-green, and even torn in parts. Holmes attempted to place his feet beside each mark as he followed the trail, but the distance between them was too great even for his long stride, and so he stopped, and frowned.

I followed the trail further, around the back of a great desk. The carpet behind it was stained with worse than algae.

"Blood," said Holmes. "So, this is indeed the room where Sir Theobald was found. His killer walked through the front door and right up to the old man's desk without interruption."

"Are you saying those marks were... footprints? Impossible, Holmes. They would have to have been made by a giant."

"I make no supposition just yet, Watson," said Holmes. "The facts, as I know them, are thus: Harding was found dead on the floor behind his desk. His neck was snapped, not from throttling, but from the sheer force of the blow to the head. The police surgeon in Ipswich thankfully makes up for in diligence what he lacks in skill, and his report is thorough, though his conclusions are flawed. Still, it cannot be denied that a blunt metal object caused the damage.

Traces of bronze were found embedded in the man's broken skull."

"He would not have allowed someone to walk up before him and murder him so, surely?" said I.

"No alarm was raised, according to Mrs. Lafferty. The front door was unlocked, and the key was found in Harding's pocket."

We made a brief survey of the ground floor. Atreus Manor was no ordinary house. The garish surroundings combined with the unbearable summer heat to produce an atmosphere of oppression. Every room was irregular in proportion and shape, great arched windows casting strange shadows in a most disorientating manner. Walls and ceilings leaned at odd angles, statues leered from niches, and carved pillars broke up every open space. Pilasters and baroque buttresses jutted from walls both indoors and out. Every inch of wood panel was carved with grotesque faces and strange sigils; every expanse of plasterwork was painted with frescoes of unsettling design. The only room not so embellished was the one sited in the octagonal tower, a windowless lounge sitting betwixt kitchen and hallway. Here, though, on each of its eight walls was a pair of levers, which I was tempted to throw until Holmes stayed my hand, warning me that nothing must yet be touched.

Holmes went next to the staircase, pausing at several family portraits, particularly interested in the more recent additions near the top of the landing. He lingered over the portraits of Sir Theobald's late wife, Sir Theobald himself, and the dead man's errant brother, Erasmus. Holmes issued a cryptic "A-ha!" before proceeding across the balcony and down the corridor, whereupon he flung open every door into one over-embellished room after another. Several times he stopped, pacing methodically as though measuring the distance between the rooms, and yet he did not enter any of them.

At last we came to another staircase, narrower this time, leading up to an attic room. For all the summer warmth, I at once felt a cold funk about me as I entered the dingy chamber, for it was quite unlike the rest of the house. It had once been a bedchamber, though it had seen no occupancy for some time. A small four-poster stood against the middle of the back wall, draped in cobwebs and musty linen. A child's cot, rotted and broken to pieces, in one corner, though as far as I knew the Hardings had ever been childless. A sad testament to more hopeful times, perhaps?

A lady's things were laid out on a small dressing table, before a cracked and filthy mirror. Holmes examined the items of jewelry and bottles of scent, with his magnifier, and then swept his eye around the room.

"There are no photographs or paintings in this room, Watson," Holmes said. "It was clearly a lady's bedroom, and has been singularly untouched for many years, and yet it is the only room in this gaudy manor without a single picture. Why?"

By the small attic window sat an invalid-chair, and I had no time to answer his query before Holmes made for it.

"Look, Watson! The brakes are still applied to the chair's wheels, and here..." he pointed to the leather straps about the arms of the chair.

"Restraints," I said. "So, the occupant of this room was a danger to themselves. Perhaps, a lunatic?"

"So it would seem. The scrapes on the floorboards indicate that the chair was moved back and forth from the bed to the window frequently, occasionally with some resistance. And from its position at the window we see... Good Lord, Watson! How did we miss it?"

Through the window, plain as day, we saw a rose garden, hidden in a hollow, bordered on one side by the walls of the orchard and surrounded by tall hedges, such that from the ground it would have been difficult to access. The garden was overgrown, although I could make out four winding paths converging upon a marble plinth, upon which a great bronze statue reclined languidly, one hand raised to the heavens, a finger pointing. Pointing, it seemed, at us.

— «» —

Holmes stood at the foot of the verdigris'd statue, which was perhaps more unsettling than any of Erasmus Harding's other creations, such was the look of lifelike fear and sorrow etched upon its life-size features. The shadow cast by the pointing hand was barely visible amongst the tangle of rose-bushes, as the sun now slipped behind the tall hedges that masked the garden. Holmes risked thorny scratches and forced his foot into the undergrowth, placing his heel directly at the tip of the shrinking shadow, and pacing methodically back to the plinth upon which the statue rested.

"I was mistaken again," Holmes said. "This is not Atreus after all, but his brother, Thyestes. The motive is beginning to come into focus, Watson, though I cannot fathom yet the method."

"Motive? Method? To what crime do you refer?" I asked.

"What time is it, Watson?" Holmes ignored me.

I sighed and checked my pocket-watch. "Three-fifteen," I replied.

"Three-seventeen, then," he said. "Your watch loses two minutes each day on average when you forget to wind it. I have not seen you do so today. So, we must calculate the shadow's length at noon."

Holmes took out a notepad and pencil, and made a quick sketch of the garden, before scribbling equations all over it. How his mind retained such miscellany I will never understand, but presently he paced clockwise from the angle of the shadow.

"A pretty trick!" said I. "Having us arrive here at noon, and then make the clue impossible to find."

"Not impossible. Indeed, the calculation of a shadow's length is a simple one, and the sun's position at noon constant. I almost wonder if the finding of the attic, which showed us this statue, was the real point of the clue. Nevertheless..." Holmes paced to where his calculations had guided him, stepping over more roses. "There, Watson," he pointed.

I tackled the undergrowth myself and discovered a number of tiny headstones hidden amongst the roses. I shuddered.

"A pet cemetery, it seems," Holmes said. "What are the names on those stones?"

"Cherry, Wolf, Herne, Paws—"

Holmes bounded over before I could finish.

"Herne. Remember, Watson, the clue read 'beneath the bower of the one who hunts'. Herne the Hunter is a famous legend. He is known locally by another name."

"Jack o' the Green..." I muttered, feeling most ill at ease in that tiny graveyard, with the grotesque, greening statue staring at my back.

"This headstone is loose," Holmes said, wobbling it back and forth. "Let's lift it out."

We worked together. Once the stone was removed we peered into the hole it had left, and saw a dirty, rusted tin. Holmes nodded to me. I sighed as I fished into the worm-infested earth and pulled out the tin.

"This has been moved, and recently," Holmes said. "Even the lid is loose. I wonder if Miss Harding's cousins got this far after all."

"Mrs. Lafferty suggested otherwise," I said.

"Indeed. Either she is lying, or someone else replaced this clue. Or..." he paused.

"What, Holmes?"

"No, never mind for now. Look here."

The tin contained only a faded Daguerreotype of a man in his late forties. His eyes were piercing, his brows strong, his expression singular in its intelligence. Holmes turned the picture over. On the back, though hard to discern due to the stains of dirt, was a number.

"Thirteen," Holmes said.

"What does it mean?" I asked. "What does this have to do with a cuckoo?"

"This picture is of Erasmus Harding. Even had I not seen the portrait hanging in the house, I would have recognized his eyes; which he has passed on to his daughter."

"Yes, I see it now. But the 'cuckoo's hour'... I did not see a cuckoo clock in the house, although we could have easily missed it amongst the clutter."

"I don't think it is quite so literal, Watson. But... wait! Watson, you are ever of singular use to me."

"Why, I try my best, Holmes..."

"Whenever my mind seeks to untangle the thickest puzzle, you point out to me the simple solution. And sometimes, Watson, that solution may even be near the truth."

—- «» —

Holmes crouched on the landing, his head within the cabinet of the grandfather clock.

"There is a mechanism of some kind at the back of the case," Holmes said. "Its purpose is unclear to me, and the design intricate. I would expect if we set the time to the 'cuckoo's hour', something will be revealed."

"I suppose the 'thirteen' could be military time," I offered. "We were in the grounds at thirteen-hundred hours. Perhaps we missed it."

"No, Watson. That would serve the late Sir Theobald no purpose in his little treasure-hunt. And besides, we know from Miss Harding that one in the morning is significant."

"That makes no sense."

"It makes perfect sense when one advances the clock and sees that the hands point to twelve and to one. That makes thirteen. As I said, a simple solution."

Holmes reached behind the clock face and wound on the hands until it was almost one o'clock, and then stood, and waited.

The clock chimed softly. Then it chimed again, and again. On it went, and Holmes counted with me, until thirteen chimes had struck.

"Good lord, Holmes," I said. "The clock strikes thirteen. What misfortune does this herald?"

Holmes held up a hand to silence me, and we listened carefully. From both above and below us came soft clunking sounds. Holmes bounded up the stairs that instant, shouting "Watson, go downstairs, see what you can find!"

Trying my best to find the location of the sound, I dashed downstairs. And then I saw it: the paneling in the wall under the stairs was ajar — a hidden door had creaked open and revealed itself from the wainscoting. I threw open the panel quickly, encouraged by Holmes' urgency, lest the door lock again suddenly. A dark passage faced me, and I did not relish the thought of entering it. I searched around for a candlestick. When finally I had a light burning, I turned back to the passage. A pale, angular face loomed from the shadows, features ghastly in the candlelight. I jumped back, before recognizing Sherlock Holmes.

"What kept you, Watson?" he asked. "Ah, you found a light. Good man. Now come along."

I followed Holmes through a corridor, not wide enough to walk through without turning sideways. The ceiling too was low, encroaching further still due to a tangle of thick metal pipes that shot off in all directions. I held the candle aloft as much as I could to light the way, although Holmes seemed accustomed enough to the dark. At the end of the passage was a steep stair, but Holmes stopped before it. He began rapping on the walls, then pushing against the wooden panels.

"There is a room behind this panel, Watson, but I cannot see how it is opened. Up the stairs there is another passage, like this, which runs between two bedrooms. In it I found a small tin box full of keepsakes. Beneath the box was taped a sequence of numbers. Come, I'll show you."

I followed Holmes up the narrow stair, and was thankful when he led the way out of the passages altogether, and into one of the bedrooms where we might examine the box he had found in daylight.

"Those passages are most interesting," Holmes said. "There is no way to open them from the inside — they open only when the clock strikes thirteen, which must be once every night. The clock mechanism operated on a twenty-four-hour cycle, not twelve."

"When Miss Harding spent the night here, surely she would have heard the chime?"

"No, if you recall, it is a very soft chime. This, I am certain, was Miss Harding's room on that night, and I doubt the clock can be heard from here. Any noise in the secret passage, however, could be heard. Look."

Holmes pointed at the unusually large air-vents, which I realized now must lead into the passage.

"Is that what the pipes are for?" I asked, for they were somewhat unusual even in a very modern house. "I thought perhaps they were for heating."

"I doubt they serve either purpose, Watson," Holmes said with an air of mystery.

He passed no further comment, instead rifling through the contents of the tin. He handed to me various knick-knacks, from costume jewelry to scraps of scented notepaper, from torn squares of old lace to a lock of hair.

"I think that is Miss Harding's," Holmes said, "judging by the color and curl."

"What? How?"

"Either she gave it to someone as a keepsake, or it was taken from her while she slept."

I was aghast at the thought of someone entering the young woman's bedchamber as she slept, and looked with renewed suspicion upon the passageway we had discovered. When I turned back to Holmes, I saw that he held one final artifact: a letter.

"This is most interesting, Watson. It is but a scrap of something longer. The paper is perfumed, but different from the other fragments in the box; it is older, for the scent has faded considerably. The ink, too… I would place this note as perhaps fifteen years old. The hand is a woman's."

"What does it say?"

"It is hard to discern. The woman who wrote this note was in a state of great distress. But the message is in some form of code. This segment here is most telling: 'He cannot keep us apart forever, darling boy.' I think this message was written by the late Jennett Harding."

"Sir Theobald's wife, writing to… a lover? Surely not, Holmes. We have already seen that the woman was not of sound mind or body."

"Not a lover, no — not in this instance at least. A loved one, certainly. And one that she was forbidden from seeing. Watson, this house holds a secret most sinister — a secret I am sure was meant for Sir Theobald's niece to find, and that we must uncover in her stead."

"For Estella Harding? Why ever would you think that?"

"Too much of what we have found already pertains to Miss Harding or her father. I think the whole pursuit of inheritance was a sham — Theobald Harding wanted Estella to find the treasure, and ensured that the clues were so weighted as to allow her to do so. But I wonder how far Miss Harding's cousins got before their search was foiled? Not this far, I'd wager."

Holmes held up one more trinket, which I had not seen before. A cufflink. I took it from him, and a chill ran through me as I saw the initials engraved upon its surface. "R.H."

"Ralph Harding," I muttered. Holmes nodded. "So, who put this here? Who collects these things? The Laffertys?"

Holmes shook his head, and leaned in, speaking very softly. "Be careful what you say, Watson." His eyes flicked to the vent and back. "I do not think we're alone. And I suspect we can be heard, and possibly seen."

"Seen? I..." I stopped short, looked about furtively, and nodded. I recalled at once Miss Harding's assertion that she had felt she was being watched whilst in Atreus Manor. Now, whether out of genuine prescience or the power of Holmes' suggestion, I felt it too.

"What do you think became of Ralph and Peter Harding?" I whispered.

"They got almost as far as we have, Watson. But I think they waited until one o'clock in the morning for things to unfold naturally, and that was their undoing."

"But there is no clue, Holmes. Where do we go from here?"

Holmes smiled a thin smile, and turned over the tin in his hands. On the underside of the rust-spotted box was a neat row of numbers followed by pairs of repetitive figures of the Chinese style, punched into the metal, thus:

1 陰陰 2 陰陽 3 陽陽 4 陽陰 5 陰陽 6 陽陰 7 陽 8 陰陰.

"That looks like something from the *I Ching*," I muttered, recalling the letter forms from a monograph Holmes had once asked me to read over.

"You are right, Watson," Holmes whispered. "The 'yin' and 'yang' of *I Ching* are related to the old forms of binary arithmetic, if you recall."

"By Jove, Holmes, I think I have it!" I cried. "The octagonal room... the levers."

Holmes placed a finger to his lips and frowned. I reddened at my own foolishness. The thrill of the treasure hunt had got the better of me.

Holmes placed a hand on my shoulder, reassuringly. "Well done, Watson, you cracked it. Now, we must hurry."

We returned to the octagonal room, which Holmes measured as being some six-and-a-half feet from the secret passage we had uncovered, and therefore whatever was behind the panel we had found lay directly between this room and the passage itself. Holmes paced around the circumference first of all, as much as was possible given the clutter. Each of the eight walls was set with a pair of large levers. On seven of the walls they were close together, though on the wall by which we had entered the levers were either side of the door. On the ceiling was a painted mural in the classical style, depicting some scene of Roman mythology, signified by the Roman numerals dotted about. Each numeral, I to VIII, was situated above one of the eight walls. I made at once to the wall marked "I".

"The inner dimensions of this room are smaller than would be expected for the breadth of the tower," Holmes said. "I expect the reason why shall soon become apparent."

"Now, we start at the levers marked 'I'," Holmes said. "Look here at the first set of Chinese characters." The first part of the code was: 陰陰 "Identical symbols, both signifying 'yin' or 'dark', used in some cyphers as the binary number zero. In a system of switches, this is usually represented by the downward or 'off' position."

Holmes threw both switches down. The second set of characters was: 陰陽 or 0-1, and he threw the switches to 'down-up'. This process he repeated, until the sixteenth and final switch was pulled downwards.

There was a loud clunk. The very floor shuddered. The door slammed shut. The light flickered then dimmed.

"Good lord, Holmes, what's happening?"

"Courage, Watson — we are surely close now!"

The floor swayed like the deck of a ship, and the rumble of machinery, though muffled, could be heard. The room revolved! I tried the door, but it was locked fast. After a minute or two, the juddering ceased and I breathed in relief when I heard the metallic clunk of locks being released at the door. That relief turned to apprehension as I saw the darkness that now lay beyond the door.

"The other side of the passage..." Holmes muttered. "Watson, take up the candle. The only way is onwards."

The pitch-dark void smelled of ancient dust and the air was so hot and thick that my breathing at once became labored. Our candlelight revealed a set of steep stairs winding downwards into further gloom.

Holmes pointed first to a handle on the wood-paneled wall. "As I thought. The passage under the stairs can be accessed from the inside. But from there, the rest of the house is sealed off until the clock strikes thirteen."

"But why?"

"Security, I should think, in case someone gets as far as we have. Which means the true prize lies down those stairs."

Holmes led on fearlessly with a lightness of step I struggled to emulate. The stairs delved deeper than I would have thought possible, and at last Holmes and I emerged into a circular chamber, dark and dingy, cobwebs tangling in our hair as we gasped for breath in the dusty cellar.

"Here, Watson, light this." Holmes pointed to a sconce on which a pair of stubby candles sat, almost burned away, but sufficient for our needs.

When our eyes adjusted to the half-light we surveyed the chamber before us. It was another octagonal room, rough-hewn from old stone, undoubtedly the base of the tower. In the center of the room was a round table, smooth, but dusty. Above it hung a thick tangle of wide, lead pipes, which spread upwards, across the ceiling and through the walls, like inverted tree roots. The sealed ends of the pipes were positioned some three feet from the surface of the table, and each had a pair of small valves near its closed aperture.

"Look, Watson. The dust on this table has been cleared frequently, by the sweeping motion of an arm. The smooth surface, therefore, must be important, and I think I know why."

Holmes turned a valve. A pipe unshuttered, projecting a beam of light onto the table top. Holmes adjusted it further, and the surface of the table lit with a dim glow, a picture slowly coming into focus. A picture of Sir Theobald's study.

"Good heavens, Holmes! It is a *camera obscura*!"

"Indeed," Holmes replied. "Each of these pipes must contain an ingenious configuration of mirrors, acting rather like a periscope. I wonder just how many rooms this device is able to spy on."

Holmes adjusted the valves, one at a time, discovering the attic room, the hallway, and the bedroom believed to be used by Estella.

"That's just scandalous!" My color rose at the implication of our discovery.

"I agree, Watson. But think for a moment about the first image — that of Theobald Harding's study. If someone were down here the night he was killed, they could have seen the murderer."

"They most likely were the murderer," I said.

"Likely, but not certain. Ah, now what's this?" Holmes looked to the floor, where he had kicked a sheaf of dirt-stained papers. As he stooped to pick them up, he spied something else. He pulled open a cupboard set into the pedestal and his eyes lit up. "If I am not mistaken, Watson, our search is at an end. Here is our treasure!"

I held my breath, wondering what riches Holmes had found. Yet, when he stood, it was with neither treasure chest, nor handfuls of jewels, but instead rolls of paper and a stack of musty books. Ignoring my surprise, Holmes unrolled what appeared to be architectural plans of the house and grounds, and weighted them down with the books.

"Here we see it, Watson! The passages that were built into this house — where we stand now is not the fullest extent. There are other routes also, leading to the grounds, and here, look — one that goes directly to the so-called 'Devil's Forge'. Some were added later — you can see the ink is heavier and of a different hue — and there are handwritten coded notes. They must reference the various puzzles by which the passages may be opened."

"So, whoever occupies these passages has free roam over the house and grounds," I said. "Our murderer must have used these passages to commit his crimes."

"Not the murderer of Sir Theobald, I think. It looks as though most of these passages can only be opened from the outside, as we've already found. Whoever is down here, with these plans, must surely be able to see the object of their salvation, but is unable to open the passages until someone outside allows it."

"Or the clock strikes thirteen," I added.

"And here..." Holmes traced a finger over the diagram of the room in which we stood, frowning over some puzzle written in gibberish. "There are passages leading away from this chamber, if only I can find how to open them."

As he studied the code, I idly looked at the books he had withdrawn. One in particular caught my eye — it was bound by hand, its title stamped on the cover. 'A Treatise on Advanced Coated Bronze Sculpture', by E. M. Harding. And then I noticed something more.

"Holmes," I said, although my friend was so engrossed he did not pay me heed. "Holmes! There is a stain on this book. I think it is blood."

Holmes took out his magnifier and checked the book cover, his mouth tightening. "You are right, Watson, and it is not so very old. I wonder..."

But even as Holmes mused, there came a soft click. A panel in the wall behind us opened a fraction, revealing darkness beyond.

Holmes looked to me, and I to him. "Your pistol," he whispered.

I drew it immediately. Holmes advanced stealthily, more silently than any other man could, and I followed. I aimed my pistol at the secret door as Holmes reached across and pulled it open. It swung slowly, revealing nothing but a pitch-black void. We stood in silence, peering into the inky dark. Finally, when nothing came forth, my finger relaxed on the trigger. Holmes breathed a relieved sigh.

And then, with sudden violence, a face appeared. A hideous visage, large and green, gnarled like tree-bark, with cascades of ivy trailing from it. It roared like a beast, and this... thing... barrelled into me, sending the pistol flying from my hand, and me crashing into the *camera obscura*. I struggled to my feet, half-dazed, half in fear. I saw the hulking, green form struggle with Holmes. I saw Holmes fall to the floor. In that moment, I cried out with rage and leapt forward, swallowing my fear in an effort to save — or perhaps avenge — my friend. I found myself at once in the grip of something powerful; a man, I thought, but one possessed of great strength. He smelled of fetid earth. Great hands encircled my throat, choking the life from me. My vision swam. I clawed at the face — a mask, of wood and foliage, like some far-distant tribal shaman might wear. My strength ebbed and at last failed.

I whispered "Holmes," as my vision went dark, and I succumbed to the power of Jack o' the Green.

— «» —

I awoke to blistering heat. I was upright, but bound to something in a pose akin to crucifixion. Acrid smoke stung my eyes, cloyed at my throat and nostrils so that I could barely see, or breathe. The smell of brimstone was overpowering. The sounds of industrial endeavour clanked and whirred all around. For one terrible moment, I thought I was in hell.

I detected movement nearby. I blinked furiously, trying in vain to turn in the direction of the sound. A shadow lurched awkwardly nearby. As my streaming eyes adjusted, I saw a huge, hunchbacked figure wrestling with levers, cranks, and bellows. A flare of light fair blinded me as molten metal was released from a cauldron, pouring in rivulets towards a central reservoir near my feet. Man-sized. Coffin-like. At this realization I tried to struggle, but I was tied fast.

At my muffled cries, the hunchback turned to me, his great wooden mask and cascades of green even more monstrous than I remembered. He limped to a great wheel, and turned it slowly, with no small effort. At each revolution, the cross to which I was affixed jerked downwards, hinged at my feet, while my face drew closer and closer to the molten metal. Molten bronze, I now believed. I was in the Devil's Forge. My eyes flashed around in panic, alighting on other figures. Bronze statues, gleaming in orange light. Disfigured, warped. What some might have mistaken for discarded failures of the sculptor's workshop, I saw now for what they really were, and for what I was about to become. Human remains, sealed for eternity in bronze. The terrible truth almost made me pass out, my mind unable to process the sheer horror of my predicament.

Closer still I went, until my eyebrows singed and my jacket began to smoke. I prayed for a swift end.

Some other sound arose nearby. Thudding, grunting. A great crash, then another. I turned my eyes, my tears now evaporating as quickly as they formed. There were two shadows now, whirling in a deadly dance. Statues toppled; voices were raised. A gunshot, then another, deafening in the confined space.

And then, mercifully, my cross jerked upwards; the squeaking of the great wheel heralded salvation as I rose further and further away from the liquid bronze. Moments later, I was free. I collapsed into Holmes' arms — my dear friend, who I had thought dead, now appeared as a guardian angel in that hellish place. What exactly happened in the immediate aftermath of my release I cannot say, for I was concussed, and nigh insensible with shock.

— «» —

Stanley Hopkins puffed out his cheeks and shook his head. At first light, two local ironmongers had been summoned to break apart the statue of Thyestes, and now those two stout men staggered away from the remnants in disbelief.

Sherlock Holmes nodded grimly as the human remains within were revealed — bones indelibly fused with bronze.

"Erasmus Harding," Holmes said.

"I'll be blowed..." Inspector Hopkins muttered. "How did you know?"

"My suspicions were aroused by the various references to classical mythology. In my experience, even the most disturbed mind would never be so precise in its symbolism unless that symbolism had deeper meaning. In this case, the very name of the house, Atreus Manor, was a clue. Atreus was a king of the Mycaenae, if my classics do not fail me, who was infamously cuckolded by his brother. Guess the name of the brother, Watson."

"Thyestes?" I ventured.

"Indeed. The very statue in which Erasmus Harding's remains were hidden. Sir Theobald's mysterious note from the night he died is an even more explicit clue. He refers to himself as Zeus, and to his lover Europa — surely Jennett Harding. He made for her a tower overlooking Crete, and summoned Hephaestus to create for him a Talos. Talos is a bronze automaton, sent to protect Europa from pirates when Zeus hid her on Crete. The parallels are clear. But what happened here was not truly borne of love, but of bitterness and jealousy.

"I posit that Erasmus and Jennett fell in love, and their affair produced a son. Those references to the cuckoo's hour are most telling. The cuckoo, after all, lays its eggs in the nest of another bird. Sir Theobald must have discovered that he was not the father and plotted a terrible revenge. He used his brother's own remarkable casting techniques to coat him in bronze, creating a statue from a living man."

"Living!" I exclaimed with horror.

"You should understand that better than anyone, Watson, for the same fate almost befell you. Such an act would require Erasmus to be living still, to fully understand his brother's wrath. And I imagine Jennett bore witness, even while she was pregnant. The sight would have shattered her mind, putting her fully under Sir Theobald's control. He confined her to the attic room, and built the rose garden, so she could look out on the statue that was once her lover. When the child was born — deformed, no doubt due to a combination of its mother's great constitutional shock and the drugs Sir Theobald had administered — he took it away and confined it to a secret part of the house that he had constructed especially for the purpose. This final cruelty was the end of Jennett Harding, but only the start of the tragedy for the nameless boy.

"Who knows what led the boy to dress in such a manner, donning a tribal mask from one of Sir Theobald's expeditions.

Perhaps he was bidden to wear it, by a guardian who could not bear to look into the boy's eyes and see the eyes of his wife and brother staring back at him. This wretched boy was allowed to see the other occupants of the house living normal lives; to see the beautiful Estella Harding pay a visit to her ailing uncle, who perhaps the boy thought of as a father. And yet he could only leave the darkness when Sir Theobald allowed it, when the clock struck thirteen. What frustration, what anger, must have grown in that boy's heart? What regret and sorrow must have festered within Sir Theobald over those long years? These feelings eventually bubbled to the surface, resulting in Sir Theobald's demise."

"Why did Sir Theobald create this elaborate treasure hunt?" the inspector asked.

"To confess. Oh, I imagine he and Erasmus plotted something along these lines from the day they completed the house — a fun game to entice the heirs at some later date. They never intended it to be so morbid. After he did away with Erasmus, Sir Theobald completed the house alone, with various modifications of his own devising. I think he was always fond of Erasmus's little girl, and later Estella became fond of her uncle, although her affection was misplaced. As some sort of recompense, Sir Theobald hid the girl's legacy in the house, and set the challenge as planned, knowing that only she would solve the clues, and become the true heir. Or perhaps he was truly evil, and counted on her never surviving the reunion with her half-brother."

Inspector Hopkins blew out his cheeks. "The other statues in the forge. Are they…"

"Most likely, Inspector," Holmes replied. "At the very least, I'd wager Ralph Harding is among them. We found one of his cufflinks at the house."

"Why would the boy become such a torturer?" Hopkins asked.

"The only books he had to learn from these past twenty years were manuals on casting bronze over subjects of flesh and blood. These books were perhaps his bibles. And his instructor was a cruel man, who surely must have intimated what had become of his brother, especially as his grip on sanity left him. The boy imagined he was carrying on the family tradition."

"But he didn't do the same to Theobald."

"No," said Holmes, somewhat distractedly. "He did not."

— «» —

"The only thing I regret," I said, when our carriage had made good distance from that sinister house, "is that we were unable to secure any endowment for Miss Harding. When she learns of the terrible things we found — of the brother she never knew — she will be devastated. And with no fortune... it is a crying shame, Holmes."

"Oh, but she has a fortune, Watson. I shall see to it that she receives it."

"How?"

"The treasure we found in that house — the plans, the books, the formulae — these are in evidence now, but after all is said and done these belong to Miss Harding. Sir Theobald always intended his niece to inherit all, as I said. And how? Because those items belonged not to him, but to his brother, Erasmus. They cannot be held as part of the estate, because they were never Sir Theobald's to bequeath."

"But Holmes, they are grisly things, are they not? Would Miss Harding even want them?"

"They are grisly only because of the use Sir Theobald put them to. If Miss Harding wants no part of it, then I shall persuade Paxman to auction them and give to her the proceeds, anonymously if need be. Justice shall be served."

We traveled in silence a little further as I mused on that. "There's just one thing I don't understand," I said at last.

"Oh"

"The murder of Sir Theobald... it could not have been conducted by the hunchback. The length of stride that the assailant took across the study floor, not to mention the sheer size of the footprints, are not consistent with even my hulking attacker. The cracked tiles in the hall were suggestive not just of immense size, but also of weight. I am at a loss to explain what could have done it, but surely it was not that unfortunate lad."

"Why, Watson, I shall make a detective of you yet. I believe some things about this case may never be explained satisfactorily. In view of the fact that Sir Theobald's murderer will never be caught, it is well that the hunchback be blamed. One more murder on that poor wretch's record hardly matters."

"Whatever do you mean, Holmes? Why won't the murderer be caught?" It was unlike Holmes to admit defeat thus.

"Watson, do you not think it odd that the sightings of this so-called 'Jack o' the Green' always coincide with the hottest months of the year?"

"I had not really thought about it. Is that significant?"

"Perhaps. It was in such heat that the misfortunes of the Hardings began, leading to rising passions, jealousy, and rage. These feelings are among the most powerful drives to murder, you must concur. The violence of Erasmus Harding's death, the cruelty inflicted upon his illegitimate son, the mistreatment of Jennett Harding, whom both Erasmus and Sir Theobald loved — why, these are crimes of such severity that their magnitude echoes through the long years after the act is done. As I said, it was in such heat as this that the crimes were originally committed. And it is in such heat also that bronze has a tendency to become more... malleable."

"Holmes, whatever are you..." I began, and then stopped myself. For I realized all at once that the answer was something I had no wish to hear.

———— « O » ————

Mark A. Latham

Mark A. Latham is a writer, editor, history nerd, proud dogfather, frustrated grunge singer and amateur baker from Staffordshire, UK. An immigrant to rural Nottinghamshire, he lives in a very old house (sadly not haunted), and is still regarded in the village as a foreigner.

Formerly the editor of Games Workshop's *White Dwarf* magazine, Mark dabbled in tabletop games design before becoming a full-time author of strange, fantastical and macabre tales. His Apollonian Casefiles series, and his first Sherlock Holmes novels, *A Betrayal in Blood* and *The Red Tower* are available now. Visit Mark's blog at http://thelostvictorian.blogspot.co.uk or follow him on Twitter @ aLostVictorian.

The Spirit of Death

David Stuart Davies

Initially, the death of Joseph Bradshaw aroused no great interest in the press, although his demise was somewhat unusual. He had been dining at home with friends when he seemed to be overtaken by a strange fit. Suddenly, he half rose from his chair in an agitated fashion, his body shaking, his mouth opening and closing wildly as though he were choking, while he emitted a growling, strangulated cry. His guests looked on with horror as his complexion turned purple and the eyes bulged, almost bursting from their sockets. And then with a final violent sigh, he fell face downwards on the table.

The doctor who attended could find no apparent cause for Bradshaw's death. Even a post mortem failed to reveal anything out of the ordinary. The man had not been suffering from any illness, his constitution and heart had been sound and further investigation revealed that he had not been poisoned. It was then that the police had been summoned in the form of Inspector Tobias Gregson. He was as baffled as the medics regarding the cause of death. "But it can hardly have been foul play — murder — not under the circumstances of his passing. Unless some other information comes to light, I see no way forward in this matter," he averred with a shake of the head, before returning to his warm office at Scotland Yard for a good strong cup of tea.

The second death caused the Inspector more consternation.

Sir Eustace Carabine was giving a talk on recent developments in psychoanalysis in the lecture theatre at Bart's Hospital when he too was overcome by a strange choking fit. I had attended the lecture and therefore was witness to the tragic occurrence. Sir Eustace had reached a very pertinent point in his presentation when he stopped, as though he was about to sneeze, and then his whole face twisted weirdly and his body shook as though caught in the throes of the palsy. Indeed, in his contortions, his whole body seemed to elevate itself several inches above the platform, jiggling like a man-sized marionette. A hoarse croaking sound emerged from his mouth for some seconds and then he collapsed on to the platform. The audience was filled with doctors and many rushed forward to his aid. I remained where I was for I was fairly convinced that medical attention was useless at this stage. It was clear to me that the poor fellow was dead.

What had brought about his demise confounded me as it did the others. The symptoms of his death agony were not only puzzling but I believed that they were unique. I surmised the only solution to the mystery must be that the fellow was poisoned. If this was the case, then a murder had been committed.

I conveyed my thoughts to my friend Sherlock Holmes that evening as we enjoyed a post-prandial pipe together in our Baker Street rooms. I related the whole incident to him in detail and waited for his verdict.

"It is a remarkable tale and has several aspects of interest," he said, puffing gently on his old black clay pipe. "Your suggestion of poison is, I grant you, the most obvious one and indeed the only solution that appears to fit the scenario as you described it. I should need more data before I could suggest any other explanation. It will be interesting to see what the official police make of the matter."

"Very little, I suspect," I observed with a wry grin.

"Tut, tut, Watson. It is not like you to be cynical."

"It is sharing rooms with you that has so affected me."

He returned my grin. It was at this moment that there came a sharp rap at our sitting room door.

"Come," cried Holmes and a burly figure in a shabby Ulster entered, clasping his hat in both hands. It was Inspector Gregson of Scotland Yard.

"Good evening, gentlemen. I hope I do not disturb you."

"Not at all, Gregson. Pull up a chair and join us," said Holmes cheerily.

Gregson did as he was bidden.

"Now what brings you here tonight?" inquired Holmes, throwing a knowing glance at me. We were both well aware that unlike Inspectors Lestrade and Hopkins, who would occasionally call on us for some relaxing idle chatter to help them unwind after the labors of the day, Gregson was very much a man of business — Scotland Yard business. It was clear to us that his appearance in our rooms meant only one thing: he had a knotty problem on hand which was defeating his detective powers.

Gregson seemed somewhat embarrassed by my friend's question and so Holmes took pity on him.

"Tell me about it?" he said.

Bradshaw gave a shy grin. "There's been a death today. A strange and puzzling death, which may or may not be murder, but the circumstances of the fellow's passing are quite baffling."

"Give me the facts," said Holmes, his features alert with interest.

"It happened at Bart's hospital today…"

"Sir Eustace Carabine…" I cried. "I was there. I saw the whole thing. I have just been telling Holmes all about it."

"Oh, you know all about it, then?" said Gregson, addressing my friend.

"Probably in greater detail than you. I have the benefit of hearing an account from a first-hand witness."

"So, what do you make of it, Mr. Holmes?"

My friend puffed his cheeks out in a nonchalant fashion. "Very little at the moment. I have too little data. Watson and I were just considering the use of poison."

Gregson shook his head. "I don't think that is likely. Poison certainly was not present in the other case."

Holmes sat forward with a jerk. "Other case! You mean there has been another death in similar circumstances."

Gregson nodded. "Yes, about a fortnight ago. Joseph Bradshaw, a journalist on the *Science Times*. He was dining with friends when, like Sir Eustace, he seemed to choke and tremble, his body juddering and shaking inexplicably. Then he just fell stone dead. The post mortem revealed nothing suspicious, and certainly no poisons."

Holmes cackled with merriment and rubbed his hands with glee. "Excellent. This seems a mystery worthy of our steel."

"You'll look into the matter then, Mr. Holmes?"

"Certainly. I thrive on such challenges. Stimulating brainwork keeps one alive. I presume the body of Sir Eustace is currently lying in the morgue back at the Yard."

"Indeed, it is."

"Then let us waste no time in going there so that I may examine it. You'll come with me, won't you, Watson? Your medical knowledge will be invaluable."

"Of course," I said eagerly, rising from my chair. "I wouldn't miss this for the world."

— «» —

As one might expect, the morgue at Scotland Yard is a grim place. It is situated in the bowels of the building and is a dank and chill chamber with a low vaulted ceiling, illuminated by gaslight that throws a range of weird shifting shadows along the old brick walls. We were shown into the main section by a gaunt, paper-thin constable who looked as though he was well past the age of retirement. There were six tables playing host to dead bodies, each covered with a white sheet.

The old fellow pointed to one of them. "That's his Lordship."

"Thank you," said Gregson, "you can leave us now."

"Happy to do so. I was just about to boil the kettle for a cup of tea." With these words he disappeared like a will-o'-the-wisp.

Holmes pulled back the sheet to reveal the naked form of Sir Eustace Carabine. Even with my medical experience it was a shock for me to see this poor man laid out like a fish on a slab. He seemed so small and insignificant. Death does indeed rob man of his humanity. It was difficult to reconcile this skinny corpse with the lively, erudite and articulate man I had seen at Bart's earlier that day.

Taking out his magnifying glass, Holmes leant over the body and examined it in close detail, muttering gently to himself as he did so. He studied the man's hands and his face in particular. And then he stepped back from the table with a strange cry, one which indicated to me that he had discovered something of significance.

"Well, gentlemen," he said turning his attention on us, "it is clear to me that Sir Eustace Carabine was strangled to death."

Gregson gave a snort of derision. "That's impossible! There was no one near the fellow when he had his fit and dropped dead."

"Watson, come here," Holmes said, beckoning me forward and holding his magnifying glass close to the corpse's neck. "Look at these marks. I know they are faint but nevertheless they are visible under the lens."

I peered at the pale flesh around the neck of the dead man and observed a series of faint marks. "Great heavens — bruises!"

"Indeed. Bruises which have materialised post mortem. Look at their arrangement." He spread his hands around the man's throat. "They have been produced by the force of a tight grip which strangled the life out of him. See, here is the placing of the thumb and here the four fingers."

I had to agree with the theory. The dark marks on the deceased's neck were certainly as Holmes described, but how could that be? I had seen the man standing quite alone on the stage at the time of his death.

"What have you spotted, Mr. Holmes?" inquired Gregson, moving in closer.

Holmes passed the magnifying glass to the policeman and indicated the bruises.

"What the devil are they?"

"Bruise marks. This man was strangled."

"Strangled! How?"

Holmes shook his head. "I have no idea."

— «» —

On returning to Baker Street, Holmes slumped down in his chair by the fire. He had been silent on the journey home, his stern features drawn in thought. In fact, after he assured the Scotland Yarder that he would give this strange matter some further consideration, he had fallen into a silent reverie. I was well acquainted with this mood. When faced with an apparently insurmountable problem he would draw into himself in order to let his mind tussle with the issues, untainted by any extraneous diversions. I knew it was time for me to keep quiet and make no effort to engage him in conversation. Such an attempt would be fruitless. However, Holmes' silence allowed me the opportunity to consider the facts pertaining to this strange affair. Much good it did me. However hard I allowed my mind to wander into strange realms, I could not come up with any rational theory that explained how a man who was standing alone in front of a crowd of onlookers could be strangled and the murderer not be seen.

"Remind me, Watson," Holmes said at last, reaching out for his cherrywood pipe, "what prompted you to attend Sir Eustace's lecture today?"

"Well, as you know, I am most interested in the work of Sigmund Freud. I am particularly intrigued by his theory of the importance of the unconscious mind and his belief that it governs behavior to a greater degree than people suspect. He says that the mind has a hidden power that has not yet been fully tapped. Sir Eustace has a strong interest in Freud's work but is critical of it, too. He believes that Freud overstates the case. I read a fascinating article in the current edition of *The Lancet* by Sir Eustace. The concept intrigued me, so I decided to attend the lecture in order to learn more."

"I see. Is the copy of *The Lancet* to hand? I would like to peruse it."

I retrieved the magazine from the shelf.

"Thank you, Watson. Now I suggest you leave me to my contemplations. I have much to consider," he said, retrieving some shag tobacco from the toe end of the Persian slipper in the hearth.

"As you wish," I said kindly and retired to my room.

Later that night, as I lay in bed, sleep refusing to visit me, I heard the gentle wail of Holmes' violin from below. He had obviously given up on tobacco as a stimulant for thought and resorted to music.

When I went down the following morning, I found that Holmes had already breakfasted and had gone out. The remains of a half-eaten boiled egg and an empty coffee cup confirmed this fact. Sometime later, when I had finished my own morning repast and was enjoying the first smoke of the day, my friend bustled in, carrying a sheaf of papers. Flinging off his coat, he thrust the papers down on the table. His whole demeanour was a direct contrast to that of the previous evening. His face was flushed with excitement and his eyes sparkled brightly. It was clear to me that my friend had made some kind of breakthrough in the case. I said as much to him and he laughed.

"Breakthrough is too strong a word, I think, but I believe some progress has been made." He lifted up one of the papers he had brought in. "Do you know the *Science Times*?"

"I know of it and have observed copies of it at my club, but I cannot claim to be a reader of it."

"There was a fascinating article in last month's issue by Joseph Bradshaw on the subject of Freud and the power of the mind."

"Really, but... wait a minute, did you say Joseph Bradshaw?"

Holmes nodded with a smile.

"That's the fellow who met a similar fate to Sir Eustace Carabine."

"Indeed. The similarities do not end there. Bradshaw's article, while touching on Freud's work and theories, spends most of its time criticising, belittling and lampooning the work of a certain Alexander Karswell."

"I can't say I've heard of the name."

"Tut, tut, Watson." Holmes held up a second set of papers. "He has recently published a pamphlet extolling the untapped power of the mind. In this learned paper, he maintains that the mind can not only move physical objects but can control another's will simply by training the mind to focus. I have read through this risible document also and I have to agree with Bradshaw's verdict regarding Karswell's claims. I am in good company, for apparently Sir Eustace Carabine was of the same view."

"Really?"

"There is a letter from Sir Eustace in the current issue of the *Science Times* not only supporting Bradshaw's comments on Karswell, but he goes further, branding him a 'scurrilous charlatan' whose work is imbued by 'farcical psychobabble'."

"Good heavens. Strong words indeed."

"Words that could not only wound the sensibilities of Mr. Karswell but also his credibility and reputation."

Holmes gave me one of his piercing glances, which I knew was a prompt for me to consider the evidence he had presented to me and pronounce upon it.

"You are suggesting that Karswell has a motive to hurt these two men — to kill them, in fact."

"I believe that is a distinct possibility. Both men, Bradshaw and Carabine, have attacked the credibility of Karswell's claims in print, seriously undermining, if not destroying, any reputation that he had within the scientific community and beyond. And now both men are dead. They died in a similar strange fashion. Surely that is too much of a coincidence. Whether their slurs on Karswell's theories were sufficient to prompt the man to take the law into his own hands is still a matter of conjecture, but it is one that bears investigation."

"I understand your thinking, but there still remains the problem of how the crimes were actually committed."

"Indeed. And that may mean that we have to take a great leap of faith."

"What do you intend to do?"

"Visit Mr. Alexander Karswell and find out for myself."

— «» —

On our journey, Holmes questioned me further about Sir Eustace's death. "It happened so quickly and without any warning," I said, forcing my mind to recall the scene.

"There was no sound or anything visible that seemed unusual?" Holmes asked, leaning forward in the cab.

I shook my head. "No, nothing that I was aware of. It just seemed like some force, some brute force had taken hold of him."

"Some invisible brute force."

"Yes. There was no shape or shadow but, if pressed, one could imagine an unseen thing attacking him."

"An assailant, not visible to the human eye, had grasped him around the throat?"

I gave a grim smile. "Indeed, it was as though Mr. Wells' invisible fiend was at work."

Holmes pursed his lips. "It is all very interesting and suggestive," he observed, darkly.

— «» —

Karswell lived in a small town house along a narrow thoroughfare in Islington. It was an undistinguished property bearing signs of neglect. The paint on the door was flaking, the small garden was uncared for and the windows were smeared with grime. Holmes rapped on the door with his stick and we waited for a response. Eventually the door was opened by a small balding man, with a drooping gray moustache and a pair of silver pince-nez parked on the end of his beaky nose. He wore a shabby brown velvet jacket, gray trousers and his feet were adorned by a pair of dusty carpet slippers.

He peered at us through his pince-nez in an inquisitive manner. "What can I do for you gentlemen?" he asked in a light whispery voice.

My friend presented his card. "I am Sherlock Holmes and this is my associate Dr. Watson. We are very interested in your views on the power of the mind and would very much like to converse with you on the subject."

"Oh, really. You are a believer then?"

"I am in the process of conversion," my friend replied.

Karswell gave a throaty chuckle. "A clever response. Well, well, do come in gentlemen, I always have time to talk about my theories, especially to those who have minds open to such possibilities."

Karswell led us down the corridor into a cluttered sitting room. There were papers and books everywhere. "Do take a seat, gentlemen," he said, clearing a couple of chairs of errant documents. "Would you care for a sherry?"

To my surprise, Holmes beamed and nodded. "That would be delightful, eh, Watson?"

I felt I had to fall in with my friend's response. I knew that he was not particularly fond of sherry but had accepted the offer to appear a friendly, amenable fellow in order to create a relaxed atmosphere — one which may well put our host off guard.

I nodded. "That would be most kind." When we were supplied with our drinks, Karswell sat opposite us at a large oak desk. "You have read my pamphlet, I trust," he said, before taking a sip of sherry.

"Indeed, I have, and found it most fascinating. The possibilities presented by your findings are quite re-markable. They would be a great boon to someone in my line of work: the detection of crime. However, I must admit it is difficult to comprehend how the process is achieved."

"Oh, yes. One has to have an incredibly receptive intellect to fully understand and accept the propositions that I expound in the publication."

"Quite so. For example, your claim that the mind can be trained to actually move physical objects..."

Karswell smiled. "Yes. It can. I have done it. It is a matter of summoning up the energies of the mind and projecting them to carry out your will."

"That is remarkable, eh, Watson. Quite remarkable."

I nodded enthusiastically.

"Is it possible for you to demonstrate such a feat for us now?"

Karswell paused and his features darkened. "I am not a circus performer, Mr. Holmes. This is not an entertainment but a major scientific breakthrough."

"Oh, I agree. But, as you yourself intimate, it is a facility that is difficult to comprehend. I am always keen to observe a genius at work."

Holmes' fulsome praise quickly softened Karswell's reserve. "Very well," he said, "I see no harm in giving you a simple demonstration. Please pass me your sherry glass."

Holmes did as he was requested and Karswell placed it on a small side table. "Now, gentlemen, I beg that you remain silent. Any extraneous noise will disrupt my concentration and the demonstration will fail."

So saying, this strange little man leaned forward in his chair, pressed the long fingers of each hand to either side of his head and stared at the wine glass. We waited in silence for some moments and then, almost imperceptibly at first, the glass began to move across the surface of the table. Gradually it built up momentum until it reached the edge and fell to the floor. With a gasp, Karswell slumped back in his chair and emitted a large sigh.

"Bravo!" cried Holmes. "That was quite remarkable."

It was some time before Karswell could respond. He seemed drained of energy and was breathing heavily. At length, he pulled himself forward in his chair. "I am glad you appreciate the power that I possess," he said. "Of course, that was a simple experiment. I believe it is possible that the mind can be trained to move objects much further afield."

"You mean that while you remain in your room here, you can project your thoughts elsewhere, to effect changes in a distant location?"

Karswell gave Holmes an enigmatic smile. "That is something that may come in time. My work in this field is in the very early stages."

"Work that is most remarkable," said Holmes warmly. "That demonstration certainly convinces me of the credulity of your theories concerning the power of the mind. What a pity that Sir Eustace Carabine and Joseph Bradshaw could not have witnessed such a phenomenon."

At the mention of these two names, Karswell's body stiffened and his eyes narrowed. "What do you know of those villains?" he snapped with a surprising ferocity.

Holmes gave a nonchalant shrug. "Only what I read in the press. I know they denigrated your researches and referred to you as—"

"I know what they referred to me as. The crass devils."

"And now they are both dead."

Karswell gave a harsh laugh. "Divine retribution."

"Hardly divine," said Holmes. "I believe there was human involvement in their demise."

"What do you mean?" cried Karswell, his fingers gripping the arms of his chair.

"Oh, I think you know what I mean," said my friend, leaning forward and picking up the sherry glass from the floor. He placed it on the edge of the table and then casually knocked it off so that it landed on the ground once more. "As you say, the power of the mind has many uses and over significant distances."

Karswell rose from his chair, his body shaking with fury. "Get out! Get out of my house, you vermin. I can see now why you are here. Holmes, the detective? Holmes, the snooper? Here trying to find out how those two scoundrels died."

"Well, sir, I believe you have provided me with the explanation."

"Ah, but you'll never prove it was me. You might have your fancy theories. Go to the authorities with those and they'll laugh at you. You haven't got the evidence and never will." He gave a loud braying laugh. "I was too clever for them and I'm too clever for you."

Holmes ignored the taunt and turned to me with a gentle smile. "Come Watson, our job here is done. I have learned all I need to know." With these words he swept from the room with me in swift pursuit.

— ‹›› —

"There is no doubt that Karswell is a genius, but a twisted and corrupt one," Sherlock Holmes observed as we sat in the cab on our way back to Baker Street. "And similarly, there is no doubt, he was responsible for the deaths of Carabine and Bradshaw."

"You mean he used the power of his mind to strangle them?" I could hardly believe the words I was saying.

My friend nodded. "I know it sounds incredible, but we both witnessed the experiment with the wine glass.

Obviously Karswell has developed his mind in such a fashion that he can project himself as a kind of invisible mind creature, a mental force which has the power and physicality to kill. The spirit of death, if you like."

"It really is difficult to comprehend."

"But not impossible, as the sherry glass trick proves. And, as I've observed on many previous occasions, once you have eliminated the impossible, whatever remains, however remarkable, must be the truth."

"But you still have no proof."

"Sadly, no, but that will come. However, what is of more immediate concern is my safety."

"Your safety?"

"Indeed. Because Karwell is aware that I know of his guilt and his power, he will no doubt attempt to destroy me before I have a chance to work out how to expose him. He will try to murder me in the same manner that he employed to kill Bradshaw and Carabine. He will send out his mind creature to destroy me."

"Great heavens," I cried, as a thrill of fear ran through me. I saw clearly that Holmes was correct. By confronting Karswell, he had placed himself in a perilous position. "What on earth will you do?" I asked.

"It is more a case of what you will do, my dear Watson. Now listen carefully to my instructions…"

— «» —

It did not take long for Karswell to make his move. It happened that very evening, as both Holmes and I expected. After a small repast, we sat quietly around our fireside, Holmes annotating one of his reference volumes while I attempted to read a novel, but was failing miserably. The words swam before my eyes. I could not concentrate; my mind was too tense with apprehension. Occasionally I gazed over at my friend. His face appeared serene and he seemed to be fully occupied in his task, but I observed from time to time a nervous flicker of the eyes which told me that he too was far from being relaxed.

We sat in silence, waiting for the dark inevitable.

It was just after nine o'clock that it happened. I felt a sudden chill in the room and the curtains rippled as though they had been disturbed by an unseen force. I was just about to comment on this when Holmes suddenly dropped the book he was working on and it fell to the floor. He gasped loudly and then, with a sharp cry, his body stiffened.

"It's beginning," he managed to croak as his whole frame shook. And then the invisible thing took full control of him. His arms began to flap wildly as though he was trying to defend himself against the unseen force that was bearing down on him. His mouth gaped in agony as the mind creature began to throttle him.

I was horrified, and for some moments mesmerised, by the nightmare vision of my friend writhing in his chair, his eyes wide with fear and his mouth champing silently. Eventually I regained my wits and rushed to his side in readiness to carry out my instructions. I withdrew my pistol from inside my coat and fired two shots into the ceiling. The deafening noise filled the room, the sound reverberating like a series of violent thunderclaps that echoed in my ears. There then followed a moment of absolute stillness as though time itself stood still. I gazed down at Holmes and he was breathing normally again, rubbing his neck, his face a ghastly white.

Then, for a flickering instant, I glimpsed a milky white shape hovering by my friend's side, it shimmered in a fluid human form for a moment and then swiftly faded from sight.

"You saw it, Watson. You saw it," croaked Holmes.

"I did."

"The spirit of death: Karswell's mind creature, a damned projection of his own corrupt brain. Well, it has now returned to its source."

"Let me get you a brandy, old fellow. You've been through a great ordeal."

He nodded his approval and drank down the brandy in two gulps. "That's better," he said at length. "I needed to lubricate my vocal chords."

"I think I'll join you," I said.

"Indeed, you deserve a drink, for you saved my life,"

"But how exactly?" I asked.

"You remember when we were at Karswell's and he performed the trick with the sherry glass."

I nodded.

"He stated that any extraneous noise would break his concentration. That was the key. He sent his mind spirit here to kill me tonight. That must have taken a great effort to focus all his energies on the task. As such he would be extremely sensitive to 'extraneous' sounds, especially those of loud pistol shots. They broke the beam of his concentration and the spirit had to retract, return to its source."

"So, you were fully convinced that he had developed the power to carry out such acts?"

"Well, I was fairly sure. He became very cagey when I raised the subject of the power of his mind projections over a distance. It was clear to me he had already reached that advanced stage. Therefore he had not only the motive but also the method to kill Bradshaw and Carabine."

"And you too! Great heavens, Holmes, you were taking an awful risk."

"Such things are part of my trade. Now then, hats, coats and sticks and off we go."

"Where to?"

"Karswell's house, of course. We have to see what damage our work has done."

—— «» ——

We found Alexander Karswell lying on the floor of his parlour. He was dead. There were severe strangle marks around his neck.

Holmes knelt down and examined the body. "The mind creature returned to its source and carried out its appointed task upon its master," he said. "Karswell must have focussed his mind to such a refined degree that the invisible force he had created formed an almost independent identity of its own. Denied of its original victim it turned on its creator."

"That is fantastic."

"Isn't it! We live in a world of marvels, Watson. We poor mortals are only able to decipher a paltry few. Well, Karswell is dead and so is the mind creature that he was able to conjure. His secret dies with him — for the time being at least."

He gazed down at the crumpled form of the dead scientist. "Violence does, in truth, recoil upon the violent and the schemer falls into the pit he digs for another."

———— « O » ————

David Stuart Davies

David Stuart Davies is the author of six Sherlock Holmes novels and *Starring Sherlock Holmes*, which details the film career of the famous sleuth. His non-fiction work *Bending the Willow: Jeremy Brett as Sherlock Holmes* is regarded as the definitive work on the subject. David's two successful one-man plays, *Sherlock Holmes — The Last Act* and *Sherlock Holmes — The Life & Death*, have been recorded on audio CD by Big Finish. Currently, David is the general contributing editor for Wordsworth Editions Mystery & Supernatural series. He is a Baker Street Irregular and a member of The Detection Club. He has given talks and dramatic presentations at various festivals, libraries, and conferences and has been a guest speaker on the Queen Mary II.

Father of the Man

Stephen Volk

Lestrade,

I am aware of the very great burden of responsibility you take on, dear friend, when I entrust to you yet another sheaf of scrawled pages with the express wish, as before, that they shall not see the light of day in my lifetime. Furthermore, the document I enclose herewith for safekeeping in the vaults of Scotland Yard's Black Museum contains a secret so alarming and so incredible that it may cause your steady hand to waver from the loyalty I have demanded. I can only say it caused mine to tremble, too, in the writing of it.

You cannot imagine — nor would wish to — how it felt to stare down at a grave by lamp light, my cheeks chilled by the night air, knowing that my friend Edgar Allan Poe, whose body lay beneath me in the earth, had been committed to a premature burial. Further that I, Sherlock Holmes, was entirely responsible for his ghastly fate.

But I must wind my mind backwards, as one might reset the hands of a clock, the better to help you understand the events that had led me to that moment, to that spot, and that awful, unimaginable deed . . .

— H.

It began in the year 1878, soon after Easter: I can be exact, for reasons that will become apparent. I was alone, furthering my research into tobacco cuts — Ribbon, Navy, Flake — that late afternoon in our rooms in the Rue de la Femme-sans-Tête. Since his clandestine arrival in France many years previously, Poe had effectively maintained a false identity, that of Auguste Dupin, his great ratiocinator in fiction, leaving his problematic life and apparent death behind him, much like a snake sheds its skin. He was his own invention now, and it was the best of him: applying logic to extraordinary cases where the methodology of the police proved sorely lacking. Thus, long having decried poetry and prose as outlets for his intellect, his obsession and preoccupation had turned to crime in all its guises, and some years earlier he had, by peculiar happenstance, taken me under his wing.

The case taking the lion's share of Poe's attention at this time was a singularly brutal murder that had taken place in the Rue Beaugé, a notorious neighborhood of brothels and seedy lodging-houses. Fabienne Gagnon, a late riser, had not been seen all day Easter Sunday, but by the following day her friends came knocking. They found her prone across her bed, throat slashed open, nose cut off and the contents of her abdomen dispersed around her like a flower in bloom. A bowl of ruby red water indicated that the murderer had washed his hands. The police could find no weapon, but upon the dressing table was an apple with a bite taken out. Poe insisted a cast be made to ensure the clue was not lost as the fruit rotted. His inevitable but gruesome deduction, since the indentations did not match the victim's teeth, was that the killer had taken pause to admire his handiwork. Given the savagery of the attack, the event had swiftly attracted the hyperbole of the press, who variously dubbed it 'La Maison Maudite' or 'La Maison Sanglante' (translated in *Lloyd's News* — literally, but without subtlety — as 'The House of Blood').

Our door bell tinkled and I heard our manservant answer it. No doubt a caller had come to consult Dupin, and was being furnished with the information that, in the absence of the great mind, a lesser mind would have to suffice. Myself.

I closed the book on my knee, stepped into the vestibule, politely dismissed Le Bon, and invited the tall man — I'd say slim, even skinny, if not for square, athletic shoulders — to join me in the study.

"I presume, as an American, you would prefer to speak English?" I said with my back to him, observing his figure via the mantelpiece mirror, a simple trick, the better to visually assess a stranger whilst making them unaware of scrutiny.

"I'd prefer to speak American," he said in a drawling accent that proved my deduction correct.

"I'm afraid that is a little beyond me." I smiled.

"In that case go ahead. I'll do my best to decipher."

As he removed his gloves to shake my hand I discerned nicotine stains on his fingers, and immediately proffered an open cigarette case.

"You wear a felt U.S. slouch hat, the enlisted version — two rows of stitching as against the officer's slouch which has ribbon round the brim. That and your ankle-length duster sets you apart from current Parisian fashions." I struck a match and he raised an impressed eyebrow. "I also note you are preoccupied. Preoccupied enough to cut your right cheek shaving. And you are a Pinkerton, since you wear a badge under your left lapel, lifting it slightly, but noticeably, away from your Anderson tartan waistcoat — excuse me, *vest*."

The man inhaled and blew smoke, flipping back one side of his coat to reveal a silver shield with the eye emblem of the national detective agency on it, together with its motto: *We never sleep*.

A quick hack of a laugh followed.

"I thought I was the damned detective."

He produced his letter of credentials and certificate of membership from an inside pocket. I checked the information against the man in front of me. I'd have estimated his age at around thirty — a few years older than myself: jaw clean-shaven, moustache dark, skin so free of blemishes as to seem almost feminine. The female sex would no doubt find him strikingly handsome: on the one hand boyish, on the other stern and somewhat aloof and impenetrable.

"Ezra P. Dugdale."

"So I see. What does the P stand for?"

"Patience. Persistence." As deadpan as they come, if humor was intended. Perhaps it wasn't.

"Excellent qualities. My name is Sherlock Holmes. I must say, I've paid great interest in your organization's role in the fight against crime over the past few years. Especially its pursuit of the Younger Brothers, which I've followed avidly from afar. I detect a small reaction. Were you by any chance involved in that activity?"

"No, sir. But my good friend Orion Hodge was shot and killed by those miscreants." A dark cloud passed over his demeanor, and his eyes did not let me in.

"I'm sorry. That was inept of me, and inexcusable."

Dugdale waved away my apology. "Goes with the shield. Job can be tough, and it can be dirty. Like the Molly Maguires business. Not my kind of trade, drumming up goon squads and infiltrating unions, being duplicitous amongst salt of the earth working men. You ask me, miners deserve an honest wage just like every other bag of bones. I don't take kindly to being used as muscle by folks just 'cause they can pay for it. Workers ain't the enemy. The enemy's the likes of Jesse James and the Reno Gang."

I could only agree. "What brings you to Paris? Not the Reno Gang, I trust."

"No, sir." He settled in his armchair, expelling more cigarette smoke from the side of his mouth. "Missing person. One who seems to have vanished into thin air, over twenty-five years ago. And it's my obligation to find him. I know it sounds like what it is — a nigh-on, gold-plated and polished-so-you-can-see-your-face-in-it Impossible Task, but from what I hear, well... C. Auguste Dupin relishes impossible tasks. The more impossible the better, by my reckoning."

It transpired that the lawman had come across Dupin's name recently when Poe had solved a sensational and bizarre crime from halfway across the world simply by reading about it in the U.S. dailies. The baffling mystery came to light when mariners cutting and bailing a sperm whale off the Azores came to an alarming discovery: inside they found a dead man. Even more alarmingly, the corpse showed obvious signs of a violent attack, leading the police to conclude he had been murdered before being consigned to the sea, subsequently being imbibed by the giant of the ocean, its capacious maw trawling for plankton. Poe had pointed out the error of their ways. Calling his response 'A Nantucket Murder', he argued that gouges on the lining of the whale's stomach indicated that the man had been swallowed *alive*, and, starving over a period of days, had satiated his hunger by feeding off the 'plum pudding' as pike-and-gaff men call it (parts of the flesh adhering to the blubber; rich, mottled and as edible as royal venison). The shape of the wound in the man's head, shown by diagrams in the original report, further led Poe to deduce that the murder weapon was arrow-shaped and barbed, the exact shape of a whaling harpoon which had pierced the Leviathan's epidermis. In short, he meticulously demonstrated that the sailor, Jonah-like, had been alive in the whale's belly when, tragically, a harpoon had penetrated and — by a cruel quirk of fate — struck him through the left temple, killing him outright. My friend and mentor had signed the letter in *Le Figaro* simply: *Dupin*.

The Pinkerton extracted a battered Daguerrotype from his coat pocket and handed it me.

"You will acquire some semblance of my difficulty when I tell you the object of my search is an American man who went missing in October 1849. Last seen in Baltimore, on October 3rd at Ryan's Tavern, sometimes known as Gunner's Hall, where he lost a game of poker."

The year 1849 triggered something in my brain, but it wasn't until I examined the photograph that the reason for its familiarity set off a mental explosion. At that point, it took every ounce of effort to stop my hands from shaking uncontrollably and giving the game away. But *what* game? What *exactly* was I looking at? What I saw was surely impossible.

But C. Auguste Dupin relishes impossible tasks...

I tried to focus my eyes upon the man in the Daguerrotype, smiling, seated as he was next to his wife or fiancée in a deeply unremarkable pose. Ah, but so — *so* remarkable! For, I could hardly credit it, the face that looked out at me, and stilled the very breath in my throat, was the face of *Edgar Allan Poe*.

"His name is Julius Jack Reynolds," said Dugdale.

Of course. Of *course,* it was! I almost tittered with glee, for it began to make some kind of sense. Some kind.

This was the man Poe had *replaced* on his last day in America, as he had told me innumerable times: the unfortunate fellow, almost his exact *double,* whom Perversity or Destiny had introduced to the plot during a day mad with electioneering and free booze. Poe had stolen his identity as the drunkard lay expired in an alley, thinking it a bizarre act of providence — divine or otherwise.

I was beginning to think 'otherwise'.

"Reynolds," I repeated blankly, knowing that Poe had felt his doppelganger's pulse and found none, taking thenceforward the courageous or foolhardy opportunity to reconstruct his life thousands of miles away, by the good grace of a ticket for a transatlantic voyage. One way.

Laying his doctor's distinctive Malacca cane across the reprobate, and furnishing him with other items to identify him as a dissolute version of Poe in a state of 'beastly intoxication', the real Poe had escaped across the seas to a fresh start in Paris. Meanwhile, back in Maryland, a delirious and incoherent Reynolds, salvaged by a printer called Walker and a doctor called Snodgrass, called out his own name to futile effect as he breathed his last at 5 a.m. on 7th October, in Washington College Hospital. And Edgar Allan Poe was pronounced dead by the attending physician. In short, the man in the Dageurrotype — the man the Pinkerton sought — was the man with whom Poe had swapped identities all those years earlier. The poor man who now lay in Poe's grave.

"Tell me what you know," I said quietly, not offering the fact that I undoubtedly knew more than my guest. But I needed Dugdale to talk for a bit, if for no other reason than to gather my racing thoughts and enable me to keep my sense of incipient panic in check.

Without hesitation, the Pinkerton apprised me of the extent of his inquiries to date. At the outset, I could tell he had been thorough, diligent, indefatigable, and I estimated months of dogged questions and foot-slogging had preceded his eventual arrival at our door.

He'd had it confirmed that Reynolds had purchased a cabin passage ticket on the *Gloria Scott*, a steam packet ship due to sail from New York to Liverpool, a trip that would take roughly ten days and sixteen hours. He showed me an etching of a two-hundred-and-eighty-foot vessel, single stacked, with three square rigged masts. He'd further discovered that a 'Julius J. Reynolds' was ticked off the list upon boarding.

I almost felt sorry for his ignorance. This had evidently been Poe.

"He was seen drinking heavily."

Yes, this was *definitely* Poe.

"I obtained a copy of the passenger manifest from the Collins Line. I then took it upon myself to visit each of those I could track down, in the hope of any clue to his present whereabouts. Tantamount to seeking a needle in a haystack, I know. There was no record of who might have shared his cabin, but at least he was not sequestered in steerage and lost amongst the rabble. By my reckoning, over the course of ten days he *must* have had contact with *someone*. Someone who might remember him. It was an arduous job, granted. Some had died in the intervening twenty-five years, not surprisingly. Others' memories failed them. Others turned out to be untraceable. And every name I crossed off the list took time, weeks, months, and as tenacious as I am when I get my teeth into a case ..."

"You reached a dead end."

He sighed and leaned forward. "Luckily, not. As a last resort I placed an advertisement in several newspapers, in both New York and Liverpool, citing the *Gloria Scott* and the date of the voyage, offering a substantial reward for any information arising. The Purser, Irishman name of Muldoon, came forward. Remembered clearly a man of Reynolds' description being a drunk and a boor towards diners." That sounded more than credible, I mused. "Later he saw the same man on deck, staring out to sea, and feared he was contemplating jumping in. Muldoon talked him out of it, persuading him instead to commit to the waves the empty bottle he was nursing. The man said, 'Should I put a message inside it? And if so, what would it say?' He confided in the Purser that the only friend he now had in the world lived in Paris, and that was all he dared desire: 'A new life, leaving my old one behind. The failures, the disappointments, the paltry and meaningless successes. And those I have hurt too much.'"

The words brought a lump to my throat. For a moment, I could not speak. The thought of Poe considering suicide was unbearable, albeit in the past. It nevertheless felt, just the idea of it, an obscene and pitiful waste.

"And so the trail leads to Paris."

He nodded. "Where it runs dry. And here I am. Begging bowl in hand."

"Not much to go on."

"Almost nothing."

"How much time have you spent …?"

"On a wild goose chase? I dread to contemplate. But I tell you this, Mr. Holmes, I won't let go of it. They say certain dogs have jaws that lock when they bite into their prey, so much so that they can't let go even if they want to. I think I'm bred from that stock."

"But you don't even have your prey. Let alone your teeth in it."

He consigned the last half inch of his cigarette to the open fire. "I am cognizant of that detail. What can I say? My heart drives my head. You get the picture." I did. The Pinkerton Agency did not easily embrace failure, and this gentleman would rather sever his left arm without a tot of rum than return to his superiors with his tail between his legs.

I wanted to end the conversation rapidly. I was not even thinking of how we could help him. Quite the contrary. I wished he had never darkened our door and I couldn't wait to get him out of it. I certainly was not minded to aid his investigation in any way. How could I, when the solution would only point to the criminal subterfuge of my dearest friend?

"It seems your options are few," I said.

"I'd like to know *your* options. That's why I'm here."

"Let me ask the obvious question. What if Reynolds is dead?"

"My client is emphatic on that matter. I must go back to him with incontrovertible proof, either way. Dead or alive, as they say on those outlaw posters out west. He wants to know the truth. That's what's important to him. That's why he pays our daily rate. Money no object. Those are my orders. To stay until I have solved the mystery of what happened to Julius Jack Reynolds, and, should my beard grow long and gray in the process, I will. But Lord knows, I am a stranger in this city, it's not my native tongue, my inquiries have fallen on fallow ground, and I need eyes and ears, and a fresh brain, and a good one, which I will reward accordingly."

He mistook my silence for deep contemplation and did not interrupt it, and I was glad of that. I did not want to arouse suspicion by rejecting his plea out of hand, though I sorely wanted to. Instead, I decided it was better for him to believe we might aid his search, then for us to reveal at some later stage that our efforts too had been inadequate.

"I can promise nothing, but we shall do what we can. Leave it with me. Rest assured I shall discuss the case fully with Dupin on his return." I stood. He stood, and we shook hands. "May I keep this?"

The Daguerrotype.

He said I could, then gave me his address, the Hôtel de Laâge, and said he would await any illumination. That was his word — *illumination.*

The tragic truth was, I could have given him it there and then. But what would have been the hellish consequences?

As I saw my guest to the door, and the noises of the street drifted up from the courtyard, he paused thoughtfully and turned to shake my hand yet again, this time making sure he held my eyes with his.

"I must impress upon you, Mr. Holmes, the son, now a grown man, is at his wit's end over this sorry business. He has become a wealthy merchant, wealthy enough to enable him to pay for my unlimited endeavors. Anonymity is the deal, but I see no reason for secrecy if it sways you and your partner in your commitment to my goal." He blinked and nodded slightly as if to provide a full stop at the end of a sentence he was loath to have spoken, but of which he was now unburdened. His eyes drifted off me. "My father died when I was ten years old. It leaves a chasm. And not to know? Well, that is unrighteous cruel." After hesitating, he tweaked the brim of his slouch. "I'll bid you good evening, sir."

I bade him the same, more grateful to see him gone than he could ever imagine.

— «» —

Unlike Barnaby Rudge, we had no pet raven, only a parrot named Griswold, who welcomed his master home with a habitual squawk of *'Vive la France!'* I knew immediately he was in a sullen mood — Poe, that is, not the parrot — as always when a case was proving opaque, let alone when there was a dangerous murderer on the loose. Though it would be incendiary, I could waste no time in recounting to him the conversation I'd had earlier, and did so as soon as we sat down to dinner.

To my surprise, he seemed to absorb the information with admirable restraint — that is to say, complete silence and utter stillness for several seconds. Whereupon he stopped eating, declared the lamb chops so raw as to be 'gamboling in the fields' and pushed the plate away from him, pressing his index fingers to his temples and shutting his eyes.

When he opened them, it was to see the Daguerrotype I had placed in front of him.

I feared what might happen next. Since an element of the legendary 'boorishness' — as recounted by the Purser of the *Gloria Scott* — had never entirely left Poe, I was terrified he was within a hair's breadth from smashing said dinner plate against the wall and possibly laying waste to the entire room.

Instead, to my alarm, he erupted in the most uncontrollable fit of giggles, for all the world as if he had inhaled a gigantic lungful of nitrous oxide. He positively rocked in his chair. And I almost rocked back in mine, dumbstruck.

"Touché!" he cried, raising his glass of *citron pressé* heavenwards. "What a master stroke! If I were inclined to

prostrate myself to a deity, which thankfully I am not — *you*, sir, have proven yourself the court jester to end all court jesters! Indeed, it could be said," (he continued addressing the ceiling) "—it *shall* be said; you have had the last laugh! Or rather *I* have, at this very moment! *Ha ha ha ha!*"

Superfluous to point out, this reaction could not have been further from my expectation.

"Why, Holmes, your countenance is grave, not to say bereft, or bee-stung. You cannot see the *humor* in the situation?"

"Frankly, no. I find the predicament horrible. But the more so for you, being in the eye of the storm, and the one clearly to suffer from it."

"There is that."

"'There is that,' he says!"

Poe rose, strands of white hair combed across the great dome with unsurpassable vanity even at the age of sixty-nine, searched for his clay pipe, and gouged the contents of Henry VIII's head into the coal scuttle.

"What is there to do?"

I was astonished. "What would you *propose* to do? Give in to your fate? Embrace the scandal and ridicule over your deception coming to light, your selfish utilization of a dying man lying in a back street of Baltimore? What do you imagine the public's response to this fraud will be? This imposture you have perpetuated for nearly thirty years?"

"It may be the perfect end to a perfect charade." His theatrical indifference annoyed me intensely.

"Well, I'm not having it," I declared.

"*You?* Of what interest is it to *you?*" He talked as if I was a complete stranger, and I was enraged almost to the point of tears.

"How dare you! It is of *every* interest to me. I simply cannot — *will* not let you go back to face the music. It would be an act of... of blatant self-destruction."

"On the contrary, the critics might approve wholeheartedly. Some might pronounce my transportation of C. Auguste Dupin from the printed page to reality quite the most creative thing I've ever done."

"You think it fitting to *joke* about this?"

"Certainly," said Poe calmly. "What is the alternative?"

"To *do* something. Do *anything* to get this relentless bloodhound off your tracks. Anything, everything in our power to send him packing, with some kind of explanation that satisfies him and draws the line under the whole so-called mystery."

"And how, my dear Holmes, do you suggest we do that?" He blew through the Gambier, clearing its airway. "It's a singular conundrum, and I would posit, an impossible one."

But C. Auguste Dupin relishes impossible tasks

Now it was my turn to laugh.

"Vive la France!"

"Shut your beak, Griswold!" I left my chair and swiftly covered the parrot's cage with its blackout cloth. I almost wanted to do the same to Poe. Instead I raided the decanter of Tiffon, emptying the balloon snifter in one gulp, then dumped my body into the fireside chair, elbows on knees.

"Damnation."

"Very likely," Poe confirmed, with disarming nonchalance. Except the fact that he turned away indicated to me that under that veneer there resided a palpable degree of terror. This was a mask. Certainly. A supremely irritating one at that. But I had no doubt that beneath the haughty bluster there churned a sea of turmoil. One he couldn't allow to be seen, even by his closest friend.

In any case, if he was not ashen, I am sure I was. "Look. If we could prove Reynolds dead, the story would go away. We could forge a death certificate…"

"You really think that would pass muster under the Pinkerton's eagle eye?"

"No. No, I don't. I don't, at all. It's a stupid idea." I drew my hands down my face. "So, all right, what if we forge a *man*? We forge a duplicate of Reynolds. We get an actor. We pay him handsomely to play the part. One night only. The performance of a lifetime."

"An actor? How could we be sure he could be even remotely convincing? And what if this *actor* smells a bigger reward from the National Detective Agency and spills the beans? Furthermore, in case it has escaped your notice, there exists a Daguerrotype. An exact representation. Do you truly believe we can drag someone off the street and create a silk purse from a sow's…Even if we *did* perform a miracle on him, the best actor in Paris couldn't pull it off being interrogated by a trained Pinkerton. The accent alone would be beyond a Garrick. And, consider this; what if he *did* convince? Would he be happy being hauled back to Baltimore to face Reynolds Jr.— or a judge? At that point, he'd be sure to give the game away. I certainly would."

"Very well, Poe. Very well! I admit I haven't thought this out…"

"To put it mildly."

"And you have a better idea? Other than to roll belly-up and let this house of cards of your ingenious fabrication fall about our ears?" I was shouting now, and I didn't care. If the whole world would soon be privy to this mad façade, what did it matter if the servants knew? Then, like a blinding flash, it came to me.

"My dear Holmes, I appreciate the mental dexterity you are applying to this problem, but there is no solution, other than me telling the truth, or waiting for the hand of the law to clamp down on my—"

"Wait. Wait a minute and listen. The answer has been staring us in the face. There *is* an actor who can do it. Who resembles Reynolds exactly, who has impersonated him once, and who can do so again. Faultlessly."

I gripped my friend by the shoulders and spun him round so that he could see himself in the mantelshelf mirror.

I watched as his perplexed expression gave way to dawning horror.

"I thank the Lord that neither Dugdale nor his client are readers," I said from his shoulder. "Had either of them opened up a volume of *Tales of Mystery and Imagination* they would have been greeted by a facsimile of the face of Julius Jack Reynolds looking straight back at them."

And there it was. Who else could possibly stand in for the man who was Poe's double — *other than Poe himself?*

"No, it's preposterous. I couldn't pretend to be a man I know next to nothing about. I'd be found out within seconds of opening my mouth."

"But that's the beauty of it! You don't need to open your mouth. Don't you see? Because you are dead!"

Poe turned to face me, backing away as if I were a madman, when in fact I was certifiably sane. I gripped him by the sleeves.

"This is the story we tell. We report to Ezra Dugdale that we have tracked down Reynolds, yes. But not alive. We take him to a grave. We show him the body. We convince him, utterly and completely. It will work. I know it will."

"All it needs is for me to be dead."

"To *appear* dead."

"Ah! We create a tableau. We commandeer a photographer's studio. I lie in a coffin. Post mortem photography is all the—"

"No. That won't hold water. It's too risky. Photographs can be faked. And isn't it so, *so* convenient that Reynolds got his corpse photographed? And by whom? Dugdale will smell a rat in an instant. What's more, it will arouse his suspicions that we are hiding something; as good as an admission of guilt writ large."

"Then— my brain is exploding... pray tell, what *will* convince him?"

"Why, the real thing of course! Your dead body. Dug up from six feet underground. Your corpse. *Reynolds'* corpse. He'll only believe what he can see with his own eyes. He said as much."

The cogs turned. The eyes shone. The breath quickened.

"I will have to be buried alive," pronounced Poe, "...and exhumed."

"It is the only—"

He raised a single finger to his lips. His countenance took on the aspect of an ancient philosopher deep in the rumination of some occult algebraic calculation. On such occasions he went I knew not where.

"It *will* work," I whispered, not knowing if he heard me. He gave no indication at all that he had.

He walked over and replaced his pipe in its rack.

Returning, he pondered the fire dogs. Then looked at me as if I had appeared in a room in which he had previously been alone. But I was grateful to see his dark eyes now twinkled, reflecting the firelight, and his mouth curled into that mischievous, if not wicked, smile I recognized so well as he stated:

"The absurdity alone makes it irresistible."

— «» —

Paris was now called the 'City of Lights'. Fifty-six thousand gas lamps illuminated streets and monuments all over the capital, making our task all the more difficult: to find a cemetery (or churchyard, as the English have it) hidden from the public eye, ill-lit, and far from a general thoroughfare, in a location where the surrounding buildings had little or no vantage over the graves below. Luckily, I eventually found one in a district with a sparse and sedentary population, blocked from prying eyes by aged cypresses, and a day, or rather evening, when the light of the moon was forecast to be the mere slice of a crescent. I also found a gravedigger compliant to our needs — for the appropriate remuneration.

"There is something satisfying to a hand-dug grave," the old man wheezed, admiring his handiwork as he leaned on the handle of his spade.

"Not if you are the occupant," said Poe, uncoiling the thick woolen scarf from his neck.

It was now three weeks after my meeting with Ezra Dugdale, since our investigation could not be seen to have advanced at too fast a pace, and the bone yard we stood in dated from the Middle ages, not a modern-day park or pleasure garden offering respite to a stroller or a museum of the famous. On my first visit and on this, I saw no promise that Nature's beauty would assuage the mourner's pain. It was embellished with no green spaces, just a sense of grim stone and haphazard infinity. Unforgiving and inevitable.

The one statue that by happenchance presided over us, Death, held its ubiquitous hourglass, not a macabre icon but a plain agent of destiny. Ideas once diffuse and vague embodied in a single remorseless figure who, as Poe always showed in various guises, from Prince Prospero to King Pest, holds ultimate reign over us all. The rest of the sober landscape, picked out by our lanterns, lay strewn with disc-shaped stelae of the Merovingian type, and Cathar crosses inscribed with the insignia of the Company of Jesus, popular in the days of the Counter-Reformation. Other headstones sported symbols of baroque vocabulary— scythe, ploughshare, the snake eating itself, symbol of resurrection — while family tombs sat surmounted by religious scenes, praying figures, grieving angels, sometimes a patron saint. Their grandeur all the more pronounced in contrast to the simple wooden cross before us, reduced to its plain four arms, topped with a little roof. No name attached.

Poe stared down into the bleakness of the empty grave, then circled it with all the casual scrutiny of a man buying a *chaise longue*. He handed his scarf to me and buttoned the breast of his great coat.

"Holmes, you have excelled yourself. It is perfect. *Horribly* perfect. I feel as though my entire work and life has led to this act. Almost as if it were pre-ordained."

He must have then seen the expression I wore; that a preoccupation with mortality had seeped into my bones, together with an unshakable worry about the enterprise upon which we had embarked.

"Your heart is beating too fast," he whispered.

My face tried to make him believe that deduction to be false. Notwithstanding, he laid his hand upon the center of my chest, and smiled for some seconds without removing it.

"That's better." He patted my shoulder, chuckling lightly. "My dear fellow, hold your nerve. You are more trepidatious about this adventure than I am."

I could not smile back.

He took the scarf and wrapped it about my cheeks, the way a doting mother might for her schoolboy son, and moved closer to me, sufficient that the gravedigger would not hear, as he looked at the frayed cuff of his greatcoat. It had belonged to Reynolds and was the same one the man wore in the Daguerrotype the Pinkerton brought — perhaps his favorite, or only, heavy coat. Poe had worn it during his voyage from America and hours earlier I had watched him remove it from the bottom drawer of a wardrobe where it had lain folded, in mothballs, ever since. I wondered whether he'd held onto it as a nostalgic talisman or a guilty reminder of the man whose life he'd usurped.

"I have not told you this before, but when I was crossing the vast Atlantic on the *Gloria Scott*," he said softly, "I lapsed for days into the most volcanic, debilitating fever. Nothing I have experienced before or since compares to the onset of that *delirium tremens*. My very body did not want to be free of drink, and my reason, my sanity, had no hold over its plight and desperation. So much did it resist my will to sobriety that it took my sickness to the very point of death. My powers to fight it diminished with terrifying rapidity. There seemed little or nothing worth clinging to. Facing what I thought could only be the end, I was nursed in my cabin by an American Spiritualist. She held my hand, saying: '*I will see you in the morning, either way.*' But, Holmes — I did not die. I arrived. In a new land. Life had not done with me yet. Nor has it."

I nodded my understanding, for the benefit of settling his mind. If it failed to have the same result upon my own, I tried not to show it.

By now our friend *le fossoyeur*, filthy and toothless, had positioned a weathered oak coffin next to the hole. He wore the habit of a Franciscan friar and I didn't wish to inquire how he came by such apparel as he was as far from a Holy man as could be imagined: nor what he had done with the previous incumbent of the oblong box, the lid of which he removed with accompanying squeals and creaks, some from the wood and some from his own decrepit anatomy.

I examined Poe as a dresser might examine a Shakespearean actor before they step out on stage. At the outset, he was a facsimile of the Daguerrotype Reynolds, over twenty-five years on, to a tee. And resembled a dead man uncannily.

I had painted his face with zinc oxide for paleness, even penciling fine blue lines to make his skin look translucent, and had used lead and antimony sulphide to darken the orbits of his eyes. Over the past weeks we had together devised — like a grotesque and indulgent hobby — every possible artifice to hide any remnant of a healthy glow. The gravedigger, at our explicit bidding, had even acquired a dead cat which he now lodged at the foot of the coffin, to exude all the excesses of decay to the nose of any future beholder.

"A black one," said Poe, holding his nostrils. "How appropriate."

He dug into the greatcoat's pockets, knowing what he would find there. Turning to me, he decanted the contents of his right hand to my own: two half cents, a Coronet cent dated 1848, a Liberty seated dime, and a double eagle. Upon those coins he placed a small book of poetry from the other pocket, its leather, embossed cover made brittle by age: *Sonnets from the Portuguese* by Elizabeth Barrett Browning.

His forefinger opened the cover to reveal an inscription in a woman's hand.

I read aloud: *"From AP to JJR, with fondest love."*

He took it back and recited from memory:

> *"I love thee with a love I seemed to lose*
> *With my lost saints. I love thee with the breath,*
> *Smiles, tears, of all my life; and, if God choose,*
> *I shall but love thee better after death."*

With that, he walked over to the coffin and lay in it, hands crossed, palm upon palm over the book of poetry on his breast.

I knelt beside him, fighting the noxious stink of the dead feline, cradled his head, and administered a solution of chloral hydrate in ethanol, a narcotic that slows down the activity of the central nervous system. The dilution was crucial, as an overdose could lead to stupor, even coma. I was by no means an expert but I was no novice, having taken to imbibing certain substances of my own.

I told myself I acted in the tradition of Priestley, Hooke and Boyle as I pressed the brown syrup to his lips. I did not have an exact idea of how long it would sedate him, but I knew, if nothing else, that it would slow his heart rate and keep him calm. Which is not a wholly irrelevant objective when said person is about to be buried alive. The worst that could happen would be for him to become fully conscious, alert and — not unreasonably — panic, using up the available air much more rapidly and putting himself in danger of suffering a respiratory attack, with dire, possibly fatal, consequences. I tried to put such a possibility to the back of my mind, but my hands were shaking.

I stood back and brushed the mud from my knees as the gravedigger re-sealed the coffin lid using the original, rusted nails. When the time came, I was well aware it would be my job to ensure Ezra Dugdale didn't put an ear to Poe's chest or stab a pin in the back of his hand. Otherwise...

"Should we — you know — say something?" The old man tottered back, his chest heaving.

"No," I said.

"I feel we should."

I sighed, but did not answer, beating my arms to get life back in them. Or perhaps to reassure myself there was life in me, in that domain of death.

Undeterred, he made the sign of the cross with gnarled, root-like hands and murmured the ancient words of the pre-Carolingian liturgy for the dead, known as the *Subvenite*: "Come, saints of God, come, angels of the Lord, take his soul and carry it unto the sight of the Almighty. Amen."

"Amen," I found myself repeating.

A high voice from inside the coffin slurred as if from too much grog: "May God have mercy on my soul."

I caught my laugh in my teeth, lest it erupt into weeping.

Without delay the gravedigger and I lifted the four cords he'd fed through the coffin handles and let them run through our hands as we struggled to lower the weight into the grave, careful that it didn't up-end itself. Far more difficult than it sounds. At times, the box hit the earthen walls as might a lifeboat against the side of a ship, causing me to inwardly apologize to Poe for the inconvenience, ridiculously like some train guard eager to placate an upset passenger. But the entire situation, as Poe accepted, *was* ridiculous. "*Sublimely, terrifyingly so.*" (I admit, the "sublime" was lost on me.)

Soil pitter-pattered on the lid of the coffin, then, once it was covered, landed in silent, thick clodges. With the monotony of every spadeful I could not help but imagine Poe lying down there in the darkness, his breathing flat and slow — *thump!*— his eyes closed — *thump!*— the chloral hopefully taking effect — *thump!* But in time, between the two of us, the grave was filled, and, for our sins, it was done.

— «» —

I was never so grateful to return to *l'esprit de Paris* as that night. The busy boulevards. The street lights. The gabbling and braying at cafe tables in busy squares. It revived me, as I stepped back, muddied and muddled, into the real world from the realm of ghosts. On arrival home I could not disrobe fast enough, and asked Le Bon to fill me a piping hot bath. I could not, of course, tell him how badly I needed to scrub the clotted scent of putrefaction from my skin.

Earlier that day, according to the plan I had concocted with Poe, I'd left a carefully-composed letter for Dugdale at the Hôtel de Laâge, urging him to come and meet me at eight o'clock sharp that evening. I'd made it clear that our inquiries had borne fruit and that we had important information to divulge.

Until then I had time to kill, over an hour in fact, so once I had dried myself and dressed in fresh clothes, I attempted to divert my anxious thoughts by reading Belot's novel *Mademoiselle Giraud, ma femme*, which had caused quite a stir of recent moral outrage. Quickly, though, I realized the depicted disintegration of a marriage and a mental state did nothing for my peace of mind, however much Poe told me subversive literature was a necessary purgative. If anything, it made me appreciably more jittery.

I took a jorum of hot rum and egg and wrapped myself in all the blankets I could find. Even so, I found I could not sit still, so circumnavigated the apartment time and again, pausing to un-crick my neck or stretch out the tension in my spine.

Our library, ever over-spilling, opened into Poe's inner sanctum, his scientific collection, which filled the densely-packed shelves: dozens upon dozens of bottles of evidence and oddities, making the spacious room resemble nothing so much as a museum of anatomy — or curiosity. *Tales of Oddity and Curiosity*, I thought as I hesitated at a pair of conjoined twin lambs, suspended in formaldehyde, whom Poe had dubbed 'Roderick and Madeleine'. I sometimes longed to have a simple peasant's admiration of God's miracles, of Life, rather than always having to examine mortality and the monstrous.

Tales of Mortality and the Monstrous...

Returning to the fireside, I sat staring at the Daguerrotype of Reynolds, pondering his poor son's intolerable loss.

How could we justify what we were doing? Did we not uphold the idea of justice, law, fairness? What was *fair* about this, to a young man in Baltimore whose only wish was to know the truth about his father?

And yet, would it do any good to tell him his father died drunk and broke on the cobbles behind a tavern? Where was the justice, or kindness, in that? Then my thoughts ended up where they always ended up — with Poe in that fetid subterranean box.

—— «» ——

Never in my life had I known a clock to move more slowly.

Eight o'clock came — and went.

I waited.

Fifteen minutes later I went to the door and looked down the stone stairs of the atrium. I saw no sign of a soul.

I returned, slamming the doors, and lit a fumbling cigarette.

Then, when it was spent, a second.

"Dugdale. Where are you?"

I cursed the air through gritted teeth, like a youth waiting on a street corner, stood up by his sweetheart.

I took to the needle. It calmed me, but not enough. Not nearly enough.

I paced back and forth even faster, checking my watch every ten seconds.

Every five.

Unavoidably, I thought of Poe's shallow breathing within his casket.

I thought of his panic. But the panic was mine — and the *fear*, like a roiling sea inside me.

What if this delay were interminable? What if I was wrong about the dose? What if he were to fully *wake up*? What if something should *prevent me from getting there in time*? Causing him to die the most horrifying death imaginable — locked, with mute screams unheard by any living soul, in that stinking, Stygian blackness?

"May God have mercy on my soul."

Dear Lord, what if those had been his *last* last words — so similar to his first?

That we had planned it together did nothing to diminish the all-pervasive self-accusation I now felt. I had made this happen, this madness, and no one else. It had been my *idea*, and mine alone.

The clock struck nine.

I could bear it no longer.

I ran full-pelt, dodging cabs and horse-drawn omnibuses along the way, to the Hôtel de Laâge. I must have looked like a disheveled madman as I ran in and approached the desk, ringing the bell franticly.

I composed myself as best I could as the *concierge* — a worn beauty with a noble forehead — emerged from *la loge*, her apartment on the ground floor, brushing crumbs from the shawl around her *décolletage*.

"My name is Sherlock Holmes. Please let Monsieur Dugdale know immediately that I am downstairs waiting for him."

She replied with her nose in the air that she was quite able to remember my name from that morning. "But I'm afraid Monsieur Dugdale has been out all day. As you can see behind me, your letter is still in his room's pigeon-hole, exactly where I left it."

My heart hit the immaculately-swept floor.

I felt light-headed. I told myself not to faint. I asked if she had any idea where Monsieur Dugdale had gone, or when he was likely to return? She said she did not, on both counts. I asked her what she *did* know. She told me she did not like my tone of voice. That did not concern me in the least, I mumbled.

Turning away, I gathered what paltry thoughts and decorum I could, then spun back and apologized profusely, offering that it was a matter of grave importance.

"I can see that," she said, but still knew nothing. I'm not sure what she said after that. I was busy thinking of that bleak, deserted cemetery — that *occupied coffin*. I was thinking how I might live with being the man who killed Edgar Allan Poe...

The next thing I knew, a cuckoo poked out its stupid head, sounding its mocking gong of half past the hour.

Nine thirty!

How much air? —how much *time?*—

Why was I even debating it? I couldn't waste another second. I had to get to that grave and save him: to blazes with the plan — we would have to think of *another* plan. The fact was, I might *already* be too late! I ran for the door and stopped in my tracks.

"Dugdale!"

He acknowledged me with perfect calmness, then a smile, and, after stroking each side of his moustache, an outstretched hand. "Holmes. What a surprise. What are you doing here?"

"Where have you been?" I blurted.

My demeanor must have given him pause. He frowned, laughing. "Why, pursuing my investigations. As a matter of fact, I have a strong lead, up in . . ."

"Never mind that now! You must accompany me—"

"Whoa! Hold your horses!" He placed a small package tied with a bow of pink ribbon in front of the *concierge*. "Keep this behind the desk 'til I return, will you, please? My wife'd have my guts for garters if I came back from *gay Paree* empty-handed."

I dragged him by the sleeve out into the street.

Hailing a fiacre, I told the driver to take us to the St-Lazare *embarcadère*, where we boarded the Ouest Company's *Ligne d'Auteuil* to the western outskirts of the city, via Pont-

Cardinet, Courcelles, Neuilly, Avenue de l'impératrice and Passy, into the 16th arrondissement and to the final stop on the line.

The journey afforded me time, highly-strung though I was, to apprise him of our researches: that is to say the entirely fictitious line of breadcrumbs which, I needed to convince him, had led us to Julius Jack Reynolds' grave. Dupin's stroke of genius, I explained, took us to a bookshop named 'Queequeg and Yoji', which specialized in selling American novels, poetry, and magazines. Dupin had been positive that an American abroad, however much in exile, would still hanker after keeping cultural ties with the nation of his birth. "And so it proved," I lied. "The bookshop owner, when shown the Daguerrotype, recognized Reynolds instantly as a regular customer over the years who called himself James Quaperlake." All of this was completely bogus information, yet I watched Dugdale absorb it gravely, without interruption. I continued to describe, as rehearsed, how we had followed the trail of this 'Quaperlake' from address to address...

"Did he marry? Does he have children?"

"No," I said. Then added nuance to the blunt statement to say we could find no record of such. Reynolds, I said, seemed to have lived a solitary, perilous and frugal existence, from what we could understand (i.e. invent), dealing sporadically in antiques, losing money as often as he made it, lurching from financial feast to famine due to his inveterate vice. Gambling.

"So, where are we headed?" Dugdale's eyes shone with expectation. "Have you found where he lives? Arranged a meeting?"

"Regrettably not." I unfolded a sheet of paper from my inside pocket. "He died in Emmaus a month ago. In circumstances where there is no will or mortgage but a lease involved, the *bureau des hypothèques* is invaluable." I handed it him. "When the death of a lessor is reported, all children and surviving spouses are recorded in the register called the *Mutation par Décès*. This includes the full name — James Quaperlake — and the date of death — March 18th, 1878."

He pored over the lines of writing. I handed him another piece of paper. A death certificate with that very date, which Poe and I had procured weeks beforehand. (Hence our necessary use of the peculiar name upon it: 'James Quaperlake'.)

"He suffered from underlying *angina pectoris*," I embellished. "But the cause of death was Bright's Disease, a form of disease of the kidneys, characterized by albumin in the urine and especially acute and chronic nephritis. Luckily for us, he didn't end up sewn into a cheap *serpillière* and deposited into a pauper's mass grave without the grace of a coffin, but benefitted from the charitable work of a local fraternity who take it upon themselves to bury the poor, and those without family or friends, with some kind of dignity."

Dugdale looked up.

"This is mere paperwork. I need proof."

"You shall have it."

The hands of the *clocher du village* showed midnight as Dugdale and I raided the shed at the gates of the cemetery of the Église Jésus-le-Roi, finding two long-handled spades there, as I knew we would. Of the gravedigger there was no sign. That again was pre-arranged. I did not want even the faintest risk of him letting the cat out of the bag.

Bad metaphor.

I thrust the shovel into the Pinkerton's hands, assuring him how the attendant had been paid off for turning a blind eye, while explaining that getting legal permission for exhumation from a magistrate was a long-winded process and by no means a *fait accompli*. I then led him swiftly to the relevant plot, where I saw that the old man had covered our excavations with stone slabs. No mean feat for the two of us to shift. How that wiry bag of bones had done so without assistance was beyond me.

Our blades cut in deep. It had rained earlier, an advantage in lessening the possibility of Dugdale finding the softness of the loam suspicious.

As we dug with vigor, I couldn't help feeling sick with fear. I had told Dugdale we would find a dead man, but would that prove to be a hideous self-fulfilling prophecy?

How many hours and minutes has he gone without air? I asked myself as my heart thudded louder and louder in my chest.

What unspeakable horror may we find when we lift the coffin lid?

"Slow down."

I attempted to explicate my nervous frenzy between gulps of air, and another lie mattered little. "I don't fancy being arrested as a grave robber."

"If it comes to it, I have my badge to show."

"Let's hope it doesn't come to it."

Our shovels scraped the last remnants of soil away from the aged wood of the narrow box. Dugdale dropped to the head of the coffin and begin to lift it. I did the same at the foot. A combination of wetness and decay oozed out as we hauled it up. The nails were so rotten that we did not need a claw hammer, many either snapped or fell out as we pinched them with our fingers. I lifted off the lid and it was like unscrewing a jar of putrid pond water.

Dugdale reeled back a step, his cuff to his mouth, coughed, then turned his cheek away. When he turned back I observed his reaction as he looked down at Julius Jack Reynolds in all his *post mortem* glory.

Poe, that was… with no more life in his gray cheeks than had the funerary carvings that stood gawping down at us.

My stomach turned over. The bleak question gnawed.

Is he dead?

I'd brought a lantern from the gravedigger's store. Now I lit it with trembling fingers. A flickering amber fell upon the stony features in the coffin.

They did not move. The repellent stench of the black cat caused me to splutter and bite on my handkerchief to stop myself spewing, but in fact the action also secretly stifled my sobs.

I handed Dugdale the Daguerrotype he had given me, of Reynolds and his beloved.

"Proof positive," I affirmed, my teeth chattering.

The Pinkerton held it in his eye line, then moved it slightly aside, as if placing the smiling immortality of the photograph and the corporeal reality of the corpse side by side.

The comparison done, he thrust the Daguerrotype back at me and moved closer, staring down at the body with great intensity, his breathing a low, growling murmur. Before I could stop him, he had swiftly bent down and extracted the book of poetry from under Poe's cold hands.

He straightened up and opened its cover.

"From AP to JJR, with fondest love."

"JJR." I repeated. "Julius Jack Reynolds."

He grunted through his nostrils.

I thought it a strange, almost dismissive punctuation with which to end his odyssey. And I wondered why he dropped the book of poetry to the dirt, when it was quite clearly an item of evidence his client in Baltimore might think of some worth. As it was, I was thinking about the wrong thing. As it was, I had no time to catch his arm, or prevent him in any way, before he had done the very last thing I expected him to do at that precise moment.

He scraped the back of his throat and spat hard and viciously into the dead man's face.

Only then, too late, did my fingers tighten on his arm. Not that he moved in the slightest. I don't think a regiment could have dislodged him.

In spite of my grip, Ezra Dugdale did not look at me. He simply fixed his gaze upon the face of the cadaver with the gout of phlegm trickling down its cheek, clearly relishing what he saw. As an impulsive act, it was loathsome; as a premeditated one, baffling. Frankly I was lost as to what to do or say. Mercifully, I was saved from saying or doing anything.

"Bury him," he said, devoid of compassion.

And by the time I'd registered what had just happened — staring down at Poe, my heart pounding, wishing I could tell if he was *alive or dead*, watching the spit create a blemish on the chemicals I had applied, wondering if that had been pointless, wondering if the man I had lived with for years would *open his eyes* — wondering why Dugdale had done what he'd done, what emotions had erupted, or been kept in check — I looked all around me, and the Pinkerton was gone.

— «» —

"Lazarus, come forth!" The unmistakably musical accent caused a pang in my heart. "O Grave, where is thy victory, O Death, where is thy sting?" A graceful, almost feminine hand reached out of the coffin, like the Arthurian Lady of the Lake. I was grateful for the darkness, that he did not see the tears in my eyes when he opened his own.

I pulled Poe to his feet, very unsteady feet though they were. Not entirely unexpected, after the chloral. Almost immediately the strength in his legs seemed to go and he toppled, but I managed to keep him upright, using one of the spades as a crutch while I picked up the book of poetry, wiping it in his greatcoat, which was too slithery with mold and damp to notice the difference of an extra bit of mud. I chose not to encumber him with questions. I was too delirious, almost hysterical, that he was alive to care.

Before we left, he insisted on pausing at the grave edge. He held out his open palm. Instinctively sensing what he wanted to do, I handed him Reynolds' coins and he cast them with a gentle flourish into the deep rectangular hole.

"Requiescat in Pace."

Whatever the symbolism, whatever the motive, he intoned these words without cynicism — a rare feat for him. That excluded, to my relief, he was as uncommunicative as I was. Hardly, in fact, had the energy to stand, let alone talk.

I let him lean his weight against me and carried him like a war veteran to the nearby hostelry, Le Mouton Blanc, in which we had booked a room. Once inside, the nausea hit him and he began retching. Again, the chloral. Again, not unexpected. I asked for a bucket. I asked for two buckets: one with water and a sponge. I peeled Reynolds' greatcoat off him — not sure it was fit for the laundry or the incinerator — and plied him with copious amounts of water to clear the drug from his system. The minute he was safe to leave alone I sped back to the cemetery and filled the grave (coffin, cat and all) though by the end of it I only had the strength to heft half the slabs back in place. I'd have to rely on the gravedigger to tidy up after me.

When I returned, utterly spent, I collapsed upon the bed where Poe already lay, I suspect with the room circling round him. The first hangover he had had in years. Whether he was sleeping, I could not tell: I had extinguished the candle before entering, and noticed only that his breathing was shallow.

The irony was not lost on me. Death and resurrection had become a habit for Poe. I pondered whether, lying in his premature grave as the clammy air ran out, there beckoned a peace unknown in life. I wondered if fear transformed into a kind of bliss, a final acceptance of the indifference of the universe — no more penance, guilt, terror, obligation to normality, repentance, faith, or lack of it: just the utter perfection of oblivion. And whether, as the coffin lid cracked open, and he felt the icy night air, that dream, that terrifying *comfort* of a dream, had vanished. After an hour of sleeplessness, I had to satisfy my curiosity.

"Poe? Your experience... of being buried alive," I whispered in the dark. "What... what did it feel like?"

I heard only silence. Then, in a measured slur, another side effect of his sedative, just three precise words:

"Read... my... story."

—— «» ——

The landlord of the hostelry reported, as I rushed downstairs, that my father had already left. How my "father" had risen and performed his ablutions without me noticing, I had no idea — but then, I was out for the count. A herd of elephants could have danced the can-can at the foot of my bed and failed to rouse me.

I hurled myself into a train carriage, trying to ignore the reactions of passengers to an otherwise respectable-looking young man who stank to high heaven. But that was nothing compared to what was to come. When I arrived home, I was greeted by a sight so strange it almost made the past few days seem a glowing picture of normality.

"Poe!"

Still cadaver-like and even more rancid than myself, he was down on all fours like a dog, tongue hanging out and his face red with exertion through the ghoulish make-up, running his hands over the floorboards as if searching for something quite invisible. Insanity, all this time the author's bedfellow, had finally consumed him. Of this I had not an iota of doubt. His experience in Emmaus had been far more dramatic than I'd thought.

"Holmes!"

"What is going on?"

"Why did Dugdale spit in what he thought was Reynolds' face?"

"Excuse me?"

"Have you been asking yourself that question? And if not, why not?"

"I… "

"Evidently, because he has despised his father all his life."

"What?" I blinked feverishly. "Are you telling me Ezra Dugdale is, in fact, the man he espoused to be working for? Reynolds' *son*?"

Poe sprang to his feet, dashed to his bureau and waved an Atlantic cable in the air like a signalman's flag.

"Not questioning for a second your ability to discern whether his credentials were genuine or not, the moment you told me of your first meeting I decided to check his authenticity for myself by contacting my old acquaintance Nathan Bullhouse of the Pinkerton Agency in Philadelphia. I received this reply today. You'll find that Ezra Dugdale is indeed the name of a Pinkerton: but one who went missing during his investigation in Baltimore into the death of Annie Phelps, and three other women similarly butchered. I read of the crimes a few months ago, and simply filed them away as an intriguing case, but an unsolved one."

He extravagantly swept a newspaper from our rack and laid its swan wings before us.

"Wait. I don't understand." I could hardly focus on the print. "Are you saying this man, this imposter, stole Ezra Dugdale's identity? To what end?"

"To what end do you think?"

"You… you cannot mean he is responsible for those murders in Baltimore."

"I can. And more than that." He took the soggy and misbegotten book of Elizabeth Barrett Browning poetry from his great coat, and showed me once again the handwritten dedication inside.

"From AP to JJR." He expanded: "From *Annie Phelps* to Julius Jack Reynolds."

Now it was my turn to extract something from my pocket. The Daguerrotype. I looked at the smiling face of the pretty young woman therein.

"Annie Phelps," said Poe. "Murder victim."

I was shaken. "So, Reynolds is his father, and Annie Phelps . . ."

"His mother. And that was only the beginning." Poe gestured towards the door, where he had been on his hands and knees. "If you look closely at the floor you will find tiny indentations left by Dugdale, or rather, Reynolds *fils* in all but name. From the various scuffs and blemishes I would attest he wore roper style boots with a smooth leather outsole, a wider than average toe box and a heel between half an inch and three quarters high, with a nail or piece of hard material embedded in it. Indentations identical to those detected in the floor at the premises in the Rue Beaugé."

"The House of Blood!"

"Precisely so. My dear Holmes, he is not merely a murderer but one compelled to do so repeatedly from insatiable lust. And has brought his foul trade from Baltimore to Paris."

I could hardly absorb the revelation. My head swam. "The cut on his cheek! —dear God, which I so foolishly deduced to be a shaving scar — in reality, the defensive claw mark of a woman's fingernail as she fought off her attacker!"

"Again, precisely so. We must stop him."

Poe reached for his hat and cane, but lost his balance and had to steady himself against the wall with his shoulder, then his forehead.

"You're weak from the chloral and you look like a corpse," I said, forcing him to a chair.

"Nonsense." He got to his feet.

"Stay here!" I was insistent. "If he sees you it will be like Banquo's ghost. And the very reason for all this deception will be blown asunder."

He saw the logic in what I said, which, for him, was a miracle on a par with the parting of the Red Sea. He sank back into the cushions, head lolling in his hand, as I headed for the street.

"Holmes." His croak made me turn. I don't know if the paleness was from the vinegar I'd applied or that some pernicious thought had drained the color from his cheeks. His eyes were sunk in coal-dark pits, the irises coal-dark themselves. "This man is a beast. It is nothing to him to snuff another flame." This was his way of saying: *be careful*. Armed with my baby dragoon, I had every intention of doing so.

"And Holmes . . ." I looked back a second time, and Poe seemed even more forlorn. "Look in his suitcase."

—— «» ——

I dashed from the building, thumped in the shoulder by a squat, bearded figure entering in such haste he didn't register me, though I recognized him instantly. The only Hebrew in the *Préfecture*, four uniforms by his side. He blundered past without apology, but I grabbed his arm.

"Solomon Grotowski."

"I need to see Dupin."

"Tell me why." I saw his hesitation. He looked sickly. "Tell me, man."

"There's been another murder, same as the last. Nose cut off. Entrails out."

"Where?"

"Body found round the back of the Place de la Croix. Marie-Louise Desmet, known as Cléopâtre. A mulatto." Offensive word some imagine derived from the Spanish for a mule, but in fact from the Arabic *Muwaladeen*, meaning white mixed with Moor.

"Come with me." I was about to ask if the policemen had firearms, but I saw that they had. The rest I explained along the way.

Hearing that our quarry was due to check out upon the hour, Grotowski told the *concierge* to stay in her room. One of the flatfeet escorted her. I was already climbing the stairs.

I knew what room Reynolds was occupying because I'd seen in which pigeon-hole my letter had been placed. It wasn't hard to find. The hotel was tiny. Homely. Family run. I thought of the other guests, secreted here for a quiet stay with lovers, wives, husbands. All that about to be disrupted. Probably by gunfire. Possibly by maiming, or death. Only one staircase. Good. No escape route.

I pressed my shoulders to the wall outside Room 9. The door to Room 11 opened opposite. Seeing my pistol, the female guest screamed. Grotowski's men exploded into action. A boot loosened the door handle. A second sent it flying ajar.

A suitcase lay on the bed, packed and ready to go.

Beyond it, Reynolds — the upright young American I'd heretofore known as Ezra Dugdale — stood combing his hair in the mirror, sarcastically whistling 'The Marseillaise', as unruffled as if a maid had arrived with the room service he'd ordered. He calmly slid the comb into his breast pocket as three cold barrels of carbines pressed to the nape of his neck. The police, fingers on triggers, trembled far more than he did.

On the chest of drawers next to him I saw an apple with a chunk bitten out of it, making a mental note to ensure it was taken as evidence. Reynolds could see me via the mirror but did not turn his head, simply raising his arms as if mildly inconvenienced while Grotowski patted him down for weapons.

Look in his suitcase.

I turned my back, unclipped the fastenings, and lifted the lid.

It was packed neatly with clothes. Nestled in the center under a folded shirt was something wrapped in newspaper. I gave Reynolds a sideways glance, but he showed no interest.

I undid the bow of pink ribbon that held it together and gingerly peeled away the outer layer, then the one under that. The newsprint next confronting me seeped dark, glutinous stains. My immediate thought was of meat purchased from a butcher's shop. Grotowski must have come to my shoulder, for I heard his intake of breath close to my ear as the shiny contents were unveiled. I felt the gorge rise like lava in the back of my throat.

We beheld the disgusting offal of a human uterus and womb.

— «» —

To think, whilst I had been waiting on tenterhooks for 'Dugdale' the night before, the man had, in fact, been removing the body parts of Marie-Louise Desmet; a foulness confirmed by our finding a set of butcher's knives in the self-same item of luggage — one of which was later proven to match the wounds on Fabienne Gagnon. It would seem he shared the trade of another notorious criminal, Dick Turpin, though with none of the attendant folk-heroism. And while I felt sick with guilt at Cléopâtre's tragically avoidable fate, this loathsome creature did not so much as even deny his actions.

"It was worth it," were the only words he said before Grotowski escorted him to the wagon.

The police got their confession, and some weeks later I visited Patrick Paul Reynolds in his cell. (Whether he liked it or not, his birth certificate had that as the surname of his father. And so it appeared on the arrest warrant.) He was confined in a narrow waistcoat, shackles on his ankles, bruises reducing his face to a distorted pulp. Whether the confession had been hard to come by, or his custodians wished to mete out their own kind of justice before a court did, I could not know. But he exhibited no glimmer of contrition, his face purely a mask of contempt. I wondered why he had agreed to answer my questions. Perhaps he wanted to be in the history books alongside Dick Turpin after all.

"Why pose as a Pinkerton?"

He sighed. "It opened doors. It accelerated the chase."

"You sailed close to the wind. It was your undoing."

He shrugged. "I had faith in my abilities."

"You didn't think we'd check you out?"

"I thought I was convincing enough."

"As a Pinkerton, or as a human being?"

He laughed sourly and his grin remained long after it had faded, as though the remark was entirely predictable and that he had expected better. "You're staring at me. Do I have flesh on my teeth? It's hard to get a toothpick in this establishment. I do like to look my best. For the ladies."

He was toying with me. I was dashed if I'd give him the satisfaction of showing my unease. In fact, I would disarm him back. "Annie, your mother."

"Oh— *her...*" He groaned. "It was her *insides*, see. Wanted to see what they looked like, all laid out in a row. When you've worked in a slaughter pen, you realize we are all made of the same filth to wash down the drain when it comes to it. The joke is, we conspire to think ourselves angels."

I kept my composure.

"Why did you seek your father?"

"My dear old Pa? Why, to kill him, of course. Death cheated me of that pleasure."

"Why not simply live in ignorance? Why was he so important to you?"

"Do you deny what's in your breeches, Sherlock, like those other eunuchs out there? You live in darkness, but there's nothing I haven't seen. I was born and raised in a bordello — and that's the world, if you but knew it — one big whore house, one big engine of coupling, steaming and grinding away. As a child I ran and fetched like a negro. And I ask you this: where was my father when the others had theirs to clip the ears of the bullies? To tell me right from wrong? To put hot food on the table every night? How could I answer the question of who I was, without asking first, who was he?"

"Did your mother not tell you?"

He grunted as he looked away, fixing dead eyes on the bricks of the wall.

"She said she never knew his name. She'd get angry, and drunk. Tell me to stop asking or get another whipping. So I got another whipping. Plenty, till I got a job in Mount Clare in one of the abattoirs near the railroad yards — the area known as 'Pigtown'. Learned pretty quick I enjoyed it more if an animal had a spark of life. No satisfaction in chopping up a dead thing. Thus, I got apprenticed in heralding meat while my mother got the disease of her kind. Some would say God's will. Her nose rotted away. Not many paid to kiss her after that. Some did. The wrong kind. Beat her. Made her meaner." His face distorted with bitterness and pain. "Few months ago, death rattling in her lungs, she finally told me his name: Julius Jack Reynolds.

"She'd known it all that time. Showed me the photograph the day they got engaged. Handsome couple. At first, I thought she told it to make me happy, but she hadn't. Said the moment he heard she was pregnant carrying me, he flew into a rage and cancelled the wedding. Marriage meant everything to her. Escape from a dark life, safety, security, love. Now there was nothing and he was gone. And all because of me, she said. 'I could have had a *good* life if not for you coming along and spoiling everything.' So, you see, her last act in life wasn't one of love, oh no — it was to vent her bile on her only son.

"And I guess I inculcated somewhat of a rage too, because I killed her and cut her up, and tore out the stinking part of her that produced me. Then ran. Then hid. Then prayed. Oh, I *prayed* in those days! Fancy! Other whores knew me and could point the finger, so I killed them too. They meant nothing to me, just like she didn't. Far as I was concerned, they didn't deserve to walk this earth. If I existed and they do not, it is unimportant to God and to me. Which of us sinned the more?"

I did not answer.

"I cared only about one thing," he continued. "And that was to find him, my father, but the Pinkerton came looking so I finished him too. Took his credentials and badge and cattle drover clothes. Traced the ship's manifest, just like I said, talked to the Purser, came to Paris. My quest got frustrating so I found a bar, tot-hunting, succumbed to a spoilt little dirty puzzle and played Cupid's kettledrums to the wee hours, then strew her crinkum-crankum to the four winds."

I thought of 'La Maison Sanglante' with its blood-dripping walls and the woman's corpse with its nose sliced off.

"Made me feel better for a while. Taking my hurt out on her all over again. Blood over the sheets like the very day she gave birth to me. Fatherless. The feeling went away. Not forever though. Always comes back. Like eating. You can only starve so long, then you need a real good steak."

"Perhaps your father didn't desert you," I suggested. "Perhaps he had other reasons. Perhaps he loved you."

He shook his head at the ridiculousness of the notion and held me with the reptilian eyes I had once perceived as attractive. "There is no love in the world, Sherlock. Just obtaining and suffering. The only choice in life is choosing which. Every man would rather make love with a knife than his lips. Just most won't admit it. Truth be told, you look at me and you envy me."

"I don't envy a man going to the guillotine," I said.

"Then you have a very poor imagination," said the murderer of many.

—— «» ——

My meeting confirmed everything Poe surmised. That it was the killing of his mother that had been the catalyst for Patrick Paul Reynolds' trip to France, and that he chose, knowingly or not, his other victims as her surrogates, by way of re-enacting that one primal and all-consuming hatred. His motive, however, was to find the father who had rejected him. The one he blamed for all the ills of his life. If alive, he'd intended to kill him. As it turned out, when he reached Paris, the savage urge within him built up again and he was compelled to satiate it on innocent women.

"How did you know to look in the suitcase?" I asked.

Poe exuded pipe smoke, crossing his legs in the comfort of our rooms. "To a certain kind of murderer, the homicidal act is akin to the high attained by a powerful drug, and the comedown just as precipitous. The taking of objects from the crime scene, biological or otherwise, is almost always part of such a person's *modus operandi*, as Vidocq would have it. Such deviants use them as fetishes to prolong the pleasure, or to keep as a sentimental memorial of the deed."

"I did not think him capable of sentiment."

"Criminals, as a breed, excel at it. But only as regards themselves, never others."

I smiled, but Poe grew silent and sank into a reverie that was not light. And I knew why.

Back in 1849 he could not, of course, have remotely known what was to come in that Paris spring of 1878, but he did know that he had left Reynolds, the father, gasping his last in a Baltimore backstreet. And if he had *not* done so — what? Would the bastard child of that man have grown up any differently? Would the poor women, and the Pinkerton, now dead, be alive? Poe had taken the circumstances before him, and tailored a new life for himself. Yet out of that same cloth, though no one could have predicted it, a monstrous son was made.

"Did I create him?"

I could only answer, as some insignificant recompense: "You created me."

— «◊» —

I give thanks that Poe was spared, by death, the knowledge that Patrick Paul Reynolds would strike again, and this time create a whirlwind of hideous slaughter that would beguile and astonish the world.

Wanted for the murders in America, he never did reach the guillotine. The U.S. government did a deal. In return for a French criminal incarcerated in New York being returned to face justice on his own home soil, Reynolds was deported to stand trial in Richmond. En route to Calais he escaped and was never seen again.

Except he was, of course. By the eyes of those he killed ten years later.

Their names toll like a funeral dirge in my mind, even now...

Mary Ann Nichols. Annie Chapman. Elizabeth Stride. Catherine Eddowes. Mary Jane Kelly...

Where he had been in the intervening years, and what he had been doing, I could not possibly know, but that he was in Whitechapel in 1888, and a fox amongst hens, I knew for absolute certain. The mutilations — his *modus operandi*, 'as Vidocq would have it' — were identical to that of the Rue Beaugé. The unspeakable brutality as unique as a fingerprint. And as brazen as a name on a calling-card. The name the public had spoken in hushed tones then — *L'Anormale*, 'The Abnormal One' — was horribly apt again.

It is the greatest regret of my life that I failed to catch him. The wolf eluded the hunter at every turn. I could only watch as blood ran in rivulets through London streets and fear held unfettered dominion even unto the limitless shores of history.

I knew who he was. I had his name. I knew his past. I knew his method. But I told none of this to the police. Or to Watson. I wanted to solve the case myself, without their help. Not through arrogance, or vanity, but a deep and unshakable sense of duty. He was mine in the most vile, possessory sense, and it was my job, mine alone, to bring him to justice.

It was personal. He had made it so. The carnage and wickedness divested upon the innocents of the East End, to him, was a mere spectacle for my benefit. To show that, even though I had unmasked him a decade earlier, he was the more powerful. That he was in the ascendant, and I was impotent to stop him. He reveled in that, I knew.

So long ago.

And yet he was the architect of a fear that endures. His name — or his acquired one — is still whispered by children's lips: a bogeyman, a specter synonymous with ghastly murder. But fear, as Poe once told me, is not all. It is only a fragment of Man, and the greater is Reason. And Reason is our champion, our guiding light against the encroachment of Chaos.

I knew this even as, weary and in my darkest hour, I took a package addressed to 221B Baker Street from the postman, and opened it alone while Mrs. Hudson fetched me tea and fresh-baked scones to revive my spirits. The contents had the opposite effect.

Wrapped inside a double-page of the *Illustrated Police News* I found an apple with a bite taken out, accompanied by this note:

To Mr. Sherlock Holmes

Well, well, "Boss!" They say I'm an American now because I use that word. How near and yet so far! I see I've got a new name too. Sells papers, eh? And my Daddy's name, too! Who'd credit it?

Apologies for the enclosed… I planned to send you a kidney like I did for Lusk. Then I thought I'd remind you of Paris. Of course, none of them is quite like my dear old Ma.

The writing on the wall, that wasn't me, by the way. Still it got Warren in a good old lather. Ha ha! The boys in blue will 'not get nowhere' chasing a schoolmaster and a Jew. Little do they know I was under lock and key once upon a time. But now I'm free. The autobiography of a knife continues. I'll be out tonight looking for a new sow to woo. Think of that as you sip your cocoa, detective.

Think of me in your dreams, always,
With fondest regards,
Jack

——— « O » ———

Stephen Volk

Stephen Volk is the British Academy Award (BAFTA) and two-time British Fantasy Award-winning writer of the infamous BBCTV 'Hallowe'en hoax' *Ghostwatch* and the acclaimed ITV drama series *Afterlife*. His many other screenplays include *The Awakening* (2011), *Gothic*, and *The Guardian*, as well as the TV mini-series *Midwinter of the Spirit*. He has published three collections (*Dark Corners*, *Monsters in the Heart* and his latest, *The Parts We Play*) as well as several novellas, including the acclaimed 'Whitstable' which features Peter Cushing as its central character. This will be reprinted as part of *The Dark Masters Trilogy* (PS Publishing) in 2018.

The Strange Case of Dr. Sacker and Mr. Hope

James Lovegrove

For some while, Sherlock Holmes had not been himself. Although one was accustomed to a certain irritability from him on occasion, the odd flash of sharp-tongued cantankerousness, such moods were wont to pass swiftly, like drizzling overcast yielding once more to genial sunshine. The particular disagreeable frame of mind about which I am writing, though, seemed to have set in permanently. I had never known my friend to be more sullen, nor more quick-tempered, than during the early spring of 1887.

I was at that time comfortably ensconced in my Paddington residence and enjoying newfound domestic bliss with my wife Mary. My practice, too, was thriving, so much so that on most days I required the continuous hire of a hansom in order to be able to honor all my patient appointments. Usually, when I was able to make time to call on Holmes at our old rooms at 221B Baker Street, I would be met with open arms, a cry of delight, a hearty handshake, and every other indication that my arrival was a welcome development. More often than not, I might immediately find myself embroiled in some extraordinary escapade.

On three successive visits over the course of a fortnight, however, Holmes had received me with an indifference bordering on contempt. Scarcely could I educe anything from him by way of conversation save a grunt or a noncommittal shrug of the shoulders. He radiated hostility and seemed barely able to tolerate my being there, to such an extent that I seldom stayed longer than half an hour and could practically hear the sigh of relief emanating from upstairs as I closed the front door behind me, even as I heaved my own sigh of relief to have escaped that brooding presence.

I put it down to pressure of work. Holmes was then engaged upon several investigations at once. My notes from that period list amongst others:

- the bizarre affair of the raven's feather and the missing logarithmic slide-rule;

- the strange circumstances surrounding Madame Navarre's locket and the burglar's severed hand;

- the ravisher of Cheyne Walk;

- the Penny Red problem;

- the incident of the shoeshine boy and the one-legged man;

- the mystery of the poisoned antimacassar murders.

These were merely the most prominent of the cases demanding his attention — there were countless others — and given Holmes' propensity for dogged, all-consuming obsessiveness, I could not help but think that he was overstretching himself, taxing his powers and energies to their limit, with a concomitant diminution of courtesy and good nature. I assumed that, after the glut of business had passed, he would return to his habitual ways and all would be as it was before.

My hopes were dashed when, upon a fourth visit to Baker Street on a certain Saturday morning in March, I was waylaid in the hall by a distraught Mrs. Hudson. The good lady all but threw herself upon me as I entered. "Gracious, Dr. Watson!" she exclaimed, red-eyed and seemingly close to tears. "I am at my wits' end. Thank the Lord you have come."

"My dear woman, whatever is the matter?"

"It's Mr. Holmes."

My first thought was that some tragic mishap had befallen my friend. An enemy, a convicted felon bent on revenge, had got the better of him. "What of him? What has happened? Is he well?"

"Well? If you mean is he hurt or injured in any way, then yes, he is well. Physically there is nothing amiss."

"But mentally…"

She shook her head and wrung her hands. "He is not in his right mind, Doctor. Far from it."

"Where is he?" I asked. "Is he upstairs?"

"Not right now. He is out. I do not know where he has gone. But the things he has done! The havoc he has wrought!"

I found some brandy in Mrs. Hudson's kitchen and plied her with it. Her trembling subsided somewhat and, having gulped down a second glass, she was notably calmer.

"Tell me everything," I urged. "What is this havoc you speak of?"

"Mr. Holmes' habits have always been… eccentric," said my erstwhile landlady. "You know it, as well as I do, from your time living here."

"*Eccentric* is putting it mildly. Holmes takes Bohemianism to its extreme."

"The peculiar hours he keeps, the parade of importuners tramping up and down my stairs day and night, those street ragamuffins he employs as scouts and spies, the abominable quantities of tobacco he consumes — these I can put up with. Mr. Holmes is, after all, a force for good in this world, and that goes some way to compensate for the antisocial behaviors in which he indulges. That and the very handsome rent he pays. I can turn a blind eye, and when necessary a deaf ear, to the less savory aspects of having him as a lodger. I have even forgiven him for putting bullet-holes in my wall when that fit of monarchist fervor overtook him. What I will not abide is wanton vandalism and arrant rudeness, both of which he has lately exhibited."

"It sounds entirely out of character for Sherlock Holmes to be rude to you," I said. "He is gallantry personified in his dealings with the opposite sex."

"Quite so, Doctor. But the things he said, the words he used — I was shocked to the core, hearing it, and no less so by the events leading up to the outburst."

"When was this?"

"Just yesterday evening. I have hardly slept a wink all night, worrying."

"Relate the incident in full, if you will."

"I was down here minding my own business, doing my needlepoint by the fire, when all at once a dreadful racket arose from Mr. Holmes' rooms. Objects crashing around, furniture being overturned, that sort of thing. I could only assume there was some kind of altercation going on. Mr. Holmes' guests have been known to get violent on occasion, have they not? That awful Dr. Grimesby Roylott, for instance. I remember *him* with little fondness. The noise went on and on, though, and I began to fear for Mr. Holmes' life, so I ventured upstairs."

"That was brave."

"I had to see if he was all right. I was fully set to dash out into the street and call for help if he was not. The door to his sitting-room stood ajar and I peered in, and there he was, quite alone. Mr. Holmes was causing that ruckus all by himself. He was hurling books about. Chairs lay on their backs. A table was on its side. He was growling and muttering, and his face was clouded with a tempestuous fury."

"My God," I said. I was appalled, but somehow not surprised. What Mrs. Hudson was describing seemed wholly consonant with the Sherlock Holmes I had encountered on my three previous visits. It seemed, indeed, the inevitable culmination of the resentment and aloofness he had exuded, as though he had been suppressing deeper, fierier emotions which now, at last, had erupted from within him like the pent-up lava of a volcano.

"So contorted were his features," Mrs. Hudson continued, "he was barely recognizable. Every ounce of suave charm was gone, every last shred of sophistication, and all that remained was a wild-eyed, animalistic anger. He caught sight of me, and I swear to you, sir, for one terrible moment I thought he might turn on me and use me horribly. As it was, he subjected me to a torrent of invective. It was as if I had done wrong by intruding upon him while he was wrecking the place. He told me to go away, leave him alone, never darken his door again, although those were not his exact phrases. Rather, he peppered the tirade with the very worst oaths, language such as might have made a sailor blush. I retreated, naturally, and took myself back down to my parlor. There I remained, with the door locked…"

"A sensible precaution, under the circumstances."

"Until, not long afterward, I heard him depart. The front door slammed hard enough to make every window in the house rattle, and I have been anxiously anticipating his return ever since. When you let yourself in — you have kept your key, of course — I thought you were he. Hence my delight when I heard your voice calling out a 'halloo', and my somewhat effusive greeting."

I climbed the seventeen stairs to the first floor in order to inspect Holmes' rooms for myself. Everything was chaos, as though a grizzly bear had been let loose upon the premises. Any pictures that had not been dashed to the floor hung askew. The curtains had been ripped down from one window, the pole canted at a steep angle. Holmes' library, including his scrapbooks and index files, lay strewn everywhere; there was not a shelf that was not devoid of its burden of volumes. I found the Persian slipper in which he kept his tobacco wedged beneath his acid-scarred chemistry bench, which lay inverted, legs in the air. All the test tubes, phials and beakers that had sat upon the bench were in smithereens, the liquid contents of some having seeped into the bearskin hearthrug. His microscope had survived the holocaust unscathed, as had his violin, but otherwise there was little that had not been smashed or sundered or trampled underfoot.

I was agog. "This is incredible," I breathed.

I had spoken to myself, but Mrs. Hudson, who unbeknownst to me had followed me upstairs, replied, "Is it not? It will cost him a small fortune to set things right, and that is assuming I even allow him to continue as my lodger. I have a fair mind to evict the fellow, after this."

"No one would blame you for it."

"Do you have any idea what has got into him, Dr. Watson?"

"Not a clue. I have observed that he has seemed under strain lately."

"I have observed that too."

"But never could I have imagined it might lead to this." I waved a hand at the devastation before me. "Nor to him treating you so objectionably, Mrs. Hudson. You have been nothing but supportive of him, even when he has driven you to distraction. Your forbearance as a landlady has been second to none. My advice to you is this. Absent yourself from the house for the next few days, at least until this spasm, this mania, whatever it is, blows over. Is there somewhere you might go?"

"My sister in Worthing. I have not seen her in a while. She would be happy to have me over."

"Then wire her, pack a bag, and leave by the first train. For your own good, and for my peace of mind."

"Very well," said Mrs. Hudson. "What about you, Doctor? What will you do?"

Logic dictated that someone should brace Holmes and get to the bottom of the affair and that I must be that someone. There was no other suitable candidate.

"I shall stay here," I said, "and wait for him to come home."

—— «» ——

I remained at Baker Street all that day, plagued by questions and misgivings. By chance I had brought my service revolver with me. I do not know why I slipped it into my pocket upon leaving the house that morning; perhaps I had instinctively anticipated trouble, without being aware of doing so, and had acted upon this unconscious premonition. Several times I checked the cylinder and the action, all the while wondering that I was even contemplating the use of the gun during any confrontation with Holmes. Surely, I had nothing to fear from the man who had been my bosom companion for some seven years. More than once I had entrusted my life into his hands. How come I now felt that that same life might be threatened by him?

A madness had descended upon him, that much seemed plain. He had been struck down by a brain-fever, one brought on by overwork. If he was prepared to listen to reason, I would counsel him to rest and let me treat him. I would suggest a holiday, a walking tour on the Continent perhaps, or a sojourn up by the Lakes, or exposure to the invigorating sea air of the south coast. He had fallen into an abyss and I would do my utmost to retrieve him.

Around six that evening, the front door resounded to a knocking. With trepidation I opened it, to see our old friend and sparring partner Inspector G. Lestrade upon the step, hat in hands. The sallow-faced police official inquired whether Holmes was in and, when I said that he was not, apologized for troubling me and asked if I might convey a message.

"Tell Mr. Holmes to drop by at the Yard, if he would, soon as is convenient."

"And what reason should I give for the invitation?"

"It is of no great matter. A confusion I should like to clear up, that is all."

"A confusion?"

"A case of mistaken identity, I am certain."

"I believe you should elucidate."

"I believe, Doctor," said Lestrade with some asperity, "that I am not obliged to discuss police business with you."

"I am asking not as a disinterested bystander, but as Sherlock Holmes' closest, and perhaps only, friend. Moreover, I am at present concerned about Holmes' welfare, for he has been acting in an atypical manner."

Lestrade cocked an eyebrow. "Is that so, eh? Atypical how?"

"Let me show you."

I ushered him up to Holmes' rooms and explained how they had come to be in such a dismal state.

Lestrade let out a low whistle. "And you have no cause to doubt Mrs. Hudson's claim that Mr. Holmes is the author of this ruin?"

"None whatsoever. What would the lady gain by lying? Besides, you did not see her. I did. Distress like that cannot be feigned."

"This does, I am afraid, lend some credence to the report I received today from one of my constables."

"Report?"

Lestrade deliberated, then said, "I don't suppose it can do any harm to tell you, given that you are, in your capacity as Mr. Holmes' aide and confidant, more or less an honorary policeman."

"Consider me flattered."

"It may, besides, be nothing. You have heard of the Singleton twins, I take it." My expression of disdain was the answer he needed, for he went on, "Yes, those villains. Derek and Desmond Singleton. Brothers and East End gang bosses. It is estimated that a sector of London covering three square miles, from Whitechapel to Stratford, is their turf, and not a crime occurs within it but they are implicated in some way. They rule with a rod of iron. Every cracksman, pickpocket, area-sneak and second-story artist within their domain gives a cut of his ill-gotten gains to the Singletons, and woe betide the crook who fails to surrender his tithe. We Scotland Yarders have never been able to touch them, alas. Every time we think we have them bang to rights, some underling confesses to the offence in question and serves out the gaol sentence on their behalf. But that, now, is a thing of the past."

"How so?"

"Because last night somebody took a poker to the Singletons and bashed both their brains out."

"I find it hard to feel that the world is diminished by the loss," said I.

"Me either," said Lestrade, adding, "although that is my opinion as a civilian, not as a representative of Her Majesty's Constabulary. In my role as the latter I am duty-bound to investigate the murders with all diligence and apprehend the culprit if I can. The Singletons shared a terraced house off Cable Street, and as my men were making their inquiries in the neighborhood, one of them interviewed a fellow who had been wending his way homeward shortly after midnight and had spotted a shadowy figure leaving the building by the front door in a hasty and furtive manner. It is reckoned that the killings took place roughly around that hour."

"This *figure*, then, may well have been the guilty party."

"Indeed."

"Was the eyewitness able to furnish a description?"

"He was," said Lestrade. "He caught a glimpse of the other's face by the light of a streetlamp as he flitted past. Now, the gentleman concerned may not be regarded as the most reliable of sources. My constable noted signs of alcoholism about him — a strawberry nose, thread-veins in the cheeks, above all a strong whiff of gin on his breath. It seems highly likely that he was in a state of inebriation the night before, and thus the validity of his testimony may be open to question. Nonetheless, he spoke with some certitude of a tall, thin man in his early thirties with a pair of keen gray eyes, an aquiline nose and a distinct widow's peak visible beneath the brim of his opera hat."

"Superficially that sounds like…"

"Like Mr. Holmes." Lestrade gave a somber nod.

"But, by the same token, the description could apply to any number of Londoners. And, as you have been at pains to point out, the eyewitness is a drunkard."

"I am not for one moment suggesting that it is Mr. Holmes who slew the Singletons. However, I know for a fact that he has recently been pursuing them over their possible involvement in the mutilation of a fellow by the name of Inigo Dodds."

"Yes. The burglar Dodds. His hand was hacked off with an axe, if I remember rightly, and was found in an alleyway behind a butcher's, clutching a silver locket."

"Punishment for neglecting to cut the Singletons in on his latest haul," said Lestrade. "In lieu of a piece of silverware, they took a piece of him. Dodds was fortunate to survive the maiming."

"But still he would not turn evidence against the Singletons," I said. "Holmes was looking into the affair."

"Correct, and in that capacity, he came to me last week to pick my brains. Wanted every bit of intelligence on the Singletons that I could provide."

"Sherlock Holmes," I said, unable to keep a note of incredulity out of my voice, "came to you for help?"

"I know. I know. Quite a turn-up for the books, eh? I will say, though, that it is not as if I am entirely without resources. Mr. Holmes clearly seemed to feel that it was expedient to consult me rather than do the legwork himself, and in the event, I was happy to oblige. I thought that perhaps he could finally lay a finger on the Singletons in a way that we at the Yard had not been able."

"Well, someone has certainly laid more than a finger on them," I said.

Lestrade laughed mirthlessly. "You can see, now, why I wish to speak to your colleague. At the very least it would appear that he was at the scene last night when they were murdered. I simply wish to eliminate him from the list of potential suspects. That said..." Grimly he surveyed the carnage in the room once more. "A man who destroys his own accommodation for no apparent reason might equally be capable of cudgeling to death a pair of notorious crime lords. Don't you agree, Dr. Watson?"

I shook my head in the negative, but without conviction.

—— «» ——

Lestrade left, having exacted from me a promise that I would send Holmes to him the moment my friend reappeared. I spent an hour or so putting straight what I could in the sitting-room, and then I settled down in my old armchair and resumed my wait. Evening came. Night fell. As the mantelshelf clock doled out the seconds, tick by tick, my eyelids drooped and I sank into a doze. I awoke abruptly to find Sherlock Holmes leaning over me, staring into my eyes, and there was such abundant spite in his gaze that I was fair taken aback.

"Holmes!" I gasped. "Good heavens, you gave me a fright. I did not hear you come in."

"That is because I spied a light in the window and reckoned I had an intruder," barked Holmes. "I wished to surprise him, so made a stealthy entrance. What are you doing here, Watson?"

"What does it look like I am doing?"

"Keeping vigil against my return."

"Precisely."

"With your gun handy."

I glanced down. My revolver lay in my lap, the fingers of my right hand loosely clasped around it. "You must realize," I said, experiencing a small pang of guilt, "that I needed to be prepared."

"Prepared in case of what eventuality?"

"You know what you have done. This room. The condition in which you left it. You cannot fault me for thinking that you have…" I hesitated, then steeled myself and proceeded. "Have taken leave of your senses."

"And you intend to shoot me?" Holmes snapped.

"Not a bit of it. At the same time, were I called upon to defend myself…"

My friend snorted derisively and turned away.

"Holmes," I said, rising. "Holmes, you must speak to me. What is going on? What has got into you? Come on, old man. It's me. Whatever the matter is, you can share it with me. We can deal with it together."

His back was still to me. His shoulders were hunched, and all at once his entire frame was wracked with tremors. I feared he was having a seizure of some sort, so strong did these convulsions become. I made a move towards him, hand raised solicitously, and then, on a sudden, he spun round.

It is hard to put into words the appalling alteration that had overcome him. His face was still appreciably that of Sherlock Holmes, but it was distorted to a hideous degree and radiated what I can only call *pure evil*. From the hellish glitter of the eyes to the cruel leer of the lips, it formed a satanic mask. There was nothing in it but contempt and hatred and every other vile passion to which the human condition is prey.

No less chilling was the voice which issued from that twisted mouth, a coarse, guttural croak quite unlike Holmes' customary speaking voice.

"Point that gun at me, would you?" he snarled.

I perceived that I had unwittingly reached out to him with the hand that held the revolver. It did look to all intents and purposes as though I was aiming the weapon at him.

"N-No," I stammered.

"Put a round in me, eh?" he growled on. "Send old Sherrinford Hope to oblivion?"

"Sherrinford?"

"Well, go ahead then, you blackguard." Holmes stepped forward and pressed his breast to the muzzle of the gun. "There, I've made it easy for you. Straight to the heart. Point-blank. Can't miss. Pull the damned trigger, why don't you!"

"Holmes," I said, lowering the revolver, "I have no desire whatsoever to kill you. You need help, that is all. My help."

"Holmes? Who is Holmes? Sherrinford Hope is the name. I told you that. And if you're not going to kill me, then do me a favor and leave. Blast your eyes, did you not hear me? I said get out. Go! Now! Or I shall do to you what I did to the Singleton twins, and with no less relish."

So saying, he snatched up the poker, which I had restored to its rightful position by the fireplace. He brandished it before my nose.

"How many warnings do you require?" he bellowed. "I shan't ask you again. Go!"

I went. I had no choice. I was neither going to fight Holmes nor shoot him. The outcome of either course of action would have been to my detriment. I hastened out of the house, stricken with a mixture of panic and bewilderment. Making my way to Paddington through darkened streets, from pool of gaslight to pool of gaslight, I tried to fathom the nature of the phenomenon I had just beheld, and could not. When I arrived home, Mary discerned my agitation immediately but I could not bring myself to explain its cause. I hardly understood it myself. Sherlock Holmes appeared to have been taken over by someone other, an alter ego calling himself by the not dissimilar name of Sherrinford Hope. It was as though he had been possessed by a demon who was compelling him to commit heinous deeds. I went to bed, stomach churning, head racing. My dreams, when sleep finally came, were feverish. My world had been turned upside down. Nothing made sense any more.

Regardless, I returned to Baker Street the next day, resolved to beard the beast in its lair. This time I brought along my revolver deliberately, with forethought.

"Holmes?" I called out in querulous tones. "Holmes?"

A feeble reply of "Watson?" led me upstairs to Holmes' bedroom. Still on my mettle, I nudged open the door. Holmes lay tangled up in the bedclothes, wan and pallid, skin slick with perspiration.

"I am ill," said he, somewhat unnecessarily.

"You most assuredly are," I said, putting a hand to his forehead. "You are running a high temperature. Let me fetch you laudanum."

"No. No drugs. Tell me, what happened yesterday?"

"You do not know?"

"I remember... vague things. Fleeting impressions. Nothing of substance."

"You do not recall destroying your room? Berating Mrs. Hudson? Above all, the fate of the Singleton twins?"

"I — I thought it was a nightmare," he said plaintively. "Was it not?"

"And Sherrinford Hope? Does that name ring a bell?"

"It sounds familiar."

"Holmes, I cannot for the life of me diagnose what has befallen you. It is some crisis of the mind, that much is plain, and it seems to be something an alienist might well be able to cure. I know a couple of good ones. I can give you their names. I will even make the appointment for you. But, for the love of God, man, you must get a grip on yourself. You are in no end of trouble. Lestrade has you in the frame for the deaths of the Singletons, and you as good as admitted your culpability to me last night. Whatever is going on, it has to stop. Now. And that begins with me ministering to you."

I made a cold compress for his brow, then went home to fetch my medical bag. Back at Baker Street, I found Holmes' bed no longer occupied. The entire house was empty. During the half-hour that I had been absent, my friend had absconded.

He had, however, left me a note.

"Watson," it said, "do not seek me. It will go hard for you if you do. S.H."

The penmanship was palpably Holmes' but more jagged and tortured than was his wont, the words seeming gouged into the paper rather than written. I had little doubt which "S.H." — Sherlock Holmes or Sherrinford Hope — had been their author.

—— «» ——

What had become of Holmes, I had no inkling, but over the ensuing days the newspapers provided possible clues as to his whereabouts and activities. Successive morning editions carried reports of the slaying of some noted malefactor or other. The serial larcenist Ezekiel Bodkin was found in Hyde Park, strangled to death. The drowned body of stamp counterfeiter Ned Phillips was fished out of the Thames by a ferryman at Gravesend. Lord Cecil Grenville-Rushwood, whose Establishment credentials had protected him from prosecution for a string of offences against women, wound up impaled on the railings of his riverside mansion in Chelsea, having plummeted head first from a fourth-floor window. Perhaps worst of all, Digby 'Mayhem' Maynard, believed to be behind numerous armed robberies of jewelry shops in Hatton Garden, turned up in Trafalgar Square, beheaded and with a large diamond stuffed down his windpipe.

All of the above individuals had been the subjects of investigation by Holmes, as enumerated earlier in this narrative. It was Bodkin who had been in the habit of leaving a raven's feather behind at every house he burgled, a kind of calling-card, and also of taking a single item of no intrinsic value such as a paperweight or a pair of spectacles or, as in the latest instance, a logarithmic slide-rule, in order to sow confusion amongst both the victims and the investigators of his crimes. As for Phillips, his sheets of Penny Reds were famous for being indistinguishable from those produced by the Royal Mail, but Holmes had been convinced that he had established a means of identifying them as fakes — subtle differences in the printing presses' distribution of ink — and hoped thus to be able to supply incontrovertible evidence that would guarantee the counterfeiter's downfall.

Lord Grenville-Rushwood, meanwhile, had been flaunting his roguery for years, all but defying the police to bring him to justice, and Holmes had been gradually, painstakingly assembling a case against the aristocrat which would be so watertight, not even the most compromised judge could throw it out of court. Maynard, for his part, had made a misstep, according to Holmes, by stopping to have his boots cleaned shortly after his most recent raid. The shoeshine boy had noted the miscreant's false leg and also the clay adhering to his soles; which was specific to north London, both observations together being sufficient, apparently, to secure a conviction.

Add to this tally the Singleton twins and their savage, ruthless treatment of Inigo Dodds — who had cleared out the home of the opera singer Madame Navarre of all its valuables — and you ended up with the entirety of Holmes' current caseload, save for the mystery of the poisoned antimacassar murders. In every instance, the affair could be considered solved, or at any rate brutally resolved.

Only I, however, could make this connection, for only I was privy to the ins and outs of Holmes' professional dealings. I knew beyond a shadow of a doubt that the man was going about methodically and systematically eliminating the perpetrators of the various crimes that were at present under his purview. He was not allowing any of them to face trial. He had determined their guilt and was summarily executing them.

The horror of this knowledge was quite debilitating. I had no idea which way to turn. Should I go to Lestrade and confess all? That would be a rank betrayal of Holmes, yet it was also the ethical course to take. But even if the police set to pursuing him, would they ever catch him? Surely, he could outwit them at every turn? And anyway, if Sherlock Holmes had elected to rid the world of some of its less desirable denizens, should I not be applauding him in that endeavor rather than hindering him?

Then, of course, there was the consideration that by interfering I might make myself — and indeed Mary — the target of Holmes' ire. I could hardly forget the sight of that 'Sherrinford Hope' persona which had manifested itself at Baker Street. It seemed more than plausible that that creature of wrath, if I provoked it, would have as little compunction about dispatching me as it had had about dispatching the Singletons, Bodkin and Grenville-Rushwood, *inter alia*. The warning in his note — 'Do not seek me.' — seemed one I would do well to heed.

My paralysis of indecision might have lasted I know not how long, had I not been visited late one evening, nearly a week after my last, terrible encounter with Holmes, by a certain Dr. Henry Jekyll.

— «» —

Dr. Jekyll was not unknown to me, at least by reputation. He was well liked in medical circles, famous for his gentility and generosity of spirit, and although a couple of decades my senior, he and I had mutual friends, all of whom had spoken favorably of him within my hearing and lauded him as a man of taste and a *bon viveur*. Certain rumors circulated around him that he had had a wild youth and moreover that he espoused a specific theory about the duality of man: how there were two selves contesting within each of us, one good, one evil, and how this conflict seemed irreconcilable and led only to misery. I myself did not put much store by these musings, and there were some in the psychology field who pronounced them reductive and heretical, yet Jekyll maintained them steadfastly and devoted much of his time to attempting their proof.

When Jekyll came to my door and introduced himself, he cut a less imposing figure than my imagination had drawn, based on the accounts of others. There were suggestions of stylishness in his dress, and his large frame betokened a life well lived; but he bore a haggard demeanor, and his unshaven cheeks and sunken eyes spoke of sleeplessness and acute anxiety, as did his habit of repeatedly casting looks over his shoulder, which persisted even after I had invited him indoors and set him down in the living-room with a glass of sherry in his hand.

Barely had I begun to inquire to what I owed the honor of this visit, than Jekyll blurted out, "You must help me, Dr. Watson. I am in grave peril. You, I believe, are the only person who can possibly forestall my doom. I have made a grievous error of judgement and the consequences may be fatal."

"Slow down, old fellow," said I. "You are not making sense."

Jekyll did his best to compose himself. "You are a friend of Sherlock Holmes?"

"I may lay claim to that accolade." I resisted the urge to append the adjective 'dubious' to the noun.

"You work closely with him?"

"At times."

"You have influence over him?"

"It is hard to say. I try to mitigate his somewhat less desirable traits."

"Could you shield me from him, were he to attack me?"

I felt a prickling of the nape hairs. "Has he threatened you?"

"I am undoubtedly in his bad books, and I am afraid that, if I do not comply with his wishes, the consequences may be dire."

"What have you done to merit his displeasure?"

"Refused him that which he craves."

"Namely?"

Jekyll let out a deep, sighing breath. "You are aware, I take it, of my postulation that man is a twofold being?"

"I am."

"What if I told you that I have taken that concept out of the realm of hypothesis and into practicality?"

"Explain."

"I have, Dr. Watson, developed a chemical compound — a potion, if you will — which is capable of separating one side of the psyche from the other. It is the result of years of research, and my aims have always been noble, I must insist upon that. My goal has been to eradicate the dark half of human nature so that the light half might be free to prosper. Unburdened of the anchor which drags each of us down, we may rise ever higher, enjoying lives of contentment and fulfilment. All that has been lacking, for me, is the will to test the drug upon a subject. I have considered taking it myself, but a failure of nerve has time and again stayed my hand. Then Mr. Holmes appeared."

"Holmes... drank... this potion of yours?"

"He knew of my work. He told me he was all too conscious of the darkness within him. He said he believed that by shedding it, he might pursue his labors with a clearer mind and a sharper focus. He had his demons, he said, and though he had learned to quieten them with cocaine, still they bedeviled him. The villains he faced almost daily presented him with a cracked mirror, an image of himself as he could be if he allowed his basest aspects to gain the upper hand. He spoke of a cruel streak in his nature, a chronic, deep-seated antipathy which led him sometimes to despise all mankind for its brutishness and stupidity, and at other times prompted him to sink into despondency and ennui. In its absence, he thought he might function altogether more efficiently and accomplish twice as much."

"My God," I said. "And you concurred?"

"His argument was forceful," said Jekyll. "More to the point, here was the great Sherlock Holmes, the consulting detective hallowed throughout London and beyond for his achievements, asking me to enhance his prowess. It seemed the perfect opportunity, a confluence of need and wish. How could I say no?"

"How could you say no to exposing Holmes to an untested compound, of whose efficacy you were unsure, let alone the side-effects?" I said drily. "Very easily, I should have thought. Nonetheless you did, and it is fair to say that the results were not what you might have hoped for."

"Alas, no."

"Holmes has embarked upon a killing spree, did you know that, Jekyll?"

The other gave a shamefaced nod. "I suspected as much. I read the papers."

"He has singled out criminals as his quarry. We have that to be thankful for, I suppose. Still, there is blood on his hands. Or rather, on Sherrinford Hope's hands, for that is what he has taken to calling his other self."

"Yes, his dual personality has become bifurcated, one half shearing off from the other. All his energies go into the Hope identity, leaving the original Holmes identity, when it reasserts itself, enervated and feeble. Soon, I fear, the Holmes identity will be subsumed completely. Hence I have refused to manufacture any more of the compound for him."

"I imagine Hope has found that refusal hard to brook."

"Which is why I am here," said Jekyll. "Hope has delivered an ultimatum. He has given me twenty-four hours to come up with more of the drug, or..." He succumbed to a shudder. "I shall not be so indelicate as to say what he has promised to do to me."

"Well, this is a pretty mess you have created, Jekyll," I said, "and no mistake. I am glad, all the same, that you have come to me and sought my aid. It is still not too late. Together, I feel we should be able to—"

My words were interrupted by a tremendous crash, the sound of the front door being kicked so hard that it broke free of its hinges and tumbled to the hallway floor. The next instant, Sherlock Holmes barged into the drawing-room — or I should say Sherrinford Hope, for those blazing mad eyes left no doubt that the man's wicked side was once again to the fore.

"Jekyll!" he thundered. "Did you think you could evade me? Did you think that you could run to Watson and beg him bleatingly for assistance, and I would not know? You fool! Your time is almost up. Where is my compound?"

I sprang to my feet. Holmes loomed monstrously huge, as though inflated by rage. His clothing was filthy and tattered. I could only speculate where he had been hiding out all this time. From the fetid odor he gave off and the soiled state of his boots and trouser cuffs, it may well have been the sewers, or perhaps the muddy foreshore of the Thames.

"Holmes," I declared, "you must step back. Take a moment to think. This is not you. There is still a voice of reason within you, I am sure. Listen to it. Heed it."

"Do not call me that!" Holmes cried. "Hope. I told you. It is Sherrinford Hope." He beat his breast. "That is who I am. Sherlock Holmes is a petulant weakling. Hope is the one who does what is necessary. Only Hope has the guts to deal with crooks as they should be dealt with. Only me!"

He rounded on Jekyll again.

"So?" he demanded. "Have you made it?"

The cowed, terrified Jekyll nodded. "I have. It is here." He drew from his pocket a phial containing a greenish liquid. It looked an oddly innocuous substance, yet its potent effects were plain for all to see in Holmes.

"You did not say that you had some ready, Jekyll," I muttered.

"I did not say that I did not, either," replied he. "I concocted it in case of just this eventuality. Much though I cherish the moral high ground, I cherish my life more."

"Give!" said Holmes, and he snatched the phial from Jekyll. Then, with an almost thoughtless gesture, he delivered a back-handed swipe that lifted Jekyll clean off his feet and sent him flying across the room. Jekyll struck the far wall and I heard a distinct *snap* as of vertebrae breaking. He collapsed to the floor, his head lolling at such an angle that I knew in an instant that he was dead.

"There," I said to Holmes bitterly. "Congratulations. You have killed the one man who could have kept you supplied with the drug."

"No," he said. "I mean to analyze the compound. I have a sample now, and I will retrieve Jekyll's notes from his house, and between the two I shall be able, at my chemistry bench, to reproduce it in any quantity I wish."

I did not doubt that he could do as he claimed. "Then let me appeal to your better nature," I said. "Holmes — Hope — please quit this path you are on. I can see it leading only to misery and disaster."

At that moment, before Holmes could respond, a timorous voice called down from upstairs.

"John? What is happening? What is all that dreadful commotion?"

My wife had been getting ready for bed when Dr. Jekyll arrived.

"Mary, dearest," I called back, with all the gentleness I could muster. "Stay in our room. Don't come down. I have everything under control."

"*Oh, John*," said Holmes, mimicking Mary's voice in sardonic, piping tones, "*Do you really have everything under control? Are you sure?*"

"Listen to me," I said coolly. "You can still save yourself. This homicidal ogre you have become is not you. He is not the Sherlock Holmes I have come to respect and admire. He is a travesty. You need not be him. There is still time to redeem yourself."

"You have no idea." Holmes advanced upon me hulkingly. Glee was writ large upon his face. "No idea how wonderful it is to be this way. I am liberated, Watson. My chains have fallen from me. I am no longer bothered by conscience. I no longer need bend the knee to the system that sees criminals punished only after a long and tortuous legal process. I am pure, unfettered justice! I stalk and catch and kill swiftly, like a tiger, and only the deserving suffer. Singlehandedly I am purging the city of its worst elements. I am snuffing out crime left, right and center. Soon nobody in London will dare commit any misdemeanor, for fear of retribution from Sherrinford Hope. Is that not a good thing? Can you not see the desirability of such an outcome?"

I was backing away, moving in the direction of the chiffonier, inside a drawer of which my revolver was stowed. "What I see," I said, "is that you believe wholeheartedly in this vision of yours. Some, though, might call it tyranny. The Law exists for a reason, to protect us all, and it is not yours to circumvent. We are all beholden to it equally."

"Balderdash! The Law is a blunt, ineffective tool. I am sharper and cleaner. The Law is a blunderbuss. I am a rapier."

"Holmes…"

"I can make you understand, Watson. I can make you view things from my perspective. It is simple."

So saying, he lunged for me, fast, so fast that I barely saw him move. I could not prevent him seizing hold of me. I was close enough to the chiffonier to have made a bid for the drawer handle, but Holmes thrust me to one side and shoved me up against the wall. One arm pinned me in place, with such might that my strenuous efforts to resist came to naught. Using his free hand, he unstoppered the phial, thumb popping out the cork.

"Open wide," he said, bringing the phial to my lips. "Just a little. It won't hurt. Well, not much. A few drops, and I shall keep the rest for my own use. Part those lips, Watson. Part them!"

He shook me violently, and my jaw sagged open, and next thing I knew, some of the liquid was upon my tongue. It tasted vile — salty and acrid — and I choked, but Holmes merely pressed a hand over my mouth and nose.

"It has already begun to permeate into you," he said. "You cannot fight it. The effects will start to make themselves felt shortly. Just swallow. Swallow and submit. It is not so bad. And when it is over, you will be like me. You will understand. You will see things more clearly than you ever have."

— «» —

They came to me in swift succession: memories. Memories of all the slights I had had inflicted upon me over the years. All the insults I had endured in my life. All the misfortunes I had known, such as my wastrel older brother and his miserable demise. All the horrors I had witnessed in Afghanistan, the screaming soldiers, the glistening fresh wounds. All the pain I had experienced, not least the jezail bullet that had come within a hair's breadth of killing me. All the cruel and vindictive deeds that I myself had committed, such as the beatings I had been party to meting out upon poor Percy 'Tadpole' Phelps at school. They came in a foul torrent, like a cesspool overflowing, spilling its contents across the greensward of my thoughts.

I knew hatred, then, like never before, and anger, and sorrow. I knew jealousy and despair. I knew the very blackest shades of emotion.

I welcomed them. They imbued me with a strength that was not only invigorating but giddyingly delightful. Nothing frightened me anymore; nothing intimidated me. I had been introduced to the very worst parts of myself, all at once, and embraced them, and now I felt a sudden, strange peace.

I heard someone calling out a name, faintly, as though from some distant hill.

Ormond Sacker.

That was me. That was this version of myself, this primal, blissfully unrestrained John Watson. That was his name.

Ormond Sacker.

"Ormond Sacker," I said, blinking and looking up into the eyes of my companion, who was bent over me with a paternal, almost solicitous air.

"Dr. Sacker," said he, extending a hand. "Pleased to meet you. Sherrinford Hope."

"Of course."

"How are you faring?"

My body seemed to vibrate with power, an eagerness to get out into the world and do exactly as I desire.

"I feel galvanized," I said. "I feel indomitable."

"Good man. Just as it should be."

"I feel that I have no constraints. I loathe what I used to be. That feckless, shillyshallying Watson. How did you ever put up with him? How did I?"

"It is a marvel," Hope agreed.

"How shall we begin this new life of ours? I have the urge to celebrate, to mark this fresh chapter in my existence somehow."

"There is a poisoner at large," said Hope. "The eminent young naturalist, Robert Keller. He steeps antimacassars in the venom of the African marsh viper, which can be absorbed through the skin. It is invariably lethal. He is killing, one by one, all those relatives who stand in the way of him inheriting a sizeable legacy. Let us teach him the error of his ways, why not?"

"Why not, indeed?"

Then the woman upstairs called out again. "John? It has been quiet down there for some while. Is it safe for me to show my face?"

How gratingly her words fell upon my ears. Mary, with her rosy, simpering features, her rust-colored hair, her ever-compliant bearing. She repelled me. She was a dumb, bovine thing. She was John Watson's soulmate and helpmeet but she would, I foresaw, be nothing but an impediment to Ormond Sacker.

"Give me a moment," I said to Hope, "and then I shall be all yours."

He smiled and nodded in approval. "Off you go then, old man. Don't take too long."

"I shan't."

I headed out into the hallway and began ascending the staircase, flexing my fingers and making fists of my hands. Mary Watson waited for me on the landing, all trusting innocence.

"Darling...?" she said, puzzled, and thereafter said no more.

— «» —

I write this account in what I reckon are the last few moments of lucidity remaining to me. Ormond Sacker is scratching at the door of my mind yet again, impatient to be let out. I have done things so shameful, so terrible, it is agony to recall them. Sacker, by contrast, finds them untroubling. He positively revels in the memory of them, and the performance of them. It will be a relief, almost, to give myself back over to him. This time, I feel it will be permanent. I shall never have to worry again. There is, and only ever will be, Sacker.

We have plenty of the compound, Hope and I. Should supplies run low, Hope simply conjures up a fresh batch. We ingest it on a nightly basis, and then we sally forth into the streets of London, seeking out wrongdoers and doling out our own brand of justice. Thus far, we have remained ever one step ahead of the Met. How long we continue to do so, I cannot say. It is not my concern. It is Sacker's.

He comes. I have no choice but to make the way clear for him. He crawls free.

The game is afoot. And we are the hunters.

— « O » —

James Lovegrove

James Lovegrove was born on Christmas Eve 1965 and has published more than fifty books, among them *Days*, *Untied Kingdom*, *Provender Gleed*, *Redlaw*, and the *Pantheon* series, including New York Times bestseller *The Age of Odin*. His acclaimed Sherlock Holmes novels are *The Stuff of Nightmares*, *Gods of War*, *The Thinking Engine*, *The Labyrinth of Death* and a Holmes/Lovecraft trilogy *The Cthulhu Casebooks*. He reviews fiction for the *Financial Times* and writes about comics for *Comic Heroes*, and lives with his family in Eastbourne on the south coast of England, not far from the small farm to which a certain famous detective retired in order to keep bees.

The Ignoble Sportsmen

Josh Reynolds

It was not unusual for my friend, Sherlock Holmes, to turn away a prospective client. As the most preeminent of that new breed of consulting detective, now so common in the more sensationalists newspapers, our lodgings at 221B Baker Street saw a steady stream of visitors. Their problems ranged from the mundane to the impossible, and Holmes often erred on the side of the latter.

For him, the mundane was as virulent a toxin as hemlock. The strange, the curious, the intriguing, these were his milk and meat. And the tale told to us by Sir Harold Gisburne held all three in ready supply.

It was a tale of locked rooms, and impossible deaths, perpetrated most bloodily. A tale that would have seemed strange coming from anyone, but most especially a man of our guest's bearing. Sir Harold was a sportsman born, broad but with a stoop particular to shootists. He had the reddish complexion of a man more used to the outdoors, and a wide, craggy face. A member in good standing of several sporting clubs, he had, he claimed, been turned our way by a fellow member of the Anglo-Indian Club. He clenched his hands as he spoke, as if in want of something to throttle.

Suffice it to say, I did not take to him.

Despite my instinctive distaste, his story was of exceeding interest, coinciding as it did with a number of recent, and startling, deaths. The names of several of those unfortunates, I knew, could be found in Holmes' assiduously compiled index of biographies. That alone might have been enough to perk my interest, and certainly Holmes' own.

So it was that when our latest visitor had finished his tale, I was surprised to see Holmes turn away, with a gesture so dismissive as to be insulting. "I find nothing of interest in your problem, sir, and I see little reason to bend my faculties to the proposed task."

"If it's money you're after-," our guest began, gruffly. Holmes stopped him with a withering look. I had been on the receiving end of that look and knew its potency myself. Holmes had cowed more than one blustering bully with that basilisk gaze. Our guest, however, was made of sterner stuff. He drew himself to his full, impressive height, flower pot red features growing darker still with barely restrained anger. Before he could speak, Holmes leaned forward, his hawk-like features stern.

"I regret that you have come all this way for nothing, Sir Harold. Do pass along my apologies to your fellows. Watson, see our guest out.'

I put away my notebook and rose. Though I was curious as to this unexpected turn, I refrained from the obvious questions. Holmes rarely left me in the dark for long, and I had learned a few tricks in my time with him. My friend resembled nothing so much as a coiled spring. It was plain to me that something had its hooks in him, whatever his claims.

Sir Harold beat me to his possessions. He moved swiftly, impatiently. Here was a man used to getting his own way, and now, having been stymied, was eager to express his frustration through action. He snatched up hat and coat and spun, jabbing a finger at Holmes. "I was assured that this matter would be easy for such as you. I see now that those assurances were wrong. Obviously, our problem is beyond you, sir."

"Every problem is absurdly easy to solve, when someone else does it for you. But I shall not play the part of your bloodhound, Sir Harold. There are detectives ten a penny in this city now. Seek one out. I shall even provide references, should you wish. No? Then good day, sir." Holmes turned in his armchair, as if to contemplate the glow of the fireplace. Sir Harold glared at the back of his head for a moment, as if lining up a shot. But then, he turned on his heel and was out the door, slamming it behind him.

As the echoes of his abrupt departure faded, I said, "The rent is due, you know."

Holmes snorted, but did not turn from his contemplation of the fire. "We are neither of us in danger of penury, Watson. Now, if you would be so kind as to look out the window and tell me what you see."

I nudged aside the curtain and glanced down at the wet street. The light of the lamps washed across rain-soaked cobbles, making the darkness ripple in strange ways. I saw Sir Harold signal a cab and there, in the watery light, the sportsman looked less like a hunter and more like a beast at bay. I saw that I was not the only one watching, as he climbed into his cab. "Holmes, there's a fellow down there."

"He is watching Sir Harold speed off," Holmes said. "A lump of a man. A heavy face, normally clean shaven, but now displaying a significant growth of brush." Holmes gestured about his jaw. "Do you recognize him?"

"Should I?" I asked, squinting down into the dark. The face was familiar, true, but I could not hook it to a name.

Holmes' lips twitched. "Possibly not. It was some time ago, and there were other considerations. Is he following the cab?"

"He's caught one himself," I said, watching until the shifty fellow and his trap had vanished into the gathering fog. "Look here, Holmes, who is this fellow? Obviously, you knew he'd be there."

"Of course. He's been there most of the day, in fact, on my orders. You really must learn to be more observant, Watson. Sometimes I find myself surprised that you made it out of the Kandahar Province at all." A quick flicker of a smile crossed his thin lips as he spoke, taking some of the sting out of his words.

I chuckled. "London isn't Maiwand, Holmes."

"No, it is altogether more dangerous." Holmes vaulted from his chair, smiling insufferably. "Well, Watson, that old hunter's pride will serve us well," he said. "I have set my bloodhounds on his trail. If he does as I suspect, we'll learn of it shortly." He rubbed his hands gleefully. "And then we'll have them!"

"I confess I am still somewhat in the dark," I said, more sharply than I had intended.

"I apologize, Watson," Holmes said. "These past few days, I have been tending to my practice, even as you have been tending to yours." I frowned. Trust Holmes to admonish a man for seeing to the needs of his patients.

"Does this have something to do with why you sent Sir Harold packing?"

"Quite. Did you notice the pin on Sir Harold's neck tie?" Holmes was no longer smiling. His face looked positively cadaverous in the light of the fire, and I wondered at his grim expression. "A stag's head, I believe."

"Picked out in gold, on a shield of green," I replied. I reclaimed my notebook from where I'd left it. "It seemed a bit odd to me. I made a note of it."

"Of course, you did," Holmes said, smiling slightly. "Did you recognize it?"

"Why — no. I took it for a club pin, of some sort."

"And so it is." Holmes was no longer smiling. He sank back into his chair, fingers pressed together before his face. "A very select club."

I frowned. "Speak plainly, please."

"The Fellowship of Herne," Holmes said. He looked at me expectantly.

"Sometime a keeper here in Windsor Forest, doth all the winter-time, at still midnight, walk round about an oak, with great ragg'd horns," I recited. It was from Shakespeare's *The Merry Wives of Windsor*. A favorite of mine.

"Unfortunately, we are not dealing with an antlered specter, in this instance," Holmes said. "Indeed, I would prefer it to the abominable banality before us." He began to fill the bowl of his pipe with meticulous fingers. "The Fellowship — of which I have it on good authority that Sir Harold is a member — is a sporting club of unusual focus, Watson."

The way he said it brought me up short. "Meaning?"

"They hunt men."

I stared at him in shock. "What? Surely not."

"Even so, Watson." Holmes' face was set in a grim expression, and I could not bring myself to further question the truth of his words. There were horrors in the world, and in recent years, I had become intimately familiar with far too many of them. Too, I recalled certain stories I'd heard, in my time in India, and felt a thrill of revulsion.

"How long have you known?"

"Long enough. The Fellowship is made up of those men for whom British law is but a suggestion, at best. My brother, who possesses no small amount of influence himself, is unabashedly hesitant where the Fellowship is concerned."

I was nothing short of astounded to hear this. Given what little I had been made privy to about his position, I could not conceive of Mycroft Holmes fearing anyone. That he had deigned to share those fears with his brother only emphasized the seriousness of the situation. I shook my head. "I cannot conceive of such a thing, Holmes. Surely there would be some outcry, despite their influence."

"According to what I have learned, the Fellowship has, until recently, kept its hunts relatively bloodless. At least on English soil. Less a blood sport than a curious ritual, and one supposedly dating back several centuries. Such things are often brushed off under the guise of hoary tradition." His tone told me all I needed to know about his opinions in that regard. "But, as times change, so too have appetites. Worse, their membership isn't anywhere near as parochial as it might once have been. The Fellowship counts Americans and Canadians among its number. Even a few Russians."

"But what should such a disreputable fellowship want with you?"

"Simple, Watson. Someone is hunting our hunters." Holmes sat back, legs crossed. "But we should start at the beginning." He gestured, and I sat back in my chair, notebook at the ready.

"A year ago, Sir Harold and a few others went to Canada for a hunting trip, specifically to the Hudson's Bay region.

There they met several other members of the Fellowship, from south of the border. They hired a local man, ostensibly to act as a sort of guide, and a camp cook — a half-breed named Punk. Harmless enough." Holmes' frown deepened, and I could tell he was truly angry. "I'd wager the poor devil wasn't told what he was really being hired for, but he found out quickly enough. Three days in they shot him down like a dog. Sir Harold claimed the fellow had gone mad, out there in the deep woods, and no one questioned them."

"But it was murder, surely." Even as I said it, I felt a naive fool, and recalled the number of well-off murderers Holmes and I had encountered. Money and prestige were often the best armor, and they had saved more than one deserving soul from the gallows, especially when the victim was from the lowest rungs of society.

Holmes leaned forward through a cloud of smoke. "It was indeed. But not the one which interests us. Some weeks later, the first sportsman died. A Canadian in Ontario. Then, a few days later, an American in Chicago. A second American followed in San Francisco. Three deaths in as many weeks."

"I think I can guess what linked them," I said. "They were all members of a certain club, and had recently been on a hunting trip to the Hudson's Bay region."

Holmes tapped the side of his nose. "An adequately excellent observation, Watson. The murders were, to put it bluntly, sensational. Savage affairs. The wounds resembled those made by an animal, or various animals."

Gisburne's accounts of the murders of his fellow clubmen had been similar. Mauled had been the word he used. As if by a big cat, or a wolf. Given his experience, I suspected Gisburne knew what he was talking about.

As I considered it, I felt a certain shameful satisfaction. If these men were as bad as Holmes claimed, then such a fate might well be one they deserved. Holmes smiled mirthlessly, as if he'd read my thoughts.

"But even that is not the strangest thing. The murder in San Francisco occurred in broad daylight, aboard a cable car. Witnesses reported that he had started screaming, as if he'd seen something that put the fear of God in him, and made as if to jump. It was assumed that he'd subsequently fallen off and been pulled under the wheels."

"And had he?" I asked, already suspecting I knew the answer. Holmes didn't reply. I stopped writing and looked at him. He puffed on his pipe, seemingly relaxed. He glanced at me, and his mouth twitched. "Well?" I asked. "This is only half the story, surely."

"Indeed, Watson. And here is where you and I enter the picture. The pattern has stretched across the Atlantic to England. Two deaths so far, both brutal affairs, with seemingly no connection, save one." He sat back. "Well, two. Besides the obvious one, certain parties have taken an interest."

"And would these certain parties have permanent lodgings at the Diogenes Club?"

"Among others. As I said, the Fellowship casts a long shadow, and there are many interested in escaping it." He gestured. "Responsibility fell in poor Gregson's lap, you know. It was merest child's play to wheedle a look at the scenes of the killings. Gregson was only too happy to comply."

That was no surprise. Of all the Scotland Yarders, Inspector Gregson was always quickest to look the other way, when it might benefit him. He was a calculating one, more so than poor Lestrade, or young Hopkins. "And? What did you find?" I asked, somewhat impatiently. The thought that he might've found nothing never crossed my mind.

"In both cases, the killer, or killers, left something behind." Holmes reached into his vest pocket and produced something with a flourish. It was small, and whitish, barely larger than a finger. I took it, and knew it at once for bone. "It has been carved, as you can see. And with great skill."

"Scrimshaw?" I asked, as I held the carving up to the light. It was an awful thing, bestial and hunched. Stag-like antlers curled back around a sloped skull and curved claws dangled over crooked knees. The thing had been carved as if squatting, but its limbs were long and bent awkwardly.

I felt a chill as I examined it. A sour taste bloomed at the back of my throat. I repressed a nauseated shudder as I ran a thumb over its carved form. It was so lifelike that I half feared it might bite me at any time. "Or a ritual totem of some kind, like that business last year, with the debtor, Hasselback?"

"The possibility is there. There are similarities to certain carvings made by the native Inuit of the Hudson's Bay region." Holmes stood, and began to pace, his hands clasped behind his back. "The *tupilak* or *tupilait* is a sort of sympathetic magic — a spirit bound to a carving, and set loose to avenge some slight or wrong."

I grew more uneasy as Holmes spoke. The thing in my hand seemed to twist and squirm, as if it knew it were being discussed. I wanted to cast it aside, but I could not. Instead, I closed my fingers about it, hoping to hide it from my sight.

Holmes continued. "Regardless of the origins, a carving such as this was found at the scene of every murder. Including those in the Americas."

"A calling card," I said. "Or a warning, like the orange pips?"

Holmes leaned against the fireplace, studying the clock on the mantel. "I believe so, though I am still at a loss to explain the deaths themselves." He gnawed pensively on the stem of his pipe. "Their cause is obvious, on the face of it, and yet, no perpetrator has been seen."

"Which is surely impossible, unless we're dealing with some sort of invisible animal..." I laughed, somewhat nervously, I admit.

Holmes didn't. "There was a strange case, out in the American Southwest, a year or two ago. A man named Morgan was found dead, out among the chaparral. The local constabulary thought it was murder, at first, but..." He trailed off and shrugged. "The human eye is an imperfect instrument, Watson. Some things are beyond its perception. There's supposedly a fellow in West Sussex who's doing some interesting research into such matters, but for the moment we are forced to rely on it." He tapped the side of his head.

"Perhaps I should take a look at the bodies. There might be some evidence only a thorough post mortem examination will reveal..." I stopped, as something occurred to me. "Wait

— if you were already investigating, why then did you send Gisburne off so rudely?"

"Think, Watson. How does one hunt a tiger?"

"Bait," I said, instantly.

"Exactly. A man — a probable murderer — like Gisburne wouldn't have come to me, if he wasn't desperate. That sort always thinks the answer lies in money, or the barrel of a gun. And for him to be so desperate, the situation must be grave indeed." He gestured to the carving, which I found I was still holding.

"You think he's received one of these?"

"Possibly. Or one of the others. But, by provoking him further, I hope to bring this matter to a swift conclusion, before any more lives are lost."

"How?"

"Protective custody," Holmes said. "Time is at a premium. In the hours it would take us to break the wall of silence about the Fellowship, and determine which of the remaining men is in immediate danger, the luckless victim would likely be dead. Worse, the survivors might scatter, making it all but impossible to catch the killer before they complete their grisly mission. So, when word reaches us that they have gathered, we'll have them."

I nodded. "That's why you sent him away — you knew he would run to the others."

He leaned against the window and twitched the curtain aside. "I know he will. And if all goes according to plan, we will soon — ah. There." He tapped the glass with a long finger. I joined him at the window, and saw a young boy waving from the street. I recognized one of the young rascals Holmes insisted on referring to as the Baker Street Irregulars.

Tossing on our hats and coats, we hurried out to the wet street, where the urchin enthusiastically received a couple shillings in return for a location. Holmes spoke with the lad for a moment longer before hailing a cab, and we soon found ourselves heading towards the East End. "Where are we going, Holmes?" I asked, as the cab juddered and bounced along over wet cobbles and uneven pavement.

"Where all unsavory sorts eventually wind up, Watson — Bluegate Fields. Porky Johnson has tracked our sportsmen to their campsite, as I knew he would." I laughed in sudden understanding, as I recalled the man I'd seen earlier. Shinwell Johnson was another of Holmes' *agentes in rebus* — a former criminal who kept Holmes abreast of the ever-shifting tides of the underworld. Johnson, for all that he'd broken more bones than I'd ever set, was a friendly enough sort.

Bluegate Fields was an odious slum that lay just north of Wapping. We had visited it more times than I cared to think of, most recently during an investigation into the disappearance of a young aristocrat named Gray. Conditions had not improved since then.

It was a dreadful sort of place, where extreme poverty was leavened by sudden violence. Song and supper rooms of varying quality were prevalent, and it was to one of these — The Joyful Cossack — that Johnson's careful directions, delivered via urchin, guided us.

The man himself was nowhere in sight, as we took up our position in a by-street across from the music hall. "He'll be inside already. Porky is a firm soul, and he'll do as he's promised," Holmes said, with all the assurance of a saint. "Gisburne won't be able to slip out, not while Porky has an eye on him." Having met Shinwell Johnson on several occasions, I knew that 'firm' was as apt a description as any. Johnson was a lump of a man, made hard of body and mind by a callous world, but he was as loyal to Holmes, in his own way, as I was.

Nonetheless, as we stood at the mouth of the by-street, I hesitated. My service revolver was heavy in my pocket. The old Adams revolver had seen me through danger more than once. I had come to regard it in much the same way I fancied a knight might regard his sword. Totem and tool both. I touched it idly, then realized that I'd inadvertently brought that grotesque little carving with me. As my fingers found it, I felt once more that eerie chill, and suddenly, the evening fog felt stifling. I tugged at my scarf and said, "Holmes, perhaps we should —"

The click of a revolver being cocked silenced me. "Perhaps you should explain to me why you're here, exactly." The voice was rough; American, by the accent.

I made to ease my pistol out. Holmes was between the newcomer and myself, but he made no move to step aside. Instead, he tapped my wrist gently with his cane, preventing me from retrieving my weapon. "No need for that, Watson. Leave it where it is. And you, Mr. Leverton — do put that Colt away, before someone is injured."

"How do you — Holmes? Is that you, then, Mr. Holmes? I'll be damned!"

"One hopes not, Mr. Leverton. I have always counted you on the side of the angels." Holmes smiled thinly. "Well, Watson, nothing to say to our old friend?"

I was momentarily at a loss, before dim embers of memory were stirred to new life. "Of course! Leverton, the American agent," I said, extending my hand.

"The hero of the Long Island cave mystery himself," Holmes said, with a laugh. It was a rare sort of fellow who could earn such enthusiastic approbation from Holmes. Leverton, with his hatchet face and hard smile, did not seem far removed from the Shinwell Johnsons of the world. A skull thumper, rather than a ratiocinator, but from what Holmes had told me, Leverton was a dogged investigator in his own right.

"I was not aware that there were any caves on Long Island," I said, as we shook hands warmly. "Then, perhaps that was the mystery?"

Leverton smiled, and clapped me on the arm. "Wrong Long Island, Doctor. The Bahamas, not New York." His smile faded, and he shook his head. "That was a bad one." He looked across the street at the music hall. "This one's worse though."

"But how did you come to be here? Surely this is no coincidence?" I took Holmes' smile to mean I was right. I shook my head, recalling how certain Holmes had been about the nature of the killings in America. Mycroft's reach was long, and Holmes was not above abusing his brother's privilege for his own benefit. "You expected him to be here."

"Someone, certainly, yes. Not Leverton in particular, though. My powers do not extend to prognostication, impressive as they may be." He smiled in a self-satisfied way, clearly pleased with himself. "Two weeks ago, an agent of Pinkerton's American Agency was retained, by a certain young widow in Chicago, to investigate the brutal murder of her late husband, not long after his return from a hunting trip…"

"Her husband was a member of the Fellowship," I said.

Leverton's eyes widened slightly, but he nodded. "That he was, and I can't say as I'm surprised you know of it." He shook his head. "I thought the Red Circle was bad, but the predilections of this crew are enough to turn a man's stomach." He smiled grimly. "Not that they ain't paying for it now."

"Quite so," Holmes said. "Justice, of sorts. A cruel justice, enacted on cruel men."

For some reason, at his words, my fingers found the carving in my pocket, and a shudder ran through me. Cruel was a good way to describe such a thing. Then, if even half of what Holmes had told me was true, perhaps Gisburne and his fellows deserved worse. The carving seemed to twist beneath my fingers and I jerked my hand from my pocket. Neither Holmes nor Leverton noticed, their attentions on the music hall.

They spoke quietly, and I tried to listen, but found myself distracted. The night was cold, and wet, and it seemed to weigh down on me. I kept catching something — movement — just out of the corner of my eye. Whenever I turned, whatever it was, was gone. But I could hear it, or something. A rattle, like flat sticks striking one another discordantly, or a broken carriage wheel, cracking against the street, and just beneath it, a steady thump-thump-thump, as of someone striking a drum. A persistent, dolorous rhythm.

Shivering, I looked up, and saw something white and gleaming rise above the sloped roof of the squalid building to my left. More shapes followed, and for a moment, I was put in mind of the prongs of an antler. I closed my eyes and shook my head. When I opened them, whatever it was…was gone. As if it had never been.

I realized that my fingers had found the carving again, and it was warm to the touch, almost unnaturally so. I pulled my hand out of my pocket and forced myself to concentrate on what was being said. "There were eight men in that hunting party," Leverton was saying. "Five of those men are dead now. One, in New Orleans, three weeks ago. I got there just as they were taking the body out." He shook his head. "It looked as if someone had taken a machete to him. I came to England then, following a letter that fellow had sent to someone named Gisburne, just before he passed over the river."

"And you tracked him here, like a veritable bloodhound? Most impressive, Mr. Leverton. I could not have done better myself."

"We never sleep, Mr. Holmes, and we never let a man escape justice."

"Admirable sentiments. And have you come to any conclusions as to the nature of the killer we are tracking?"

"The cook — Punk — had kin among the Inuit around Hudson's Bay, and they took his death poorly." Leverton seemed distracted, like a dog with a scent he cannot shake. "There was talk as they'd gone to a fellow, an *angakkuq*, they call them — a witch-man, as my granny used to say — and that they'd set a spirit on Punk's killers."

Holmes snorted, but I could think of nothing save the carving in my pocket. "Perhaps one of Gisburne's accomplices," I said, too quickly. I glanced at Holmes. "We've seen it before — a man turning on his fellows, out of guilt."

Holmes frowned. "Even more reason, then, to take them all into custody. Come. It is past time we put an end to this."

The Joyful Cossack was a riot of color and noise. Somewhere an out of tune piano was being tortured by someone with more enthusiasm than talent, and on stage a bevy of woman danced cheerfully, if not skillfully, to the applause of a raucous crowd. The air was thick with tobacco smoke and the mingled smells of stale beer and greasy food. The stage was set back from the floor, allowing for an arrangement of a dozen or more tables, most of which were occupied. Holmes quickly led us to one.

I saw Shinwell Johnson, lounging at the bar. The blocky man tipped his battered hat to Holmes as we passed, but gave no other sign of recognition. As we took our seats, I saw him duck towards the rear exit, as if in a great hurry. That was all for the best. Johnson's effectiveness as an informant was reliant on there being no knowledge of his relationship with Holmes or the police. "Exeunt Porky," Holmes murmured, his eyes on the stage.

I spotted Gisburne almost immediately. He was sitting at a nearby table with two other men, one of whom looked decidedly nervous. They leaned towards one another, speaking intently. "Holmes," I hissed. "Look there. It's Gisburne."

"Yes, Watson. I see them. Why do you think I chose this table? It gives us the perfect vantage point from which to watch." Holmes glanced at me. "Now stop staring — do you want to spook our quarry?"

"Well what are we going to do? Should we confront them?"

"Sounds good to me," Leverton murmured. He edged back the line of his coat and I saw the grip of a pistol jutting from a shoulder holster.

"That won't be necessary," Holmes said. "Before we even climbed into our cab, I sent word to Gregson. The police should be here directly. All we must do is ensure that Sir Harold and his fellow sportsmen do not leave."

There seemed to be no danger of that. Gisburne's companions were deep in their cups. Obviously, they had been waiting for him for some time. And given the attentiveness of the staff, I could only conclude that they were regulars. Then, perhaps that wasn't so surprising, given their other vices.

I studied them, wondering what made such men kill. Not in self-defense, or for the good of the Empire, but out of the sheer joy of the act. We had come across madmen before — individuals who struck with frenzied malice. But all of them had had some motivation beyond simple bloodlust. This was something else. A cold hunger.

For a moment, I thought of what it must have been like for their victim. Pursued through a dark forest by men with guns. The moonlight glinting off of rifle barrels, the crunch of snow. Then, a spray of crimson on white. And for what? No reason other than some animal pleasure. At that instant, I almost wanted to see them dead. This killer, whoever he might be, was simply balancing the scales. Hunting the hunters, as Holmes had said.

I stared at that table of evil men, watching as one of them, pale and sweating, downed drink after drink. Wracked by fear, I hoped he understood how his victim had felt. I doubted it. These were not the sort of men for whom such understanding came naturally.

I realized that Holmes was watching me. I tried to compose myself, but I knew he had seen my anger. "It is understandable," he said, softly.

"What is?"

"Your anger, Watson. You are wondering why we do not simply leave them to their well-deserved fate. Save the country the cost of a hanging, as Mr. Leverton might say."

Leverton chuckled bleakly, and I knew then that he shared my low opinion of our quarry. Holmes shook his head.

"I have asked myself that same question, and I have concluded that it is because they must be made to pay in full. Not for one death, but for all of the others they might have caused. They must be drawn into the light, and exposed for all to see, otherwise all of this may well be forgotten, and the names of their victims with them. So we will save them now, if we can, in order to crush them later, with the full weight of justice."

"Not quite as satisfying," Leverton said.

"No," Holmes said, "but it is our duty. My brother agrees." He extricated his watch from his vest pocket and glanced at it. "The police should be here soon. I suggest we enjoy the performance until then."

Bawdy as it was, I soon found that I could not keep my attention on the performance. Instead, I found my eye drawn repeatedly to the edges of the floor, where the crowd was thickest. Someone — something — was moving through the mass of humanity. I caught only glimpses of it — brief flashes of white bone and black, empty eyes. I was put in mind of some great beast moving carefully through the tall grass towards its prey.

I thought to warn the others, but found myself unable to speak — to move. I could only watch as whatever it was drew closer. As it moved, I could hear a persistent rattle, or clatter, and I felt an unnatural chill creep along my extremities.

I was certain Holmes had not seen it. If he had, he might have stopped me from what I did next. My hand dipped into my coat and I clamped my fingers about the grip of my service revolver. As I drew it, my eyes never left the clattering white shape, moving through the crowd. It seemed to grow as it drew near, but I could not make out its face, or anything beyond the impressions of a starveling frame and what might have been antlers, rising high enough to set the gaudy chandeliers to swinging. A headdress, I thought, and I wondered why no one could hear the harsh jangle of its approach.

I glanced away, and saw that, despite my assumptions, someone else had indeed seen the thing, for one of Sir Harold's fellows lurched to his feet with a great cry. As his chair slammed back against the floorboards, the white thing lunged. No, rather, it *stretched* across the intervening distance, reaching out with too long arms, and too long fingers, for the unfortunate fellow. And as it did so, I at last saw its face.

It was the face of the thing in my pocket. A face I have seen in my dreams many nights since. A thing of cruel hunger, contorted in a leer such as has never graced a human face. A beast's face, but like no beast which has ever lived, save in the fevered imaginings of madmen. "Watson, what are you doing?" Holmes hissed, as I hauled my service revolver out from under the table, took aim at those hateful features — and fired.

The thing, for it was a thing and not a man, whipped around, fleshless jaws snapping. I could not tell whether my shot had done anything more than startle it. An arm, bone white and long, flailed towards me, and I threw myself backwards, nearly knocking Leverton from his seat. Something cold and sharp passed over me. I tasted the harsh air of winter in the back of my throat. I heard a voice in my head, and a dim, guttural chanting, as well as what might have been the thump of rough hands on a drum of stretched hide.

As if from a great distance, I heard Sir Harold bellow something, and then the sharp crack of a revolver other than my own. A projectile tugged at the edge of my coat as I fought to stand. Holmes and Leverton both tried to wrestle me back to the floor. I knew then they couldn't see it, for if they could, they would not have tried to stop me.

I do not know, even now, what I'd hoped to accomplish. I simply knew in the moment that I could not let the thing do what it had come to do, and still retain my soul. Whatever the crimes of those it had come for, they were human crimes, and deserving of the gallows. Not this, whatever this was.

The thing towered between our tables, half solid, half spirit. I saw that it resembled the carving, but was more horrid in every way. Its head resembled the skull of a stag, and then that of a man, and then something else entirely. It was an impossible thing. I felt its hunger like a physical blow. Before I could fire again, it had turned away, back to its original prey.

Through a haze of sweat and fear, I saw that Sir Harold, perhaps fearing an attack, had produced a pistol from somewhere, and was firing at our table. Perhaps he'd mistaken my shot for an assassination attempt. I was never to find out, for the white thing gave a great cry and leapt. Claws like scythes lashed out, and then the air was full of blood. Screams such as I had only ever heard at Maiwand echoed as I forced myself upright. At the back of my head, the chanting and drumming had grown louder.

The thing — the spirit, the devil, whatever it was — seized on its prey with a shocking savagery. It tore at the hapless sportsman, pressing his writhing form to the top of the table. The creature's screams had driven Sir Harold and the others into a panic, and they discharged their weapons wildly. I ignored them as best I could, and tried to focus on the pallid abomination while it was distracted by its butchery.

I levelled my pistol, the apparition turned towards me as I did so, fleshless jaws agape and eyes as black as the pit. I heard a shout, and saw, as if in a dream, Sir Harold extend his weapon towards me, eyes wide. I wondered, for an instant, whether he could see the thing. Then I felt his bullet as it creased my arm and knocked me for six.

Losing my footing, I fell back with a shout. Out of the corner of my eye, I caught sight of Leverton, as the Pinkerton snapped off a shot. Then I saw nothing but the malign immensity bearing down on me. It plunged towards me like smoke boiling through a flue, and my head throbbed with the sound of it, and the pounding of the drums.

Its voice was soft, but enormous in volume, at once hoarse and sweet. Like a gale wind, or the crash of ocean waters against smooth rocks. As it roared, I felt the carving resonate within my coat. The thing loomed over me, antlers scraping the ceiling. It was a stag and a man and a giant, but there were feathers and claws and other things — a bone-white chimera, as vast as the world. My revolver clicked dry, and it reached for me, claws spread.

I felt Holmes' hands at my coat. "The carving — where is it?" he shouted, as if from a great distance. I fumbled at my breast pocket, even as I tried to push him away, out of reach of those terrible claws. He batted my hands aside and tore the carving free. As he did so, the looming monstrosity seemed to buckle and fade away before my very eyes.

Holmes turned, and I saw his eyes widen slightly. Then, he flung the carving into the air, and shouted for Leverton. I heard the bark of a pistol, and a sound like ice cracking, and then the pressure on my chest faded, leaving only a dim ache. The clatter of white antlers and bone was gone from my ears. I could breathe again.

I sat up with Holmes' help. As I did so, I caught sight of Sir Harold, lying nearby, his eyes wide and staring. A third eye, red and deep, occupied his brow. Leverton stood over the body, his revolver hanging from his hand. "Damn it," he said.

"Your quick thinking saved both Watson and myself, Mr. Leverton," Holmes said. "And I rather suspect you did him a mercy, in the long run."

"You misunderstand me, Mr. Holmes. I was hoping to see him hang, is all." Leverton holstered his weapon and turned away from the bodies. "Guess this'll serve well enough."

"Only time will tell, I fear," Holmes said, as he helped me to stand.

I will not bore you with the details of what followed. Suffice it to say, once the constables had arrived, the matter became a mundane one. Gisburne was dead, thanks to Leverton's skill with a pistol, as was one other man, the one I'd seen mauled by the thing. Even now, I cannot think of a fitting word. A spirit? A demon? Herne himself, come roaring up out of the dark to punish those who dared to use his name?

Perhaps all three.

No description seemed to do it justice, and when the police arrived, Holmes made no mention of it. The survivor quickly found himself under arrest for a variety of charges. He was almost pathetically glad to be in police custody. I did not blame him. Just as I did not blame him later, when he hung himself in his cell, using the sheets from his cot. Whether or not he had received one of those curious carvings while in gaol, I cannot say. Perhaps it was simply the guilt. Holmes knows, I think, but I have never asked him.

Leverton had taken his leave as quickly as he had come. I suspect now that he knew more about things than he'd shared, and I do not envy him that knowledge. I wonder, sometimes, if perhaps he went north, to tell Punk's kin of what had occurred, and to see that no more white, little figures found their way into unwary hands. I like to think so.

I hope so.

"Who sent the carvings, do you think?" I asked Holmes, after we had returned to Baker Street. The night was drawing to a close, and a pale light was stretching across the rooftops. I felt as if I could have slept for a week, but my curiosity prevented me from succumbing.

"I have my suspicions," Holmes said, "But we shall never know for certain. Given what has happened, I find myself reluctant to muddy the waters further." He glanced at me as he said it, and I heard the unspoken apology in his words.

"It was a hallucination, obviously, brought on by some toxin worked into the bone." I spoke flatly, more for his benefit than mine. Even so, the words felt hollow. What I had seen had been real enough to leave marks in my coat and bruises on my flesh. What hallucination could do that? Even now, I am sure that I saw something, though I cannot say what it was.

"As good an explanation as we are likely to get," Holmes said. "There are cases where imagined trauma results in very real wounds. The stigmata, for instance."

He trailed off then. Uncertain. A moment later, he bent to retrieve his Stradivarius. As he set bow to string, I asked, "Did you see it, Holmes? When you held the carving — did you see it?"

Holmes never answered my question.

And I doubt he ever will.

—— « O » ——

Josh Reynolds

Josh Reynolds is a writer, occasional editor and semi-professional monster movie enthusiast. He has been a professional author since 2007, and has had over twenty novels published in that time, as well as a wealth of shorter fiction pieces, including short stories, novellas and the occasional audio script. An up-to-date list of his published work, including licensed fiction for Games Workshop's Warhammer Fantasy and Warhammer 40,000 lines, can be found at https://joshuamreynolds.wordpress.com.

The Strange Adventure
of Mary Holder

Nancy Holder

The night of horror is over, but I fear that its aftermath has followed us home.

This morning, as the sun rose, the pea souper that had pressed down on us all night gave way at last. Icy sleet drenched my friend Sherlock Holmes and me as we silently descended from our hansom in Baker Street. Neither of us reacted to the punishing downpour.

The roads were choked with travelers hurrying to escape the deluge. Mud and water sloshed our ankles as we reached the door of 221B. We crossed the threshold and trudged up to the sitting room; I felt as if I were floating. I was numb from head to toe, and in such a state of shock that I could not put two words together, but lowered myself numbly down upon the wicker settee without taking off my overcoat. Holmes crossed to the fireplace and stirred a pile of smoldering ashes with the poker. He had already told me what had been burnt there. I had to look away.

The room was frigid; I could see my breath. Mrs. Hudson was in the country. No tea, no heat.

Holmes' long, hawkish face was gray; did his fingers tremble, like mine? We would be confederates always in this night's wild work — had we the right to do as we did?

Holmes cast a covert glance at the writing desk; therein lay the small Morocco leather case that held his hypodermic.

A burst of frustration mingled with some envy: had I means to achieve oblivion, I should have seized upon it, but it has ever been my policy that Holmes' drug use will be the end of him.

My words are my balm, I thought.

"Write it down, Watson," Holmes said gravely, as if he had read my mind.

The merciless grip of fear clasped my heart once more and I could not breathe. Our world had shifted onto a new axis. It was as if a curtain had been lifted and now the *real* truth would play upon the stage of our lives — from the staid sensibility of the realm to the fever dream of the Grand Guignol.

I am the chronicler. I am his Boswell. But enumerating all the events that have transpired regarding Mary Holder would give them more weight, credibility. It would make the unbelievable … possible. Once you eliminate the impossible, whatever remains, no matter how improbable, *must* be the truth.

Holmes put down the poker with a sigh and said, "Watson, old fellow, I beg you to give your mind some ease. I am a detective. You are a writer. Fall into what comforts you best."

He is right, of course. Accordingly, I have taken pen to paper, and begin this tale of murder most foul.

—— «» ——

Those who have followed my publications in *The Strand* may remember the tragic tale of 'The Adventure of the Beryl Coronet'. That mystery involved the financier Alexander Holder, who had accused his only son Arthur of stealing a fabulous diadem seated with thirty-nine perfect beryls — a public treasure that had been entrusted by 'one of the Highest in the Land' to Mr. Holder, as collateral for a loan of fifty thousand pounds. Holmes exonerated Arthur, who had chivalrously refused to reveal that it was his beloved cousin, the dark-eyed Mary Holder, who was the thief. She had conspired with her lover, Sir George Burnwell, and the cad had successfully made off with a section of the crown, which contained three beryls. Holmes managed to retrieve the stones, but irrevocable damage to the family had been done: realizing that Holmes would unmask her treachery, Mary Holder left her uncle's home with Burnwell. This, of course, cast her out of society, ruined her reputation, and broke her uncle's heart.

I had often wondered at Holmes' insistence upon claiming the one thousand pound reward that Mr. Holder had set on the return of the stolen gems. My friend is not of an avaricious nature; indeed, he often takes cases knowing full well that the client will be unable to pay. What motivates him is the puzzle to be unlocked — the deeper the mystery, the better. That, to him, is the better coin.

I therefore surmised that his close watch on that one thousand pounds was motivated by something other than personal gain. I believed that he tracked down that poor, wretched girl and gave her the funds as a means of escape. Until this new case concerning her, I had only inquired after the matter obliquely, and he had not confirmed my suspicions. Now I know that I was right. How tragic she could not take advantage of the windfall and free herself of that monster's clutches!

But I am charging ahead. This sequel to that story began last Friday, as bleak and sullen a morning as London has ever suffered, when Arthur Holder, the son of Alexander, entreated us by telegram to come down to Fairbank, their ancestral seat, as fast as we might. He gave no reason, but correctly deduced that we would move with all swiftness, and we presented ourselves at the somewhat modest residence just in time for tea.

The servants were in tears, and Arthur too, as he explained that his father was gravely ill, and not expected to recover. The old gentleman had one last request and was trying with all his might to linger until it was fulfilled.

"You want me to find your niece, Mary, so that you may let her know that she is forgiven and welcome to come home," Holmes said. We stood together at Mr. Holder's bedside. I observed the patient with a physician's eye; my hopes were not great.

"Indeed, that is what I want most in this world. I have made provision for her in my will. Arthur knows of this and approves."

Arthur busied himself with pouring his father a brandy. I could see that the conversation was much oversetting him. He had been in love with his cousin for years, and appeared to love her still. She had turned down his several proposals of marriage because of his youthful waywardness, but see what she had accepted instead!

Without looking at us, Arthur nodded in assent. The distraught young man cleared his throat and said, "With all my heart, I approve. To me, her treachery speaks of her utter feminine innocence. I, too, was taken in by the worldly charm of Sir George Burnwell. He was my boon companion in all my escapades, and it is only because he showed his hand so soon that I did not fall into deeper depths of depravity in his company. It is no surprise, therefore, that a sweet, sheltered country girl, such as my cousin, would be overwhelmed by his flattering attentions, and do his bidding."

"I should have refused him entry into this house!" Alexander choked out, his indignation muffled by a fit of coughing. "I betrayed her trust in me! I was her parent in every way and I was too gentle!" His coughing became more extreme, and Arthur rushed to his side with the brandy he had poured out. Arthur regarded his parent with filial devotion and said, "Father, please, do not exert yourself. Mr. Holmes will find her. He will bring her home."

"Indeed, I shall," Holmes told them both. "On that score, put both your minds at ease."

— «» —

We dined with Arthur — Mr. Holder being in too distressed a condition to join us — and soon after, quitted the countryside. Skeletal trees and lonely fallow fields provided our only landscape as we headed back up north on the train. Holmes was quite downcast.

"I fear they have expectations that the Mary Holder whom we find will be the same sweet child they long for," he said, more to the dreary vistas beyond the window than to me. "The world may have ... reduced her somewhat."

I chose to remain hopeful. Once we debarked at the station, we headed at once to the Diogenes Club. There we conferred with Holmes' brother Mycroft in the Stranger's Room, the only space in the club where spoken word is permitted. When the name of Sir George Burnwell was uttered, Mycroft's face betrayed his utter revulsion, much as if one had served up a rat instead of kippers for breakfast. Mycroft professed astonishment at his brother's assumption that he would know anything about Sir George; however, he eventually produced a fellow member of the Diogenes Club who did.

That gentleman pointed us toward the Royal Jubilee Exhibition, which was then taking place in Liverpool. On condition of anonymity, he allowed as how while attending the exhibition a fortnight before, his own younger brother had frequented a local gambling hell, where he had been roundly fleeced by Sir George. The lad refused to provide any details despite his relative's threats to his allowance or entreaties to his conscience. I wondered if Burnwell had threatened the young man in some dire way, and marveled at the power of such a villain that he might frighten one of his victims from so many miles distant.

"To Liverpool, then," Holmes said, and as my practice was rather unencumbered with patients, I was in a position to accompany him.

Mindful that hours, if not minutes, might make the difference in Alexander Holder's peaceful exit from this life, we telegrammed our itinerary to Arthur and left on the first train the next morning. Despite the desultory weather, Liverpool itself was quite charming, with many Tudor buildings still standing, and of course, the old castle. I must confess that when surveying the hustle-bustle of the Jubilee Exhibition, I had no idea how on earth we were to ferret out Sir George.

However, I didn't have long to wonder at it, as Holmes led the way through the respectable squares and alleys until we came to a more disreputable section of the place, and swung into a dingy pub called The Five of Clubs. Nutshells on the floor, drooping leaded glass in grimy window panes.

Surveying our fellow patrons, I took comfort in Holmes' knowledge of baritsu and the weight of my service revolver in my pocket. More than once we two have acquitted ourselves well when violent circumstances demanded it.

However, after buying a round, it wasn't long before we found someone who had intimate knowledge of Liverpool's *demimonde* and who responded affirmatively to Holmes' detailed description of Sir George. However, the bounder had moved his base of operations to a different gaming establishment and had taken the name 'Lord Exeter.' We were greatly heartened to also learn that 'Lord Exeter' arrived at the tables each night in the company of a dark-haired, dark-eyed woman who had caused a stir. This, we assumed, would be Mary Holder.

Holmes assiduously telegrammed Arthur again, and then we found a room at an inn where we might refresh ourselves and, after napping, dress for the evening — my meaning should be taken in a number of ways, for Holmes determined that we should disguise ourselves. We powdered our hair gray and applied a colored paste to our faces that gave the appearance of wrinkles. Holmes bent his frame over a walking stick. I made a quip about how we should look in twenty years, still solving cases together. Holmes shot back that I would no doubt have been married two or three times by then while he would safely remain a bachelor.

Dusk descended and with it a thick, choking fog that mingled with the gasses of industry. My chest ached for clean air. In due time, we hired a hansom to take us to the outskirts of the town, to an unsavory establishment fronted by an opium den, no trade sign in evidence, and, thanks to a well-placed sovereign, we gained admittance.

Such a sight! The furnishings were of the most exotic sort, very Oriental, with Chinese papers of scarlet and vermillion and glazed lamps, of jade and black lacquer, that lent the rooms a luxurious glow. The tables were ebony inlaid with mother-of-pearl. Couples and groups lay languidly among the pillows, recovering, I guessed, from their exertions in the opium den. Glazed, heavy-lidded eyes watched us with some curiosity and suspicion. As might be expected, the ladies present were dressed more freely than one might find in the salons of the upper classes; I hardly supposed that any who moved so sinuously on the arms of the well-dressed gentlemen were their wives.

We continued through the room observed, but not remarked upon. Thus, we made our way through the place until we came upon a small but quiet crowd that had gathered around one of the tables. Two men were playing German whist.

Holmes whispered, "It is he," and I turned my attention to the player who was garnering so much attention. I had never met Sir George; my friend had, and though Holmes had described him to me, I was unprepared for the perfect proportion of his features. In truth, he did not look like 'one of the most dangerous men in England', as Holmes had termed him. He appeared friendly, and charming, and quite at his ease.

A woman was seated beside him, and for one brief moment I thought it was Mary Holder. Like Mary, her upswept hair was raven-black, and her uncommonly dark eyes pierced the surrounding gloom. But that was where all semblance ended. This woman was exotic, voluptuous. She was swathed in black — caressed by lace of deepest purple-black, shot through with beads of jet, accessorized with a black lace shawl and holding a large tasseled black lace fan decorated with painted roses. One of her long gloves had been peeled back off her hand, revealing nails of red lacquer such as one might find on a Chinese concubine. She was fascinating; something about her drew me in and caused me to stare, though my heart was heavy as I considered that Sir George must have thrown over Miss Holder. What had become of her I wished not to consider.

The other player, a younger man most admirably attired, sat across from Sir George, a number of empty glasses at his elbow and his expression one of bleary agitation. Heavy brows furrowed across a broad forehead as he swept back his chestnut hair, peering down at the cards that he held close against his chest. Then he stared down at the smattering of coins arranged before him. Sir George's massive towers of winnings attested to my supposition that Sir George was fleecing the young man in some manner, and the stranger's pockets were sure to be turned out empty before the night was over.

Holmes murmured to me, "Watch closely," and quit the tableau. The woman in black studied the young man's face, then fanned herself. Sir George threw down a few sovereigns, an insignificant amount to him, perhaps, but to his youthful opponent, a veritable king's ransom if one judged the scattering of sad metal before him to be his entire store of remaining funds.

"I will stand you," Sir George said. After the man nodded, Sir George put down his cards with a flourish. "The fifth point," he declared to a scattering of applause.

The young man stared, and then deflated. "You have me at a disadvantage, sir," he said, his face red with mortification. "As you have discerned, I am in this moment unable to produce the sum you have won from me. But if you'll permit a visit to your home later this evening, I shall discharge my debt."

"Indeed. That will be acceptable," Sir George decreed. He swept up all the coins in front of the young man, smiling with unbecoming glee as he did so.

At that very moment, Holmes returned with two snifters of brandy, and was about to hand one to me when he stumbled, tripped, and sprawled forward, landing with arms outstretched atop the table. Coins and cards flew up, then showered those around us, who cried out in surprise. The table tipped and clattered to the ground.

"*Hélas! Pardonnez-moi*," Holmes said in a thick Parisian accent. He prattled on in French, behaving as if, in his embarrassment, he had forgotten his English: in French, he offered to reimburse anyone whose garments had been harmed by his clumsiness. No one came forward, but many were the hands that were extended to assist him up. I noticed that the dark-haired woman seemed particularly eager to participate — she moved lithely, like a snake — but several men put themselves between Holmes and her. She fanned herself, staring intently at him, and I felt strange and dizzy.

Soon I lost track of her, and Sir George as well, in the throng that gathered around Holmes. He looked about, his dark brows shot up, and he took me aside.

"Do you see either of them?" he asked.

I, too, glanced round, then rested my gaze on Sir George's vanquished opponent. Holmes followed my gaze. "It was a setup, Watson," my friend murmured. "As I wandered away from the tables, I engaged the attention of a young *demoiselle* who is a frequent visitor, if not an employee, of this establishment. She was watching the whist game from a distance, and she wore such an expression of amusement that I asked her to share the joke. For a sovereign, she told me that the loser is a fraud. His pockets are loaded to the gills with money. He did not bet one-tenth of what he has on his person. She has seen his vast riches herself. How that fortunate happenstance had occurred I did not ask."

I grunted to indicate that I took his meaning at that last statement, and he continued.

"She was of the opinion that the loser cried poor in order to obtain entry into Sir George's domicile, his object being to acquaint himself with the lady in the black lace. After our conversation concluded, I wondered at the youth's poor showing at the table, and so contrived to fall. I discovered — as I thought I might — a clutch of cards, that would have crowned him the winner, tucked into the cuff of his trouser leg."

"How extraordinary," I said. "Did this *demoiselle* share the name of this dashing trickster?"

"Mademoiselle informed me that he is called Alexei Averin, and he claims a Russian heritage. But she herself is fluent in the Russian tongue and informed me that his Russian is quite feeble."

"Lying about his poverty and his heritage," I said, delineating the clues.

Holmes nodded. "She has no interest and no motive in exposing him as a fraud, however, as he has been quite generous to her in times past. He has been an *habitué* of this establishment for approximately two weeks. Sir George — or rather, Lord Exeter — began playing here a week ago."

"Did she say anything about him? Perhaps something that could lead us to Mary Holder?" I asked, and Holmes shook his head.

"The lady in black has been Lord Exeter's only female companion here," Holmes said. "My young miss does not like her, and in fact shivered when I made mention of her. Sir George's friend is called Giaconda Manzetti, and her English is thickly accented."

"She makes me shiver too," I confessed. "There is something about her that I cannot define, but that warns me off. Looking at her is rather like regarding a viper at close range."

Now it was Holmes who shivered and said, "No mention of serpents, if you please."

"As you wish. Well, now we've lost track of them," I said, but Holmes raised a finger in the air.

"Indeed, we have not. If you recall, 'Alexei Averin' has made an appointment with Sir George to make good his debt this very night."

"Of course. And so, we shall follow him," I supplied.

"We shall follow him," Holmes concurred. "I propose, therefore, that you secure us transportation while I keep vigil over our quarry. When he prepares to leave, we shall give chase."

Our duties divided, I went outside and secured a hansom. Twin lamps flanked the door of the gambling hell, but otherwise the street was dark, and so I hoped we could trail after without exposure.

I explained to the compliant cabbie that he should be ready to take off at a moment's notice, and was about to go back in to inform Holmes of my success when the false Russian strolled out and walked toward a well-turned-out brougham. A driver climbed up just as Holmes casually came through the doors and spotted me.

After Averin climbed into the brougham and it had pulled away, Holmes gave our driver the order to follow. There was some traffic on the street. Then, when we headed out onto a road into the countryside, Holmes asked our man to douse his lamps. We set to wiping the paste off our faces so that if

Mary Holder lay within our reach, she would recognize us as friends.

Darkness cloaked us. Unease washed through me like a chill wind, and I could almost hear someone whispering in my ear to turn back. I glanced at Holmes to see if he was experiencing anything similar, but I could tell by his transfixed stare that he was sifting through what information he had gathered thus far. I was sure he had collected many more clues than I was aware of.

Driving in darkness proved to be a baleful mistake. As we trailed after the silhouette, cut but subtly out of the blackness, our driver missed a deep rut in the road and the front left wheel sank fixedly into the groove. We two were forced to climb out and help him push. In that time, Averin had put sufficient distance between us and him that we lost him at a fork in the road and had to determine which way to go. Using the lamplight, Holmes inspected the wheel tracks and determined the sinister — left-hand — path to be the fresher. We took off again, aware that we had lost over half an hour in our pursuit.

Foreboding wrapped its fingers around me more tightly. I shifted my position, quite uneasy and suddenly very nervous.

"Do you feel it as well, Watson?" Holmes asked. "As if someone were walking over your grave?"

"The very devil is plucking the strings of my spine," I concurred.

"I feel as though I am covered with ants. Can we have been drugged? We had nothing to eat or drink at the den," he said. "Perhaps there was something in the opium that occasionally wafted through the rooms."

"I only began to experience these sensations after looking at that woman in black lace," I ventured.

He was quiet for a few moments. "I too," he declared. "Most interesting."

Then our vehicle stopped. Holmes tapped his cane on the ceiling and the driver informed us that his horses had simply refused to go farther. They were afraid.

"I do see a light," he told us. "Looks like a house."

Holmes climbed up and confirmed the light, adding that it appeared to be the glow of a window. We guessed we were not far from Sir George's domicile. We arranged for the driver to wait there for us, as we two got out and went on foot. The night air was cold as marble.

I have been to war, and I have seen sights in my adventures with Sherlock Holmes that turned my blood to ice, but never had I suffered such oppressive dread as when we began to walk through that tangle of trees and underbrush. By moonlight I saw a dozen shadows that seemed to creep along behind and beside us; whorls in tree trunks became distorted faces; vines were garrotes. My nerves were screaming at me to turn back, but of course we could not. We had a serious duty to discharge to the Holders and a young woman to rescue — or so I hoped.

A jag of lightning crashed overhead, illuminating a distant pile, some country squire's Gothic folly faded to ruin: a sharp-tipped abbey with a good portion of the roof fallen in, leaded, arched windows missing many panes, stone walls dripping with ivy and moss. I thought of Mary Holder; could she have lived in such a wreck? Did she live there still?

Soon we made our way out of the trees across a weed-choked lawn, past crumbling urns tumbling with wild ivy, and statues missing heads or arms. From our vantage point, we saw that more lights were on, and shadows cast on the wall indicated movement.

Then we heard the crack of a gunshot and a woman's high-pitched scream. Together we raced toward the great front door, and found it hanging just open. Holmes dashed in first, clattering into a great hall of smashed masonry and what, in the watery light, appeared to be the rotting carcass of a stuffed trophy lion. My revolver was in my hand. Holmes turned the head of his walking stick, revealing a blade. Thus armed, we flew up a set of stone stairs that fanned outward in two directions.

There was another scream, and a woman crying out in a thick accent, "What have you done?"

We raced down a vaulted corridor. Bats squeaked and flew out from the rafters in the frigid gloom. I could barely see in front of myself, but trailed after when Holmes made a sharp left, where illumination suggested the scene of the crime.

At the threshold, I instantly clutched my stomach, overcome with nausea. Holmes, too, skidded to a stop. It was as if someone had forced poison down my throat. My blood burned; my eyes watered and the bitter taste of lemons flooded my mouth. I fought down the sensations and looked to Holmes, who staggered two steps forward, into a display of death such as we have never seen. Before us lay Sir George Burnwell, who had been shot in the face, and 'Alexei Averin', not far from him. A pool of blood spread beneath him. The woman in black — Giaconda Manzetti — was crouched over him.

Far across the room, barely visible in the light from a single gas jet, Mary Holder was pressed into a corner in a gray muslin gown, her hands fixed over her mouth, eyes wide with terror. When she saw us, she gasped. I thought she was about to faint and ran toward her.

"Don't let her touch you!" Giaconda shouted in accented English. "Stay away from her!"

Mary Holder looked at her in astonishment and reached out her arms in supplication to Holmes and me. I caught her as she collapsed against me, weeping wildly.

"She has killed them! Murdered them both!" the Giaconda woman shouted.

"I have not!" Mary Holder sobbed. "Mr. Holmes, Dr. Watson, I know not by what providential means you have arrived here, but I implore you to take that murderess into custody! She has killed my husband and seeks to kill me as well."

"*Ukraben*," the woman snarled, staring at the corpse of 'Alexei Averin'.

"The word for 'liar'. You are Romani, then," Holmes said calmly. "And *not* Italian." She glared at him, and then at me. The room began to spin. Mary let out a strangled gasp and clung to me.

I said to Holmes, "Let me take her out of this place."

Giaconda shrieked and charged at us. I was too slow to respond and she pulled Mary out of my embrace. Mary threw punches at her, some landed, and before Holmes and I could part them, they had scratched and struck each other. Hairpins flew and curls waterfalled to the floor, pieces of lace both white and black, gray muslin and ebony velvet fluttered like leaves in the chaos. I had quite forgotten my revolver in the melee.

"There, there it is!" the Romani woman shouted, grabbing at something. At that moment, Holmes subdued her, pinning her to the floor, and I half-carried, half-dragged Mary from the room. The Romani woman went still, unconscious. I immediately felt my old self again, and the palpable dread that had surrounded me disappeared.

"Escort Mary to the coach," Holmes told me. "Get her to her uncle."

"To my uncle?" Mary asked. "What of him?"

"Holmes, old man, what of you?" I asked. "That woman is more than what she seems."

"And what is that, Watson?" he asked reasonably, a smile playing at his lips. "Do you believe she has placed a Gypsy curse upon this place?"

We argued further, but Holmes prevailed upon my duty to the Holder family, as every moment might be Alexander's last. I forced him to take my revolver and reluctantly escorted Mary to the coach, aware that the forest no longer seemed fraught with horrible danger. Could it be that the Romani woman *had* performed a Gypsy curse? Did I believe that? I was glad she was unconscious — and prayed that Holmes would have the stomach to render her thus again, should she awaken and the situation warrant.

I gently explained to Mary her uncle's desire to see her. She burst into tears of joy and sorrow both, and confessed how ashamed she was for all that had transpired.

"Oh, Dr. Watson, I knew as soon as I left with George that I had made a terrible mistake. I longed to return to my family, but I could not face the two men I had so terribly wronged. My cousin had stood in for me most nobly, but I knew that Mr. Holmes would find the means to clear him. I did not know that Mr. Holmes had retrieved the three beryls and returned them to Uncle Alexander."

She began to weep in the hansom, and I comforted her as best I could. Once she had command of herself, she told me that Sir George had indeed married her, sealing her fate — she was no longer a fallen woman, but she belonged to him in all legal implications of the word. She dreamed constantly of leaving him, and had planned many escapes. However, as you know, in our country a man may beat his wife or commit her to an asylum if she is recalcitrant. She told me that she never found the one thousand pounds, and we could only conclude that someone had picked her pocket. Alas.

"Then he brought that woman home…. Giaconda. She is evil, Dr. Watson." Mary covered her face with her hands. "I believe she is some kind of witch who can read people's minds. He took her to the gambling tables as we traveled all over the country and began to win immense sums. I feared for my life — what need had he of me?"

All this I pondered, even more afraid for Holmes, as the driver delivered us to the train station. Giving him additional payment, I requested that he go immediately to the police and inform them that Sherlock Holmes was awaiting their pleasure at a double homicide. To say that the man was shocked would be an understatement, but unfortunately, I had to avoid the authorities so that I would be able to spirit Mary away to her uncle without first speaking to the police myself

The trip from Liverpool to London, and then to the Holders', was largely uneventful. I delivered poor Mary to her relatives, who embraced her joyfully.

I was taking tea in the study, to afford them privacy, when I received a telegram from Holmes with but two words: DETAIN HER.

Therefore, when I was asked if I might care to remain at Fairbank for the night, I replied in the affirmative. Mary was put into her old room, the chamber kept as it had been since the night she decamped. Unknown to the Holder males, though I was exhausted, I maintained a vigil at her bedroom door.

Several times in the night I heard footsteps behind the door, and the knob turned twice, but the occupant made no further effort to come out. My eyes drooped; I started violently as someone gently gripped my shoulder, only to realize that Sherlock Holmes himself stood before me.

"Arthur Holder is on his way to this door," he informed me. "Alexander is about to breathe his last."

I removed my chair and we stood together as the younger Holder, wan and anxious, approached us and rapped softly on Mary's door. It opened at once. Mary was still wearing her torn dress; her face chalk-white and her eyes red and sunken.

Holmes said to her, "Giaconda Manzetti — whose real name is Dorenia Horváth — has been taken into custody. You may be called to speak at her trial, but I have explained to the police what has transpired. You may rest assured that the guilty will be punished."

Her eyes widened, as she went paler still, but then she clasped Holmes' hand and said, "Thank you, sir. A thousand times."

The family reunited in Alexander's room, and Holmes collapsed into a chair. He looked positively ill. His shoulders drooped and he pressed his fingertips against the bridge of his nose as if fighting off a headache. After a few moments of this, I grew alarmed.

"Are you all right?" I asked him, and he lowered his hand to his lap.

"I am not, but I hope to be so," he replied in a voice so low I almost couldn't hear it. Then he told me this story:

"After you left, Dorenia Horváth roused, and went wild with hysteria upon learning that you had taken Mary away. She told me that she was indeed a Gypsy, and that she and 'Alexei Averin' were husband and wife. The deceased's name was Samson Horváth. Sir George's reputation — and his identity — preceded him, and the two hatched a plan to fleece him. It was easy for Dorenia to catch Burnwell's eye, but easier still for her to tailor her conversation and deportment such that he fell prey to her charms, because she could read his thoughts."

"What nonsense!" I cried.

"Is it?" Holmes moved his shoulders. "She and Horváth had in their possession a certain book. In it were supposed rituals — Romani magic — that imbued the supplicant with certain gifts. Dorenia Horváth claimed that one of these gifts was the Second Sight. Another was a sort of ward, employed to set up barriers of protection around one's home." He raised his brows. "An intruder can become discouraged easily by sensations of agitation and vertigo."

"Good Lord! Extraordinary," I blurted, then narrowed my eyes. Despite everything we had seen and done — claims by spiritualists that they had contacted the dead, and supposed vampires, and a man turned into an ape— science had provided a rational explanation in each case. So, I raised one brow, inviting my old friend to provide one now.

He did not fail me.

"Of course, I didn't believe a word." He smiled grimly. "Eager to prove herself innocent of two murders she showed me the book, turning to the page containing the arcane ritual to imbue one with Second Sight. She told me that she had used it repeatedly on Sir George, learning where he kept his vast gaming winnings, and told Horváth. Last night, as was planned days before, Horváth deliberately lost to Sir George, thus providing a reason to come to his house."

"I can see it now," I interjected. "They meant to murder Sir George and steal the money. And Mary? Did they plan to kill her too?"

Holmes grew very grave, his brows lowering over his hooded eyes as he pressed his fingertips into a steeple. "Though they are criminals, they were not murderers. They have performed this setup all over Europe, and while they are wanted in a dozen countries, it is not for capital crimes."

DETAIN HER. The words burned into my brain. "Did *Mary* commit the murders?" I was thunderstruck by the possibility.

"Mary was fearful — and rightly so — that Sir George might abandon her to the world at any moment. Over the months she was with him, she grew quite watchful. Some weeks ago, when Dorenia and Sir George left together, Mary snuck into Dorenia's quarters searching for money, or failing that, some hold she could have on her rival. And she succeeded — she found the book. She performed the Ritual of the Second Sight. And it worked."

"You are jesting," I insisted. "Such a thing is impossible."

"So I thought." Holmes fell silent again. Then he cleared his throat and continued. "Shortly after their arrival in Liverpool, Mary confronted Dorenia about her liaison with Sir George, whereupon the fiery Romani slapped her. At once, Dorenia's thoughts poured into Mary's mind like fish into a river. She immediately knew the plans of the Romani. She also knew of the many charges that had been brought against them.

"After performing the ritual several more times — the effects are cumulative — she informed Dorenia that she had known all along who she really was, and had proof. This proof had been entrusted to a secret ally, and would be revealed to the world unless Dorenia and Horváth did as she commanded — kill Sir George. She gave them leave to take all his money, save a few hundred pounds."

"But Dorenia must have read Mary's mind as well, and realized that Mary had performed the Ritual of the Second Sight," I put in. "And that Mary's claim of 'proof' was a bluff."

"Dorenia did suspect and attempted to probe Mary's mind. But once Mary had acquired the Sight, she read that to shield one's mind from the invasion of another, one had simply to keep on one's person an object belonging to the mind-reader. In this case, Mary tore a fragment of black lace from one of Dorenia's gowns and kept it tucked in her hair. Despite Dorenia's repeated attempts to find something, she never did — until the scuffle that we witnessed, when in the brawl, the lace came free. Then Mary Holder's thoughts became as Dorenia's own." His tone altered. "And they were of such a depraved nature, Watson, that Dorenia fainted." He looked as if he might faint himself.

"Good heavens." I stared at Holmes. "Surely you do not believe this story."

"I *didn't*," he said pointedly. "Until with Dorenia's help, I performed the ritual upon myself." He swallowed hard and gave his head a small shake. "And now, upon touching Mary Holder, I know that Dorenia is right." He drew breath as if to steady himself, trembling like a locomotive engine in need of a release of steam. "Watson, Mary Holder is a creature of unimaginable evil. I do not think she is even human. She is capable of acts you cannot even imagine. And what is worse is that she is totally unaware of her own true nature. She believes herself to have been nothing but a desperate victim, driven to blackmail and murder to escape a terrible fate. We have allowed other women to leave brutal men, even if they murdered the blackguard in cold blood. "

He locked gazes with me, as if to make absolutely certain that he was making himself understood. "But this is nothing like that. *She* is nothing like that. The potential is there. Lurking. If unleashed, the damage she could do... the brutality and destruction... "

"Holmes, have you lost your wits? Of course, she is human. She has an uncle, and a cousin—"

"They are neither one like her," Holmes said. "I tested each of them. She alone is a... *monster*."

He looked somewhere beyond me, gazing into a terrible future. He said again, "She doesn't know. And she doesn't know that *I* know." He produced one of the pieces of gray muslin that had been torn from Mary's dress during the fray. "By possessing this, I was able to shield my thoughts from her."

"Did she kill the two men?" I asked, and Holmes shook his head.

"Oh." He uttered a little tone of surprise. "I thought it was obvious. The blood on the floor tells the entire tale. They murdered each other. Horváth shot first, and Sir George retaliated before he succumbed. Thus, neither of the women is technically guilty of a capital crime."

"I see." I was not relieved in the slightest. "And did Dorenia advise us what to do next?"

"She did, though she was most highly distressed to learn that the moment she had been taken into custody, I burned the infernal book. But before I did, I gleaned that the advice given by Dorenia regarding what we must do coincided with that in its pages."

"And that is what, Holmes? What did it say?"

— ‹›› —

And so, we are here at 221B once more. I have asked myself a hundred times if there could have been another way.

Could we have rehabilitated the malevolence that resided in place of a human soul? A wickedness that was about to explode upon the world and wreak havoc? Could Dorenia not consult with her clansmen to find a way to destroy the thing that dwelled inside Mary Holder, or perhaps lead it to redemption?

Of course, Holmes had asked these questions as well, and found the best answer that he could. He, not I, had been the one to stare into the mind of Mary Holder.

It was done with a fall down the stairs. The look on her face — first fear, and then such rage — I felt burned by that look. And her face — it changed—

Thank God Alexander Holder had already expired. Poor Arthur is left to grieve two deaths. And we, to keep forever this dreadful secret. This story, of course, will never see the light of day. Now that it is finished, it will join the ashes of that unholy book in our grate.

Holmes is playing the violin. Such a melancholic rhapsody, a counterpoint to the endless rain. He has told me that the effects of the Ritual of Second Sight have already faded — one recitation of the words is but an introduction into the world of its influence. Would that the knowledge of what we have done fade as well.

But it will not.

It will not.

Which of us did the deed? Pushed her to her death? That I shall not say.

And though I will burn these pages, I shall never again be at peace.

—— « O » ——

Nancy Holder

Nancy Holder is the New York Times bestselling author of over 80 novels and 200 short stories and essays. She has received 5 Bram Stoker awards for her supernatural fiction as well as a Scribe award for a novel based on the TV show, *Saving Grace*. She is known for her contributions to the world of Buffy the Vampire Slayer, including the new *Buffy Encyclopedia*, written with Lisa A. Clancy. An avid Sherlockian, she has written stories and comic books featuring The Master. She is currently working on the next issue of *Mary Shelley Presents*, her comic book series for Kymera Press.

The Lizard Lady of Pemberton Grange

Mark Morris

"You will have observed the headline on page four of this morning's paper, I take it, Watson?" said my friend, Mr. Sherlock Holmes, bursting into the room.

I raised my eyebrows. It had been unusual of late to see Holmes dressed and ready for the outside world at so early an hour. Unlike myself, his general habit had been to maintain an air of dishevelment in dressing gown and carpet slippers at least until after breakfast — and oft-times until later in the day if he had nothing of note to occupy his ceaselessly questing mind.

"And a good morning to you too, Holmes," I murmured, but my reproving tone was lost on him.

"Well?" he demanded. "Have you or have you not?"

His stance put me in mind of a grayhound quivering with anticipation in the traps.

Sighing, I said, "I daresay I have," but I opened the paper and scanned the requisite page anew.

Knowing my friend as I do, my eye alighted instantly upon the headline to which he had doubtlessly referred. GRUESOME MURDER AT PEMBERTON GRANGE it ran, beneath which several paragraphs provided particulars of the appalling events in question.

I shook my head. "A heinous business."

"Heinous and grotesque," said he, but there was a spark of excitement about him, a quivering of the nostrils and a flashing of the eyes, which I recognized only too well.

"Am I to understand that we are to investigate this matter?"

He responded to my inquiry with a brief bark of laughter.

"I would congratulate you on your deductive powers, Watson, were the answer not so apparent." He extended his right arm towards me, twitching the first and second fingers of his hand to draw my attention to a telegram, which was pinched between them.

I read the proffered missive silently, all except the name at the bottom, which I spoke aloud. "Miss Lily Parrish."

"The murdered woman's personal maid," said Holmes. "She'll be with us directly. Call for Mrs. Hudson, Watson. I daresay Miss Parrish will be in need of a cup of strong tea when she arrives."

—- «» —-

Indeed, she was, although her nerves were such that the cup rattled in its saucer as she held it. Her sharp features, which would have been pleasing had there been a rose in her cheeks, were pale as curd, though the flesh around her eyes was red and raw from tears and sleeplessness. It was an early spring day, and exceedingly mild, the pavements and the row of buildings opposite our own in Baker Street made cheerful by sunlight. Miss Parrish, however, was dressed as if for winter, in a long overcoat, and she shivered as if a chill had taken residence in her bones. I gave up my chair beside the fire so she may sit in it, and watched her with all the anxiety of a boy hoping to coax an injured sparrow back to health. Holmes, for his part, regarded her as a cat might, his eyes unblinking.

After she had taken several sips of tea, he said without inflection, "It is a bad business that brings you here."

She glanced at him, and her head trembled in a series of rapid nods, causing several strands of chestnut-colored hair to fall loose from beneath the rim of her bonnet.

"It is, Mr. Holmes! Oh, it's a terrible state of affairs!"

"We have read the report in the paper," I said gently, "but the details are scant. If it is not too distressing, perhaps you could add to them?"

"It is distressing, sir," said she, "but I shall tell you all I can."

Holmes lit a pipe and leaned against the cluttered mantelpiece, watching her shrewdly, as she recounted her version of events.

"Two mornings ago, I knocked on my lady's door at seven o'clock as I always do. There are occasions when she answers my knock immediately, bidding me enter, and occasions when she sleeps on, whereupon I wait until a count of five, and then enter her bedchamber silently and draw open her curtains.

"On this particular morning — Tuesday it was — she failed to respond to my knock, and so, after counting to five, I turned the handle and pushed the door open."

She paused here, and raised a gloved hand to her mouth. Holmes waited patiently, drawing on his pipe, his eyes never leaving her face. "What I saw, standing on the threshold of that room, I shall never forget. Oh, it was a dreadful sight! It spoke of savagery and degradation beyond measure. My first impression was of a shimmering mass of green upon the pale floor. My lady liked to wear green — indeed, she barely wore any other color — and my instant thought was that she had discarded her gown upon the carpet, which struck me as strange.

"Then, as if a veil had been removed from my eyes, I saw the rest of it. The blood… it was everywhere. On the carpet, of course, but also on the bed, which had not been slept in, and on the walls, and on the furniture.

"And at that moment too I saw… I saw what had been done to my lady. To her and… and to Toby."

"Lady Pemberton's dog," murmured Holmes.

His words were couched as a statement rather than a question, but Miss Parrish nodded.

"What manner of dog was it?" Holmes asked. "The newspaper declined to say."

"Toby was a pug, Mr. Holmes. Oh, he was such a sweet little thing. He and my lady were devoted to one another. I believe she loved that little dog more than anything in the world."

"More even than her own husband?" Holmes asked slyly.

Now a flush of red *did* suffuse Miss Parrish's pale cheeks, but it was accompanied by a look of distress that caused me to bestow a frown of disapproval upon my friend.

Holmes, who it must be said is generally kind and sensitive in his dealings with those innocents ensnared in ghastly events, waved a hand, as if to dispel a troublesome fly.

"Forgive me, Miss Parrish. My question was an impertinent one. Pray continue with your narrative."

The young lady pursed her lips and clenched her hands together, as if gathering in her strength. "My lady and Toby were lying side by side, my lady's hand resting upon the dog's body, as though to protect it from further harm. But the harm had already been done... and no worse harm is it possible to imagine. The fact is... their heads had been cut off, Mr. Holmes — my lady's and her sweet dog's. Cut off and... and taken."

"Taken?" I repeated.

She glanced in my direction. "They were not present at the scene, Dr. Watson, and have not been recovered since. The police believe that whoever violated my lady and her pet took their heads with him."

There was a moment of silence in the room. I felt a pulse beating like a small drum inside my head. I had seen terrible injuries upon the battlefield, had witnessed suffering and death and degradation in many forms during my years as Holmes' friend and companion, and yet the words from that young woman's lips, and the image they conjured, struck a chord of horror in me that I had rarely, if ever, experienced.

"Appalling," I muttered. "Quite appalling. Why would someone do such a thing?"

"The heads were taken as macabre trophies, perhaps?" Holmes' voice was steady, and he directed his next question to Miss Parrish. "Were these singular injuries the sole marks of violence upon the bodies?"

"No. The police examiner concluded that it was a knife to the heart, in each case, that constituted the killing blow."

"Indeed," said Holmes, and steepled his fingers beneath his chin, his face thoughtful.

After a moment he asked, "Where was Lord Pemberton when this was taking place?"

"He was in his own room further down the corridor. My lord and lady have separate bedchambers."

"And he heard nothing?"

"He says not, Mr. Holmes."

"What of the rest of the staff?" I asked her. "How many are you?"

"We are eleven in all, sir. But our lodgings are in the west wing of the house. Even the most terrible ruckus would fail to reach our ears from my lord and lady's bedchambers."

"If Lord Pemberton truly heard nothing, then it is likely Lady Pemberton knew her killer."

"How so?" I asked.

"Think on it, Watson. The sudden appearance of a stranger would have caused a commotion. Lady Pemberton, if threatened, would have raised her voice. At the very least her dog would have barked."

"Perhaps both were asleep when the intruder struck."

"It's possible, but you recall that Lady Pemberton was fully dressed, and her bed had not been slept in."

"My lady was not given to dozing, Mr. Holmes," said Miss Parrish. "Although her sleep patterns were irregular, she never slept but in her own bed."

"And what of Lord Pemberton? Is he a light or a heavy sleeper?"

"I have no knowledge of my lord's nocturnal habits, sir," she replied, a little taken aback.

"Of course, you have not. Forgive me." Holmes smiled at her, and then asked, "Why are you here, Miss Parrish?"

She looked taken aback a second time — as, this time, so did I. "To seek your help, Mr. Holmes."

"You are dissatisfied with the police investigation?"

"Why… no. On the contrary, the police have been the very model of efficiency and decorum."

"So, what then, has driven you to seek additional aid?"

She looked momentarily uncomfortable, and then she said, "You will think me foolish."

"What I think would often astound you," Holmes replied.

Miss Parrish's cheeks flushed red again, and she hesitated momentarily. Then she said, "My lady has come to me, Mr. Holmes. Since her death, I mean. I believe... I believe her appearance to be an appeal of sorts. I believe she is imploring me to do all I can to find her killer."

"And so, you came to seek the help of the greatest detective in England?" said Holmes, with neither modesty nor irony.

"Just so."

"Ha!" he exclaimed, and tapped his pipe against the side of the fireplace.

"Hold a moment," I said, but before I could elaborate Holmes interrupted me.

"Although you have my friend Dr. Watson's utmost sympathy for the distressing circumstances in which you find yourself, Miss Parrish, you have nevertheless caused offence to his ordered and rational mind."

I admit I spluttered a little. "Not 'offence' as such, Holmes."

He smiled impishly. "You nevertheless balk at mention of spirits, do you not?"

"As do you," I retorted. "What was it you said during that business of the Sussex vampire? The world is big enough for us, and no ghosts need apply?"

My friend may have had a propensity towards arrogance, but he took delight from the rare occasions when I managed to outmaneuver him in a game of wits. Chuckling he said, "You have me there, Watson."

Miss Parrish looked at us unhappily. "So, you do not believe me? Well, it was only to be expected."

Holmes raised a finger. "It's true that Dr. Watson and I entertain no truck with the spirits of the dead, but that does not mean that we disbelieve *you*, Miss Parrish. On the contrary, I am intrigued by your claim, and more than eager to hear the details."

"As am I," I said.

Thus reassured, Miss Parrish commenced with her tale.

"It happened last night, sirs," she said. "Unsettled by two days of disruption and upset caused by my lady's death, I slept fitfully, my dreams filled with terrible images that caused me to wake several times in shock and fear. When this had occurred for the third or fourth time I decided to abandon sleep altogether, and lit a candle to dispel the darkness that seemed to be pressing in on me from all sides. With nothing better to do, I wandered to the window and looked out. The moon was full, though partially obscured by clouds. My room looks out over the croquet field on the west side of the house, beyond which, some several hundred yards distant, a stand of trees marks the edge of the woodland, which forms a natural boundary of the grounds at that side of the house. It is a restful view, Mr. Holmes, and one which has afforded me great comfort on many occasions. Although it was dark, I suppose I was hoping to glean a similar measure of comfort in this instance. It was a perfectly still night, which was why my attention was instantly drawn to movement among the trees. There was the figure of a woman standing there. From her upright stance and the way she held her hands in front of her, I gained the immediate and strong impression that it was my lady — so strong an impression, in fact, that I gave a gasp of shock and stepped back."

"You talk of the lady's hands, but did you not see her face?" I asked.

Miss Parrish turned her eyes, lambent in the firelight, upon me. "She had no face, Dr. Watson. There was nothing above the collar of her gown but the blackness of the trees."

—— «» ——

The following day Holmes and I took an early train to Somerset, where our first port of call, after disembarking at the station and arranging for our luggage to be forwarded to the inn in which we were staying, was the neat cottage occupied by Inspector Moorcock and his charming wife, Harriet.

The Inspector was a tall, stout, florid-faced man, clean-shaven, with short, dark hair graying at the temples. He greeted us warmly, and although he did not say it, I gained the idea that the Pemberton Grange murder case was the greatest and most troublesome of what had, up until now, been a fairly sedate career, and that he fervently welcomed Holmes' involvement in it.

"I know of you by reputation, of course, Mr. Holmes," said he, once we were settled in his homely parlor, "but I little thought I would ever have the honor of meeting you in person, never mind inviting you to sit beside my fire and sample a slice of my wife's excellent cherry cake."

"The delight is all mine, I assure you," replied Holmes, nibbling at the huge slice of cake that had been handed to him.

"I understand you have spoken to Miss Lily Parrish, Lady Pemberton's personal maid?"

"Indeed," said I. "It was she who implored us to attend."

"Although I believe my curiosity may sooner or later have lured me here regardless," Holmes admitted.

"It *is* a curious business, sure enough," remarked the Inspector. "For one thing, there appears to be no motive for the crime."

"There is always a motive, if one searches long enough," said Holmes.

"Oh, I daresay, though for now it remains obscured. The house was not burgled, nor did Lady Pemberton appear to have any enemies — or not murderous ones, at any rate."

"An interesting qualification," mused Holmes. "Do I gather that her Ladyship was not a popular figure hereabouts?"

The Inspector hesitated. "Loath though I am to speak ill of the dead, it would be relaying nothing but the truth to say that she was not well-liked. That is not to say she was particularly *disliked*, Mr. Holmes. She was not cruel to those she employed; nor did she ill-use those around her. But she was... austere. Yes, that about sums her up. She was an austere woman."

"Folk round here called her the Lizard Lady."

These words came from the doorway, and were spoken by the Inspector's plump and jolly wife, who had entered the room with a fresh pot of tea.

Holmes raised his eyebrows. "Indeed?"

"Yes, sir. It was partly on account of the fact that she never wore any other color but green, and partly it was due to her manner. She was a cold-blooded creature, sir. Never once did I see her smile. And she had a way about her, a slow, watchful, calculating way, that sent a shiver through your bones if ever you felt her gaze upon you."

"Quite the Medusa," Holmes murmured.

"I'm sure you're right, sir," said Mrs. Moorcock, and then she noticed the frown of disapproval her husband was directing towards her, and put down the teapot with a clatter.

"But pardon me for interrupting you gentlemen," said she pointedly. "I'll not disturb you again."

As she bustled out, Holmes called after her, "Thank you, Mrs. Moorcock. And my compliments on a most delicious cake."

Her response was a girlish giggle, which caused Holmes' lips to twitch in what might have been a smile. Then he turned back to the Inspector and was all business again.

"What of Lord Pemberton's relations with his wife? Was their union a happy one?"

The Inspector pursed his lips. "I do not believe it was *un*happy, Mr. Holmes. If I may speak frankly, my impression of Lord Pemberton is that he is a weak and somewhat ineffectual man, and that he was beholden to the iron will of his wife — not least because it was she who held the purse strings in their relationship. It is said that without the family wealth that she brought to the marriage, Pemberton Grange would have been sold off long ago."

"Might Lord Pemberton have been driven to extreme measures by her bullying ways?" I asked. "Is it possible that he committed this terrible deed in a fit of passion?"

Again the Inspector looked doubtful. "It's *possible*, but I'm inclined to think not, Dr. Watson. Having spoken to him, I am of the impression that he is devastated by what has occurred."

"Besides, the crime is not a passionate one," murmured Holmes. "To dispatch both victims and mutilate them in such a manner suggests a cold and calculating mind."

"Not to mention, a depraved one," I added.

— «◊» —

After taking leave of the Inspector, our next destination was the scene of the crime. Pemberton Grange was set in several hundred acres of undulating parkland, upon which herds of deer grazed beneath the shade of huge, gnarled branches, which reached like enveloping arms from the vast, twisted trunks of ancient oaks. The grounds were fringed on every side by dark clumps of woodland, which concealed the impressive Georgian edifice at its center from prying eyes.

Beneath a changeable spring sky, which now threatened rain, the house looked gray and forbidding. Holmes pointed out the east wing, where the crime had taken place, and the west wing, where the servants were housed. He noted that they were indeed far enough apart, from one another, for those ensconced in one wing to be completely unaware of any commotion that might be occurring in the other.

Holmes and I, who had sent word of our arrival on ahead via the Inspector, were shown into a large, book-lined study with French windows all along the outside wall, through which grayish daylight streamed. The dark furnishings of the room seemed to retain shadows to such an extent that the only note of cheer was a crackling fire set within a fireplace of white marble, whose side columns were carved into the shapes of lions' heads, their fanged mouths open in silent roars.

We waited patiently — and in Holmes' case motionlessly, his eyes narrowed almost to slits, as if his mind was occupied with some inner narrative — for several minutes, until the door opened and a portly, red-faced, scowling figure entered the room. He was somewhat squat, and he wore a brown tweed suit, and my immediate impression was that he was not a fully-grown adult, but a belligerent youth of some seventeen or eighteen years.

It was only when he moved towards us, stepping into the insipid light that streamed through the French windows, that I saw the pouches of flesh beneath his bloodshot eyes and the marks of stress and worry lining his sagging jowls, and thus revised my initial estimation. This was not a slovenly youth, but a man of forty or more years, who carried his natural boyish plumpness with a careworn weariness that may or may not have been due to recent events.

"Dr. Watson, Mr. Holmes," the newcomer said, offering each of us a damp and fleshy handshake. "I received word from Inspector Moorcock that you were on your way and wished to see me. I am Lord Pemberton."

"Please forgive us for intruding upon your grief," I said, "and thank you for agreeing to speak to us."

"How could I not? If you can find the fiend who killed my wife, I will be forever in your debt."

Holmes inclined his head. "We shall do our utmost, Lord Pemberton. And now let us forego further pleasantries and cut to the chase. If the recollection is not too painful, will you recount to us the events, as you perceived them, prior to the discovery of your wife's body on Tuesday morning?"

Lord Pemberton spread his chubby hands. "There is little to tell, I'm afraid. When I bid my wife goodnight at around eleven o'clock, all was well. I went to my bed, read for perhaps half an hour, and then extinguished my light and went to sleep. I was aware of nothing more until I was awoken by Miss Parrish's screams the following morning."

"What time was this?" Holmes asked.

"I confess my primary concern was to seek out the cause of Miss Parrish's distress rather than to consult my pocket watch, but I know my wife liked to be awakened at seven a.m., and so I assume it was around then."

"And you heard nothing at all in the intervening hours?" I asked.

"If I had I would have informed you of the fact."

There was a snappish quality to Lord Pemberton's responses, which was perhaps understandable in the circumstances, but it caused my hackles to rise all the same. "And you don't find it unusual that you slept through such a violent incident taking place mere yards from your own bedchamber?"

"I am a very heavy sleeper."

"Tell me, Lord Pemberton, do you take medication as an aid to sleep?" asked Holmes.

The portly man hesitated. "I do not, sir."

"You sound unsure."

Lord Pemberton puffed out his chest defiantly. "Like many gentlemen, I take a drink in the evening. I find a brandy or two puts me out very nicely."

"And how many brandies did you imbibe on the night of your wife's murder?"

Lord Pemberton scowled. "What do you imply, sir?"

"I imply nothing. I am merely attempting to ascertain the facts."

For a moment Lord Pemberton resembled the belligerent youth I had originally taken him for, and then he said, "I believe I may have had three glasses on the night in question, but certainly no more."

"Just enough to aid a solid night's sleep," said Holmes with a smile.

"Precisely."

"All well and good." Holmes spoke lightly, as if that cleared up the matter. "Now we come to a more crucial question: did anything out of the ordinary occur in the days or weeks leading up to your wife's death? Did she receive any unusual visitors to the house? Any letters or telegrams or messages, which distressed or concerned her in any way?"

Slowly Lord Pemberton shook his head. "Not to my knowledge, Mr. Holmes."

"Has there perhaps been any trouble in the local vicinity in recent weeks?"

His Lordship was silent for a moment, and then he said, "I did hear tell of strangers in the area, stealing horses and the like. Vagabonds passing through. Gypsies most likely."

"Ah!" said Holmes. "When was this?"

"A week ago, perhaps."

"And how did you come by this information?"

Lord Pemberton waved his hand in a dismissive fashion. "I don't recall. It was a mere rumor. I had forgotten it until now."

"No matter," said Holmes airily. "The likelihood is that it has no bearing on this case. And now, sir, if you have no objection, I think Dr. Watson and I will take a stroll around your beautiful estate."

Lord Pemberton frowned, wiping a trickle of perspiration from his flushed face with his fingers. "Of course, I have no objection, but may I ask to what purpose?"

Holmes beamed at him. "Perhaps none. But, in my experience, time spent getting the lie of the land is hardly ever wasted."

—— «» ——

"What did you make of our host, Watson?" Holmes asked, striding purposefully across the neatly cut lawn towards the thick woodland that bordered the west side of Pemberton Grange.

"It is perhaps uncharitable of me to say so, Holmes, but I didn't like him. I found him a cantankerous fellow."

"Nervous also," Holmes remarked.

I glanced at him. "Do you think he has something to hide?"

"Oh, I'm sure of it — although as to precisely what, I'm less certain."

"Surely," I said, "there is only one thing that he can be hiding? He must be responsible for the murder of his wife, and the killing of her dog, be it directly or indirectly."

"Ordinarily I would agree with you, Watson, but it is the matter of the heads that rankles me. Even if we assume that Pemberton cut them off in order to bamboozle the police into believing that a maniac was responsible for the killings, it still strikes me as far too ostentatious a gesture on his part, not to say a time-consuming and bothersome business to become involved in. Granted, Pemberton has a motive — his wife was, by all accounts, a cold and controlling woman, and he had much to gain, both in material wealth and in terms of his peace of mind, from her death — but I simply can't see it. A frenzied attack with a sharp implement would have been a far simpler way of going about things, and would have drawn less attention to his crime. Additional to which, why would he not go the whole hog and combine murder with burglary to further deflect suspicion from himself? If Pemberton did commit this crime, he would have had to remove the heads from the house, presumably in some sort of receptacle. Would it not, therefore, have been the work of moments to add some of his wife's jewelry to his grisly burden? Ah, here we are!"

Holmes had led the way across a patch of lawn shaved almost to its stubble, which was inset with croquet hoops, and now stood within the first row of trees at its far edge. Turning to face the west wing of the house, he peered up at its myriad rows of dark windows.

"Which of those do you suppose Miss Parrish looked out from last night, Watson?"

I followed his gaze. "I'm sure I have no idea."

"Well, it's of no matter. Any would suffice." Holmes had brought his cane with him today, which he used to prod and poke at the undergrowth around him. "A more important consideration is where our apparition was standing when it was spotted by Miss Parrish. Look about you, Watson. See what you can find."

It did not take Holmes long to discover what he was searching for. "Look here!" said he triumphantly, pointing with his cane at a small hole and a pile of disturbed earth between the roots of a sprawling oak tree. "Something has been buried and hastily removed. Now, what do you suppose it was?"

I squatted down to peer into the hole. "It was not the missing parts of our victims at any rate," I said. "The cavity is both too narrow and too shallow. Whatever was buried here was not much larger than…" I looked up, searching for inspiration, and my eye fell upon the close-cropped croquet lawn. "…than a croquet ball," I concluded.

Holmes said nothing, but I recognized the intensely concentrated expression on his face all too well, and knew that great mind of his was turning over and sifting through the disparate facts we had thus far uncovered.

Straightening up with a groan — I was no longer as young or as fit as I had once been — I said, "What now, Holmes?"

My friend emerged from his reverie, his eyes flashing in my direction. "Now," he said, "we shall repair to our inn and sustain ourselves with a good dinner and a bottle of serviceable claret. And then we shall wrap up warm, and under cover of darkness we shall return here unannounced and maintain a vigil, in the hope that our reclusive phantom may yet again appear."

— «» —

There was little to report of our activities that night, save that they were uneventful. After an excellent dinner and a short rest at the country inn in which we were staying, we returned to Pemberton Grange at around eleven p.m. and scaled the outer wall — Holmes more nimbly than I — with the aid of an accommodating oak tree. Making our way around to the spot we had discovered earlier, and concealing ourselves amidst the thick foliage nearby, we settled down to wait out the nocturnal hours.

Pemberton Grange was a solid block of black against the softer, velvet darkness of the sky, although for the first hour of our long vigil it was studded with small, glowing squares of yellow light, which gave a suggestion of warmth and cheer. Then, one by one, the yellow squares were extinguished, and soon enough the only illumination was the cold glow of the half-moon, which flickered like a candle in a breezy nook, as clouds scurried across its face.

Holmes and I spoke little during the hours that followed, though he did touch my arm briefly when the black shape of a stag moved silently across the croquet lawn before disappearing into the darkness of the trees to our right. At around three in the morning there was a rustle of undergrowth close by, but the instant I raised my head, the fox — for that is what it was — got wind of my presence and darted away, affording me no more than a glimpse of its sleek body and bushy tail.

At some time between five and six I must have dozed off, because when Holmes shook my shoulder to rouse me, I opened my eyes and was surprised to see pale pink streaks lightening the dawn sky.

"Our phantom was in no mood for haunting last night it seems, Watson," said he, looking as fresh and alert as he had at the outset of our fruitless escapade. "Ah, well, it is not to be helped. Let us move on from here before we take root."

Remaining out of sight within the cover of the trees, we began to make our way back round the side of the house towards the main gate. My bones were aching with cold and inactivity, and my mind was still a little befuddled with sleep. My mouth was watering at the prospect of a hot breakfast back at the inn when Holmes froze and put his arm up across my chest, barring my progress.

"Hold, Watson," he hissed.

Evidently his ears were keener than my own, for it was a second or two more before I heard the sound that had put him on the alert. It was the distant clatter and rattle of a carriage coming from the direction of the house.

"Come, Watson," Holmes said urgently, and together we moved quickly through the trees until we had reached the gates, which were standing open. We slipped out on to the country road beyond, and then, with Holmes leading the way, crossed the road, pushed through a stand of bushes and clambered over a stone wall into a ploughed field. There we crouched down, peering over the wall at the open gates, the tops of our heads visible only to one who might feel compelled to scrutinize the tangle of bushes that all but concealed us from view. Holmes seemed perfectly content among the muddy furrows, but in my fatigued and bedraggled state I found the experience unpleasant and humiliating. Not since my long-ago days of boyhood games had I secreted myself in such a manner.

"What are we doing, Holmes?" I hissed irritably. "I accept that we would have had a pretty time of it, explaining our presence here at so early an hour, but to hide like this-"

"Pish," said Holmes with a dismissive waft of his hand. "It is not personal embarrassment that concerns me, Watson."

"What then?"

"You recall the stag?"

I frowned, my mind too tired for his games. "I do. But I don't see-"

"Lord Pemberton is *our* stag. And I have no desire to put him on his guard by alerting him to our presence. Now! No more talking. Here comes the carriage."

We fell silent as the clatter of the approaching carriage rose in volume. Seconds later the vehicle itself emerged from the open gates and turned to the left. As it passed us I spied Lord Pemberton seated within, his face grim.

Holmes consulted his pocket watch and rose to his feet. "Excellent. Come, Watson. We have not a moment to lose."

Instead of clambering back over the wall on to the road, he turned and began to stride across the farmer's field, his pace brisk.

Bewildered, I hurried to catch up to him. "What are you doing, Holmes?"

He did not pause, but maintained his swift pace, leaving me with no option but to do the same if I wished to hear his reply.

"How long is the carriage journey from the railway station to the Grange, would you say, Watson?"

"I don't know," I panted. "About half an hour."

Again he glanced at his pocket watch. "A little less. Our journey from Inspector Moorcock's cottage yesterday took precisely twenty-four minutes."

"Well, what of it?"

"There is a train to London in thirty-six minutes. It is reasonable to assume, wouldn't you say, that Lord Pemberton intends to be on it?"

If I had the energy, I might have shaken my head in exasperation. "Perhaps. But I fail to see the relevance-" And then all at once I *did* see it, and it dismayed me to do so.

"From your silence, I gather it has come to you," said Holmes almost gleefully, and pointed with a long finger straight ahead of him. "The carriage journey along the roads is circuitous, but this is the most direct route to the railway station."

"How far is it?" I asked with a sinking heart. Holmes' response was brisk and immediate.

"Two and three-eighths of a mile. With the wind at our backs we should just make it. Now, Watson — best foot forward!"

— «» —

I am pleased to say not only that we reached the railway station with less than two minutes to spare, but also that once we were seated on the train we were able to partake of a most excellent breakfast of scrambled eggs, bacon, grilled kidneys and hot coffee. In order that our quarry not become aware of our presence on board, Holmes even used his influence to arrange that our meal be served in our carriage instead of in the breakfast buffet car.

"For what reason did you suspect that Lord Pemberton would come to London today?" I asked Holmes, once our bellies were full.

Holmes puffed contemplatively on his pipe, the smoke wreathing about his head.

"I did not suspect it, Watson. While you were slumbering last night, I remained alert by memorizing the local railway timetable, having procured a copy on our journey here. It is always useful, in cases such as this, to familiarize oneself with the limited travel options available to one's potential quarry. It is clear to us both, is it not, that Lord Pemberton has something to hide? Did he kill his wife and her little dog, or arrange to have them killed, or do his secrets lie elsewhere? Only time will tell. But one thing is indisputable: he is a nervous man, and nervous men are rarely able to sit still. I felt certain he would make a move sooner rather than later, and when he did I was determined you and I would be at his heels. Just as much is achieved through dogged persistence as by the powers of observation. You know this, Watson."

"I do, Holmes."

"That is why we are such an excellent team, my dear fellow!" he said, beaming. "You have an abundance of the one quality, and I of the other!"

Upon arriving in London, our main concern was to ensure that our quarry remained unaware that we were following him. However, Lord Pemberton appeared so preoccupied with his own concerns that did not prove to be a problem. He looked neither left nor right, nor over his shoulder, as he departed from the station, but simply moved straight ahead, intent on whatever errand had brought him to the capital.

After watching him climb into a cab, we boarded one ourselves. Although the London streets were clamorous with life, it was not difficult to keep him in sight; indeed, the bustle of vehicles and people worked greatly to our advantage, as it meant that we did not stand out. We pursued our quarry for several miles, until eventually his cab came to a halt outside one of the many public houses that occupy Upper Street in Islington. Holmes motioned to our driver and he too pulled into the side of the road, some twenty or thirty feet away.

From our vantage point we watched Lord Pemberton's portly, red-faced figure emerge from his vehicle, speak briefly to the driver, and then scurry in through the door of the public house. I looked to Holmes for guidance, but he remained seated and silent, his eyes fixed unblinkingly ahead. The public house was named The Dancing Bear and seemed an unremarkable place, entirely in keeping with an area which was considered neither eminently desirable nor particularly low. Indeed, perhaps the only remarkable thing about the establishment was that Lord Pemberton should visit it at all.

After ten minutes, he emerged and clambered back into his cab, whereupon Holmes suddenly came to life. I expected him to inform our driver to continue his pursuit, but instead he opened the door of the cab.

"Continue to follow our quarry, Watson," said he. "Do not lose him. I'll see you back at the inn in Somerset."

So saying, he stepped nimbly down onto the pavement and closed the door behind him.

"Dash it all, Holmes," I called after him. "Where are you going?"

"I would have thought that was obvious. While you see where he's going, I shall investigate where he's been."

He raised his hand in a gesture of farewell, and before I could comment further he was gone.

—— ⟨⟩ ——

Although my room at the Crown and Mitre was most agreeable, by midnight that night I had come to loathe its four walls. Since our hasty parting some twelve hours previously, Holmes had neither reappeared at the inn nor sent notice of his whereabouts.

The rest of my own day after Holmes' defection had proved eminently unremarkable. I had followed Pemberton's cab, as instructed, but it had simply returned him to the station, from where he had caught the next available train back to Somerset. I had boarded the same train, but upon arrival at our destination had been unable to continue the pursuit of our quarry, for the simple reason that to have done so along the country lanes that lay between the railway station and the Grange would undoubtedly have attracted Pemberton's attention. After observing him clambering into the self-same carriage that had conveyed him to the station that morning, therefore, I arranged for a carriage to transport me to the Crown and Mitre, in the hope that Holmes would presently appear. However, some eight or nine hours later I was still kicking my heels, by which time the inactivity had driven me almost to distraction.

After a late supper, I considered retiring, but knew that, exhausted though I was, I would only spend the long hours of the night tossing and turning in my bed. Instead, therefore, I stoked up the fire, lay a blanket across my knees, and attempted to lose myself in a book.

My next memory is of being shaken vigorously awake. I opened my eyes to see Holmes glaring down at me.

"Make haste, Watson!" he cried. "We have an appointment to keep!"

"An appointment?" I murmured, my head a muddle. "Where?"

"There is no time to explain now! We must go!"

Within minutes I was in a carriage, with Holmes sitting beside me, early morning sunlight flickering through the trees and falling across my face.

"What is this, Holmes?" I asked him. "Where are we going? And more to the point, where have you been?"

"I shall explain when we reach our destination, Watson," was all he would say.

After perhaps half an hour of negotiating a variety of twisting country roads, we pulled into the courtyard of a charming roadside inn called The White Bull. Holmes consulted his pocket watch and gave a satisfied cry.

"We have time for breakfast before our appointment! Excellent!"

Holmes was in the type of mood I recognized only too well from previous adventures. His exuberance was due, no doubt, to his having achieved a satisfactory conclusion to his investigations in London yesterday. However, I knew that his sense of the dramatic would prevent him from revealing what he had discovered until what he considered the apposite time, and that questioning him on the subject would prove a pointless exercise.

The interior of The White Bull was just as charming as its exterior, and the breakfast a sumptuous delight. We had barely finished our last mouthful when there came the sound of a carriage drawing to a halt outside.

"Aha!" cried Holmes. "Here is the third member of our party! And perfectly on time!"

We waited, I with barely concealed impatience and Holmes with an indulgent smile, as the newcomer disembarked from the carriage and entered the inn. Hurried and heavy footsteps were heard in the entrance porch, and then the door to the room in which we were seated burst open — and there stood Lord Pemberton on the threshold!

His eyes widened in shock when he spied Holmes and me at our table.

"Good morning, Lord Pemberton," said Holmes pleasantly.

Pemberton's piggy eyes swept across the room, as though he expected another to be present, before alighting again upon Holmes. Struggling to compose himself, he said, "Mr. Holmes, Dr. Watson. This is a surprise."

"I expect so," Holmes replied.

"I did not realize you were staying here."

"Nor are we." Holmes smiled. "We are here to meet you."

A range of further emotions swept across Pemberton's face — at first confusion, then realization, and then an expression of wariness combined with fear.

"I don't understand," said he.

Holmes feigned puzzlement. "Oh? Are you not here in response to my message?"

Now Pemberton's mouth dropped open. "*Your* message? I thought..."

Suddenly all of Holmes' friendliness was gone, and his face became cold. "Sit down, Lord Pemberton."

For an instant, Pemberton looked as if he would obey without question, but then his red, perspiring face twisted into a sneer. "I shall not," he said. "Who are *you* to give *me* orders? I have wasted enough of my time on this fool's errand. Good day, gentlemen."

He turned towards the door, only to find Inspector Moorcock, with a broad-chested Sergeant in his wake.

"I would do as Mr. Holmes advised, if I were you, your Lordship," said the Inspector mildly.

Pemberton's face turned a shade redder, and he looked for a moment as if he might protest, but then, without another word, he staggered over to the nearest chair and dropped into it.

"You took the train to London yesterday morning, did you not, Lord Pemberton?" Holmes said.

Pemberton glared at him, but said nothing.

"It is of no matter whether you admit it or deny it. Watson and I were on the same train, so we know it to be true. Upon our arrival in London we then followed your cab. Is that not so, Watson?"

"It is," I confirmed.

"After a short journey, you halted outside a public house, The Dancing Bear, on Upper Street in Islington, whereupon you disembarked and entered the establishment. After approximately ten minutes you emerged from The Dancing Bear, re-entered your cab and returned to the station, where you caught the train home."

Pemberton looked around, his sweating face defiant. "Well, what of it? A man can find refreshment where he pleases, can he not? It's a free country."

Holmes' only response was a brief nod. Then he continued.

"As you entered The Dancing Bear, I observed that your left hand was pressed to a slight bulge in your jacket, over your ribs, as if you were concerned about, or perhaps protective toward, an item in your inside pocket. Perhaps you noticed this too, Watson?"

"I did not," I admitted.

"No matter. During the period in which you were inside, I counted a total of fourteen men, some in groups of two or three, emerge from the building and walk away in various directions. The last of these men had a bulge in his jacket pocket, which caused me to wonder briefly whether he had forcibly relieved you of your burden. Less than a minute later, however, you yourself emerged from the building, none the worse for wear, and climbed back into your cab. It was here where Watson and I parted company — Watson in order to follow you back to the station, and me to discover what manner of business you could possibly have in such an establishment.

"From my observations, I concluded that you had passed a package to this other man. The landlord of The Dancing Bear not only confirmed this, but informed me that upon entering the premises you had asked him to recommend a trustworthy man who would be prepared to run an errand for a small fee. The landlord recommended William Dwight, a local furniture-maker and an upright citizen, albeit one a little too fond of his drink. The landlord assured me that Mr. Dwight would be back presently, to spend his unexpected windfall, and so I settled down to await his return.

"Sure enough, Mr. Dwight returned to The Dancing Bear within half an hour. I found him an amiable companion, and more than willing to talk for the price of a glass of ale. Mr. Dwight informed me that you had instructed him to deliver a package to a nearby address in Bewdley Street. When he asked why you did not deliver the package yourself, you had told him you did not wish to be seen."

Pemberton continued to glower at Holmes, his chubby hands squeezing the edge of the table before him, as if he wished it were Holmes' throat and not insensible wood beneath his fingers. Unperturbed, Holmes carried on.

"I discovered the address in Bewdley Street to be occupied by a Mrs. Martha Bullimore, a lady of around sixty years of age, and two young children, who it transpired were the offspring of her daughter, Hetty Meadows, who had been absent from the family home for several days. When I inquired as to the contents of the package delivered by Mr. Dwight, Mrs. Bullimore informed me that it had contained two hundred pounds and a letter from Hetty, which she duly presented to me. In the letter, Hetty said that due to circumstances beyond her control she had had to go away, but was sending money for the care of her children. Mrs. Bullimore further informed me that Hetty had been employed as a waitress at a somewhat exclusive gambling club in the West End — a club frequented by rich young gentleman, and of which I subsequently discovered that you, Lord Pemberton, were a member."

Pemberton was trembling now, but he remained defiant. "So?" he snarled.

"After some investigation, I managed to locate and speak to another of the club's employees, a rather charming young woman by the name of Florence Bishop. According to Miss Bishop, you had struck up a friendship with Miss Meadows, which in subsequent months had developed into a deeper relationship. Indeed, Miss Meadows confided to Miss Bishop that you had made her certain promises — namely, that you had assured her you would find a way to unburden yourself from your wife, in order that you and Miss Meadows could be permanently together."

Enraged, Lord Pemberton leaped up from the table, the movement so sudden that the chair upon which he was sitting flew backwards and toppled over. "It's not true!" he cried. "The girl's a damnable liar! I refuse to listen to any more of this nonsense!"

At a nod from Inspector Moorcock, the broad-chested Sergeant stepped forward and placed a hand upon Pemberton's shoulder.

"Please sit down, your Lordship," he said politely.

Pemberton huffed and growled, but it was clear he would be no match for the Sergeant should it come to a physical struggle. He therefore sighed and nodded, whereupon the Sergeant righted his chair and Pemberton slumped back down in to it.

Holmes, meanwhile, rose from his own seat. "Excuse me, gentlemen," he said. "I must speak briefly to the landlord. I will be back in a moment."

He exited the room, nodding to Inspector Moorcock as he passed by, who nodded back at him, as if the two were colluding over some previous arrangement. He was gone for no more than a minute, during which not a word was uttered by anyone. Then he was back, rubbing his hands. He crossed the room and seated himself once more beside me.

"What was all that about, Holmes?" I asked, a little put out that he had apparently chosen to confide in the Inspector and not in me.

If Holmes detected an acidic quality in my tone he did not show it. "We are to be joined by one other." He pointed at the ceiling. "Hark!"

From above us came the creak of footsteps, which moved across to our left and then descended what I could only assume to be a flight of stairs. As the footsteps reached ground level and approached the room in which we were gathered, Inspector Moorcock turned and pulled the door open.

"Please enter, madam," he said.

The woman in widow's weeds on the other side of the door, who was now revealed to us, froze in apparent surprise. It was not possible to interpret her expression, for her face was concealed beneath a thick black veil. I wondered briefly for whom she was mourning, and then it struck me — she was not in truth a widow at all. Her somber attire was merely a disguise to avoid detection!

I gripped Holmes' arm and hissed, "Hetty Meadows, is it not? So, she and Lord Pemberton committed the crime together."

Raising his voice, Holmes ordered, "Remove your veil, madam."

The woman's veil rustled as the face beneath it turned towards Pemberton, but he offered his lover no solace. Instead he was now slumped forward across the table before him, as though resigned to his fate.

Slowly the woman raised her hands and peeled back her veil. The face beneath was older and more severe than I had imagined. Inspector Moorcock gave a gasp.

"Lady Pemberton!" he exclaimed.

The woman in question ignored him, but instead fixed her husband with a withering look. "So, our deception has failed. I should have known better than to place my fate in your fumbling hands."

"The fault was not mine," Pemberton protested in a wheedling voice.

"No? Whose was it then?"

"If you had not allowed yourself to be seen by that dratted maid of yours, she would never have involved Mr. Holmes."

"Do not blame Miss Parrish," Holmes murmured. "It was a singularly intriguing case. I may have become involved regardless of her intervention. You returned under cover of night to procure some item left for you by your husband, I presume, Lady Pemberton? A package of money, perhaps?"

"Money, yes," said she bitterly. "I was forced to leave the house hastily, and had little at my immediate disposal. It was unfortunate that Lily happened to peer from her window at just the wrong moment. I pulled my veil over my face in the hope that she would not recognize me."

"She did not recognize your face, but she knew your stance well enough," Holmes said. "The fact that you wore a veil only consolidated what she thought was her last memory of you; that of a corpse missing its head."

"I assume the real victim of this crime was Hetty Meadows?" said I.

"Yes," replied Holmes, "clad in one of Lady Pemberton's dresses and with her head removed to lead police to the obvious conclusion. The fact that Miss Meadows worked her final shift at the gambling club on the night of her death, but then did not return home afterwards, leads me to conclude that, no doubt on a wild impulse, she caught the last train from London. She arrived at Pemberton Grange, perhaps having walked all the way from the station, only after its staff had retired to bed in the west wing of the house. This would ensure her presence here was unknown to all but her murderers. Indeed, if it hadn't been for Lord Pemberton's journey to London yesterday — an admittedly philanthropic undertaking, albeit driven by the guilt of having deprived two children of their mother and a family of their sole breadwinner — there would never have been reason for Hetty Meadows to have been connected to this case at all, and subsequently the identity of the victim may never have fallen into question. It was a stroke of calculated genius on your part, Lady Pemberton, to allow your pet dog, on which you doted, to be killed and mutilated in a similar manner to the murdered woman, thus further deflecting any possibility of suspicion from yourself."

"It was a difficult decision to make — and now it seems," she replied, casting a bitter look in her husband's direction, "an unnecessary one."

"I suppose Lord Pemberton identified the corpse as his own wife," said I, "thus further consolidating the fact?"

Holmes nodded.

Inspector Moorcock looked with distaste from Lady Pemberton, standing imperiously in the middle of the room in her widow's weeds, to her husband, a broken, sniveling, red-faced man lying sprawled across the table.

"So, which of you is it who murdered the poor girl?" he growled. "Which of you struck the killing blow?"

Pemberton raised his head and pointed a trembling finger at his wife. "It was her! She did it! Poor Hetty turned up to have it out with me — she claimed I'd been leading her on, but that was never my intention, sirs, I assure you — and *she* stabbed her through the heart with a letter opener in a fit of rage and jealousy. Then she made me... she made me..."

At this, Pemberton was overcome and collapsed into a fit of sobbing.

Lady Pemberton looked down on her husband with cold disdain, before turning her dispassionate gaze upon Holmes. "My husband is a mountebank and a philanderer, Mr. Holmes. I am the injured party in this instance. From the outset, he regarded our union as nothing more than a way of averting his own financial ruin, and has treated me with contempt throughout our marriage. Yet, despite this, I have not only turned a blind eye to his dalliances, but have continued to support him financially and to maintain a façade of decency and solidarity. But when that *woman* came to *our* house... well, it all suddenly became too much. And so, I struck out. I did not mean to do it. For a moment, I... I lost myself."

"And yet you recovered your composure admirably quickly," Holmes remarked. "It required a cool head to do what had to be done afterwards."

Her gaze never wavered. "That is true, Mr. Holmes. My father was a hunter of big game in Africa, and like him I have a practical mind and a strong survival instinct. My only mistake in life is that I made a bad marriage."

— «» —

There is little else to add to my account of the Lizard Lady of Pemberton Grange. It is ironic in a way that the undoing of the Pembertons hinged on a moment of passion in a largely passionless life for Lady Pemberton, and a rare pang of conscience in a mostly selfish life for her wayward husband.

Lady Pemberton's ultimate plan, before it was undone by Lord Pemberton's inability to bide his time and maintain his discretion, was to live modestly in London, in rented accommodation and under an assumed name, until the furor of the investigation had died down and interest in the gruesome case had waned in the public imagination, and then for Lord Pemberton — still ostensibly the grieving widower — to sell Pemberton Grange, and for the two of them to begin a new life, either together or apart, somewhere in Europe.

As for the grisly question of the missing heads, Lord Pemberton admitted that they were to be found, together with a bundle of bloodstained clothing belonging both to Hetty Meadows and to himself, at the bottom of a disused, overgrown and boarded-up well in the woods to the east of the house. This, indeed, turned out to be the case — which left only one aspect of the mystery still unresolved.

"How did you know Lady Pemberton was residing in The White Bull, Holmes?" I asked of my friend one night in Baker Street, with spring rain lashing against the windows and a glass of fine port at my elbow.

Holmes, sitting in the armchair across from me, looked up from the lepidopterology journal he had been studying.

"It was a simple matter of deduction, Watson. Her departure on the night of the murder was hasty and unplanned. It was too late to catch a train, and any attempt on her part to have done so, disguised or not, in the days immediately following her apparent death may have aroused comment or suspicion. Better then to take a room at an inn and to remain there unobserved for a while. But which inn?

It could not be one too close to the Grange, for she was well known in the local vicinity, and may have been recognized by her bearing or her voice. On the other hand, she needed to remain close enough to the house to easily pick up provisions and messages from her husband. This narrowed the options down to four choices, and when I discovered that a heavily veiled widow had taken a room at The White Bull, at a very late hour, on the night of the murder, I knew that we had our woman."

I nodded somberly. "It is a sad case in many respects — a triangle of love, in which there are only losers."

"Love is a destructive force, Watson," Holmes remarked. "It muddles the thinking, and often makes fools of those who become tangled in its threads. That is why I have never had any truck with it."

And so saying he returned to his moths, and I to my glass of port and my contemplation of the flames.

———— « O » ————

Mark Morris

Mark Morris has written over twenty-five novels, among which are *Toady*, *Stitch*, *The Immaculate*, *The Secret of Anatomy*, *Fiddleback*, *The Deluge* and four books in the popular *Doctor Who* range. He is the author of three short story collections and several novellas. His short fiction, articles and reviews have appeared in a wide variety of anthologies and magazines, and he is editor of *Cinema Macabre*, for which he won the 2007 British Fantasy Award, its follow-up *Cinema Futura*, two volumes of *The Spectral Book of Horror Stories* and the upcoming *New Fears* (Titan Books). His script work includes audio dramas for Big Finish Productions' *Doctor Who* and *Jago & Litefoot* ranges, and also for Bafflegab's *Hammer Chillers* series. His recently published work includes the official movie tie-in novelizations of *Noah* and *The Great Wall*, the novellas *It Sustains* (Earthling Publications) and *Albion Fay* (Snowbooks), and his *Obsidian Heart* trilogy (Titan Books).

The Magic of Africa

Kevin P. Thornton

If you are reading this, I am dead and so is my good friend Sherlock Holmes.

I pray that I do not sound too dramatic. As both the literal and literary sounding board of the great detective, I am often placed in the situation of having to decide which of his adventures will be forwarded to the publisher for the public's edification and which will not. I have, I hope, been a scrupulous chronicler and if there are tales held back from the readers' eye it is, on the whole, due to various reasons of discretion. Some investigations are protected by the Official Secrets Act of 1889, some others at the request of the party or parties involved. There are a few that Sherlock Holmes has asked me to keep '*in pectore*' as the Papists might say, close to the heart. I have done so to honor his wishes and to protect his descendants.

And then there is this case. Unless science has changed dramatically, I feel confident that both of us are long gone. I base this deduction on the hope that my family, executors and publisher have all followed my wishes as to when this story will see the light of day. Its embargo is lengthy, and some might even say capricious.

When I sat down to write the complete version of this tale from my notes some fortnight after the event, I chanced to look at the cricket in the newspaper. The touring South African Cricket team were playing Hampshire. The score at the end of the first innings had the home team leading by a score of 111 to the visitors 82. It was the Hampshire score that caught my eye. The 111 looked like the unlucky sight of a batsman's wicket sans bails, signaling he was out. They also reminded me of the claw marks found at the home of the adventurer and hunter, Arthur Neumann, whose death was surely Sherlock Holmes' strangest case. I have kept this one close to my own heart out of honor and friendship. I do not wish to tear down, even slightly, what I have spent so many years helping to build up in the eyes of the world, but I feel that eventually the truth must be told.

— «» —

The morning of the 29th of May 1907 was quiet, reflected in the paucity of news in the paper. Most of the back page was occupied with the Touring South African Cricket team and their match against the M.C.C. The visitors were using four leg spinners to great effect, an unusual tactic when pace bowling was all the rage.

The front page was taken up by idle speculation about a string of burglaries which had baffled Scotland Yard. The police, from the Commissioner on down, all seemed to be flummoxed as to the means and manner in which they had been propagated, and the editor had even suggested that they might wish to bring one Mister S. Holmes back from retirement.

As if the thought gave fulfilment to the wish, a telegram dropped through the mail slot. My wife gave it to me with a humored, yet quizzical, look. Gone were the days that a missive from Holmes would have me speeding away into the night and gone too were the days when I received such messages with any frequency. Since his retirement to the Sussex Downs, all he ever sent was the occasional letter discussing his research into the recuperative and revivifying powers of the product from his beehives. These I kept next to my bedside to cure my insomnia. This, however, was the first request from him in some time, and my anticipation must have been obvious to my wife, who sent the maid to hail a cab immediately.

The telegram was typical of Holmes; brusque, and to those who didn't know him, impertinent even. 'Watson, meet me at the Officers' Club on Haymarket, I have need of your medical eye. Holmes'.

I was dressed, out the door and into the waiting cab before my tea had cooled. I rarely traveled much farther than the corner of the street anymore, so the bustle of the city, with all the new construction and the concomitant loss of open land, was eye opening and even disconcerting. As we drew near our destination, a circus that had been using one of the few free spaces as yet unbuilt on was tearing down its tent and moving on. The posters remained up, advertising, inter alia: The Amazing Treblini Trapeze Act, Udo the Lion Tamer and the acrobatic Runty and the Small Frys. I was wondering idly whether Mrs. Watson might enjoy a visit to the show when I was interrupted by our arrival.

The uniformed policeman standing in place of the doorman was the only indication of anything untoward. Upon mention of my name he opened the door and pointed to the stairs. "Top floor, sir," he said cheerily, pointing at four flights, and I silently cursed my advancing years.

The room at the top differed in architecture from the rest of the building. It was a corner-piece tower and it looked as if it had been built as an afterthought, an added edifice that had no architectural merit. There were two windows looking out from the small landing, made smaller by a short, rotund man in ill-fitting day wear, who looked to be about half my age and twice my weight.

"Doctor Watson, I presume? Delighted to be working with you. I am Detective Inspector Pound, of the Yard. Your esteemed colleague is inside already." He made as if to move out of the way, but the constraints of the walls prevented such a maneuver, so he opened the door, beckoned me forward, then stepped in behind me.

The accommodation itself was simple, some sixteen by sixteen feet. The walls seemed to indicate the former use of the room. They were of unfinished rough brick and the look was more of a storage space than a bedsit, yet the furniture gave lie to this. The surrounds were furnished, barely, with a cupboard and desk, an easy chair, and another table on which stood a washbasin and some male toiletry items. The center was occupied by a bed that dominated the room as it was raised some two feet by building blocks. Holmes was by its side, closely examining the floor, and I was so delighted to see him that I nearly missed the reason for his presence. Behind the bed lay the body.

Holmes stood up and turned. "Ah, Watson, good of you to come. What do you make of this?" He moved behind the bed and I followed.

"Permit me to introduce the late Arthur Henry Neumann," said a voice behind me. It was Inspector Pound. Holmes frowned, and I discerned that his opinion of the police force, never very high to begin with, was unlikely to be improved by this latest manifestation.

I looked at the body on the floor. "The famous hunter?" I asked. Holmes nodded.

I bent to look closer. He had died a terrible death, as if his throat had been ripped by some machete or clawed device. His head was half severed from his torso, and I could see the beginnings of three sharp cuts on his skin before they bit deeper in, creating a commingled gash. There was a large pool of blood from this horrendous mutilation all over the floor next to where he lay.

"He died quickly," I said. "Whatever was used to do this likely killed him almost before he hit the floor, and it was done here. His throat was torn open and he fell, the blood pooling next to him."

"Well spotted, Watson," said Holmes. "Inspector, please reiterate your meagre notes for the sake of my friend."

If Pound was insulted, he didn't show it. "One of the club servants delivered his breakfast at precisely 6:15 this morning. He knocked, and on hearing no answer, left the tray outside, a common enough occurrence. Thirty minutes later, when he came back to remove the plates, he found them still untouched outside the door. He knocked and there was no reply. He called the senior servant, and after several attempts to arouse Major Neumann they realized the key was still on the inside of the door in the keyhole. They placed a sheet of newspaper under the door at the bottom, jiggled the key with a stiff wire so it fell onto the paper, pulled it out and opened up. They found Neumann, as you see him now, and called us immediately."

There was no mention of how Holmes came to be involved. Before I could ask, the most singular part of the case occurred to me. I looked around again. Unlike the landing outside, there were no windows in the room and when I looked up, the strangeness of Neumann's final home continued to perplex. The walls were some twenty feet high, culminating in a solid roof with a solitary circular skylight, scarcely more than twelve inches across.

"So, if the door was locked from the inside," I said, "how did the murderer get away? There is surely no space for any man to get through that skylight. It is far too small. And even if it were possible to climb in and jump down that distance, landing on the bed, say, there is still no way out. Was there some trickery with the lock?"

Inspector Pound continued reading. "According to the staff, this room was originally a storeroom, and there was one key only. When Captain Neumann returned from Africa he specifically asked for this room, and double-checked there was only that one key."

Holmes watched me carefully as if waiting for me to catch up with him. I said, "Did he ever explain the blocks raising the bedstead to anyone?" Holmes smiled, and Inspector Pound looked sheepish.

"I, erm, assumed it was to get closer to the cool air from the skylight. It has been unseasonably warm." Holmes said nothing, so Pound continued. "There was also talk from the gentleman downstairs of a possible supernatural element involved, some form of African leprechaun. I was not able to ascertain too much from him. Perhaps you can help us there, Mr. Holmes? He is your friend, is he not?"

I waited for Holmes' retort. When it came, I was surprised by how mild it was. Age may have lent my friend some patience at last.

"Come, come, Inspector. Why would Neumann insist on this room with no adequate ventilation, then arrange for those forty-pound blocks to be carried up all those stairs to get closer to the fresh air? I admit the reason for the raised bed is not yet apparent, but there is definitely a reason why he was living in this strange room. I'll warrant if you put in your reports that it had to do with leprechauns from Africa, your next job will be working the streets down Whitechapel Road, strolling a uniform beat. Neumann wanted this room because it was a fortress, one that in the end did not defend him from whatever he feared. But this was no imp, no goblin, no fairy and certainly no leprechaun that killed him."

He turned to the door. As he did, something on the wall caught his eye. It was about eight feet off the ground. Holmes stood on a chair to see it. When he stepped down he said to me, "Watson, see what you make of this." I looked. There were three deep scratches, about two inches across. They were vertical, and at first looked like the number 111.

"Could the implement that made those scratches on the wall be similar to the one that gouged the body of Mister Neumann?" Holmes asked.

"By Jove, Holmes, I think it could." I measured the width, then clambered down and compared the measurements with Neumann's wound. "I can't be definite without proper examination, but it's likely. Does that mean the weapon was thrown across the room by the perpetrator?"

"To what end?" said Holmes. "There was no blood, so it did not occur after the murder, and why would the murderer do so before? Come, Watson, we are done here. Inspector, if I have any ideas as to how this event occurred, you will hear from me."

We went down the stairs to one of the club rooms. The man who was waiting turned to the door as we entered.

Holmes said, "Watson, may I introduce my old family friend, the Honorable John Guille Millais. Johnny, this is my dear friend and confidante, Dr. John Watson."

Even after so many years, I knew so little about Holmes and his family that my astonishment at such an introduction must have been obvious. More than that, Johnny Millais was a distinguished artist, and son of Sir John Everett Millais, the renowned landscape artist and Pre-Raphaelite. For Holmes to have considered them close and to never have mentioned them to me was typical of the man, and also hurtful. Millais must have seen what crossed my face. He walked towards me and said "We both know Holmes so well. Who should be hurt more? You, because he has said nothing to you of me? Or me who has had to listen too much to his thoughts on you and your close friendship? Let us both accept that Sherlock is difficult but captivating."

"Agreed," I said, liking the man instantly. "My wife and I went to your latest exhibition. Delightful, absolutely delightful."

"Oh come, Watson," said Holmes in his more familiar impatient manner. "I have told you my mother was a Vernet. Anyone can see that Johnny's father trained in the ways of Horace Vernet, my great Uncle, and could therefore deduce that the family friendship began back then."

"Of course," I said. "It is so obvious when you point it out in such a manner."

Millais smiled. "I see sarcasm is also your defense against the mind of Holmes. I have traveled that road myself."

"How did you come to be drawn into this?" I asked.

"I was listed as his next of kin," said Millais. "The Neumann and Millais families go back in time as well. He had been staying with my family in Horsham until this lodging was ready. He had been desperate to move as he said his presence endangered us. When he told me why, I didn't believe him. Anyway, I asked Holmes to join me because of what I know about Neumann's fears."

"Ah, yes," said Holmes, "the leprechauns from Zululand. What on earth made you think that telling Inspector Pound about these figments of the imagination would be helpful? Let us now hear what you have to tell us, and why you asked me to look into your friend Neumann's death. It is intriguing, no doubt. A locked room, a man confining himself to a defensible position, yet a hunter with no weapons in his room. How was he supposed to fight back?"

"You are right, Holmes," said Millais. "A hunter of Neumann's status should have had guns and other weapons to hand, and the Arthur Neumann I used to know would never have retreated into a storeroom, hiding from his fears. Yet when he came back from his last trip to Africa he was a changed man. The reason was not a leprechaun, but *Tokoloshe*."

Neither of us said anything. Millais continued. "I can see by your looks you have never heard of it. Until Arthur's recent return from Southern Africa, neither had I. This is what he told me. *Tokoloshe* are believed to be gnomes or imps that can be controlled, as a means of vengeance, by a tribal medicine man or witch doctor. They are supposed to be small, yet immensely powerful, dark of skin and nature, with a protruding horned spine, and are capable of great feats of athleticism and strength. They are the avenging angels of these witch doctors, and once they are set on a path they will not stop. Neumann told me that he had dealings with the local *Sangoma*, for that is what witch doctors are called in that part of Africa. The deal did not go well and both parties felt they had been robbed. Neumann decided to accept his losses, the *Sangoma* did not."

"He was attacked, was he not?" said Holmes.

"Yes," said Millais. "He would not give me any details, save to say that *Tokoloshe* is a musky and dusty smelling creature and after the first attempt on his life, which he barely survived, it was the smell of it that saved him subsequently. He was warned by the odor on two more occasions. After the third attack, he packed up and left, thinking London to be safer for him."

"And it wasn't," murmured Holmes. "*Quod erat demonstrandum*. Pray continue, please."

"Naturally," said Johnny, "there are superstitions that surround *Tokoloshe*. They can cause people to drop dead from fear alone. They can jump and climb great distances, yet perversely cannot seem to clamber onto a raised bed or sleeping hammock. When he stayed with us, he insisted on building up his bed from underneath, and I'll wager he did the same here." He saw me nod in acknowledgement. "And although they are tiny, they are human in likeness; except for their claws, which are razor sharp and three to each hand and foot."

I started, and Holmes smiled, shaking his head slightly as if he knew what I would say. My temper had risen a little, as it does when I am given evidence of secrets kept from me by one whose trust I felt I had earned many times over. I therefore jumped into the conversation, to a place where Holmes likely did not wish me to wander.

"Your friend was killed by something claw-like, and there was a similar mark on the wall. If such a monster were to exist, he certainly sounds small enough to climb through a skylight, exact the revenge he was asked to seek, and use the rough wall as a springboard to propel himself back to his means of egress."

Millais was silent for a moment. Holmes seemed to be struggling to control his comments. Eventually he spoke, but it was a calm and reasonable Holmes, not the impatient investigator I had first known all those years back.

"If *Tokoloshe* exists, and I do not believe it does, why did it create a locked room conundrum when it would have been far easier to leave through the door?"

It was Millais who answered. "I have been to Africa, Holmes. The thatched huts and rondavels *do not have* doors that lock. It may be that Tokoloshe *was not* familiar with locking mechanisms and unable to operate the key."

And thus returned the old Holmes. "Hah," he barked. It was a sound of derision I knew so well and judging by the look on Millais's face he too was familiar with it. "There is no *Tokoloshe*," said Holmes. "There is no magic save the superstition of people who cannot explain something that defeats their senses. Watson, do walk with me outside. I need to check one more item before I unmask the killer. Johnny, ask the bumbling Inspector if he will join us in Neumann's room in thirty minutes, when I will tell you how the murder happened."

"I wish you wouldn't do that," said Millais. "One last thing I remember about *Tokoloshe*. They often return to their last place of mischief, some say to gloat and some so they can find and kill family members as well, if the *Sangoma's* spell calls for such action. Would you rather not meet in the bar?"

But Sherlock Holmes had already left. The Honorable John Guille Millais and I shrugged our shoulders to each other and set about our tasks.

When I arrived downstairs, it was to catch a glimpse of Holmes leaving the porter's desk, having engaged the man to send some telegrams. I walked out the front door to see my friend already turning the corner.

Wherever Holmes was going, he was doing so at speed. I nearly had to run to catch up. "What the devil's the rush?" I shouted.

He paid me no mind, heading for the common with a rapidity that would do the youthful Holmes proud. He was easy enough to follow, his head above most others, so I gave up trying to catch him. He headed for the common, where the big top was nearly packed away, and I saw him speak to one of the peg boys for two or three minutes. Whatever he told Holmes was worth it as I saw a bank note exchange hands, much to the delight of the youngster.

"My apologies, Watson. I needed to talk to a member of the circus staff before they left and I was just in time. Now we have some minutes to spare. Come, old friend, let us stroll back. I can do nothing more now until my telegrams are answered."

For the next ten minutes, we walked along the edge of the common, exchanging pleasantries and comparing lives. Holmes seemed happy on the Downs. Already parts of his research into honey had restored some of his vitality and alleviated his arthritis, and he promised to send me some of his curative teas and rubs.

The conversation led me to ask him, "Holmes, why are you so sure there is no such thing as magic? Surely it is possible for fairies and guardian angels to exist, maybe even *Tokoloshe*? After all, the results from your studies into bees may be seen by some as magic."

Holmes took a moment to answer. "All my life I have trained my intellect to deal with evidence and logic. Even my studies in beekeeping have had, as a starting point, a theory based on the longevity and soothing properties of honey; all I did was discover more than anyone else has done heretofore. Yet you speak of other realms and creatures as if there is a logic to their possibility, and I refute it, Watson. I refute it! When we get back and the answers to my telegrams confirm my hypothesis, you will once again see that the elimination of all impossibilities will eventually lead us to the truth."

We crossed the road back to the Officers' Club. Holmes received the answers to his telegrams from the porter, smiled as he looked at me and said, "Come, my dear Watson, let us repair to poor Neumann's fortress above." He dashed off ahead, leaving me to catch him as and when my old bones would allow.

Word had spread through the corridors of Scotland Yard. Unlike the old days when the Inspectors had taken their time to come around to Holmes' way of doing things, distance had definitely lent enchantment to their view. The room, where the death had occurred, and landing were now teeming with policemen, all come to see the legendary detective at work. I counted at least four inspectors — with Pound trying unsuccessfully to land his spot near the center — as well as six other policemen, and Johnny Millais. I stood at the entrance to Neumann's strange room, watching my friend in his element. The air was stuffy, so I opened the landing window.

"No doubt," said Holmes, "Inspector Pound has regaled you with the fanciful tale of the mythic African creature, *Tokoloshe*, and how it has all the skills to have committed the crime. There is a motive, of course, the *Sangoma's* rage, and there is the belief that *Tokoloshe* have been employed in this way before… in fables. It had the means to do so as well, as by now you are all *Tokoloshe* experts, knowing all about this vile, villainous murderer, this ghostly goblin, that an hour ago you had likely never heard of. The only fact is that this creature is certainly the reason why Arthur Neumann holed himself up here. He came here because he believed in *Tokoloshe* and thought the creature powerful enough to harm him." Holmes paused and then looked wearily at each one of us.

"Arthur Neumann was the victim of a robbery gone wrong. That is all this is."

He had their attention now. "There have been a number of burglaries recently, places that have been broken into in ways no one can see. But I saw. Did anyone notice the circus posters today? All around the streets?" Some of the policemen nodded.

"One of the acts was an acrobatic troupe called Runty and the Small Frys. Now, what unique talents would be useful for a string of impossible burglaries? Millais? Anyone? Anyone?"

"The small frys," I said. "Runty. Acrobat midgets. Able to get in anywhere."

"And acrobatic enough to climb anything," said Holmes. "Well done, Watson. While we were downstairs I checked by telegram on the location of the previous burglaries. The traveling circus that just left the common here has been in the vicinity of all of them. Inspector Pound, your murderer will be among the number of that troupe."

"But why kill him, and how?" said Millais.

"Typically, burglars of this skill look their target over before they actually break in," said Holmes. "The details will be confirmed after a search of their caravans, but I suspect they were tempted to break into Neumann's fortress because it looked a challenge, and such a protected room must hold something of value. They were mistaken, just as they were wrong about the occupant. Far from being asleep, he was waiting to be attacked by a small, strong creature. In a panic, as Neumann defended himself, one of the burglars must have lashed out with the tool that they had fashioned to add purchase to their climbing, also the reason for the mark on the wall. Mountaineers fashion similar devices for the Alps, normally not to such devastating effect."

"So that's it?" said Millais. "Neumann let the heat of Africa fry his brain, so much so that he was scared of an attack by a mythical creature, and he was accidentally killed because, in protecting himself from this creature, he set himself up to be burgled by midget thieves who looked like *Tokoloshe* to him."

"I don't know that he was just protecting himself," said Holmes. "Neumann really believed in *Tokoloshe*, and he set himself up here because he believed staying with you may have endangered you and your family. He sat here, with a skylight only his perceived enemy could get through, unarmed. He didn't believe his weapons could defeat the magic, so he didn't bring them. However addled his mind, he died trying to do what was right for his friend."

It all seemed so logical the way Holmes described it. The acrobatic circus team with burglary as a second career, and their temptation to see what treasures Neumann had walled up in his eccentric suite, which in turn led to his accidental demise.

I leaned back from the stifling room to catch a breath of fresh air from the landing window. As I glanced across the parapet I saw, briefly, a small dark creature scampering across the roof. But for its protruding spine and black skin I would have thought it a large cat, even as I could hear the scratching of its claws as it ran. It traversed the roof at an astonishing speed. Rushing to the next building, it scrambled across with unbelievable dexterity, swung itself directly over the parapet, one clawed hand catching halfway up the wall and springing it over. Then it disappeared from sight.

I stood, dumbstruck, contemplating what I had seen. Who could I tell, what could I do? Had it come back to the scene of its crime to hunt again?

My heart rate slowed and my brain stopped throbbing. I was just about to dismiss my own witness to the existence of the murderous monster, when I caught the faintest of whiffs of sun dried dust and stale musk.

— «» —

If *Tokoloshe* stayed in England, I never saw anything that might have been attributed to it. This salves my conscience. But for Holmes to have been so wrong sits uncomfortably with me. I do not wish to publish his failures, but he would have insisted, for the sake of constancy and verity.

The timing, however is my own. As I said at the beginning, if you are reading this I am surely dead, because the embargo I placed on this story was the mark of the claw and the score that Hampshire made the day I wrote this down, 111 years. If my executors have not failed me, this tale is being read for the first time in 2018. What brave new worlds have you wrought?

— « O » —

Kevin P. Thornton

Kevin P. Thornton has lived or worked in Nairobi, Upper Hutt, Boksburg, Ladysmith, London, Dubai, Pretoria and other places he has chosen to forget. Now in Fort McMurray, he is currently a writer and poet, and formerly a soldier, military contractor and logistics specialist. He is a member of The Keys, the Writers Guild founded by G.K. Chesterton and Msgr. Ronald Knox, as well as the Crime Writers of Canada, the Arts Council of Wood Buffalo, the Fort McMurray Heritage Society, the Crime Writers Association, and the International Thriller Writers. He spends his life attending meetings.

A Matter of Light

Angela Slatter

"Mr. Holmes," drawled the butler with a haughty sniff, "is not best pleased."

Kit Caswell raised one fine eyebrow; she'd given her name so he could not have been ignorant of who she was. Besides, how many visitors might be expected this late at night in fashionable Piccadilly? And how many might have been received with this level of disdain? The written summons had come from John Watson, so technically it mattered not a jot what Mr. Holmes might or might not be displeased about, but she kept the thought to herself. For some reason servants seemed to like Holmes rather more than their betters did. She was unsure as to why, but thought perhaps it had something to do with the Great Detective's ability to make fools of said betters, all of which caused much amusement and satisfaction below stairs.

The good doctor's missive had been brief and finished with the admonition 'to dress like a lady'. Although the temptation to disobey had been strong Kit'd controlled herself. She wore a neat purple plaid stuff walking suit, a confection of a hat she couldn't really stand but upon which her housekeeper, Mrs. Kittredge, had insisted, a cloak against the chill evening air, and black kid gloves which she removed one carefully plucked finger at a time.

"Indeed?" she said and, leaning close enough to catch a whiff of a not-unpleasant odor, draped her cloak over the man's shoulder, enjoying his look of outrage. She slapped the slim gloves into the palm of the hand he raised in surprise; he had no choice but to grab at them, or let them drop and thereby failing in his professional duty. Her reticule — containing house keys, handkerchief, several sovereigns, and a set of brass knuckles — she retained. "Well, I have been summoned — I've not inflicted myself on this household uninvited — and thus I am arrived. Be so kind as to conduct me to Doctor Watson. We'd not want Mr. Holmes discontented any sooner than needs must."

There were a few tense seconds when she thought he might instead shove her out into the night for sheer spite, but apparently his training was too ingrained. He choked, "This way, Miss Caswell."

A slight, pretty maid wearing a very clean white apron over a black dress — whatever had happened in this grand house meant that neither maid nor butler had a chance to change into their nightclothes though it was past midnight — appeared from a darkened doorway. She gathered the garments from the butler's hands, barely glancing at Kit beyond a measured flicker, yet it was enough to convey her opinion of the late-night visitor. Clearly it matched that of the butler.

Inwardly, Kit sighed and wished she'd stayed at home reading the book on Eastern European folklore. The light of her notoriety hadn't dimmed in the three months since she had, in no particular order, run to ground Jack the Ripper, become the fosterling of Sir William Gull, and been discovered masquerading as a man in the service of London's Metropolitan Police Force, much to the consternation of her superiors. Everyone, from low born to high, seemed to think they had a God-given right to comment on her behavior, either by verbiage or action. Mrs. Kittredge had a saying about opinions being like fundamental orifices: everyone had one and they produced much the same substance.

Kit grinned as she followed the butler's astonishingly straight back along a corridor filled with closed doors. Behind one she could hear in passing the sounds of muttering and pacing; from behind another came sobbing. An elegant house, noted Kit, big enough to accommodate an impressive entry hall, at least two drawing rooms, a library, a study, a formal dining room, and other reception rooms besides on its ground floor. There'd be a kitchen and laundry below, and bedrooms above, with servants' quarters above that. Which made her wonder at the lack of other domestics — surely a legion would be required in a place like this? Shouldn't they be gathered in corners, whispering and milling?

When there was no further to go, the butler threw open the very last door with what might have been aplomb tinged with contempt: *There! I've done my duty but I take no pleasure in it!*

"Doctor Watson, Miss Caswell has arrived," he announced darkly.

Kit stepped past him into a dimly lit room lined with books and redolent of hair oil, pipe smoke and paper. John Watson, on the shortish side, in his late thirties, moustache and hair touched by dignified, though perhaps premature, gray snow, sat at a desk that, had it been a person, could only have been described as "disheveled". He looked up and smiled, hands filled with disparate folios and envelopes. She was fairly certain he'd not found what he was looking for, whatever that might have been. Parallel with the edge of the desk, a silk-lined box held a gleaming silver letter opener with a sharply honed edge, the placement of which suggested a missing twin, perhaps lost beneath the papers through which Watson was searching.

"Thank you, Peterson. That will be all. Oh, is Mr. Holmes still in the north parlor, and your mistress in the south?"

"Yes, sir. Shall I carry a message?"

Watson shook his head. "Thank you, no." He waited until Peterson had closed the door behind him and said in a low voice, "It's always best to know where he is before one discusses him."

Kit smiled. "Are you well, sir?"

"Well, enough. My apologies for this late hour, but there is a matter which I believe will only respond to your particular talents, Miss Caswell." He rose and came to offer his hand, which was square, his grip firm. His eyes brightened when he smiled.

"I'm happy to help you if I am able, Doctor Watson."

"Well, helping me involves helping Holmes…"

Kit pulled a face. The Great Detective had, like many others, made his opinion of her known, supplying quotes to any newsman who had asked. She was irresponsible, a girl playing at dress-ups, at best a hoyden, at worst some sort of jezebel or suffragette. Kit thinned her lips. She'd met Watson at a dinner party at Sir William's and found him kind and clever, surprisingly non-judgmental (some of her foster father's guests regarded her as a curiosity to be gazed upon much like Mr. Joseph Merrick or a bearded lady in a traveling show). The good doctor had made it clear he didn't share his friend's opinion, in this matter at least, and they'd gotten along famously. She relented and said, "Tell me what the problem is, Doctor, and I'll decide if I'm willing to assist." She grinned. "You mentioned my talents?"

"Let us call it your open-mindedness."

"What has happened?"

He led her to a burnished walnut sofa covered with blue and gold brocade in front of the hearth where a fire burned low. "Holmes has been … out of sorts of late. He does not do well when bored and you might recall my mention of his … tendencies." In a moment of confidence, he'd let slip the man's recreational habits, how they had almost destroyed him and how he, Watson, had been at pains to keep his friend distracted. Easily solved cases provided some relief, but only temporarily, like feeding an enormous hunger with tiny rare meals, or attempting to extinguish a raging fire with thimblefuls of water. Such small successes, such easy gains merely increased Holmes' thirst for challenge, made him more irritable and, Watson knew from old and painful experience, more susceptible to the siren song of his demons.

"And you believe this one to be one of those easily solvable, quickly digested puzzles that give him but brief satisfaction?" asked Kit.

"I fear now that it might be better if it had been." Watson shook his head. "I thought it might provide more fit meat for him to chew upon, but alas I fear it will only result in further frustration."

"The details, Doctor?"

"Of course. Just the details." He smiled. "We are in the home of a Mr. and Mrs. Harrington. Mr. Harrington is a shipping magnate of some note and considerable fortune. His wife is a society beauty, or rather was in her day," he said, gaze softening, displaying signs of diverting from topic. "Still, in a certain light—"

Kit tapped him on one wrist before he waxed lyrical about the lady's bygone loveliness. "It's always a matter of light, Doctor, in all aspects of life and perspective."

He raised a hand in surrender. "Of course, irrelevancies. Here is our problem: Ezekiel Harrington is dead."

"Thoroughly dead?"

"Very dead indeed, but rather improperly."

"Aha. So, you and Holmes were called in hope of discretion?"

Watson nodded. "I have known Ezekiel for some time — we shared a club — and his wife sent for me. I brought Holmes along in the hope of staving off yet another crisis in his confidence."

"And why have the police not yet been called in?"

"We have the weapon and the murderer, but— he will not confess." John Watson shook his head. "And Holmes cannot seem to divine the means to make him do so."

"Ah. And if Mr. Holmes cannot gain a confession, he cannot perform for the public and bask in their adoration."

"That is harsh, Miss Caswell."

"But true, dear man, do not deny it." Kit had on occasion wondered if half of Holmes' prey simply caved in and confessed, beaten down by the impression the Detective gave that he knew all one's sins as if they'd been written down in a book.

"Not untrue, no." He sighed. "Yet there is something else, Miss Caswell, something I cannot quite put my finger on. Something is just not right about the young man we have in custody."

"Apart from the fact you believe him to be a murderer?"

"Beyond that." He shook his head. "We could hand the lad over to the police and be done with it, but ..."

"Your intuition renders you uncomfortable." She smiled gently "What makes you think I might gain disclosure where Sherlock Holmes cannot?"

Watson paused, pursed his lips. "You've a gentle way with you, and besides, you've seen things that others have not. You are willing to accept something alternate — more things in Heaven and Earth and all that — where more rational minds will not consider any explanation that does not conform to particular parameters."

Kit sat back, away from the dying flames that were suddenly too intense. Pearls of sweat broke out down the line of her spine. No doubt her benefactor, Sir William, had let slip matters that Kit had entrusted to him in confidence. She asked calmly, "What makes you say that, Doctor? Who has spoken out of turn?"

Watson looked guilty, then revealed: "I have been for some years an acquaintance of Inspector Makepeace."

"Ah." Kit offered a silent apology to Sir William. Edwin Makepeace, her former superior at the Met, had taken her under his wing and acted as a mentor. Though he'd figured she was a girl well before the secret was out, he'd still listened to and acted upon her theories. And it was he who'd carried her, bruised and bloodied, from the London sewers after she'd helped destroy Jack the Ripper, burning him in a witch-fire kindled by his victims — unfortunately not before that notorious killer had stabbed her. "Talking out of school."

"Don't judge him too harshly, he was… perturbed by what he saw."

He should have experienced it, thought Kit, not entirely bitterly. Her shoulder where the knife had entered still ached. "So, you think my gentle touch and an open mind might hold the key to your mystery?"

"Perhaps." He shrugged. "Or perhaps you might simply lead Holmes in the right direction."

"I strongly doubt Mr. Holmes will listen to one such as I, Doctor, but I'll do my best for you." She smiled. "Kindly introduce me to the Widow Harrington."

— «» —

"I'm terribly sorry for your loss, Mrs. Harrington," said Kit, examining the woman who sat on a red velvet chaise longue —

or rather it seemed she'd draped herself on the furniture like a cat, conscious of how she appeared even at this late hour. Indeed, conscious and careful of how the illumination from the lamps fell upon her; Kit couldn't help but wonder how much time the mistress of the house had spent examining the way light and shadow mingled, and which position would show her fading charms to their best advantage. Unlike the servants, she'd obviously been to bed at some point, and wore an elaborate house coat in midnight blue over a white nightgown; embroidered slippers covered her tiny feet. Golden curls tumbled artlessly over one shoulder. It was interesting, though not surprising, that even under a weight of grief the woman had taken time to make herself look pretty. Augusta Harrington was not a unique creature; her looks were her currency, no matter how devalued.

"I don't understand why you're here, Miss Caswell. Why is she here, Doctor Watson?" Her voice was a fluttering thing, like a wounded butterfly. Large, limpid, green eyes blinked at Kit in confusion. The woman seemed barely awake, yet she must have been up for some time since news of her husband's demise had been brought to her.

"Miss Caswell is here to help, Mrs. Harrington. Please tell her your tale. Indulge us."

A snort came from the gloomy corner in which the Great Detective had sequestered himself. His leather wingback chair groaned each time he shifted with restless energy. His hawk-like nose and high forehead were silhouetted against the light of the window. *How long would he sulk?* Kit pondered, but didn't bother to cast a glance in his direction.

"Please tell me how you found your husband."

The woman gave a sob, then buried her face in a handkerchief. John Watson knelt beside her and grasped her free hand with chivalrous enthusiasm. Kit managed not to roll her eyes. The doctor's weakness for pretty faces — faded or not — was well-known, but his admiration brought a response, which Kit doubted her most patient questioning ever would.

"Emily woke me," she choked.

"The maid," explained Watson.

"Emily said Ezekiel had been murdered. That … the boy was responsible."

"And what did you do?"

"Went to his bedchamber and found him … found him …"

"The room is as we found it," said Watson. "I'll show you when you wish."

"Who is the boy?" asked Kit.

"Some wretch in whom Ezekiel had taken an interest," sobbed the woman. "How could he repay my dear husband so vilely?!"

"And what did you see?"

"My poor Ezekiel in bed, cold and dead."

"What's his name? The boy."

Mrs. Harrington appeared nonplussed at the change of direction. "Milo."

"Nothing else?"

"No. Not that I ever heard my husband say." She sniffled, appeared to wonder why she'd never asked for it herself.

"Had your husband's habits changed since the boy joined the household?"

"That boy was never part of this house. I would not allow it. He would… visit Ezekiel in the evenings." The woman's tone was sharp.

"I see. Had your husband adjusted how he conducted his daily life, Mrs. Harrington? Changes in appetite and action, in ways small or large?"

Mrs. Harrington paused, as if considering new aspects of her marital state that had not occurred to her, then said, "He slept in, went to the office much later. He was… short-tempered on occasion. His appetite has not been what it was for some weeks." She bit at her lips then opened her mouth as if the words caused her pain: "And he wanted no company but Milo's."

"And where was the boy in the bedroom? In relation to your husband's body?"

That question broke the woman and she began to sob. When the flood did not abate after several minutes, not even under John Watson's tender hushing and there-there'ing, Kit went to the door to call for one of the servants. She found the young maid already waiting anxiously, as if she'd been on the verge of charging to her mistress' rescue but had not quite yet found the courage.

"Emily," – Kit assumed it was she – "please see to Mrs. Harrington."

— «» —

The bedroom was large, decorated in dark masculine tones; part of its area was utilized as a sitting room furnished with two armchairs in front of the cold fireplace, a low table, a mahogany secretaire and a chocolate-colored recamier set between a pair of high arched windows with thick brocade curtains drawn. Also accommodated were a canopied bed, a chest of drawers and an armoire. A mirror sat above the hearth, all gilt and glamour. The marble-topped washstand seemed somewhat redundant when a door sat ajar showing where a closet had been converted to a small bathroom.

The air was thick and redolent with the iron odor of a red death. Yet from the doorway where Kit stood, she could see the lumpen shape of a body beneath the covers on the right-hand side – her left – of the bed, but no sign of a struggle.

"Where's the boy?" asked Kit.

"Locked in the coal cellar."

"Did he go quietly?"

"Very. He was somewhat stuporous."

Kit scanned the room. "And where are all the servants, Doctor?"

"Most have left to prepare the Harringtons' country house. The family were meant to go tomorrow morning." The clock on the mantle struck one, and Watson corrected himself: "*This* morning."

"When was Mr. Harrington found?"

"Mrs. Harrington was somewhat hazy on that, but the maid said about eleven-thirty."

"Why did she check on him then, the maid? Was she called for?"

"She said she noticed the light burning under the door rather later than was the master's wont."

"Aha." Kit stepped into the room and approached the bed.

Ezekiel Harrington had been a dignified looking man in his early fifties and remained rather handsome even with the spatters of dried blood on his face. His neck had been cut, left to right, with the silver knife remaining in the wound, its hilt resting on the red-stained pillow beneath the man's head. Kit's eyes followed the path of the arterial spray, on the wall and the bedclothes.

"He did not fight back."

"It would appear not," came Holmes' voice from the corridor.

"Where was the boy when you first saw this?" Kit frowned.

Watson cleared his throat. "Beside Ezekiel, on the bed, curled like a child against him."

Kit made her way around to the other side, leaned over the coverlet and noted how the mattress appeared to have barely borne the weight of another body. "But the boy was not *in* the bed, surely?"

"No," said Watson in surprise. "How can you tell?"

"Because there is a void on the linens where no blood has landed – presumably where another body lay – and then there is blood on the edge of the coverlet. Not to mention that the rug beneath my shoes feels rather wet and squishy." Kit straightened. "Surely you noticed that, Mr. Holmes?"

The silence from the hallway spoke volumes.

"So, you think to test me rather than to share what knowledge you have gleaned, sir?" She sighed. "Help me, Doctor, if you please; let us not derange the scene too much."

Carefully, she and Watson pulled back the covers, folding them at the foot of the bed.

Ezekiel Harrington lay in his nightshirt, which was rucked up around his thighs, one of which was flecked with pricks marks and blood.

"Good Lord," said Watson.

"You've not seen this, Mr. Holmes?"

His voice was closer when he said, "No."

Holmes had moved into the room and was bending over the dead man. He pointed at the patches of dried blood, then said with certainty, "False starts."

"This is a new habit?" asked Kit, and Holmes nodded, meeting her eye for the first time.

"Related to the young man?" ventured Watson.

"Let us ask him. Would you mind fetching the mysterious Milo, Doctor?"

"But of course."

"Take Peterson along, just in case."

"He's a slip of lad, barely half of my weight dripping wet."

"Nevertheless, humor me. Oh, and kindly send the maid Emily up first of all."

When the good doctor had departed, Kit and Holmes stared at each other for a few moments.

"A respectable man's reputation might survive a private drug habit," observed Kit. "But not being caught with either a dead girl or a live boy."

An unwilling snort of laughter came from the tall man's mouth.

"Where is his paraphernalia?" asked Holmes. "There should be a syringe and one vial, at least, for the morphine."

Kit restrained herself from saying *You would know* and instead said, "I wonder about this" — and pointed to the sprays of blood — "Correct me if I'm wrong, for your experience will be greater than mine, but does not this pattern appear... weaker than it might?"

"Opium and its derivatives will slow the heartbeat, the pulse, the strength at which blood is pumped out. I believe that's the effect we witness here."

"So. We must locate the paraphernalia to support our thesis."

"Yes."

"Was this murder the result of a drug-induced rampage, Mr. Holmes?"

"Not if we're dealing with morphine: it is not something to excite the system, Miss Caswell." He smiled ruefully. "But then, I suspect you already know that and are humoring me."

In his smile was a sweetness she'd not expected. Grudgingly, she decided the Great Detective couldn't be all bad if someone like John Watson gave his devotion to the man. Kit did not nod, but gave an answering grin. "The good doctor said Mr. Harrington was a shipping magnate?"

"Yes."

"Where do his ships sail?"

"All over, but with especial interests in the Baltic and the Balkans."

A timid knock on the door interrupted anything further he might have said.

"Come in," said Kit, noticing how the lanky man took up position by the curtained windows, finding refuge in shadow once more. Was that the truth of Sherlock Holmes? That he was only happy in the light when he was confident of his truth? Any uncertainty might risk the exposure of the ragged edges of him, the shattered nerves. No one but Watson was allowed that sort of intimacy, to view what Holmes obviously considered a weakness in himself.

The door opened to show the young maid, hovering on the threshold.

"Do come in, Emily, please," said Kit firmly.

"Yes, Miss." The barely-hidden contempt the girl had shown her in the entry hall had disappeared. Her eyes slid away from Kit's and went to the bed where Ezekiel Harrington lay. The girl's shoulders began to shake and tears welled. Kit put her arm around the maid and turned her away from the scene.

"I know it's very upsetting, Emily, but you must be brave. I'll not keep you long."

The maid nodded, pale blue eyes blinking, but Kit could tell she was fighting the urge to look over her shoulder at the body again. "Tell me what you found, when you came in here."

"The first time, I brought him his hot toddy about nine after he'd gone to his room, like I always do after Mr. Peterson prepares it. I knocked and entered and put it down on the table, then I left. Later on, about half-eleven, I was on my way to bed when I saw the light under the door burning late. I thought Mr. Harrington might need something else. I knocked, like I always do, and went in. I saw them on the bed — I hadn't realized *he* was here. Mr. Peterson must have let him in." Her lower lip trembled.

Kit asked, "And why did you approach the bed, rather than depart immediately?"

"I was going to leave, but I saw…" the girl frowned as if trying to remember precisely. "Neither of them was moving. Not one bit and it made me pause. Then I went over to the Master's side…" Her trembling increased.

"How long has Milo been in Mr. Harrington's… orbit?"

"A month, Miss," said the maid with a lick of vitriol. Kit wished she could bottle the timbre of the girl's words; the acid could be used to etch steel or glass.

So.

"And where was Milo? On the covers or beneath?"

"On them, Miss."

"Thank you, Emily, you may go."

The girl dropped a hasty curtsey, threw one last look at the recumbent figure, then made for the doorway, which was suddenly filled by the bulk of Watson, Peterson and a slender youth no taller than the maid. His hair was a wispy blond that hung to his shoulders; his face was as pretty as a girl's; his clothing appeared new, albeit crumpled, as if heedlessly slept in.

The little maid hissed "Murderer!" and Kit feared she might strike, but then the moment was gone, the girl out in the corridor, the boy in the room, and Watson closing the door in the butler's face as Kit said, "Thank you, Peterson."

The boy blinked and blinked, stared around him, his gaze attaching to the body on the bed and Kit saw a terrible sadness take up residence. The full lips trembled. Kit grabbed at the boy's sharp chin and stared into his eyes.

"His pupils are pinpricks. Did you notice, Doctor?"

Watson nodded. *This time*; before they'd been too busy looking at the blood spatter. Holmes, by the window, grunted.

"I don't use it," said the boy, tightly, his thick accent pointing to somewhere in Eastern Europe.

"Use *what*?"

The boy looked away. He wasn't really a boy, thought Kit, but a young man so fragile-looking that he seemed younger.

"You are showing signs of having used either opium or one of its by-products. You woke disoriented, did you not?"

The boy nodded slowly.

"Tell me what happened last evening," asked Kit quietly.

"Last evening... I arrived after nine-thirty. Ezekiel has given me a key to the back door. We have tried to be... discreet."

"Unsuccessfully," sniped Holmes.

Kit gave the shadowy shape a sharp glance and there was no further comment. She sighed, and looked at the mirror over the fireplace, taking in all the inhabitants of the room, and then drew the young man to sit on the recamier.

"Please continue, Milo."

"We spoke, then he fell asleep. And then I slept." The boy was lying, or mixing omissions with slivers of truth. His slender hands with their long fingers were clasped in his lap, tightly interlaced.

"You said you did not use opium. But Mr. Harrington did. We have surmised it was a very recent development." When the boy's mouth tightened, Kit hurried on, "Milo, please trust me that your friend's reputation will suffer no more than the three of us in this room will allow; we are each here to help in our own fashion."

Still the boy remained silent.

Kit tried a change of tack. "Had Mr. Harrington been ill lately?"

The bottom lip trembled, then Milo nodded.

"Ezekiel has been in such pain." He sighed. "I have urged him to seek the advice of his physician, but he has — had — proved obdurate."

Kit nodded. "I've known men who'd prefer a slow death to asking for aid and thinking themselves seen as weak. Did you buy the morphine for him?"

The boy shook his head but avoided her eye; another half-truth, half-lie. He had not made the purchase, but knew who had.

"And how did you come to suffer the effects of an opiate, Milo?"

"I did not—"

Kit held up a hand. "I do not doubt you did not take it by intent. Think on it."

He puzzled, pale brows meeting over dark eyes. "I drank only… the girl brings every night a hot toddy. Ezekiel had lost his taste for it with the illness, but I found I liked it. I drank that, as I have most nights here, and I slept." Again, Kit had the sense that he was picking through the truths he knew, careful to keep others back. Giving up only what he felt he could afford to part with.

"Where's the glass?"

"On the table." He pointed in full expectation of the object being where he'd left it, but it was not in evidence. Milo frowned, genuinely puzzled.

"Has Peterson been in here?" Kit asked.

"He said not," Holmes answered. "He's a stout fellow."

"Aren't you all? And never an evasion or an untruth for the sake of honor? A devoted butler who would not gaze upon his master's death, even if only to attempt his desperate saving? Doctor, would you mind acting as my Mercury once more? Ask our erstwhile butler if he happened to fib."

As Watson disappeared, Kit returned her attention to Milo. "No one but Ezekiel knew that you'd taken to drinking the hot toddy?" He shook his head. "Where did you meet Mr. Harrington?"

"On the docks." He cleared his throat as he realized how that sounded, then amended: "In his office. I had been a sailor, but wished for other work. I saw the sign for his office and sought him out. I can read and write, do figures, I thought perhaps to be on dry land for some while."

Kit laughed aloud. The boy was never a sailor; oh, he might have been on a ship but that didn't make him anything more than a desperate person seeking a way out of an unpleasant life. She took his hands in hers and examined them, turned them over to caress the smooth palms; no sign of calluses or blisters, no proof of old injury such as a mariner would have experienced more than once in a life at sea. Another lie, then. The boy was running from something in his past, but probably unconnected with Ezekiel Harrington. Harrington was a new phase, a new problem, a new loss.

The door opened to reveal Watson and a shame-faced butler.

"Peterson has something to tell you."

The butler addressed himself to Holmes. "I'm sorry, sir. I found Mr. Harrington. I found him and didn't want him being put down as no suicide, nor dying like some stupid woman."

"Miss Caswell asked you the question, Peterson. Do her the courtesy of answering."

The man blushed red as a beet, but turned his gaze to Kit; his expression said he wasn't sure if he should repeat what he'd just said, as if she'd not been in the room the entire time. Kit stared at him for a long moment, then said, "Suicide?"

"Yes, Miss. No way the Master would have taken such a cowardly way out."

"Peterson, *how* do you think Mr. Harrington died?"

"Laudanum, Miss. I came to check on him about eleven and found him too deep asleep to wake. It became clear that he'd taken to using laudanum like the Mistress, to help him sleep." The man looked at his shoes. "I could smell it in the dregs of the hot toddy, Miss. Must have added it after Emily brought it up."

"And where was Milo?"

"Asleep beside the Master." Peterson did not look at the boy; Kit had the feeling it was not the first time over the years that the servant had seen such company in this room. "To be honest, Miss, I thought he was dead too. I thought they'd both..."

No, thought Kit, something was missing. There was something else he was hiding.

"Did you take the syringe and vial, Mr. Peterson?"

Startled, he stared at Kit.

"He was still alive, your master, but you feared him soon to die. Not from the laudanum but its mixing with something else... something else you knew he had because you'd purchased it for him."

"How can you—?"

"You're a trusted employee and I imagine you've served many years with Mr. Harrington. You knew he'd become ill, that he suffered. Where Milo refused his request for the drug, as employed servant, you had no such choice." Kit took heart as he nodded, a sharp, shamed movement. "I smelled the sweetness of opium smoke on you when I arrived, yet you did not strike me as a user. Ergo you'd been in a den for another purpose: seeking out a stronger solution for a man too fearful to consult his physician." Kit clasped her hands in her lap. "Yet when you found him deep in its grip you feared less that he had overdosed than you would be found out as having provided him with the means to do so."

The man paled.

"Never fear, Peterson, he's no suicide. What did you do with the toddy glass?"

He blinked hard. "Smashed it, buried the pieces in the garden. I can show you where."

"Perhaps later. Thank you, Peterson." Kit smiled.

"Is that all, Miss?"

"For the moment. You were cowardly, Mr. Peterson, but I do not believe you a killer."

When the butler had shuffled from the room, Watson barely kept his oath inaudible.

"Well, Miss Caswell?" asked Holmes from the shadows.

"Peterson still thinks his master died of an overdose; he feared that would be the outcome and lo, he assumed that the cause of death was drugs. He does not know about the knife."

"How can that be?"

"There would be no reason for him to enter the room a second time. He believed his master to be on the way out. After Emily discovered Mr. Harrington dead, Peterson believed he knew the cause. The death was no surprise to him. Mrs. Harrington said Emily brought her news, accompanied her to this room; the lady of the house was not especially coherent, so I've no doubt she did not give any great detail. Peterson, you can see his shame. That would be enough to keep him away."

"Then we are no closer to a solution than before you arrived, Miss Caswell." Watson sighed.

Holmes corrected him, "On the contrary, we know considerably more, yet this wretch continues in his refusal to confess."

"And he is right to do so," said Kit.

— ‹› —

"Hello, Emily."

"What's he doing here?" Kit had knocked and opened the door to find the maid sitting on a narrow bed, an old petticoat spread across her lap, needle and thread in her hands. Behind Kit, Holmes and Watson crowded, Milo between them.

"We can't just leave him roaming about. Never fear, Milo will be dealt with justly soon enough." That seemed to soothe the girl's feathers. "Darning before wash day?" asked Kit with a smile, which the girl did not bother to return as she nodded.

At the foot of the bed was a wicker laundry basket. The room was scantly furnished, but for a small set of drawers and a washstand. Kit quickly looked them over, and dismissed them. On the top of the drawers was a tiny posy of dried flowers and a few trinkets, cheap glass cleverly cut. Gifts from a suitor no doubt.

Yet it was to the basket of dirty clothes Kit gravitated, kneeling in front of the receptacle.

"Oi! You've no right to do that!" shouted the girl rather more loudly than she should.

"Caswell, that's most unsavory and unnecessary," Holmes said, apparently horrified at the sight of a woman's unwashed garments.

"Bachelors," said Kit, "are afraid of the strangest things. Remain calm, Mr. Holmes, no one is asking you to undertake washday duties."

Kit continued to excavate the contents of the basket until at last she came to a white apron, which had been rolled into a tight bundle. Carefully she removed it and laid it on the floor, unwrapping it meticulously as if it might contain something precious.

When at last Kit was done, the apron lay open on the threadbare rug. In its middle, a field of red blossoms — bloodied finger and handprints — marred the snowy fabric. "Now, gentlemen, do you require instruction in the differences between ordinary blood and menstrual blood? This is most certainly the former."

"Really, Miss Caswell," Watson tutted, turning a deep crimson.

Holmes' dark eyes were fixed on her face, keen and sharp. "Well? Tell us, you've earned the floor."

"But the girl was with her mistress all night," objected Watson.

"No. You merely assumed that, yet Emily herself said she'd gone to her master's room twice that evening: once to deliver his drink, the second time to check on him. And Mrs. Harrington was clearly under the influence of laudanum when I tried to question her — Peterson told us she used it." Kit smiled. "She'd have no idea if the girl was there or not."

She began to tick off points on her fingers.

"When Emily spoke of finding Mr. Harrington murdered, she said she knocked and entered. The girl is methodical in her descriptions, gentlemen: she lists each step she has undertaken. Were you to ask her how she might achieve a future task, you would discover she does the same thing as when she recalls a past action. Now, you'll recollect when she knocked on the door downstairs at my summons, she waited to be told to come in. When she described her two trips to her master's room, she did no such thing: she said she knocked and went in. That suggests, to my mind at least, some degree of intimacy; she knew he was in there. That on numerous other occasions she knew she did not need to await permission."

She saw Holmes jerk in surprise. Watson hid a smile as he groomed his moustache. Kit turned to Milo.

"Were you intimate with Mr. Harrington?"

"Not in any way you might recognize, Miss."

"When Emily spoke about this young man, she bitterly resented his intrusion into the life of the household — you've seen how she reacts to his presence — but at no point has she mentioned her poor mistress as his 'victim'. As if Mrs. Harrington was not the one displaced. That suggested to me that she cared not a jot for the position of the lady of the house."

One more finger was tapped.

"The direction of the cut on Mr. Harrington's throat could only have been made by someone standing to his right — if that had been Milo there would have been blood spray on the covers. Yet he lay there creating a void and you'll note, if you look carefully, the dark patches on his jacket where the blood spurted. He could not have been the murderer."

One last finger was folded away.

"And I could not help but question what maid has such a pristine apron on after midnight?" Kit tilted her head as she surveyed the girl who sat so very still on the bed. "Unless she didn't want anyone to see what she'd wiped on it. Emily, why?"

"Because once he met *that* he never looked at me again! Not once." The girl began to sob angry gasps, not sad ones; rage at being caught. "I looked after him! Me! I was the one he looked to for comfort. Then this thing came and turned his head and heart. After all our time together, after all the lovely gifts he gave me." She threw a hand towards the pile of cheaply glittering trinkets.

"You cared for him. You brought him the hot toddy every evening. You knew he'd been in pain..."

Emily nodded. "I put some of the mistress's laudanum in it last night, to help."

"But he'd stopped drinking it."

"Didn't know that, did I? But then I found *them* asleep together. Him" — she glared at Milo — "in *my* spot, laying where I used to, ought to. And I thought how Ezekiel threw me aside so easily and what if I killed two birds with one stone? Revenge on both of them, the one for casting me away, the other for taking my place."

"And of course, you'd had the foresight to take one of the silver letter openers with you from Mr. Harrington's desk earlier," said Kit smoothly.

The maid jerked back as if slapped by proof of her obvious premeditation.

"And so." Kit sighed and re-wrapped the apron, then stood, and handed the bundle to Watson. "Perhaps now would be the time to send for the police. I'm sure you can explain it adequately, gentlemen. As I am rather unpopular with the Met in general, and Inspector Makepeace in particular, I think it best if I depart."

"Miss Caswell—"

"Mr. Holmes, I suggest you allow this young man his liberty. I do not believe he will do well under another round of questioning from the peelers. Milo? Perhaps you will be so good as to escort me?"

Downstairs, Kit found that Peterson had acquired a hansom cab; she shooed Milo ahead of her.

Kit bade farewell to the good doctor. "Good evening, Doctor Watson. I feel almost sorry that I was unable to find anything more in Heaven and Earth for you."

He smiled, relieved.

Holmes led her down the front stairs, and before she could climb into the cab he grasped her hand. "Thank you, Miss Caswell. You have delivered a salutary lesson in observation." Then he leaned in close and whispered almost beseechingly, "That boy. There's something odd about that boy, isn't there?"

Kit nodded slowly. "Do you want to know what it is? I warn you, sir, it's not rational and will not fit well in your view of the universe."

There was a long hesitation before Holmes shook his head and gave a rueful smile. "A man must know his limitations, Miss Caswell."

He helped her into the cab, then waited on the footpath to watch as the vehicle rattled away.

Inside the cool dimness of the cab, faces occasionally lit by the streetlamps they passed, Kit and Milo sat in silence for several minutes, until Milo said tentatively, "When... when did you know?"

"In the bedroom."

"When both Peterson and Emily said they thought I no longer breathed?"

She laughed. "No. They both said you did not *move*; neither mentioned breath. It was when I noticed you had no reflection in the mirror above the fireplace."

He gave a chuckle of comprehension. "That was why you moved me away from it, yes?"

She nodded. "I have read about your kind, Milo − do you have a last name?"

"Albescu. My true name is Sorin Albescu, but I am Milo to this world."

"Aha! Well, Mr. Albescu, I am aware of your kind."

"And yet you've put yourself in close proximity with me? Are you not afraid, Miss Caswell?"

"Only a fool would hurt me when we were last seen together by the World's Greatest Detective and the World's Most Devoted Physician. Is my instinct that you're not a killer wrong?" Kit slid her hand into her reticule and grasped the handle of the remaining silver letter opener which she'd 'souvenired' from Ezekiel Harrington's desk, in case of just such an exigency. Silver was one of the things that sources seemed to agree on as a *deterrent* to the undead.

"You will know, if you have done your research, that my kind must feed. I feed, yet I have never killed. I do not begin a *relationship* with an unwilling partner, Miss Caswell. I fed on Ezekiel last night as I have every time since I met him."

Kit slapped her knee. "Of course! The marks on his thigh — there seemed too many for one night's injection site."

"It was easy to camouflage the needle pricks amongst the marks of my teeth, they are very similar. Our intercourse was not sexual, at least not as you might understand. He was my friend. He gave me shelter — rented rooms for me where I might safely sleep during the day — and in return..."

"Did he think your kiss, your bite, might save him?"

Milo nodded in the brief light. "I tried to explain that what I have — what I *am* — is not a gift. That my immortality was not of my choosing. That the price was, and has always been, too high."

"Desperation will make people refuse to see what is in front of them." Kit sighed.

"That was his tragedy — and mine — to have met when he was at his most needy, his most vulnerable. What might we have had in other circumstances?" Milo asked wistfully.

"If I'm to let you go in this city, what will you do? Propagate?"

"That has never been my way, Miss Caswell." He smiled and it seemed impossibly bright in the dimness of the cab. "A creature who lives like that — who does murder and makes others like itself — will soon be found out." He gave a sigh containing untold centuries of regret. "We are but scraps and echoes, Miss Caswell, things that have fallen from humanity, but remember our old shape too well to let it go entirely. I would not condemn anyone else to this life."

All she'd read suggested beings like Milo were soulless, yet she'd seen nothing in the past hours to support that. Kit took a deep breath. "Then you'd best go. The sun will not be kind to you, will it?"

"The matter of light is a constant for the living and the undead."

"If you ever need help, Mr. Albescu, seek me out."

"Thus, I will say the same to you, Miss Caswell. I thank you for this evening's kindness." He bent over her hand and she felt only the touch of his cold, cold lips; no breath escaped them. Then he was gone, the door of the cab opening and closing with terrible swiftness, and Kit was alone.

How you viewed life was, she reflected, all a matter of light.

—— « O » ——

Angela Slatter

Angela Slatter is the author of the novels *Vigil* and *Corpselight* as well as eight short story collections. Angela has won a World Fantasy Award, a British Fantasy Award, one Ditmar Award, and six Aurealis Awards. She's been a Queensland Writers Fellow and the Established Writer-in-Residence at the Katharine Susannah Prichard Writers Centre. She has an MA and a PhD in Creative Writing. Her work has been translated into Bulgarian, Chinese, Russian, Spanish, Japanese, Polish, and Romanian. The film rights to her novelette 'Finnegan's Field' have been optioned by Victoria Madden (*The Kettering Incident*). The character of Kit Caswell first appeared in the novella *Ripper*.

The Song of a Want

Lyndsay Faye

From the Office of Mr. Henry Wiggins
Wiggins, Perry, and Tilton
4 Grosvenor Place, London
October 14th, 1904

My dear Mrs. Rachel Caine,

It is always gratifying to hear unexpectedly from an old friend, and in particular one in whose career I can take justifiable pride. Therefore, first: congratulations upon your, I daresay, meteoric rise in the ranks of feminine journalism! Your accolades have not gone unnoticed by your humble servant, and when I think of our earliest days as colleagues so long ago…

You know everything I have to say on that subject. There is too much in my heart for a young solicitor to express. It defies English.

Naturally, I received your letter of the eighth of last week with great interest. You are the best possible candidate to pen the article you described. Felicitations! Of course, on the occasion of a remarkable man's retirement, curiosity regarding his life and career — though I can't say we've ever seen public curiosity wane regarding this particular individual — naturally increases. Questions regarding early life and influences arise. Origins take on the proportion of myths.

Are we myths, Mrs. Caine? Are we a part of something grown so huge that we are now fictional, nothing more than a carefully tapped out collection of two-dimensional letters on a page? Have we been irrevocably flattened? Or do we still exist as flesh and blood, if only to ourselves?

The wind moans in the hearth I just stoked, the mice at my small office whisper their secrets quite audibly tonight, and the thought of becoming a mere fable is unsettling. So, to the point: your project is a dear one. When I reflected on your queries, however, I came to realize that my own humbler beginnings were very much tied up with those of the great man in question; and furthermore, I had never before sat down and done the tale justice with nib and foolscap.

It has taken me, therefore, some days to write this. I am penning it all out clean again now. But our mutual exposure to storytelling from a tender age drives me to give the full account — in a more complete manner, I daresay, than you bargained for.

I find I cannot tell it any other way than as myself, as I was before. Because I have never previously revealed any of this, and now I ache — yes, I suffer, Mrs. Caine — for someone to know of it. It writhes in my guts like a worm, so that whenever I am not composing this letter, I can think of nothing save what to write next. The plot was a right smasher, if admittedly dark and, dare I say, even hopeless.

How hopeless were all our lives, then? How hopeless would they have remained if not for him?

So. The first time I ever saw Scott Williamson, he was in a bad way and no mistake.

We were all huddled about the fire barrels that night — in a horrid, tight, frozen corridor, a crack in London's face — near Shadwell Market. Wind sharp enough to freeze your blood to your bones, and every so often you'd catch a whiff of chestnuts roasting, or some lucky bugger's thermos of hot coffee. Something other than the stench of the sewer driftwood and the mudlark coal we were burning, and your belly would tie itself into a knot over something as insubstantial as a smell. But I don't need to explain that to you.

January of 1880 wanted every man jack of us dead, though I think you're too young to remember? When it wasn't snow, it was sleet, which was worse. Snow could freeze your finger-ends, but the sleet left you shaking like a flag in the wind, with a hard hurt in your bones that never quite went numb and made a gentle end of you.

That's how my best mate, Meggie, came to fall sick and vanish. And if it hadn't been for Scott Williamson, the Lullaby Doctor might have gone on doing whatever he wanted with nobody the wiser. But it's best to begin stories at the beginning — we've all had that drilled into our pates, haven't we? And the beginning for me was January 21st, 1880, around those awful stinking fire barrels that kept the life clinging to our bodies like the muck on our boots.

Because that was the night we met Scott Williamson.

"Cold, innit?" said Meggie, appearing at my side out of the gloom.

"It must be. Your jokes are getting feeble, and they was bad enough at the start," I retorted, tucking a friendly arm about her. "Any luck?"

"Not I. Corner shop's boarded up, chophouse bins clean, and the chestnut men glaring at everyone what gets closer than ten paces, like they's regular peelers. It's more'n your liberty's worth to steal a bite tonight."

"Told you, didn't I?"

"You did. But trying anyhow passes the time till the light's strong enough for us."

"So does standing here, you daft little thing."

"Aye, but I favor trying. Even if it comes to naught. Work is the best cure."

"For what?"

"Nighttime. Cold. Anything o' the sort what ails a girl."

"Freezing to death?"

She made no answer. Though already philosophical, Meggie was nine, scrawny as a sparrow, and I eleven. Meggie's dad was a great kindly brute, Irish bred, a coalwhipper down dockside way. I met him half a dozen or so times. Back when she was only a fire-headed lass of five, and he still coming home to their digs in the shadow of the bridge, with his eyes scarlet from the dust and his hands blacker than any gloves.

Then when Meggie was around six, he didn't come home one day. And he stayed away the next. And soon after that, you'll not be too staggered to learn, there wasn't a home anymore. Not for her.

Myself, I'd never known naught but the orphanage, and the workhouse, and the streets. And the streets beat the other two with a twelve-inch tawse. So, when I found my mate Meggie curled up under a potato sack in Brick Lane, I took her in. As best I could do, you understand. Which was in the hold of a barge where I paid the lighterman tuppence a night to let me sleep behind the saltpeter bags and the bundles of whalebone, whatever the sad old sot was delivering that day. And whenever I had pennies.

So that made about three years we'd been together, on that night. Thicker than thieves. Thicker than blood.

"Anyhow. Early start this morning would be best." Meggie clapped her hands. Tossed her red curls.

"Don't I know it. Beat the rest of 'em to the shoreline and set to."

We'd slept rough in the shadow of a carpenter's barrow for the first half of the night, but that was risky as soon as the dawn crept over the garbage-choked river. The sooner Meggie could clamber up my shoulders between the barges and knock some coal onto the shoreline, the sooner we could sell it and eat something.

"Give us a tune first, luv." The voice came from the other side of the fire, where a toothless crone with a rotting straw bonnet stood dribbling down her own chin. "Pretty please? Just a ditty or two. For luck, like."

Meggie drew her shawl closer. "My luck or yours?"

"It's all one, dearie. I ain't partial. Any fair fortune is better than none, says I. It's like sunshine. Where's the harm?"

Smiling, Meggie started to sing, in that peculiar piercing lilt she had, as if you were listening to a wind chime or a silver spoon struck against crystal. It sent icicles down your spine. She started with a rouser, one to whip up sluggish blood and make the night shine. But in her voice, it came out high and queer and prickling. Pleasantly eerie, like watching a candle snuffed without any draft, or a door creak open with nary a soul to push it. And of course, the subject was drear despite the jolly melody.

We didn't know any other songs.

> *Now, gentlemen, be you all merry,*
> *I'll sing you the song of a Want;*
> *I'll make you as merry as may be,*
> *Though money begins to grow scant.*
> *A woman without e'er a tongue,*
> *She never can scold very loud;*
> *'Tis just such another great want*
> *When the fiddler wants his crowd.*

The old witch cackled with glee as Meggie reached the chorus, and anyone with strength in their lungs croaked and wheezed and howled it out along with her. It must have sounded like a dust-up in Bedlam. But for a small sweep of the second hand, we were in a pub with a roaring hearth and a frothing pint. Not dying in Stepney.

> *Good people, I tell unto you,*
> *These lines are absolute new;*
> *For I hate and despise the telling of lies—*
> *This ditty is merry and true.*

Cracked shoes and flapping boot soles tapped. Our own hardened bare feet jigged on frozen dirt. The meager blazes spat and fizzled, the wind shrieked against the suffocating smell, and there were worse ways to speed along the sunrise. Meggie quickly warmed her voice, if not her fingers, and it rang out sharp as a knife in the back.

> *A bell without e'er a clapper,*
> *Will make but a sorrowful sound;*
> *And he that has no land of his own,*
> *May work on another man's ground.*

We had just finished another chorus when a strange voice — one that could pronounce the letter *H* and had vowels as smooth as a lady's silks — exclaimed, "Well done indeed. Brava!"

We peered into the dim, startled. A very tall, thin fellow hove into view.

"Young lady, that's a fine instrument in your throat," the intruder continued. "But it should serve you far better in Tottenham Court Road, supposing you wish to profit by your innate musicality. And I don't see why you shouldn't."

"Who in blazes are you, then, what wants me to be taken up for begging and, like as not, packed off to the reformatory?" Meggie scoffed.

"Mr. Scott Williamson." Even in the darkness the man's pale eyes glittered, his words came fast as bullets, and he'd a violin case tucked under one arm. "Lately of Cambridge, but the victim of unfortunate circumstances. At least until my fiddle here can earn me back my proper clothing, and I can visit the employment offices; then all will be right again."

Meggie and I exchanged a look. It held, puzzled.

Because this Scott Williamson fellow was lying.

Murky as the night was, it might have worked; I might've taken Scott Williamson for a Distressed Scholar type, except that his togs were too grand. The regular dodge of the chap who makes his way shamming to be an unlucky academic is simple: compose a letter of recommendation with dollops of Latin and wave it about, and claim you only need get your proper gear out of hock. Then beg for what you will — railway fare, generally. But this fellow had actual gentleman's clothes. They were mended, but they were never cheap, so the fabric alone he could sell to a jerry shop. He wasn't a beggar, therefore. Not on a night like that one. And I didn't think him a true street musician either — not at three thirty in the morning, two blocks from the Thames, talking of greener pastures.

No, this chap was off his kilter. He had long fingers, like a conductor's, and was waving them as if he didn't know he was doing so. Mr. Williamson's voice was rapid. But the energy with which he spoke seemed leashed by only the flimsiest of leads. It bucked and reared. I could equally imagine the man bursting into a pool of scattered starlight or taking flight like a bird. Either a raven king of old had just landed in our alley, or it was worse, and some sort of lunatic was paying us a call.

"Well then, Mr. Williamson, this here's Henry Wiggins, and I'm Meggie Hart," my friend offered.

"Never mind all that, I've a marvelous idea." He unsnapped the case and tucked the violin under his neck, as if he'd never been so keen to do anything in his life. "Oh, come, I'm accounted better than decent. I'll bring no shame to your esteemed concert. On my honor. Nothing, really? Here, I'll lead us in!"

The man rattled like an express train. An instant later, notes poured out of his instrument. Crazed ones, quicker than Meggie's tempo had been and twice the number, dancing around the melody like demons poking at a lost soul.

Meggie's eyes turned saucers. Then she laughed, and struck up the next verse.

> *A Blacksmith without his bellows,*
> *He need not rise very soon;*
> *And he that has no clothes to put on,*
> *May lie in his bed till noon.*
> *An Innkeeper lacking in custom,*
> *Will never get great store of wealth;*
> *And if he has ne'er a sign to hang up,*
> *He may e'en go hang up himself.*

The dregs of London bellowed in harmony and the fires hissed their approval. The world changed, as if a great curtain had been swept aside. This was a genuine performance. The barrels were footlights, and Mr. Williamson swayed to the music while Meggie sang words about empty spaces that would never be filled.

I wish I could better describe to you what happened next, or how he did it — but one second we were hunched around the barrels, and the next we were edging out of the alley behind Mr. Williamson, inching towards the awakening street. He was our Pied Piper, leading us off into some godless horizon.

At the mouth of the corridor, he stopped. And we behind him, framed as if by a proscenium.

That was when coins began to hit the straw and the stones. *Plink clink plink clink* around us, like the beginning of a thunderstorm, the starving folk squealing and diving at the mud. And me not being simple, well, I looked to Meggie and whipped off my cap to hold out, and she stepped up brazen as you please next to Scott Williamson, and he arched his back like a great black cat's and the metal rain fell harder.

> *A warren without e'er a coney,*
>   *Is barren, and so much the worse;*
> *And he that is quite without money,*
>   *Can have no great need of a purse.*

Fingernails tore and bled as our neighbors scrabbled for ha'pennies and my hat filled. Minutes passed. The stranger smiled as he played, a melancholy moonstruck look, and his fingers flashed faster as we hurtled towards the final chorus.

> *Good people, I tell unto you,*
>   *These lines are absolute new;*
> *For I hate and despise the telling of lies—*
>   *This ditty is merry and true.*

The song concluded with a flourish on his part and a high note on my friend's. Wild applause erupted. We were in a jungle, Meggie and Mr. Williamson our idols. Cheers went up likewise from the crowd of some two dozen which had assembled.

I clutched my hat to my chest as Meggie grinned at me with sweet, crooked teeth.

"What did I tell you?" Scott Williamson gasped, sweat beading along his gaunt temples. He staggered, lithe back hitting the bricks, and swished his bow at the pair of us. "If you're blessed with a talent, why not earn a few quid by it, is what I say? You can whistle while you work, but if you can be paid for merely the whistling, then so much the better! Supposing the whistling is superior to everyone else's. There's no call for meadowlarks to go away to war, or for angels to dig ditches. The very fabric of the universe frowns upon such degradations, don't you agree?"

We couldn't, not having the faintest idea what he was saying. His head drooped. He slumped down to the rough stones gracelessly, though careful of his instrument — he cradled it, and the bow he likewise guarded in his lap as he hung his head over his knees.

We shifted our feet.

"What in bloody hell is wrong with this 'un?" Meggie wondered.

"Gives me the morbs, he does," the crone rasped. "Knows things as no man should. You can see it in his eyes. Best to steer clear."

"Knows things he shouldn't or not, he made us half a crown," I whispered urgently to my friend. "We can't just leave him for the bobbies to pick up."

"Mr. Williamson." Meggie stooped, touching his shoulder. "Sir? Do you know whereabouts you are?"

"Hell." Shuddering, he raked a trembling hand through his hair and regarded the blank skies. "Specifically, Stepney. But I know of a worse one. This isn't the lowest by far."

Clip clop clip clop rattle rattle scrape.

A carriage slowed to a halt before us. Briefly, I thought of nothing save running, with my coins clutched against my chest and Meggie's frail hand in mine — the newcomer could herald the onset of police. It was a toff's two-wheeler, with peeling paint and dirty windows but matched sorrel horses. The driver stared unseeing over his drooping whip.

Then the owner swung the door open and stepped down, and the sour iron taste of fear rose in my throat.

"Not him again," Meggie murmured, crossing herself.

The Lullaby Doctor, or so we all called him, stepped down from his derelict conveyance with a lit bullseye lantern. Using it to pierce the gloom of the fissure we occupied made him all but invisible. But I'd spied him some half a dozen times before. He was a spindly-legged man with a round, hard, distended belly, like a ruined woman's, which he patted continually, as they often do. His face was clean shaven and I couldn't imagine hair growing on it, so childlike and smooth was his skin. Watery blue eyes, a curiously cocked head, blond hair he wore in lank curls to his shoulders, and a weak mouth completed this picture of warped innocence. One which made every last one of us want to make tracks whenever we saw him.

"My name is Dr. Manvers," he called in a soft squeak. "Some of you know of me, I daresay, yes, yes, yes, and some do not. I am here to ascertain whether any child present among you is seriously ill, one who might qualify to be treated *pro bono* at my practice? I provide free services for the young and the destitute."

He walked down the alley — bending over a quaking heap of rags here, touching the face of a lice-ridden street Arab there, murmuring questions. Everyone shrank from him. But no one ran.

"Now, *that* one," Meggie breathed, wrinkling her nose. "That one gives *me* the morbs."

"Who the devil is he?" Mr. Williamson inquired, glaring in disgust — insomuch as he could focus at all.

"That there's the Lullaby Doctor," I said. "Comes round every few months, sometimes driving up to us bold as brass here in Stepney, sometimes walking yonder on the Rotherhithe side. Finds the sickest, he does, and takes 'em off the streets. Treats 'em. For a price. Them as come back can't remember much save being warm and kept in vittles. They don't always pull through once they're set loose again."

"Not worth it," Meggie muttered.

"Why would you say such a thing?" Mr. Williamson's eyes slit like a feral tom's. "It's a life, it isn't a handkerchief. There's no coming by another. Isn't any chance better than none, mathematically speaking?"

"It's on account of her hair," I explained.

"Beg pardon?"

"He takes it away." Meggie shivered. "When they come back, it's gone."

Brushing my friend's copper tangle off her shoulder, I pressed rough fingers against her neck, meaning only comfort. It spilled to her waist, Meggie's hair — corkscrews, matted in places, a crown worn by a wild animal. Meggie was practical about most things: work, food, shelter, all the daily dozens of tiny pragmatic considerations that kept us alive. Whether to buy a cone of fried fish from the chap who might easily sicken you, and still have a space on the barge that night, or whether to spend all on a fresh kidney pie and walk the waterfront till the stars retreated. She was no mewling kidlet.

But about her hair, she was as vain as a duchess. Meggie would comb it with fork tines, scrub it with ash and rinse it in rain barrels, steal grease from the dockyard mechanics' tubs to make it glisten.

"Takes it?" Mr. Williamson seemed sharper, all his angles jutting.

"Aye," Meggie assured him. "Cross my heart."

"Just a moment. Workhouses shave hair as a hygienic measure against parasitic infestation, prisons and madhouses for that and a number of other reasons, including discipline and dare I say even deliberate cruelty. Why should a doctor of medicine require a child's hair?"

"Says it's part of the therapy — ain't said how," I replied.

"He's a rotter, that one," the haggard old woman interjected. She had retreated behind a barrel, and we could see the glints of sickly light off her own locks but little else. "Thank Christ I'm old as dust, and he wants none of me. Small mercies. They're like luck. Take any as come along, is what I say."

"Why do you call him the Lullaby Doctor?" Mr. Williamson wanted to know.

"When any o' the ones what he takes pull through, they says it was all like a dream," Meggie answered. "And sometimes…"

"Yes?"

"Some of 'em have said they saw others of us. Still there, like. Where he lives. But they can't have done." Peering into the polluted mist, I gritted my teeth.

"And why is that?" Mr. Williamson persisted.

"Because the ones as they saw were dead and buried already."

Mr. Williamson pressed twitching fingers to either side of his face, lips pressed into a line as if he might be ill. "I shouldn't have asked. Not in this state."

"Been wondering what state this is, guv," I admitted.

"Oh, a touch of this, a dram of that, all meticulously prepared to the exact specifications I require. This…I was testing something." He dropped his hands. "I dabble in chemistry."

"Looks like you do more than dabble."

"Sir," Meggie attempted again, "are you—"

"Well, well, well, and how are you faring this morning, my dear?" a sickly-sweet voice interrupted.

My belly slid towards my bare feet. Dr. Manvers wouldn't have loomed over us if we two hadn't been underfed children, and Mr. Williamson hadn't still sat on the frozen ground with his wrists draped over his knees. But as it was, I shrank back, drawing Meggie with me.

"Hale enough, sir, and with promise o' better," she replied, tossing her head.

"That is excellent news! I am very glad to hear it."

"Thank'ee."

He leaned down and whispered in her ear. Meggie made a face, but did not turn away.

"Plenty of tea when you can come by it, and no whiskey yet for one so young, I hope? Ah. Try not to overindulge, then? You will remember, I trust, that should you ever find yourself in direr circumstances, I am your friend? Good, good, good."

A flash of light seared my eyes. I shouted something, hand before my face. It was as if the sun had risen all at once. When I could see again, I realized that it had been the sweep of the bullseye, which Dr. Manvers had been aiming low, and furthermore that it was now held in the tenuous grip of Scott Williamson. His attention was as fixed as the Pole Star, and pinned to the Lullaby Doctor before him — brightly illuminated now, every follicle and crease on display.

Glancing down, I saw with watering eyes that the violin and its bow had been placed carefully behind a few disintegrating bricks.

"What is the meaning of this?" Dr. Manvers exclaimed. Now the full light shone on him, I saw that his complexion was a gelid gray, and that his suit was mottled with stains. "Who are you, sir?"

"No, that's — that isn't," Mr. Williamson attempted. "Not remotely. The point, I mean. Not at all, you see. Who are *you*?"

"I have already explained," the medico snapped, arms akimbo. "I am Dr. Vincent Manvers, and in addition to my regular researches, I do charitable work amongst the street urchins of the London docks. Return my dark lantern at once!"

Mr. Williamson was shaking his head urgently. "I can't. You had better go."

"Go?"

"Yes, and quickly, too. Something might befall you in one of these wretched alleys, something you wouldn't like."

"And what might that be?" the repellent man questioned, quailing.

"Well, I might knock you down, you know." Mr. Williamson teetered again, then righted himself against the wall. "I've knocked other chaps down, quite a few, and none of them liked it. Here, quite right, I've no wish to rob you — just take your lantern back and be on your way. These are dangerous streets. Particularly for men who aren't themselves, I ought to know it, and you're about as far a cry from you as…from anything else I can think of. It's all far too much to explain at present, don't ask it of me, I fear I cannot oblige. Go! I shall give you ten seconds."

Most of our companions of the night had scented danger and slunk further into the shadows by this time. The few remaining, the crone included, leered at the scene with reddish gleams in their pupils, awaiting the crowning of the victor.

Dr. Manvers snatched his bullseye back, stepping away, and again we were lit and he a black cutout.

"Very well. You, sir, must not excite yourself to violence before innocents. Seeing none who require my professional services, thank God, and pugilism being against my principles as a doctor, I shall withdraw," he said. "You will not try to impede a philanthropical physician again, however. No, no, no. Consider yourself warned!"

I could hear the ripple of fear in his voice, like spying an eel slithering through calm water. You recall as well as I do the effect our mutual friend could attain when he liked.

"Oh, thank heaven, you were making me dizzy," Mr. Williamson moaned, descending back to the frozen ground. "Everything about you. Whatever you are — I frankly don't know. If you'd wanted to scrap with me, you might accidentally have landed a blow or two, and I should never have forgiven myself. Disgraceful."

"You dare too much, sir, you really do!" Dr. Manvers squealed.

"I disagree. We certainly needn't trouble over violence in front of innocents, for instance. If that lot there are innocents, then I'm an itinerant Cambridge tutor. This is Stepney. May you have every bit as good a morning as you deserve, and not a whit better."

The violinist's lids fell shut, and his breath came shallowly. He tented his fingertips before his prominent nose. With a sound between the snarl of a terrier and its whimper, Dr. Manvers turned on his heel. The steady percussion of the horses' hooves fell immediately after his slamming the door.

I knelt before our baffling new acquaintance, riveted. He always had that effect, of course.

"What did you mean just now, sir?" Meggie appeared at my side with the violin case. "About him not being himself?"

"Dr. Manvers, if that is his name? He wasn't." Mr. Williamson managed a spasm of a smirk. "Neither am I, to be fair, though I meant no harm and that scoundrel could have meant anything. Steer well clear of him, promise me that you will?"

"Why?"

"Detectives know things, it's my business to know things, I cannot help but know things, it's my sole *raison d'etre*. God knows I haven't any other." Opening his eyes, Mr. Williamson rolled his skull against the brick and then slammed it backwards, hard. "What the devil are you imps staring at? You've money enough now — go and spend it. There are shoes to be bought, dare I say even stockings, and I'm fatigued."

"I've ne'er seen a detective before, only constables. It's interesting. And y'can't sleep here!" Meggie, for all her vast knot of hair and blackened toes, looked scandalized. "You'll freeze for sure. Sure as this girl's talking sense at you."

"Then I'll freeze," he whispered. Blinking, he rubbed at the crook of his left elbow. "How long would that take, I wonder? It'll be an experiment. I'll write it up for the *Scientific Review*."

By this time, I had all our precious new coins secreted in three separate hidden pockets, and I slung my cap back on with loyalty renewed. "Bollocks. Up you get, Mr. Williamson, and we'll see you safe home. It's the least we could do. Whereabouts do you live?"

"In Bloomsbury. Montague Street, three twenty-six, flat D."

"Well, sod this, off to Montague Street, then!"

"No!" His eyes, which had struggled against closing, flew open. Mr. Williamson buried his face in his hands. "I can't go back there, I can't."

"Don't be daft, that's your—"

"Please. Anywhere but there."

I think it was the entreaty that caught our notice. You could touch it, sure as you could have reached out and touched his face.

"But—" Meggie attempted.

"It's four walls. Do you understand?" Mr. Williamson pushed his hand over his mouth as if stifling a smile. "You couldn't, could you? No. I apologize for that. But God, only four walls, and nothing else of consequence, and they're shrinking. Every day. Sometimes I am almost tempted to measure it. Then I'd have some empirical proof. If you could only see them, getting smaller. It's like being Alice without the company. In Montague Street, it's only me and the walls. I can't, not tonight. It would kill me."

"I told you." The old woman, bones creaking, made her way past us, shaking her head. Her stooped silhouette continued toward the mouth of the alley and the brightening day. "Knows too much, he does. Things as he shouldn't. Leave him to sleep, luv. The devils are at that one, something fierce. It'll be kinder in the end."

"Yes," Scott Williamson whispered. He smiled at one side of his mouth. "Yes, go on, I'll be right as rain soon. I always am, you see. You needn't worry. I only need to rest a moment. It's terrible, those four walls. I never get any rest at all."

His lips were turning blue as Meggie's eyes. The trembling had stopped. Scott Williamson was lax and listless in an abandoned Stepney alleyway in January, and I knew what happened next, supposing he didn't take shelter or keep moving.

Meggie looked at me, and I looked at Meggie, and we made a decision.

You've already guessed what it was.

We got Mr. Williamson to his feet and started off towards the barge we called a shelter, if not a home. After a feeble protest, he went like a lamb. He was monstrously tall, and tense as a whippet — but we could make a slow progress tucked up under his arms, steering him like a dandy who'd been all night at the lush. He didn't smell of gin though, and he kept muttering nonsense when a drunk would have been long asleep, thank Christ, or we'd never have made it a quarter mile to our dock as the sun slashed the sky's throat in a thick band of crimson.

When we stumbled onto the deck, the lighterman proved to be snoring great whiskey clouds in the pilot's cabin. No morning deliveries, then. We could pay him when next we saw him conscious, or he kicked us awake in a dull rage.

"We can sleep," Meggie sighed happily.

"We can all sleep," I agreed, worn to a nubbin.

The stairs were problematic and Mr. Williamson nearly squashed us twice. Below deck, the air was always foul. But we'd last transported tallow and coffee, so that morning it smelled strangely of bitter roasted fat, which was better than most days by leagues. The pile of tarpaulin where we slept lay blessedly near the engines. We deposited Scott Williamson on the outside and curled up together with our backs to the hull, our skin burning as the nerves sparked back into life, all thought of food forgot in our weariness.

"What did the Lullaby Doctor say to you?" I inquired.

"How to contact the blighter. Fat chance o' that, says this girl."

Mr. Williamson convulsed gently, winced, buried one hand in oil-dark hair and held on as if for his life.

"Do you suppose he's this barking when he's sober?" I mused.

"I don't figure as he's barking, Henry," Meggie whispered. "Just alone."

She began to sing, and Scott Williamson settled into fitful oblivion, and I fell asleep thinking of Wants.

> *A peddler without e'er a stock*
> *It makes him look pitiful blue;*
> *A shepherd without e'er a flock,*
> *Has little or nothing to do.*

When we woke, as you can imagine, there were only two of us. But as I sat up, checking our lucre was safe, I saw by the sulphurous light that Mr. Williamson had left us a message. Crawling to the edge of the tarp, I laughed.

"What d'you have to wake an honest girl for?" Meggie mumbled.

"Cheer up, my lass, and think over what color ribbons you fancy. We're rich, that's what!"

She laughed in her turn. We couldn't read, of course — I had my numbers and name and anything else was a right head scratcher, and Meggie signed her mark with an X — but the communication was perfectly clear. It was a middling quantity of odd coins piled next to a chalk drawing. Two neatly sketched pairs of boots, surrounded by three arrows and underlined for emphasis.

"Guess Mr. Williamson wants us to scare up two pair o' secondhand bats somewhereabouts." Meggie yawned. "Christ save us. We'd never have charged him so dear. This must've been everything he had on him, poor blighter."

"He ain't as poor as all that," I reminded her. "He's a 'tec. The Distressed Scholar dodge were just for show. Cor, been so long since I had boots, I've like as not lost the knack of it. Let's spend it on summat else?"

"Yes, please," she agreed, blue eyes flashing. "What first? Chops or a bloody great pie? Or a proper fry-up with runny eggs? D'you reckon it's still morning?"

Chops proved the readiest to hand, with onion gravy, and we stuffed our faces till our ears stuck out. But as for the rest of our money — it went to neither boots nor ribbons. About a fortnight later, Meggie began to cough.

Just a bit, at first, the sort of wheeze everyone acquires from sleeping on a boat floating on pure coke sludge, and from climbing up my shoulders to knock coal off of barges for a living. She refused to let us survive off our savings after a few nights. So, we went back to the mudlarking. We kept our precious treasure hidden onboard, behind the fuel storage — the plank I'd loosened, unmarked, in full shadow, and discernible only by counting five grooves to the left of starboard.

Though I will not dwell on that time in detail, we'd need every penny.

After a month of coughing, Meggie started to shrivel. The money dwindled. The ailment worsened. I paid a nurse to visit, and she left ingredients for mustard poultices and told me to pray. It got bad enough that Meggie would stay abed, and after I'd paid the grumbling lighterman, I'd race to a new apothecary. Sometimes I found the barge where I'd left it; sometimes I'd catch it in Rotherhithe after sprinting over a bridge; sometimes I'd meet her upriver. I didn't dare to take her to a workhouse, lest she be trapped there, nor to take her to a proper doctor, lest she be turned away and have wasted her strength.

"That makes rubber," Meggie announced on the night she vanished. We were playing cards on the barge in the early evening, and though I'd wrapped her in potato sacks and bought her a boy's secondhand woolen jumper, she still crouched like our friend the old crone. "Have y'any explanation for losing three hands o' whist in a row when I'm this poorly?"

"You cheat," I accused gamely.

My heart wasn't in it. It only beat for my friend.

A brief fit stole Meggie's breath, and then she smiled. "If you've naught better to do, you could fetch a girl some soup? I think I could eat today, if we've the coin, and supposing y'go on losing at whist so as to keep me cheerful, like."

When I arrived back half an hour later with a clean little pail of pea soup and a spoon to share between us, provided I returned both to the market stall, she was gone.

You had best believe, Mrs. Caine, that I searched high and low. A stale rain fell, filling the cracks between cobbles until my naked feet threatened to slip and I could no longer gauge the depths of puddles that aspired to be lakes. She wasn't in any of the saloons that granted us custom, any of our usual haunts.

"Henry! Henry, luv, over here!"

I skidded at the sound of my name. The ancient woman stood under the archway of a door on Upper Shadwell, her rags draped shapelessly about her and her face half-hid by a muffler. I stopped, panting.

"Your friend went with him," she rasped, both hands resting on the stout stick she used for a cane.

"With who?"

"With the Lullaby Doctor."

At first I stood there, stunned speechless. But she knew his address, I realized — he had whispered it to her the night we met Mr. Williamson, and though Meggie couldn't write, she'd plentiful friends who could if she needed writing done. So did I. And she'd hardly been in my sight every moment, foraging for river coal to keep us tenants of the barge, same as I'd been doing. We'd only a shilling left of the strange violinist's money.

"She was afraid of him," I protested. "No, it ain't sensible."

"Always trying, that one was, never believed that giving up can make for a softer end," the old woman sighed. "I'm sorry for you, luv. But there's about as much hope in the Lullaby Doctor as blood in a brick."

"Where did—"

"I saw wee Meggie get into a hackney with him." She shook her head, spittle from her pendulous lower lip trailing a cobweb to her scarf. "No telling where. If she comes back, give her a kiss for me, would you? She brought an old woman comfort. And comfort's like sunshine, you know."

"Is it?"

"Yes, it is. Take it as it comes. Whenever it comes. It can't do nobody no harm."

The lovely hag wandered off, leaving a terrified boy of eleven with chest heaving and throat thick with terror. I had to find Meggie. I had, at least, to try, and succeed or fail.

And if I failed — well, then my heart would be broken, and how anyone could live with a broken heart I didn't know. It seemed to me a vital organ, one that if injured would ruin the whole mechanism, like a train with a shattered engine. But Meggie always tried. Work could cure anything, she said.

So, work I must, I determined, but how?

Five minutes later, I recalled I knew a detective.

326D Montague Street.

It took me an hour, hopping on the back rails of cabs until I was thrashed off of them, to reach Bloomsbury. But it took me two hours more to locate Mr. Scott Williamson, Detective. He had a landlady, then as later, only this one was a shrew, with a staring circle of a mole above her left brow and an expression sour enough to turn your milk into cheese.

"What's your business?" she asked when I knocked.

"I need to see Mr. Scott Williamson," I answered, trying to look as if I was straightening a jacket I wasn't wearing.

"Do you take me for dense? There's no such person as lives here."

My only hope was slammed in my face. But I knew she was wrong — he'd been too far past sense to be prevaricating, he really did live in Montague Street.

So, I tried.

I banged and I banged and I banged on that door. I had hot dishwater thrown out at me, and dodged most of it. She threatened me with a dog. Then the police. Never once did I think of giving up, because it was for Meggie, but just when I was ready to start sniveling, the door flew open and there he was. Tall as a scarecrow, perfectly brushed tails, snowy collar, and his prominent chin dropping in surprise.

"By Jove!" His voice was as clipped as I remembered, but much more piercing, and his strange eyes were as clear and calm as ice blocks.

"Thank Christ," I breathed. "Mr. Williamson. You ain't forgot me, have you? It's Henry Wiggins, from Stepney. You remember?"

"Yes, yes, of course I do, I've an exceptionally keen memory. But what in the name of the devil can you be doing on my doorstep?"

"Looking for you."

"Oh, no!" He held a palm up, one steady as a painted signboard, and young though he was, you'll believe me when I say I almost flinched. "There will be absolutely none of that, if you please. It simply won't work."

"What won't?" I asked, dazed.

"Look here, my dirty little chap," he continued snappishly, "if you think you can somehow find out my address and extort payment from me over the regrettably botched experiment I was performing on the night we met, you needn't bother."

"But I ain't of no mind to—"

"I am on my way to complete a particularly complex branch of my studies at the British Museum, and I won't be detained by a guttersnipe."

"Mr. Williamson—"

"'Tention!" he barked. "March straight along, young rascal, you aren't wanted."

"You've the wrong end, I tell you, I—"

"Fine, yes, very well, here is…let me see, three shillings." He fished coins out of his waistcoat pocket. "Go and buy yourself a pie. Or half a dozen of them. And some soap, while you're at it, you are in dire need of the substance. If you attempt to blackmail me again, you shan't enjoy the results, and if you attempt to blackmail my family, he'll have you transported. He is well aware of my peculiar scientific studies, and should you threaten me, he would think nothing of snapping his fingers, and then where would you be? Shanghai. Good afternoon."

"Please," I begged, ashamed the tears were starting. "It's Meggie, she's gone. I think she went to the Lullaby Doctor, the one as you said ain't right."

Mr. Williamson's face changed — first to a blank, you know the look well — and then a mark appeared between his dark eyebrows and he pulled his lips between his teeth.

"You had better come in." Whirling, he held the door.

I don't know what I expected to find as we trotted up three flights of stairs and he whipped out the key to his flat. But so far as I was concerned, the space was a generous one. Under the window was room for a bed for a renter like me, and there too under the desk, or past the chemistry set, and over there if a body were to move books out of the way.

There was nothing else, though. Only space.

"She got sick and run off yesterday and I ain't seen her since," I reported, as Mr. Williamson threw newspapers into one corner seemingly devoted to that purpose. "It's not like her. And one of our folk said she got in a cab with the Lullaby Doctor."

"From the beginning, please," Mr. Williamson requested.

He lit a small pipe, sat down and crossed his legs on the uncarpeted floor. You could have knocked me over with a swift puff. I was that staggered.

You are speculating, my dear Mrs. Caine, that our great affection for his subsequent address makes my recollection biased against his Montague Street rooms; but apart from serving to keep the rain off his head, they were quite barren. Two shabby armchairs faced each other, and a lone brandy decanter with a pair of snifters rested on a shelf. The single grime-streaked window looked out on a crumbling back area. An intricate chemistry set rested on a cheap deal table, scores of books were neatly arranged on the plain shelves, and the violin case sat propped against the wall near a cold hearth. Other than these items, there were no personal touches whatsoever, and it seemed from the oppressively solitary feeling that only one of the snifters and one of the chairs was ever put to much use.

"You're upset and I'm rushing you. Do sit down," Scott Williamson ordered, as he himself stood. "Let us put our heads together and try to puzzle it out between us. What do I have in, heavens, there's…yes, we shall have a little brandy and water, with more water than brandy for you, of course, but enough to be fortifying, and here's some cheese left from my supper, and just enough bread to suit. Now. When did young Miss Meggie go missing?"

As he bustled about gathering refreshments, I told him everything. About Meggie's ailment, and the Lullaby Doctor's personal interest in her, which was so disturbing as to make me nauseous, and the gentle witch's report that she had gone off with the repulsive fellow in a hansom.

"Hansom— you're sure she said that? Not a carriage?" Mr. Williamson, having deposited a small hunk of Stilton and the heel of a bread loaf on a plate for me, folded himself into the opposite chair with one knee drawn up under his angular jaw.

"Certain sure," I avowed. "Though I can't vouch for her eyes, mind."

"Oh, she had excellent vision, she dove for any shillings that came within a yard of her, and with admirable accuracy in such poor light. As well as two ha'pennies." Mr. Williamson linked spidery fingers around his shin. "I suspected that wasn't Dr. Manvers' carriage, and this confirms it."

"It does?" I asked, swallowing the rude luncheon.

"Beyond the shadow of a doubt. I haven't any carriage or matched horses either, but if I did, I would take enough pride in them to keep my conveyance clean. Additionally, if some unruly young musician stole my bullseye and threatened to knock me down, I should expect my driver to at least do me the courtesy of looking alarmed, if not rush to my aid. The Lullaby Doctor's coachman was a complete stranger to him."

"But you said as he weren't a doctor."

"He wasn't." Mr. Williamson pressed at his left brow. "He didn't make a whit of sense, nothing about him. I'd…well, as you know, I was not quite myself that night."

I thought he'd been very much himself, nakedly so.

"But the data was altogether bizarre. Sometimes the act of detailing observations aloud can be quite useful, and since you're here, I may as well try it — one wearies of talking to a Stradivarius. Let me see," he mused, shutting his eyes. "Medical men are occasionally shabby, but they are seldom unclean, as it goes against their training, and he sported a rather astonishing variety of marks, which I was able to see when I turned the dark lantern on him. Wax in both liquid drop form and in hardened shavings on his sleeves. Clay, or what I thought must be dried clay because of the dusty patina, on his fingernails. Plaster stains on his trousers. The residue of what appeared to be an oil-based paint on his shirt cuffs. It was an embarrassment of clues. I've never witnessed anything of the kind before."

"And you…that's the sort of thing you notice, then?" I confirmed, destroying the last of the bread. "As a 'tec? And that's why you done warned Meggie off?"

"Yes, for all the good it did," he replied dispassionately. "The detail of the missing hair from his 'patients' is likewise alarming. If I could deduce his profession, we could gamble that he employed his real name due to lack of imagination, and cross reference it, considering the fact he lives in Rotherhithe."

"Does he?"

"Yes, you mentioned you'd encountered him on both sides of the Thames, but on foot in Rotherhithe and in a carriage in Stepney. When he journeys further afield, he rides in style. Look here, my unwashed young acquaintance, would you do me the favor of not speaking for as much as perhaps half an hour?" Unfolding himself, he retrieved his pipe. "I need to smoke. And ruminate over the highly distressing number of substances this man comes into contact with. And then we'll see that Meggie comes to no harm. All right? Yes, yes, very well, another splash of brandy for you, but that is the end of it. I haven't the means to keep street Arabs in their cups."

In the end, it wasn't half an hour at all — he sat still as a bust for fifteen minutes, emitted a noise like a choke, smacked his pipe against his palm, and then covered his mouth with his hand.

"What?" I cried. "What's the matter, then?"

"I beg your pardon, I — it's possible that I'm wrong." Scott Williamson flung himself out of his armchair and pulled down one of the impressive directories from his bookshelves. "Manvers…no, no, excellent, no…ah."

I could see him calculating as he raised his eyes, staring into the middle distance as if it contained the solutions to the deepest mysteries of the human soul.

"My dear, dirty young fellow, I imagine you should like to accompany me," he said softly.

"Bet your life," I confirmed. "But where?"

"An artisan's workshop in Rotherhithe. You'll be quite safe, I assure you, I wasn't exaggerating when I claimed to have something of a talent for fisticuffs. Admittedly, at times

I wish for nothing more than a comrade with a serviceable weapon — but on this occasion I've confidence in our powers, and anyway it doesn't do to indulge in the fantastical."

We left Bloomsbury in a cab hailed by Mr. Williamson. It occurred to me belatedly that I would have to pay for these services, but not knowing how, I kept my mouth shut. So long as Meggie was all right, I could face debtor's prison, the workhouse, anything. When we pulled up to a shop front surrounded by warehouses and dockyards, with peeling gray paint and heavily curtained windows, I fought the urge to be sick on the cobbles, so tense was the set of Mr. Williamson's face.

"Allow me to handle this, if you please," he instructed, stepping down. "I do not believe us to be in any physical danger from this Dr. Manvers, and pray God Meggie isn't either, but if I am right, this could be touch and go. Do nothing rash."

There was a sign next to the door: MR. VICTOR MANVERS' RESTORATIONS AND CURIOSITIES. Mr. Williamson strode, in that headlong way he has, to the entrance and rapped. When no answer came, he pounded with the stick he carried, sending staccato booms down the windswept street. I heard commotion within, and then Dr. Manvers himself opened the door, and as little as I knew of society, I knew that was wrong. A maid ought to have greeted us, not the master of the house.

"Ah," Scott Williamson said. "I thought as much."

"Heaven save me!" Dr. Manvers gasped. "I had half convinced myself you were a nightmare, and here you are upon my doorstep, and with a child from the same hellish morning. I shall cry for a policeman."

"Dr. Manvers, or rather Mr. Manvers, for you are no doctor, by all means summon a policeman." Steel had threaded its way into Mr. Williamson's tone. "Where is Meggie?"

Mr. Manvers' lank blond hair was tied back in a queue, his pasty complexion bright with sweat — he had looked unhealthy, but respectable, until the detective uttered that query. He shrank back as if from a hooded serpent. His lips grew white.

It frightened me.

"Yes, go on," Mr. Williamson commanded. "Lead us to her. If we find her unharmed, I may yet have mercy on you."

Mr. Manvers bowed his head. He turned away. The wallpaper was stained with sooty rain from cracks in the ceiling, the carpeting dotted with mold. All along the entry hall were installed glass cases. Scores of unseeing eyes stared back at me, glittering as coldly as jewels, and the unliving skin painted with blush and with brow and lip stain reminded me of the single occasion I saw a corpse dressed for burial. These undead creatures wore immaculate clothing, and their lips parted as if about to speak, and their tiny hands reached for me. Never having seen anything like them, I shrank back in terror.

"It's merely a display," Mr. Williamson said quietly. "They're the children of his profession — Mr. Manvers is a dollmaker. Wax molding, plaster casts, clay modeling, and finally paint. I don't know why I didn't see it at once, I was unforgivably slow. Come along, Wiggins. Bear up. Let us take Meggie home."

Fighting the urge to cower behind his coattails, I obeyed. We ascended a staircase, each step groaning like a tormented ghost. When we reached the first floor, Mr. Manvers gestured to an open bedroom, and Mr. Williamson hastily ducked inside.

Meggie lay on a bed with a threadbare but warm quilt covering her depleted form. Her eyes opened only a crack — but upon seeing me, she gasped, and attempted to pull her arms from the bedclothes.

I could see freckles on her scalp, tiny new constellations I'd never had cause to witness before, because her head was entirely shorn.

"Henry!" she rasped. "What in the name o' Christ are y'doing here? And with Mr. Williamson?"

"Removing you from this establishment." Mr. Williamson delicately lifted the tonic bottle resting on the bedside table. "Simple laudanum. Better than I had feared, as we might have been dealing with ether or chloral. Very good. Mr. Manvers, you will now show me your collection. As Miss Meggie gathers herself and prepares to depart, young Wiggins here will accompany us. I require an eyewitness of the correct age to spread news of this back to the urchins of Stepney. In order to ensure that nothing of the sort ever happens again."

Mr. Manvers already boasted a juvenile face, a cringing demeanor, and a repulsive aura. But at this edict, he collapsed still further into himself, strings of hay-like hair drooping in front of his eyes.

"You…you know about that?" he whimpered. "But how? How could you possibly?"

"It is my business to know what others cannot discover. Or at least, I sincerely hope that it will one day be my business, as well as my preoccupation. Lead the way, sir. I mean to remove your latest victim from your premises with all speed — but first, you will show my friend Wiggins here what you have been about."

We followed his hunched back down the hallway, then up another staircase. A peculiar aroma drifted down to meet us, one reminding me of tallow candles and the more astringent smell of turpentine.

"I can take 'em as they comes generally, Mr. Williamson," I whispered. "But I ain't—"

"He is a dollmaker," Scott Williamson said without inflection. "Specifically, he molds wax figures, which require the use of paraffin, plaster, and paint. His public occupation need not concern us — regarding what I suspect to be his private collection, however, you and I are going to put a stop to it."

When we reached the attic level, Mr. Manvers withdrew another set of keys from his pocket, jangling them like a church bell at high noon. I felt sorry for him.

Then he opened the door and I could never feel sorry for him again.

I cannot dwell upon that chamber. Not even to describe it to you. Dozens of children, some of whom I had known or still knew, stared back at me from that wretchedly perverse room. Their waxen faces may have been blank, granted. And their eyes fixed. But they were perfectly, even immaculately, rendered, and some grotesque part of me was able to marvel at it. In a corner beneath a window, a new mannequin stood with her new face drying, a matted but genuine head of red hair meticulously attached to the scalp. Given a few more seconds, I discerned that all the false children had real hair, and then I knew as much as did Mr. Williamson.

"When they're sick, you feed them laudanum, and…and then you copy them? With their real hair?" I stammered.

Mr. Manvers said nothing. But he sat fully upon the floorboards, scarcely breathing, his palm caressing his spherical belly.

"God in heaven," Mr. Williamson marveled. "I cannot… this is unspeakable. You may well have justified it by telling yourself that they needed warmth and drugs more than they needed their hair, but to pretend to be a physician and return them to the streets…it's monstrous."

"I never meant any harm!" Mr. Manvers protested, clasping his hands prayerfully. "I'll never do anything of the like again. I swear it, I'll swear it on a Bible. Only keep these, and be finished for all time. Yes, yes, yes. I never hurt Miss Meggie, only took what I needed."

"Needed?" Mr. Williamson cried. "Whatever for? No, no, don't tell me, I entreat you, but these will have to be destroyed, you must know that. They are the product of a diseased imagination."

"Please," Mr. Manvers whispered. "Ruin my reputation, stop me from making more, but don't take them away. They're all I have."

Mr. Williamson took half a step back. "No, they cannot be all you have. You're a respected dollmaker, with a lucrative profession aside from this hideous hobby. I found you quite easily in my latest directory. You've an occupation, and you are your own man. That must mean something."

"Not as much as they do. Please."

"No, there must be a line somewhere!" Mr. Williamson cried. "You took a little girl and you took two dozen other children and you lied to them, they call you the Lullaby Doctor, and it may not be a crime precisely, but it's a violation, an *assault*. These must be destroyed."

"I can't," Mr. Manvers claimed, his lips trembling.

"You haven't any choice!"

"Yes, I do." Our grotesque host hoisted the lantern which lit the room.

Then he dashed it at his feet.

The reek of kerosene flooded the small chamber. Mr. Williamson shouted, and dove, but the spilt fuel licked at Mr. Manvers' togs, quickly ate its way through the carefully dressed waxen figures, ignited against the paint and the plaster until within seconds the attic space was a conflagration and Mr. Manvers was shrieking.

Mr. Williamson tucked me under his arm and fled for my life. I cannot imagine that he was fleeing for his.

On the instant I was out of the room, he began flinging doors open in search of a basin, a pitcher, some source of water. But by the time he found a single carafe, the doorway had been engulfed in flames, and he dashed the vessel to pieces as he snarled in frustration.

"Meggie," I coughed. "We have to..."

"Yes, of course." Taking my hand, Mr. Williamson shook himself. "Run with me. On the double. I'll carry her, and you lead the way."

We did precisely that.

When we emerged from that terrible building, Meggie still wrapped in the quilt, and I shivering not from cold but from terror, Mr. Williamson turned to look behind us. The house had already gone up like a tinderbox, and neighbors were shouting.

"Her figure looked newest," Mr. Williamson said. "At least we need not worry there were other children in the building."

"Who would do such a thing?" I demanded, digging my nails into my palms.

"I cannot tell you. It was revolting. But I think it was the song of a want. In a way. In a terribly wrong way."

Luckily, there was a firehouse nearby, and the blaze was soon extinguished. We three made our way to a charitable hospital Mr. Williamson knew of, where Meggie was made warm and comfortable. She passed into God's care a fortnight later.

Because as false as the Lullaby Doctor had been, her ailment was not.

Afterwards, Mr. Williamson once said to me, before asking me to be his lieutenant, "In spite of everything, and my sincerest sympathies, I thought you were lucky."

I, of course, demanded to know what he meant.

Mr. Williamson still lived in Montague Street at the time. So he said, "You would have done anything for her. No one will ever feel that way about me."

He was mistaken.

He employed more children. Others followed, my dear Mrs. Caine, which of course is the reason I may confide in you. Yourself, in 1885, and what an asset you proved at the ripe age of seven! Rabbit, three months later. George, Lizzie, Gunn, Hollins, and Lacy in 1886. Jack Tilton, who did more with one leg than most any chap I've ever met could do with two. Bessie, who was lost to us so young, and who not even the good Doctor could endeavor to save.

You will note that in my caution over this missive falling into enemy hands, I have confined all personal references to pseudonyms — which happily comes naturally to me, as Scott Williamson was the name by which we were first introduced. Nevertheless, I beg that you will burn this letter after culling what you will from it. My anticipation of your forthcoming article could not be more keen, and may I presume upon your kindness so far as to request that you will inscribe a copy to an old friend?

For at the end of every man's long, lingering twilight, what have we of more value than old friends? It gives me great joy that we are yet young, and that many more decades of mutual admiration lie before us.

I remain, my dear Mrs. Caine,

Very sincerely yours,

Mr. Henry Wiggins

———— « O » ————

Lyndsay Faye

Lyndsay Faye is the twice Edgar Award nominated author of *Dust and Shadow*, the Timothy Wilde trilogy, *Jane Steele*, and the Sherlockian short story collection *The Whole Art of Detection*. A proud member of the Adventuresses of Sherlock Holmes, the Baker Street Irregulars, and the Baker Street Babes, she lives in Queens with her husband and cats.

If you enjoyed this read

Please leave a review on Amazon, Facebook, Good Reads or Instagram.

It takes less than five minutes and it really does make a difference.

If you're not sure how to leave a review on Amazon:

1. *Go to amazon.com.*

2. *Type in Gaslight Gothic by edited by J. R. Campbell and Charles Prepolec and when you see it, click on it.*

3. *Scroll down to Customer Reviews. Nearby you'll see a box labeled Write a Review. Click it.*

4. *Now, if you've never written a review before on Amazon, they might ask you to create a name for yourself.*

5. *Reviews can be as simple as, "Loved the book! Can't wait for the Next!" (Please don't give the story away.)*

And that's it!

Brian Hades, publisher

About the Editors

J. R. Campbell

J. R. Campbell is a Calgary based writer and editor. His short fiction has appeared in *Tesseracts 20: Compostela*, *Rigor Amortis*, *The MX Book of New Sherlock Holmes Stories Vol. 2 & Vol. 4*, *Challenger Unbound*, *A Study in Lavender: Queering Sherlock Holmes* and *Fantastical Visions IV*. He has also written three episodes in Imagination Theater's *The Further Adventures of Sherlock Holmes* radio series. Along with his brother in arms, Charles Prepolec, he has edited the anthologies *Curious Incidents Vols. 1 & 2*, *Gaslight Grimoire: Fantastic Tales of Sherlock Holmes* (2008), *Gaslight Grotesque: Nightmare Tales of Sherlock Holmes* (2009) and *Gaslight Arcanum: Uncanny Tales of Sherlock Holmes* (2011), and *Professor Challenger: New Worlds, Lost Places (2015)*. His latest project *By the Light of Camelot* (2018), with co-editor Shannon Allen, explores the lives of the Knights of the Round Table and the Arthurian world.

Charles Prepolec

Charles Prepolec is a former Mystery bookshop owner, currently freelance editor, writer, artist and reviewer with published contributions in a variety of books and magazines. He is co-editor of five Sherlock Holmes anthologies (with J. R. Campbell) — *Curious Incidents Vols. 1 & 2*, *Gaslight Grimoire: Fantastic Tales of Sherlock Holmes* (2008), *Gaslight Grotesque: Nightmare Tales of Sherlock Holmes* (2009) and *Gaslight Arcanum: Uncanny Tales of Sherlock Holmes* (2011); as well as co-editor (with Paul Kane) of *Beyond Rue Morgue:*

Further Tales of Edgar Allan Poe's 1st Detective (2013) for Titan Books. His most recent anthology (with J. R. Campbell) is *Professor Challenger: New Worlds, Lost Places* (2015) for EDGE SF&F. Charles has been an active Sherlockian for more than 30 years and holds memberships in The Bootmakers of Toronto, The Sherlock Holmes Society of London, The Sydney Passengers of Australia and an investiture in The Baker Street Irregulars (The Man with the Twisted Lip). He lives in Calgary, AB, Canada with his wife Kristen and their cat, Karma.

About the Cover Artist

Dave Elsey

Dave Elsey is an Academy and Saturn Award-winning creator of special characters and creatures using special Makeup Effects and Animatronics. He is known for his work in movies such as *X-Men: First Class*, *Ghost Rider*, *Star Wars*, *Hellraiser*, *Alien 3*, *The Wolfman*, and *Mr. Holmes*. A keen Sherlock Holmes enthusiast, he has provided cover art for the comic book series *Sherlock Holmes: The Dark Detective*, as well as the books *Gaslight Arcanum: Uncanny Tales of Sherlock Holmes* and *Professor Challenger: New Worlds, Lost Places*.

Need something new to read?

If you liked Gaslight Gothic, you should also
consider these other EDGE-Lite titles:

— «» —

Terminal City
(Book One in the Terminal City Saga)

by Trevor Melanson

Mason Cross never wanted to be anything like his father, a famous professor who, it turns out, was also a necromancer. But death changes people.

Now Mason is following in his dead dad's footsteps, down a dark, solitary path between two competing lives: one as a student at Terminal City's top university, the other as a necromancer.

But will he find the answers he's looking for? Or will he find only death, caught in a hidden war between necromancers and a religious inquisition?

As the gravity of both worlds bears down on him, Mason will need to discover not just new power — but what a human life is really worth.

Praise for Terminal City

"Mason Cross is embarking on a new life in more ways than just going to college. When he moves in to the house he inherited from his dead father and an odd stranger comes calling, he discovers that death is just another beginning.”

“Once introduced to the world of unseen things, Mason is delivered as a complex hard-edged young man who takes joining the ranks of his father’s powerful friends, the Necromancers, in an epic battle against the Inquisitors in stride.”

“This is a fast-paced, well-written entertaining book and a good way to pass time. The plot never lags, and it is pleasantly easy to stay immersed in the darkish underworld of the book. I am looking forward to the next in the series!”
— A. Volmer

“Riveting read from start to finish. Highly imaginative romp into the dark side with complex characters. I found myself liking the bad ones as much as the good ones; indeed the lines between ‘good’ and ‘bad’ were often blurred. Action packed, and never a dull moment; the author paints incredible pictures of an alternative Vancouver (Terminal City) as well as other layers of the necromancer’s reality, and the flow back and forth between the two.”
— Linda Nickerson

“Terminal City delivers. Every character had me hooked. They challenged me to think beyond popular preconceptions of protagonist/antagonist paradigms, to what shapes a person’s character and their approach to their unique situations.”
— Ariane Fleischmann

For more on Terminal City visit:

tinyurl.com/edge2086

—— <> ——

White Death

by Jack Castle

Ravenous Predator hunts Arctic Expedition

Coined by early explorers as the Atlantis of the North, the Arctic is a desolate, intense land colder than even Antarctica.

Anthropologist Kate Foster accepts a job at an isolated research facility on a remote island surrounded by a vast ocean of crushing Pack Ice. Her scientific expedition becomes a mission of survival when she is joined by Detective Jack Decker with the Alaska Bureau of Investigations. Kate and Decker's team of criminologists race against time to solve the gruesome and multiple homicides of her colleagues while someone, or something (thought to be extinct), is hunting them.

Praise for White Death

"Chilling, both in terms of absolute terror and frigid conditions where the action takes place."
— Spokesman Review

"When Jack Castle delivers a new adventure he draws his readers in with creative story lines that unfold in realistic settings. The descriptive nature and action packed details of his stories are riveting and spell binding. I'm anxiously awaiting his next journey through the unknown."

— Major Dennis Allen (Ret) and recipient of the Distinguished Flying Cross

"I'm not a sci-fi fan, but I read Mr. Castle's first book, Europa Journal, in one sitting, (I actually found the book on a seat at the airport on an unexpected layover). And I didn't think he could top his supernatural thriller, Bedlam Lost. But that's exactly what he did with his latest book, White Death. This time around the story takes place at a remote facility in the Arctic. A team of criminologists are flown in to investigate a brutal massacre of scientists when something begins picking them off one-by-one. I haven't been this on the edge of my seat since watching the movie Jaws as a kid. Three different books, three different genres and the author managed to knock it out of the park every time!"
— Liz Garrick

For more on White Death visit:

tinyurl.com/edge6015

—— <> ——

Lethal Influence

by Susan Bohnet and K L Webster

Unknown to humans, a friendly alien society lives among us. Kai, a young Trebladore male, has unusual abilities that are lethal to humans. Different factions of the Trebladore Society begin to vie for the use of his powers, and he discovers disturbing things about his species and their methods. When humans start dying and the woman he loves is in danger, Kai must make desperate choices. Choices that will change the future of mankind forever.

Praise for Lethal Influence

"From the moment I read the brief description, I knew I was in for a good read. This book takes you through SciFi, Romance, Mystery, Intrigue and Suspense. With a bit of Humor here and there. I can definitely see this becoming a series (one can hope) as there is more that can be told. But if it is only to be one book, it is still worth the read"
— Amazon Customer

"I often wish/hope/imagine that some 'guardian angels' are out there, ready to influence bad guys to be better. Susan does a GREAT job of building this in a believable way. I don't want to introduce a single spoiler, but the story builds up and ends up with a satisfactory ending."
— Xubbycat

"We follow our main character Kai, who is a Trebladore
and his friends; a group of aliens with the power to influence
humans, as he comes to term with the fact that he is different
from his fellow Trebladores and that his own influencing
power is much more than he realises. We see him struggle
with this knowledge and how to best use his influencing
powers for the greater good as it's what's been ingrained into
him since he was a small child and is the Trebladore way."

"Some action, plot twists that you may or may not see
coming with a bit of romance thrown in, it will definitely
make you ponder what it means to be human and how far an
alien race would be willing to go in order to help us."
— MyBookishRealm

For more on Lethal Influence visit:

tinyurl.com/edge6019

For more EDGE titles and information about upcoming speculative fiction please visit us at:

www.edgewebsite.com

Don't forget to sign-up for our Special Offers